Always Forward

January – October 1867

Book # 9 in The Bregdan Chronicles

Sequel to Shifted By The Winds

Ginny Dye

Always Forward

Copyright © 2016 by Ginny Dye
Published by
A Voice In The World Publishing
Bellingham, WA 98229

www.BregdanChronicles.net

www.GinnyDye.com

www.AVoiceInTheWorld.com

ISBN # 978-1530760596

Printed in the United States of America

For Suess – who told me this is my best work to date ☺ - But mostly because she is the most awesome friend in the entire world, and I am so grateful for all she means to my life!

A Note from the Author

My great hope is that *Always Forward* will both entertain, challenge you, and give you courage to face all the seasons of your life. I hope you will learn as much as I did during the months of research it took to write this book. I have about decided it is just not possible to cover an entire year in one book anymore. As I move forward in the series, it seems there is so much going on in so many arenas, and I simply don't want to gloss over them.

When I ended the Civil War in *The Last, Long Night*, I knew virtually nothing about Reconstruction. I have been shocked and mesmerized by all I have learned. When I got to October of 1867, and I already had close to 500 pages, I knew I needed to close the door on this book and start fresh in October with the next volume of *The Bregdan Chronicles*!

I grew up in the South and lived for eleven years in Richmond, VA. I spent countless hours exploring the plantations that still line the banks of the James River and became fascinated by the history.

But you know, it's not the events that fascinate me so much – it's the people. That's all history is, you know. History is the story of people's lives. History reflects the consequences of their choices and actions – both good and bad. History is what has given you the world you live in today – both good and bad.

This truth is why I named this series The Bregdan Chronicles. Bregdan is a Gaelic term for weaving: Braiding. Every life that has been lived until today is a part of the woven braid of life. It takes every person's story to create history. Your life will help determine the course of history. You may think you don't have much of an impact. You do. Every action you take will reflect in someone else's life. Someone else's decisions. Someone else's future. Both good and bad. That is the **Bregdan Principle**...

**Every life that has been lived until today is a
part of the woven braid of life.
It takes every person's story to
create history.
Your life will help determine the
course of history.
You may think you don't have
much of an impact.
You do.
Every action you take will reflect in
someone else's life.
Someone else's decisions.
Someone else's future.
Both good and bad.**

My great hope as you read this book, and all that will follow, is that you will acknowledge the power you have, every day, to change the world around you by your decisions and actions. Then I will know the research and writing were all worthwhile.

Oh, and I hope you enjoy every moment of it and learn to love the characters as much as I do!

I'm constantly asked how many books will be in this series. I guess that depends on how long I live! My intention is to release two books a year – continuing to weave the lives of my characters into the times they lived. I hate to end a good book as much as anyone – always feeling so sad that I have to leave the characters. You shouldn't have to be sad for a long time!

You are now reading the 9th book - # (*Walking Into The Unknown*) will be released in November/December 2016.. If you like what you read, you'll want to make sure you're on my mailing list at www.BregdanChronicles.net. I'll let you know each time a new one comes out so that you can take advantage of all my fun launch events, and you can enjoy my BLOG in between books!

Many more are coming!

Sincerely,
Ginny Dye

Chapter One

January 1, 1867

Carrie heard the sound of crackling flames, but she refused to open her eyes. She snuggled deeper beneath the heavy quilts, knowing the fire would have done nothing to diminish the frigid cold. She lowered the covers just enough to blow breath into the room, and then cracked her eyes open to confirm her suspicions. The plume of foggy air made her pull the covers over her head again. She had seen enough of the rosy sky through the window to know dawn was kissing the Virginia countryside awake, but she had no intention of watching it happen. Carrie sighed, and then moved over closer to Robert's warmth. Her eyes sprang open when she realized his side of the bed was empty, but she still refused to lower the covers.

"Old age is a terrible thing."

Carrie heard Robert's voice as he poked at the fire, creating a loud snapping as the flames shot higher, but she didn't move.

"I can hardly believe my wife is still in bed," Robert continued sadly. "The same woman who used to greet every New Year's Day on the banks of the James River is still in bed. I'd say this is the first sign of old age," he teased.

"I am not old!" Carrie protested from beneath the covers. She was, however, stunned to realize it truly was New Year's Day. With the exception of the war years, she hadn't missed a sunrise with Rose down by the James River since she was seven years old. Her efforts to produce the energy to join Rose for their annual tradition just wasn't there, though.

"Are you still feeling sick?" Robert's voice had changed from teasing, to concerned.

Carrie thought about the question. She laid her hand on her stomach, relieved there was no pain. Then she took a deep breath, even more relieved when there was no feeling of nausea. The last three days had been a blur of queasiness and sickness. "I think I'm feeling better," she responded, hoping she was right.

"Well enough to start a new tradition?" Robert asked.

Carrie considered the question for a moment, and then pulled the covers down just enough to peer at her handsome husband outlined by the blaze from the fireplace. She couldn't see his thick, dark hair, and she had to just imagine his bright blue eyes, but there was no mistaking the broad, muscular shoulders. "A new tradition?" In spite of still being fatigued, she was intrigued.

Robert strode over to gaze out the window. "There are two horses that seem tired of being tied to the hitching rail."

"Two horses?" Carrie was enjoying the game, but she still wasn't about to leave her cocoon of warmth.

"Granite and Eclipse," Robert continued. "Of oouroo, thoy don't loolt quite tho oamc through a curtain of snow."

Carrie gasped. "Snow? It's snowing?"

"Well, if thick, white flakes falling from the sky is snow, then I suppose the answer is yes." Robert edged closer to the bed.

Carrie gripped the quilt to her more tightly. "Don't even think about it," she warned.

"Think about what?" Robert asked innocently. "I do believe you were the one who was hoping for snow on New Year's Day. Are you really just going to lie in bed?" His voice was a mixture of playfulness and concern.

Carrie thought about her answer. She had not felt sick in the few minutes she had been awake, and her mind certainly seemed to be clearer. She was not at all sure she would encourage any of her own patients to go riding in the snow so soon after being sick, but the urge to do just that was growing. "How much snow?" she asked.

"Six inches, so far," Robert said with a grin. "It is still coming down hard."

Carrie sighed. "It sounds wonderful." She felt a twinge of concern when she realized even the prospect of riding through fresh snow wasn't enough to make her spring out of bed. Maybe she *was* getting older. She shook her head hard, black wavy hair spilling over the pillow. "I will not act old!" she said vehemently.

"My feelings exactly," Robert agreed. "Obviously, you need some help this morning."

Carrie heard the warning in his voice, but before she could react, Robert had pulled the covers off her, laughing as he evaded her groping hands. "Robert!" she gasped as the cold air from the room washed over her. "You'll pay for this!"

"Not unless my old woman wife gets up." Robert laughed harder, dodged her kick, and then thrust a bundle of clothes at her.

Carrie grasped them to her closely when she realized they had been warmed by the fire. Since there was no chance of burying herself beneath the quilts again, she jumped up with a groan, and then dashed over to stand by the flames.

Robert grinned. "I'll meet you downstairs, Mrs. Borden. Annie has hot coffee and ham biscuits waiting for you. She knew you would need something before the brunch later this morning."

Carrie nodded, pulling on clothes as fast as she could while Robert strode from the room. The coffee sounded wonderful, but she wasn't sure her stomach was ready for ham biscuits.

****

Carrie started laughing as soon as she stepped out onto the porch. Granite, her towering, gray thoroughbred, and Eclipse, the bay plantation stallion that matched Granite in size, were both tossing their heads and pawing at the snow that surrounded them. Granite snorted as soon as he saw her. "I'm coming," she called, starting down the steps as soon as she heard Robert open the door.

"Young lady!"

Carrie stopped short. The command was not coming from Robert. She turned around sheepishly. "Hi, Annie."

"You ain't going out on any long ride without some food in that there stomach!" Annie glared at her. "I been watching you the last few days. You ain't eaten enough for one of them cardinals flittin' around in the woods. You ain't got no business bein' out in this cold without some breakfast."

Carrie knew she was right, but she also knew the warning signs her stomach was giving her. "I can't, Annie. I already know it's not going to stay down."

"But you figure you ought to go gallivantin' around in the snow? Why you figure the Good Lord gave you sense if you ain't got no plans to use it?"

Carrie sighed, and met Annie's eyes, woman-to-woman. "Because my husband and I are starting a new tradition, and I refuse to mess it up."

Annie's glare softened. "I reckon that be a right good reason," she admitted gruffly. "The two of you done been through enough hard times for a lifetime."

Carrie nodded. "I know I'll go back to homeopathic school eventually. I want to make as many memories as I can before I do." She tried to control the grimace that wanted to twist her face when another spasm gripped her stomach. She took a deep breath, praying Annie wouldn't notice.

Annie's sharp eyes told Carrie she hadn't missed a thing, but her voice was soft this time. "Ain't nothin' wrong with takin' care of yourself, too."

Carrie pushed aside the niggling thought that told her she should stay home, and waved her arm at the snow as she managed a bright smile. "And miss this?" She breathed a sigh of relief as Robert stepped from the house bundled in a warm jacket, with a hat pressed down firmly on his head to protect him from the snow.

"You ready?" Robert asked with a grin.

Carrie's answer was to run down the steps, brush the accumulating snow from her saddle, untie Granite, and quickly mount. "What are you waiting for?" she called. "Getting old?"

Robert laughed, released Eclipse, and vaulted into the saddle. "We'll be back in time for brunch, Annie!" His words were still floating on the breeze as he urged Eclipse into a gentle canter.

Carrie gave a whoop of delight as Granite surged forward to catch up. Both horses were eager to gallop, but deep snow could strain tendons. Cantering side-by-side down the road, snowflakes swirling in flurries around them, she caught a deep breath of joy. She had dreamed about having these times with Robert while she had been trapped in Philadelphia for school. She wasn't going to let a little stomach flu keep her from having them. In truth, the cold, crisp air seemed to have settled everything. She felt fine.

They were content to ride in silence. Carrie admired the barren fields, glistening beneath the blanket of snow. They stretched for miles before blending into the deep woods that bordered them. She looked up when honking Canada geese caught her attention, barely able to see their outline through the cascading flakes. Only the black on their necks and heads stood out against the gun-metal gray sky. Vivid splashes of red revealed the cardinals were not letting a little snow stop them. Granite moved smoothly beneath her as he and Eclipse cantered along head to head.

Robert finally pulled the stallion down to a walk, but he said nothing to break the silence. Carrie was happy for the cocoon of quiet that wrapped around them. In spite of how much she loved having a houseful of people, she had also been yearning for peace and solitude. She knew Robert wasn't just starting a new tradition – he was giving his wife what her heart craved.

"Thank you," she finally said. Robert nodded. She knew that he knew what she was referring to. In just the two months she had been home – taking a sabbatical from school – they had grown closer than she thought possible. Their love had been strong almost from the day they met, but so much had conspired to keep them apart during the war, and during his long recovery after the conflict ended. These two months together had been the longest stretch of time they had been together without trauma and worry.

"Any regrets?" Robert asked after another long silence.

"Not a single one," Carrie assured him.

"You're certain?" he pressed.

Carrie looked into his eyes, touched by the vulnerability she saw lurking there. She knew Robert still questioned her decision to not go back to school. "I didn't stay home for you, you know."

"No?"

"No," she said firmly. "As much as I loved being in medical school, my heart ached every day to be here on the plantation with you." She tipped her head back to let the snow cascade onto her face. "I dreamed of moments like this, and was afraid we would never have them." She straightened, and gazed into his eyes. "I love you with all my heart, Robert Borden. The future may be a little murky, but I wouldn't choose to be anywhere else in the world right now."

Robert smiled, reached out to take her hand, and then pulled Eclipse to a stop. Carrie eased Granite closer, and then bent forward to meet his lips, her heart melting with love. When she finally pulled back, she tried to hide the gasp that came with the spasm of pain rippling inside her. She took a deep breath as she fought back the nausea.

"Carrie?" Robert's voice was deep with concern.

Carrie tried to reassure him with her eyes, but she was afraid to speak.

"We're going back," Robert said firmly.

Carrie made no protest as they walked home. She was grateful for the slow pace. By the time they returned to the house, the fresh air had done its magic again.

"Better?" Robert asked.

"Better," Carrie responded, but she knew it could hit her again at any moment. She had never had a stomach flu quite like this. She would check her books when she got upstairs to determine what homeopathic remedy would make her feel better. She had tried several over the last few days, but she was still struggling. What was wrong with her?

The house was bustling with activity when they entered. Warm air swirled around them, as blazing fires in every room chased back the chill. Carrie welcomed the heat, but quickly realized it was making her feel ill again. She took several deep breaths before she turned to climb the stairs. She caught Robert's questioning look. "I'm fine," she said firmly. "I just want to change for the brunch." She didn't mention that if she was going to be sick she wanted to be upstairs in the privacy of their room. "I'll be down in a few minutes." Carrie could feel her husband's eyes on her as she climbed the stairs slowly. She couldn't blame him; he had never seen her sick a single day.

****

Everyone was in the parlor when Carrie, dressed in an emerald green dress that reflected her eyes, came down to join them. Abby appeared at her side. "Are you sure you feel like being down here?"

"I'm fine," Carrie said quickly, looking toward Robert who was deep in conversation with her father.

Abby interpreted her look. "Your husband said nothing, dear daughter. Do you think I can't tell for myself when someone is feeling badly?" she asked blandly.

Carrie flushed. "I'm sorry. I just don't want to spoil the New Year's Day brunch."

Abby gazed at her, opened her mouth to say something, but then closed it again. Something lurking in her eyes prompted Carrie to question her further, but Annie's call from the dining room stopped her.

"Time to eat!" Amber yelled.

"Girl, don't you know better than to yell inside this house?" Polly said sternly.

Amber grinned up at her mother. "I don't know why adults have to pretend they aren't excited to go in and eat all that food we've been smelling all morning," she announced. Her black eyes snapped with excitement beneath the ebony braids Polly had coiled around her head for the holiday.

Carrie gazed at her, continually astonished with how fast the little girl was growing up. She had gained three inches in height, but it was the look of confidence in her eyes that said she had truly come into her own since being on the plantation. She was only eleven years old, but she had already proven herself as a capable trainer with the foals.

Robert chuckled. "That's my girl," he said approvingly. His grin broadened as Polly fixed him with an admonishing look. "Why shouldn't she be honest? Aren't we all feeling the same thing?"

"I know I am," Thomas agreed quickly. "Now, can we stop talking about how excited we are to eat, and just go do it?"

Carrie slipped gratefully into her seat, and then gazed around at the gaggle of people crowding the room. In spite of how large the dining table was, extra chairs had been added to accommodate everyone. Her father's glistening silver head was bowed low to talk to Felicia, Moses' and Rose's twelve year old adopted daughter. One year old Hope, born on Christmas Eve the year before, was snuggled tightly in her father's arms, as Rose tried to calm 4-year-old John down enough to sit at the table. Simon, his five year old cousin, was doing nothing to make it easier, but the happiness on her best friend's face said she didn't mind.

Janie and Matthew, married just one week, glowed with the newness of their love. Matthew's arm was wrapped tightly around his wife as they chatted with Simon and June, who had arrived just before the meal had been announced - refusing to let the deepening snow keep them on Blackwell Plantation. They had brought along the news that Perry and Louisa wouldn't be joining them because Louisa wasn't feeling well.

She watched Abby's head tilt back with a joyous laugh as she chatted with Clint and Gabe. Polly had joined Annie in the kitchen to carry everything to the table. Annie had staunchly refused any more help. Carrie could tell by the look of pride on Clint's face that he was talking about how his colt, Pegasus, was progressing. She had seen him appear briefly at the barn door when she and Robert rode off. She suspected he had been there since dawn. He took his job as stable manager and chief trainer very seriously. The results spoke for themselves.

"I wish Jeremy and Marietta were here," she murmured to Robert when he took his seat beside her.

"I do, too, but I have a feeling they are enjoying having Thomas' house all to themselves," he said, a mischievous glint in his eyes.

Carrie laughed. "I do imagine their honeymoon week will be much more private in town," she agreed. "I'm also sure they are glad to not have to drive back through the snow today."

Janie overheard her last comment. "Matthew isn't sure we will be able to leave today."

Thomas nodded. "There will be two feet of snow before it stops," he predicted. "It won't be safe to take the carriage into Richmond."

Matthew shrugged, obviously unconcerned. "Janie and I will get back to Philadelphia when we can. I thought about leaving yesterday so we would miss the snow, but I wasn't about to let us miss our first New Year's Day brunch as a married couple." He pulled Janie tighter with his arm. "I refuse to miss a single *first*."

Janie raised a glowing face to meet his eyes. "I don't imagine the Homeopathic College will stop running if I'm not there, and the *Philadelphia Enquirer* will somehow survive without their star reporter."

Carrie's heart warmed. She was so glad Matthew and Janie had each other. They were the perfect couple. "I'm so glad y'all aren't leaving." She rolled her eyes toward Matthew. "I suppose you will want to try and beat me in chess tonight since you have failed so miserably the last few times."

"Only because you weren't feeling well," Matthew scoffed. "My mother taught me to never take advantage of an ill woman."

Carrie and Janie exchanged a grin. "I guess it's as good an excuse as any," Carrie agreed impishly. "I'm feeling better, though, so you'll have to come up with a new excuse after I beat you tonight."

"Time will tell," Matthew said complacently. "Time will tell."

John's voice rose high above the clamor. "Isn't it time to *eat?*"

Annie chuckled as she appeared in the doorway holding a huge platter of sliced ham and baked sweet potatoes. "That it is, grandson." She eyed him sternly. "But I don't feed little boys that ain't sitting down at the table."

John gave her a big grin, and scrambled into his chair. "I'm here, Granny!"

"So you be," Annie said calmly as she set the platter down on the table. She turned toward the kitchen to get more, as Polly appeared with several bowls of greens, grits, and black-eyed peas.

John frowned as the black-eyed peas were placed in front of him. "I don't like the peas," he announced.

"Doesn't matter, son," Moses said gravely. "It's tradition."

John frowned harder. "Well, then I don't like tradition."

"That doesn't matter, either," Moses assured him. "People in the South have been eating black-eyed peas and collard greens on New Year's Day for as long as I've been alive."

"And for as long as I've been alive," Annie added. "And as long as my mama was alive."

John stared at his granny for several moments. "That's a real long time," he finally said. He looked more closely at the peas. "What's so special about them?"

"The black-eyed peas bring you luck," Moses said solemnly. "The collard greens will bring you money."

John grinned with relief. "Then I don't need to eat them," he announced happily. "I'm already lucky, and I don't need any money!"

Laughter rolled around the table, but John's plate was the first to get a small spoonful of black-eyed peas and collard greens.

"It won't be a son of mine who brings bad luck on Cromwell Plantation," Moses said. Then he leaned over closer to the little boy. "I hated them when I was your age, too," he confessed.

John gazed up at him. "But Granny made you eat them?"

"She did," Moses agreed. "Just like you're going to have to eat them."

John stared at his plate for several long minutes. "So you're doing something bad to me just because Granny did something bad to you?"

The laughter was explosive this time. Rose stepped in to rescue her floundering husband. "He's not trying to do something bad to you, son. Traditions are a wonderful thing, but sometimes they take a little getting used to."

"Can I hold my nose?" John asked. "Felicia told me that they wouldn't taste so bad if I do."

Rose nodded, her eyes twinkling. "That would be okay. I used to hold my nose sometimes, too."

"We got to eat this food while it still be hot," Annie said when she reappeared with another platter heaped with fried chicken and biscuits.

Thomas reached over to put a hand on John's shoulder. "Can you and Simon be real quiet during the blessing?"

John nodded vigorously. "Yes, sir. Can you pray for a long time?"

Thomas bit back a laugh. "My praying a long time won't make the peas go away."

"Mama told me there is always hope," John said staunchly. "I'm hoping that your prayer is good enough to make these peas disappear!"

******

Quiet reigned while Thomas asked the blessing over the meal.

When Carrie opened her eyes, she knew she was in trouble. The room's heat, mixed with all the aromas of the food, was suddenly more than her system could handle. She pushed back her chair roughly, grabbed a napkin, and raced toward the kitchen, barely making it outside before her stomach rebelled. She felt Abby's comforting touch on her shoulder, as Rose's hand appeared with a damp cloth to wipe her face. Carrie leaned against the house and let the cold air embrace her. She was sure the other women were freezing, but it felt wonderful to her. It only took a few moments before she felt better. "I don't know what in the world is the matter with me," she muttered. She saw Rose and Abby exchange a look, but they just took her arms and led her back inside.

"I'm glad you feel better, but hypothermia is dangerous too," Rose observed. "Do you think you can stand being back in the dining room?"

Carrie wasn't at all sure, but she didn't want to miss being with everyone. "I want to try."

"Annie has fixed you some toast and hot tea," Abby said, tucking an arm around her waist to support her. "I told her you probably wouldn't feel like eating."

"How long do you think this flu will go on?" Carrie asked.

"Aren't you the medical expert?" Rose teased.

"I guess I'm still learning," Carrie answered. "I've looked in my books for things to help with a stomach flu, but nothing seems to be helping."

The room was quiet when the women appeared at the door.

Janie spoke into the silence. "I'm afraid you won't find anything in the homeopathic books to help, Carrie. At least not for what you are looking for."

Carrie looked at her, confused by the twinkle in her friend's eyes. She grew more confused when she saw the same humor lurking in the eyes of every woman at the table. "Am I missing something?"

"I guess it just goes to show that nobody ought to be their own patient," Annie observed.

Carrie's stomach started to churn again. "I'm afraid I don't feel up to riddles. Can someone just make sense of this for me? I'm tired of feeling bad."

"It might last a while longer," Annie said solemnly. She glanced at Polly.

"Yep. It could last a while longer," Polly agreed.

Carrie's eyes widened as understanding filtered through the curtain of nausea. "You mean I'm..."

"Pregnant?" Janie replied. "I do believe that would be the proper diagnosis."

"Pregnant?" Robert asked with a gasp, his own eyes growing wide. "Carrie is pregnant?"

Carrie sat quietly, trying to absorb the news. It certainly all made sense now. "I have morning sickness?"

Abby took her hand. "You have morning sickness," she agreed, and then looked at Thomas with a glowing smile. "We are going to be grandparents."

Carrie fought the nausea as a warm joy spread through her body. Her hand touched her stomach gently. Then she met Robert's eyes. "I guess I'm pregnant," she said softly.

Robert's face exploded with joy. "Pregnant," he said hoarsely. "We're going to have a baby." His voice was a mixture of awe and disbelief. He stared at Carrie's hand on her belly. "A baby..." he repeated.

"Congratulations!" Rose cried.

Carrie felt intense joy, but the heat from the room was making her ill again. "How long...?"

"How long will you be sick?" Polly asked. "I guess it depends on how far along you are."

Carrie did a quick calculation in her head. Now that she knew she was pregnant, she was able to think back to when her last menstrual period had been. She gasped and met Robert's eyes. The look on his face said he knew too. Their lovemaking in the clearing by the river in October had produced a child. Carrie's fears that Robert couldn't conceive children had obviously been wrong. "Almost three months," she said softly, her eyes holding Robert's as their message of love spread through her.

Polly nodded. "That's about what I figured. You're lucky this didn't hit sooner. You'll probably feel sick another couple weeks, and then it will ease up."

"Peppermint and Ginger tea will help with the nausea," Janie said helpfully. "When I get back to Philadelphia, I'll send down some *Colchium*. It should take care of the rest of your symptoms. I used it with another pregnant woman the week before we came to the plantation. It worked wonders."

Carrie smiled as the word *pregnant* resonated through her mind and heart. "We will have a baby in July."

Robert reached over and grasped her hand. "I apologize that I called you an old woman this morning." His voice was remorseful, but his face contradicted his words.

"You called my daughter an *old woman*?" Thomas asked. "And you lived to tell about it?"

"At least so far," Abby retorted. "Carrie may have been too sick to retaliate, but the rest of the women around this table are just fine."

"Amen!" Janie said with flashing eyes.

Robert held up his hands in surrender. "I was just teasing her," he protested. "I have certainly learned enough in our marriage to not be quite *that* stupid."

"That's a great relief," Rose said sternly.

"It certainly is," Felicia added. "I may only be twelve, but even I know you should never call your wife an old woman!"

When the laughter died away, Robert rose and lifted Carrie from the chair. "I can tell by the look on your face that you are about to be sick again. I'm taking you upstairs."

Carrie wanted to deny his statement, but her rolling stomach was not to be ignored. "That would be nice," she agreed with a weak smile. She made no complaint when he wrapped an arm around her waist gently and helped her up the stairs.

Robert held up a hand when Polly and Janie rose to join them. "I'll take care of my wife," he said firmly. "I certainly learned enough when I was sick to know how to handle this." He looked down at Annie. "If you'll just put a bucket of water and some rags outside the door, I would appreciate it."

"I'll do that," Annie answered. She turned to look at everyone. "Ain't none of y'all can do anything Robert can't do, and babies been coming in this world for as long as people been livin'. Y'all go ahead and eat this food 'fore it gets stone cold."

****

Robert lowered Carrie gently on the bed, and then placed pillows beneath her head.

"Can you open the window a little?" Carrie begged. The fire had done its job of warming the room, but now she found it suffocating.

Robert opened the window quickly. "I guess that means you don't need a quilt?"

Carrie's smile was shaky. "Not right now, anyway."

Robert sat down on the bed gently, and then reached out to touch her stomach lightly. "*A baby...*"

"Our child," Carrie said, full of the same awe he had. "We're going to have a child."

A smile spread across Robert's face. "I wasn't sure it would ever happen."

Carrie didn't admit just how afraid she had been of the same thing. Fatigue pressed down on her. Now that she knew why she was so sick, she could also admit how tired she was. Both she and her child needed rest.

Robert saw it, too. "You need to sleep," he said firmly. "You have more than just yourself to take care of now."

Carrie's eyes drooped as the darkness closed in. A child. She and Robert were going to have a child. Sudden terror ripped through the curtain of joy.

What kind of world was she bringing a child into?

Chapter Two

Five days passed before the snow melted enough to clear the roads into Richmond. The warmer air came with a strong wind that dried the mud quickly. Bright sunshine outlined the oak trees standing guard over their house, their silver and grey branches brushing each other in a graceful dance.

Carrie gazed out the window as she took deep breaths. "I used to hate winter."

Robert glanced up from where he knelt by the fire, emptying ashes into a bucket to haul outside. "Why?"

"I like green," Carrie answered. "It was always so sad to me when the trees lost their leaves. I saw nothing but stark barrenness that seemed to mock me. I could hardly wait until spring brought out the green again."

"And now?"

Carrie smiled. "It was something Miles told me."

"Miles?"

Carrie felt a wave of sadness. "Miles was one of my father's slaves. He managed the stables." Her voice softened with remembering. "He taught me almost everything I know about horses. He taught me how to ride... how to jump." Her voice dissolved into laughter. "He even helped me keep the jumping a secret from my mother. She would have died if she had found out."

"How did he do that?"

"He found a big clearing back in the woods that he set up jumps in. No one ever suspected a thing."

"Not even your father?" Robert asked in an amused voice.

"Especially my father. He had to defend me for so many things to my mother. I didn't think he needed another one that big."

"Did Miles die?" Robert finished filling the bucket, and came to stand beside her at the window.

"No," Carrie said quickly. "He was among the first slaves to escape before the war. Rose received word that they had made it through to Canada, but there has never been any direct communication." She brushed back the wispy curls the wind was blowing around her face. "I so wish I knew what had happened to him. I think his escape was the hardest for my father to take. He hated losing any of his slaves, but he just couldn't understand why Miles would leave. He thought he loved running the Cromwell stables."

"He loved the idea of freedom more," Robert replied.

"Yes," Carrie murmured, amazed once again at how far her husband had come. "Anyway, we were out riding in the woods one day in the winter when I was about fifteen. He made me stop and tell him what I saw in the trees."

"What you saw?"

"Yes, he told me how much he loved the winter woods because every tree became a sculpture that stood on its own without the leaves to blur its lines. When I started looking at them differently, I realized each of them had its own special magic. I quit hating winter that day."

Robert's eyes scanned the massive oak standing guard over the house. "The *winter woods*. I like that."

Carrie reached for her coat when she heard the rattle of the carriage wheels. "Everyone is about to leave. I want to say good-bye."

"You're sure you feel like it?"

Carrie shook her head. "No, but I don't think there is anything left in my system to throw up," she said with a smile. "I've hardly been downstairs the last few days. I want to at least say good-bye." She held up a hand when Robert opened his mouth. "Don't try to change my mind. Now that I know I'm pregnant I will take care of myself, but I will not be coddled."

"Your father warned me about this," Robert muttered as his concerned eyes scanned her face.

"My father is a wise man," Carrie retorted as she turned and walked across the room.

****

Abby held Carrie close before she released her and stepped back. "You'll take good care of yourself?"

"Are you concerned about me, or about your grandchild?" Carrie teased.

"Both, of course," Abby agreed easily.

Carrie caught the shadow of worry in her eyes. "My father told you about my mother."

"That she almost died giving birth to you? Yes," Abby responded softly. "He told me."

Carrie decided it would be a waste of effort to try and hide her own concern. Abby knew her too well. "I'm going to take good care of myself," she said gently. "Robert and I want this child. I'm not going to be careless."

Abby gazed at her for a long moment before she finally nodded. "You'll let me know if you need anything?"

Janie walked down to join them. "And me, too? I can't believe I'm going to be so far away while you are pregnant."

Carrie managed to laugh around the lump in her throat. "You just want to see me get fat," she accused.

"That too," Janie conceded, but then she grabbed Carrie's hands. "I know you are the last person you think about so I'm not going to tell you to take care of yourself. I'm going to tell you to take care of your child."

Thomas appeared on the porch with Matthew, loaded down with suitcases. "I trust y'all are talking sense into my hard-headed daughter."

"The best we can," Abby assured him, and then stepped forward to hug her stepdaughter again.

Carrie savored the warm embrace. She had been too sick since the discovery she was pregnant, to talk about the things that were really on her mind. She longed to have a long conversation with Abby, but now they were going to again be separated by the miles between the plantation and Richmond.

When Janie stepped away to talk to Rose, Abby lowered her head to Carrie's ear. "I know, honey. You are excited about your child, but you are also wondering about your future."

Carrie stiffened as Abby spoke the words she had fought even acknowledging.

"It's perfectly normal, Carrie, but I just want to tell you that having children doesn't have to end your plans. They will change some, but you can still be a doctor."

Carrie closed her eyes tightly as she sagged into Abby's arms for a brief instant.

"It's time to go," Thomas called. "We want to make Richmond before it gets dark."

"Thank you," Carrie whispered before she stepped back from her stepmother. She had the same questions swirling through her mind, but she no longer felt so alone.

****

The next minutes were a flurry of activity. When the carriage finally disappeared into the distance, Carrie sank down on the step and gazed up at the sky dotted with fleecy white clouds that had danced their way onto the azure canvas.

"I will miss everyone, but I think I'm also going to enjoy the peace," Rose said as she sank down next to her.

"Yes," Carrie agreed absently, her eyes watching the flight of a hawk circling above them, the sun glinting off the red in its feathers.

"Feel up to visiting mama?" Rose asked.

Carrie watched the hawk as she pondered the question. She knew Rose felt the angst tightening her belly. She couldn't blame pregnancy for what she was feeling at the moment. Rose was offering her the chance to talk, or the opportunity to remain silent if that was what she needed. "I might get sick," she finally murmured.

"Mama and I won't mind."

Carrie was grateful for the warm breeze as they walked slowly through the woods. Sunlight transformed the grey bark of hundreds of trees a shimmering silver. Cardinals, blue jays, and an army of sparrows created bright splashes of color as they flitted through the branches. She felt herself relaxing as the forest embraced her, but the questions continued to rampage in her mind.

Carrie sank down on the log pulled in front of Sarah's grave. "I'd give just about anything to have a talk with your mama," she whispered.

"I know just how you feel," Rose answered. "Of course, she would just tell you that the baby growing inside of you is a gift from God. She would tell you that you are going to be a great mama, and that she knows you love your child already." Rose paused. "She would also tell you it's perfectly normal to be wondering if your dreams will ever come true."

Carrie drew in a shaky breath as she lowered her head. There was no reason to deny the feelings with her best friend. "You think so?"

"I know so." Rose reached over and took her hand.

Carrie gripped it tightly as the feelings she had been pushing down rushed forward and attempted to overwhelm her. "I'm afraid, Rose."

"Of what?"

Carrie appreciated that Rose didn't tell her she shouldn't be feeling afraid. "That I won't be a good mother. That I'm crazy to raise a child in this world. That everything I've done to become a doctor will have only been a waste of time." Her voice faltered. "...And then I feel terrible..."

"For even thinking and feeling that?" Rose finished. "I felt all those same things. Oh, not so much when John was born because I didn't even know enough about what it would take to follow my dreams to think it might be harder with a son. I didn't even really feel it so much with Hope, but..." She stopped to take a deep breath. "I was terrified for Moses to bring Felicia home because I thought it meant I would have to give up everything I ever wanted. I felt terribly selfish, but

I couldn't deny I felt my dreams slipping further away. I didn't want my feelings to hurt a ten-year-old girl who had just lost both her parents."

"What did you do?" Carrie whispered.

"I went down by the river to talk to my mama – the very same day Moses brought her home. She told me I was borrowing trouble before it came."

Carrie managed a smile, not doubting for a moment that Rose had heard Sarah's voice from the other side. "That sounds like her. What else did she say?" She was desperate for words of wisdom that would calm her heart. The reality that they were coming from a dead woman only seemed to give them more importance.

Rose smiled, closed her eyes, and then repeated what she had heard by the river that day. *"Ain't I teached you nothin', girl? God sho 'nuff didn't give you this burnin' desire just to let it smolder out here on the plantation. You go ahead and love that Felicia child like you love your own. You ain't got no idea what a gift she is to you. You'll figure it out soon enough. Your time is coming, Rose girl. Your time be coming..."*

Rose pulled her hand free, and rested it on Carrie's shoulder. "I reckon she would say the same thing to you, Carrie."

"Why is that my time seems to always be *coming*?"

Rose shook her head impatiently. "Now you're just being silly," she scolded.

Carrie's eyes widened, a little shocked by the sudden change in tone. "What do you mean?"

"You act like this happened *to* you, Carrie. *You* are the one who decided to stay on the plantation. *You* are the one who was afraid Robert couldn't have children." Rose took a deep breath as the hot words spilled out. "If I didn't know you better, I would think you were just looking for something to be afraid about."

Carrie shrank back, but didn't look away from the challenge in Rose's eyes. What was the point of having a best friend if they couldn't speak honestly? If Rose was speaking the truth, she needed to know it. *Was* she looking for something to be afraid of?

Silence filled the clearing as she forced herself to think about what Rose had said. The wind died down to a whisper as the sun's rays landed on Sarah's simple headstone, causing the mica in the granite to glisten and twinkle. Finally she lowered her head. "I don't know how to be two people," she admitted. "How can I be both a mother and a doctor? My mother always told me I should just be happy with being a plantation wife and mother. I think she knew I couldn't be more than that."

"Do you believe her?" Rose asked. Her voice was calm, but her eyes were flashing.

Carrie thought back over her childhood; reliving all the times her mother had tried to shape her into someone she could never be. She had already accomplished so much more than what her mother had believed a woman was capable of. She laid a hand on her stomach and tried to feel the life that was growing there. What was it about the baby growing inside her that suddenly had her doubting everything she had come to believe about herself? "How do you do it?" she asked, suddenly desperate to know. "How can you be the mother of three children, and still believe you can go to college and be a teacher?"

Rose seemed to understand the desperation in her voice. "I do nothing for my children if I choose to be less than I am," she said bluntly. "I'm afraid every day of raising my children in this world, but what choice do I have? This is the world they were born into. They are going to have more opportunities than I could have ever believed possible when I was their age, but they are probably also going to encounter more hate and danger than I even knew existed when I grew up on the plantation." Her voice grew firmer. "The only way I can make things better for them is to help change things. The only way I can make things better for all my students is to help change things."

Carrie shook her head impatiently, the angst she felt swelling in her chest and throat until she was afraid she couldn't breathe. "But *how*? I know the reasons why, but you're not telling me *how*."

Rose sat back and stared at her for a long moment, obviously trying to formulate words that would answer her question. "The same way you survived the war," she finally said as she grabbed one of Carrie's hands. "How many times did you feel you couldn't possibly go on when the wards at Chimborazo kept filling with wounded men fighting for their life? How many times were you so tired that you just wanted to curl up somewhere, but somehow managed to pull forth the energy to keep going? How many times did you have to choose to simply *do it* because you didn't really have any other choice?"

Carrie met her eyes steadily. "Every day of the war," she admitted.

"How did you do it?" Rose asked quietly.

Carrie managed a smile. "I understand."

"Do you?" Rose persisted. "You're not answering my question. *How* did you do it?"

"I just did what needed to be done," Carrie replied slowly. "I didn't really think about the how. I just did it because there were people who needed me. I did it because I wanted to be a doctor. I did it because I saw Robert's face in every single soldier I treated."

"So you just figured it out each day?" Rose asked keenly, her black eyes snapping with passion.

"Yes," Carrie whispered, the knot in her stomach unraveling as the truth of Rose's words and questions penetrated her fear.

"And that, Carrie, is exactly how you will be a mother and also a doctor. The how is not important. The *why* is everything. You will figure it out as you go." Rose's gaze softened. "We both will." She turned back to stare at her mother's grave. "I wonder every day how I'm going to go to school with three children," she admitted quietly. "But then I remember the *why*, and I know I'll just have to figure it out as I go. Mama used to tell me I could spend all my energy worrying about something, or I could just go do it."

Carrie sat quietly for several minutes, gripping Rose's hand tightly as she stared at Sarah's grave. Gradually, new understanding replaced all the angst and desperation. She placed her hand on her stomach, and turned her head to gaze into Rose's eyes as tears filled her own. "I'm having a baby," she whispered.

"That you are," Rose replied joyfully. "The morning sickness will go away soon. Then you're left with months of feeling a new life grow inside you. It's the most amazing feeling in the world," she said hoarsely, memories filling her eyes.

Carrie smiled brilliantly "Even when I'm sick, I think about who is growing inside me. I wonder what they will look like? I wonder what they will become." Her smile dimmed. "I also wonder what kind of world I'm letting them be born into."

"A world they can help make better," Rose said firmly, and then sighed heavily. "I would give anything to protect Felicia, John, and Hope from what the world is like right now. I can't imagine any parent not feeling the same way."

Carrie nodded. "I hoped our country would be so different after the war. I thought everything would be alright once slavery had ended. We went through so much during the war..."

"But it hasn't ended," Rose finished grimly.

Carrie suddenly realized how petty her own fears were. "I'm sorry!" she cried.

"What are you talking about?" Rose demanded. "What are you sorry for?"

"For being so upset about how I was going to be a mother and a doctor," Carrie answered, her mind spinning furiously. "At least my child won't have to worry about being treated badly just because of the color of their skin. I don't have to worry about my child being denied the right to live the life they want to."

"Only if it's a boy," Rose said dryly, a hint of amusement lurking in her eyes. "Women have to fight for everything, no matter what color we are."

"I'm serious, Rose," Carrie insisted. "As much as I try to understand, I know it's not possible for me to truly understand what it is like to be black in America."

The amusement faded from Rose's eyes. She turned to look back at Sarah's grave. "It is what it is," she said finally.

"I heard Jeremy and Matthew talking yesterday," Carrie admitted. "They both think matters are going to get worse."

Rose sighed, but remained silent.

"It's not right," Carrie said fiercely. She wanted to protect her best friend's children as much as she wanted to protect her own. "We have to make it different." She was startled when Rose spun to look at her with eyes full of bold strength, determination, and an odd desperation.

"And we will," she announced. "We don't have a choice. Our children are depending on us."

Carrie gazed at her, almost overwhelmed with the strength she felt flowing from her best friend. The words penetrated her soul, and filled her heart. "You're going to be a great woman, Rose."

"Yes, I am," Rose agreed easily, a tiny smile erasing the desperation. "We are both going to be great women because the time we are living in requires great women. We can count on others to change things, or we can just do it ourselves."

Carrie let her words fill the clearing. The barren trees seemed to reach out to capture the words, and hold them suspended over their heads where they could be carefully examined. The weak winter sun cast a glow over them as their truth spun a cocoon to envelop them.

Carrie finally nodded, a new strength and purpose filling her. "We will be great women," she agreed. Then she frowned.

"What?" Rose asked, a little impatiently.

Carrie turned to look back at Sarah's grave. "Your mama told me one time that greatness comes from great suffering." She paused, not really wanting to put into words what she was thinking, but pulled forward by the desire to hear what Rose's answer would be. "Do you think we have suffered enough yet to be great, or do you think more is coming?"

Rose shifted her eyes to her mama's grave. "Right now I'm just wishing my mama wasn't always right," she said hesitantly. "We're both not quite twenty-five years old," she added slowly. "I wish I could believe we have both suffered enough to be truly great women, but..."

Carrie continued to hold her best friend's hand. "I can handle anything as long as we handle it together. I will always be here for you, Rose," she promised.

Rose turned to her with a glowing smile. "And I will always be here for you, Carrie."

The promise wrapped Carrie in a blanket of warmth that held her close as they walked back to the house. She smiled, as she always did, when they broke free from the woods and she saw her home outlined against a sky kissed golden by the waning sun. The three-story white home with its columned porch and carefully guarded secret always made her feel safe. She tightened when a sudden burst of wind scudding across the sky sent a thick cloud to blanket the sun, plunging the house into a dark shadow.

Carrie frowned when her heart quickened with alarm. The question rose from within and threatened to swallow her. *What would she have to suffer in order to become a great woman?*

Chapter 3

January 8, 1867

Janie pulled her heavy coat closer as she hurried through the snow-clogged, Philadelphia streets. She pushed aside images of the pristine white covering Cromwell Plantation as she stepped around another mountain of grey snow that had been pushed aside, and was now covered with coal soot. The roads were fairly clear; the air filled with the clop of horse hooves as wagons and carriages jockeyed for position. Street vendors yelled for her attention, but she had become adept at ignoring them. She lowered her head and walked more quickly.

She and Matthew had only been home two days. Her brain was spinning with all she had learned that day at the Homeopathic College. Thinking about her courses made it easier to push aside memories of the peaceful plantation. She was happy to be back at school – she merely wished it was possible to be in two places at one time.

As she drew closer to the yellow-sided home she now shared with Matthew, her discontent disappeared. She was married! The surreal glow that had surrounded her since her wedding on Christmas Eve was slowly beginning to feel like reality. She really was Matthew's wife!

The warm glow from the windows told her he had arrived home early today. He had warned her he would probably be late tonight. Her heartbeat quickened with alarm. Only important news could have made him leave the *Philadelphia Enquirer* office early so soon upon his return.

Janie burst in through the front door. Matthew appeared at the door to the kitchen as she quickly unbuttoned her coat and tossed it haphazardly on the hook next to the door.

"What's wrong, Janie? I was watching you come down the street. I don't believe I have ever seen you move so fast." Matthew's blue eyes were dark with concern as he glanced at the door. "Was someone after you?" he asked sharply, and then forced his voice to relax. "Of course, maybe you were just eager to get home to your new husband," he added lightly.

"Is it good news, or bad?" Janie demanded, her soft, blue eyes fixed on his as she pulled her hat off, brown hair breaking free from her bun and cascading down her back.

Matthew didn't pretend to not understand. "Good," he assured her. "I should have known my early arrival would alarm you," he said apologetically.

Janie relaxed as soon as the words came out of his mouth. "I'm glad you're home early," she said warmly. "It's just that after so many years of horrible news – especially where you are concerned – it may take me a while to not anticipate the worst." She wrapped her arms around Matthew's waist, and pulled him close. "Hello, husband."

Matthew chuckled. "Hello, wife." He pulled her close, and lowered his head to give her a kiss. "I have a surprise for you."

Janie smiled. "It's hard to keep chicken soup and apple pie a secret when the aromas are swirling out of the kitchen like a snowstorm."

"Do they smell good?" Matthew asked hopefully.

"Heavenly!" Janie, starving now that there was no cause for alarm, turned toward the kitchen. "Is it ready to eat?"

"Ten minutes."

Janie altered her course, and went to stand beside the gas heater. "Then you have time to tell me the good news. Talk," she commanded.

Matthew chuckled again. "Am I the only one who knows you are not nearly as mild-mannered as you want the world to think?"

"It's best to keep everyone guessing," Janie said primly. "They don't pay me nearly as much attention so it's easier to achieve my agenda."

Matthew threw back his head with a laugh. "I'll remember that for the future."

"That would be wise," Janie agreed easily, her eyes sparkling with laughter. "Now, tell me what happened."

Matthew took a deep breath. "Black men were given the right to vote in Washington, DC. Congress approved it today."

"That's wonderful," Janie exclaimed, but then hesitated. "They can do that? I thought they had to pass an Amendment for blacks to get the vote."

"Washington, DC is rather unique," Matthew explained. It's not actually a state, and it is not part of any state. Congress approved the creation of a capital district along the Potomac River in 1790. The Constitution proclaimed it would be a federal district under the exclusive jurisdiction of the Congress."

"So they don't have to have anyone's permission," Janie observed. "They can do whatever they want?"

"Well, yes, but whatever they do has to pass with the majority of the Congress."

Janie thought about that for a minute. "President Johnson approved this?"

Matthew snorted. "Hardly. Our president vetoed it. Congress overrode his veto and made it law. It's just the beginning of what our president can anticipate. Now that the Republicans have such a strong control of the Congress, they can be fairly certain of accomplishing what they want."

Janie turned to look out the window, not even minding when the first flakes of new snow floated down past the oil lampposts stationed outside the house. "So it's begun," she said quietly.

"Yes, it's begun," Matthew agreed. "It's just a matter of time until black suffrage is law throughout the country."

"For men," Janie said wryly.

"Yes." Matthew stepped up to wrap his arm around her waist. "I'm sorry, Janie. But I do believe women will have the vote in this country in the future."

Janie pushed aside her retort that it should have *already* happened. She knew how much Matthew wanted women to have the vote. There was something else, though... "What aren't you telling me, Matthew?"

Matthew blinked down at her. "Not telling you?"

"Black men getting the vote, even if it is only in Washington, DC, is a truly historic event. So many people have fought for it." Janie narrowed her eyes. "Your excitement is rather underwhelming."

Matthew frowned, and then smiled. "It will take me time to get used to having a wife who knows me almost as well as I know myself."

"I have the advantage," Janie said smugly. "I've been watching you for years. I wanted to know everything about you. If you hadn't been smitten with Carrie for so long, you would have realized it." She felt a flash of sympathy at the embarrassment that flashed through her husband's eyes. "Oh, pooh, you finally came to your senses." She decided to answer the question she saw on his face. "And, yes, I know you love me desperately, and are completely over your infatuation with Carrie. You finally proved you are as intelligent as I always believed you were," she added smugly.

Matthew pulled her close. "As long as you know I love you desperately," he said tenderly.

Janie smiled as she eased away from the kiss. "I'll know it more if you will answer my question."

Matthew groaned as a grin twitched his lips. "*You* should be the journalist."

"Perhaps," Janie agreed complacently. "Right now I'll just settle for knowing why you aren't wildly excited about blacks getting the vote."

Matthew lifted his head and sniffed. "I promise to tell you, but only in the kitchen. The nose my mother trained so well in the mountains of West Virginia tells me the apple pie is done. My guess is that you don't want it to burn."

Janie turned, grabbed his hand, and pulled him toward the kitchen.

****

Questions about Matthew's response to the black vote disappeared as the steam and aromas coming from the pot of chicken soup enveloped Janie. She walked over and lifted the lid in order to get the full effect of it billowing into her face. "There is not anything I would rather have than your chicken soup on a day like today. I wish it was possible for me to thank your mother for raising such an incredible son."

"Me too," Matthew said wistfully. He gazed out the window for a long moment. "Smelling this soup puts me right back in the mountain cabin I grew up in. My mama was the best cook in the world. She knew how to make anything taste good. We didn't have much money, but we always ate well." He turned back to look at Janie. "Mama would have loved you so much. I hate that she won't get to meet you, and I hate that she died before we could produce fabulous grandchildren for her."

Janie's heart softened at the longing in his eyes, even as her heart quickened at the idea of having his children. "How many?"

"Children?"

Janie nodded. "We've never talked about that."

"Twelve would be fine."

Janie blinked, searching for words, but came up blank. "Excuse me?" she finally managed.

Matthew chuckled. "I just wanted to see how you would react. Twelve might be fine for a mountain family that requires a labor force, but I have a feeling we won't need so many."

"That's good," Janie said faintly. Having grown up an only child, she couldn't begin to imagine twelve of her own.

"How many do you want?" Matthew asked. "Since you raised the question..."

Janie thought about it as he ladled the soup into bowls, and then added a thick slice of buttered bread onto the plates beside them. "Right now even one, while I'm still in school, seems impossible, but I've actually dreamed of having four children."

"Four," Matthew repeated with a smile. "That sounds like a fine number. I hope they all look like you."

"And I hope they all have red hair and bright blue eyes," Janie replied. She paused. "I'm worried about Carrie."

Matthew cocked his head. "Carrie? Why? Women get pregnant every day."

"Carrie's mother almost died giving birth to her. She could never have more children."

"Surely that doesn't have anything to do with Carrie. She knows how to take care of herself."

"Of course she does," Janie said quickly, "but sometimes the reasons get passed down to the offspring." She paused long enough to eat some of her steaming soup. "They don't know what causes it, but some women just have a very hard time bearing children. I spoke with Dr. Strikener about it today."

Matthew frowned. "Did he have any suggestions?"

"He gave me a list of treatments to send to her, but he said the most important thing she could do is listen carefully to her body and not push herself."

Matthew's frown deepened. "I'm not sure she has any idea how to do that."

"I know," Janie said worriedly. "I wrote her a long letter before I left school today. Hopefully, she will take it seriously." She ate several more bites of soup, and then shook her head. "I know worrying will not do any good. Tell me about why you are not extremely excited about the black vote in Washington, DC." She wanted Matthew to distract her from the concern she was having such a difficult time shaking.

"I *am* excited about the black vote," Matthew insisted. "It's the first step that will lead to suffrage for all black men, but I learn more each day that tells me the road is going to be very long and hard."

Janie fixed her eyes on him, but kept eating. She knew from experience that he would explain himself if she just remained quiet. Steam hissed from the gas heater as she waited.

Matthew finally shook his head. "It took four years of war to make the slaves free. I suspect it will take far more violence before they truly have the right to actually *live* free," he said heavily.

Janie gazed at him for a moment. "We've talked before about the fact that the war is not actually over. Something has happened." It was not a question. When she saw Matthew hesitate, her voice sharpened. "I do not want to be protected, Matthew. The benefit of being married to a journalist is that I can learn things before most people. You will only make me angry if you hold back."

"I know," Matthew said with a sigh. "It's not really what has *happened*, though. It's more a feeling for what is coming."

"Which you have been right about every single time," Janie reminded him.

"I suppose so," Matthew murmured, his eyes focused on something she couldn't see. "Americans wanted the slaves free, but most of them have no intention of ever accepting them as being equal. I don't think many of them ever considered that could actually happen."

"Northerners included?"

"Yes. Oh, I know abolitionism started here, and I know members of Congress are pushing hard for black rights, but they are only a tiny percent of the American population. Most people in the North want the blacks to be free, but they also want them to be kept in their place. The South is a whole different issue."

"The vigilante groups."

"Yes," Matthew agreed, "but…"

Janie eyed him sharply when his voice trailed away. "The truth, Matthew."

"That's the trouble," he replied. "I don't know what the truth is." His eyes met hers steadily. "But I suspect it is going to get far worse. I'm afraid what we are seeing right now is just the beginning. Now that the Republicans have control, and are determined to pass new amendments to give blacks full rights as American citizens, I believe the backlash is going to be more violent and more extreme. When word gets out that the blacks have been given the right to vote in Washington, DC, I don't think it will be taken well."

"But the South lost the war," Janie protested. "I know it will take time to get used to that, but surely they won't risk another war."

"Desperate men don't usually do a lot of thinking," Matthew said flatly. "They act from their emotions and their fear. They don't usually consider the consequences. Yes," he continued, "the South lost the war, but each person in it still has their hopes and beliefs."

"And their pride," Janie added.

"Yes, their pride," Matthew agreed. "Pride is a powerful thing, even if it is misplaced. Every Confederate soldier has had their pride damaged. There are men who will do just about anything to try to restore it."

"By hurting the freed slaves?" Janie asked. "That doesn't make any sense."

Matthew managed a small smile. "None of this makes any sense. It seems that people, for all of time, have wanted someone to look down on. Someone to feel superior to. Instead of taking responsibility for their own feelings of inadequacy and failure, they blame them on someone else. They take out their rage and anger on whoever they believe is weakest."

Janie absorbed his words. She didn't want to believe him, but the last five years had taught her he was right. "What's coming?" she asked quietly.

"I don't know," Matthew admitted. "I just believe it's going to be worse than anything we have seen so far. We won't know until it happens. The vigilante groups are like the top of the carrot. We can't really see what is growing underground. But it is growing," he said ominously, his eyes dark with concern. "It is growing, and I don't believe it will be long before it is pulled out of the ground."

Janie swallowed hard. She had asked him to tell her the truth. She couldn't choose to hide from it now. "Then we will all deal with it," she said bravely.

Matthew turned his eyes on her. "Yes, but some of us will have much more to deal with. The color of our skin affords us some protection, but so many of the people we love are going to be in serious danger."

Janie could think of absolutely nothing to say so she settled for grabbing his hand, and squeezing it tightly.

****

Carrie looked up as the door to the clinic opened, letting in a blast of cold air. She pushed away the strands of hair floating down into her face as a harried-looking mother, holding two small children by the hand, entered the small building.

Polly bustled forward, her face creased with a warm smile. "Hello. How may I help you?"

"It's my kids," the woman replied, tired blue eyes peering out from a tangle of blond hair.

She looked to be in her thirties, but Carrie suspected she was far younger – probably closer to her age. The last years had aged everyone. She listened closely as she finished bandaging the hand of one of the men from Cromwell Plantation. He had cut it badly while taking down some trees for firewood, but he would recover.

"Both my kids are real sick," she said wearily. "We ain't got enough to eat, and this weather has been real hard on them."

Carrie's eyes turned to the children. Both of them had eyes glazed with fever, and their faces were flushed above their too thin coats. They were both trembling from the cold.

Polly, observing the same thing, grabbed two thick blankets and wrapped them around the children, pushing them gently down into two chairs. Then she handed the mom a blanket. "I expect you need this just as much as your kids."

The woman accepted the blanket gratefully, pulling it close. It would take a while for the warmth from the fire to stop the shivering. "My kids are supposed to start school in a couple days," she said quietly. "I don't want them to miss it. Neither one of them ever been to school."

Carrie's heart ached for her. She reached down to touch her stomach lightly. The nausea had finally eased enough for her to come to work. Robert had questioned her being around sick people, but she couldn't just ignore the patients who had come to count on her. Besides, she had been treating ill people for six years, and not once had she gotten sick herself. Seeing the young mother, however, made her ache for the other woman's pain. She couldn't imagine knowing her own child, yet to be born, would go hungry, or cold, or not have an education.

She finished wrapping the hand. "You're good to go, Benjamin. Try and keep that axe away from your hand next time," she said lightly. "Come back tomorrow so I can change the dressing, and put on a fresh layer of ointment. I'll change it each day for the next week. Do *not* let your hand get dirty," she said more firmly. "You will recover fully before spring planting, but only if you don't let it get infected. I'll take the stitches out in seven days."

"Yes, ma'am," Benjamin said stoutly. "I'll do just what you said. I don't want to have to answer to Moses."

"To Moses?" Carrie asked innocently, concealing her smile.

"Yes, ma'am. He told me he would forgive me for being careless enough to cut my hand, but he wouldn't let me off easy if I didn't do just what you says to do. Moses be a real good man, but I don't want him mad at me," Benjamin said earnestly.

"Wise man," Carrie replied with a chuckle. Moses sent every one of his men to her with the same threat. It always worked. "Now go on home."

She watched him leave, and then turned to the children with a gentle smile. "Hello."

"Did you really sew that man up?" The little boy, who looked to be six or seven, clearly thought that was not likely.

"I did," Carrie assured him.

"But you be a woman," he persisted.

"Silas! Don't be rude," his mother scolded. "I'm sorry, Doctor Borden," she said quickly.

Carrie smiled at the woman. "What's your name?"

"Amanda Williams."

"Well, Amanda, welcome to the clinic. You can call me Carrie, and your little boy can feel free to ask questions. I don't mind at all. How long have the children been sick?"

"They started feeling poorly about five days ago," Amanda answered timidly.

Carrie hid her frown as she nodded briskly, and knelt in front of the little boy, not missing the flash of gratitude in the tired woman's eyes. A normal cold would have run its course in five days. The children's had developed into something more serious, probably pneumonia, but she kept her voice light. "It's nice to meet you Silas."

The little girl, a year or so younger, seated next to him smiled timidly. "I'm Violet."

Carrie turned to her, and placed a cool hand on the burning forehead. "I bet you don't feel so good, do you, honey?"

"No, ma'am. I reckon I don't. Silas be sick, too."

"Yes, I can tell both of you are," Carrie agreed. "I think we should do something about that."

"You can make us feel better?" Silas asked weakly. "Even though you just a woman?"

Carrie glanced at Amanda with a reassuring smile, and then turned back to Silas. "There are a lot of women doctors now," she said gently. She decided there was no need to mention she wasn't an actual doctor yet. She had been working as one for the last 4 years. A diploma would make other people feel better about her credentials, but the poor people coming to her clinic only wanted to know if she could make them well. "And, yes, I can make you feel better."

Silas seemed to accept her answer. "Thank you," he said simply before he took a deep breath and erupted into hoarse coughing that seemed to cause spasms through his entire thin body.

Carrie looked up at Polly, but didn't have to say anything. Her assistant nodded, and headed into the remedy closet.

"Can you make me feel better, too?" Violet asked, her little body continuing to tremble in spite of the blanket and the warm room.

Carrie reached forward to take the little girl's hand, brushing back damp strands of blond curls with her other hand. "Yes, honey. I can make you feel better, too."

"Right away?" Violet whispered. "I'm feeling real bad."

Carrie smiled. "You're not going to feel very well for the rest of the day, I'm afraid, but I believe you'll wake up in the morning feeling much better."

Violet tried to smile back, but a wracking cough took over before she could.

Carrie looked up at their mother. "Is your home warm?" she asked.

Amanda flushed, but she didn't look away. "Not very," she admitted. "My husband tries real hard, but he ain't been able to get work since the war. He was gone the whole four years. We managed somehow. I thought things would get easier when he came home, but he can't get work."

"Can't he chop wood for a fire?" Polly asked when she emerged from the supply room.

Bitterness twisted Amanda's face. "It ain't so easy to do when you only got one arm, and your left leg is a stump from the knee down," she said bluntly. "He had to have both of them amputated during the siege of Richmond. They completely froze up during that long winter."

Carrie grimaced. She knew exactly how horrible that time had been.

Amanda continued before she could respond. "I try to cut enough, but it upsets him to see me chopping the wood." Shame filled her eyes as she looked at her sick children.

Carrie's heart squeezed with sympathy. "I'm so sorry," she said softly. She looked up at Polly. "These children are staying here tonight."

"Here?" Amanda asked sharply. "This ain't no hospital."

"No," Carrie agreed, "but it is most certainly a place where people get well. Your children need to be warm tonight if they are going to get better. We'll make up beds for them in the back room. You can stay here to care for them. I'll give you everything you need." She didn't add that at least the woman could be warm for one night.

Amanda hesitated, and then nodded, her eyes flooding with gratitude. "Thank you," she whispered. She glanced at the door, a sudden look of concern filling her face.

Carrie understood. "Go home and tell your husband I won't let the children come home tonight. Tell him I insist you are here to care for them."

"My husband is a good man," Amanda said staunchly.

"Of course he is," Carrie agreed quickly. "The war has been hard on everyone's pride. And, the end of the war has only made things harder for some people." She locked eyes with Amanda. "Let's help your children without hurting his pride any more than it already has been. Now," she added briskly, "you head on home so we can start making your children feel better. Come back as soon as you can. I promise you they are in good hands."

Amanda's smile was genuine this time. "I know that, Miss Carrie. Folks ain't got nothing but good things to say about you."

Carrie smiled gently, and then turned back to Silas. "How about if we get you and Violet into a warm bed with some hot water bottles?" she suggested.

"I reckon that sounds real good," Silas answered weakly, his body seeming to sag with relief that he wouldn't have to walk home through the cold. All Violet could do was make a little whimper when Carrie reached out a hand for her.

Chapter Four

Amanda was back within an hour. She nodded when she entered the door, her eyes even heavier with fatigue, but she didn't say anything. Carrie could tell she was simply relieved to have a warm place to spend the night. She suspected the woman had barely had enough strength to make it back to the clinic.

"The children are settled," Carrie said. "We heated a pot of water with sage, mint and chamomile, and let them inhale it while we tented a towel over them. That helped their congestion, and it helps kill off the cold virus."

Amanda listened closely, but remained silent, her strained eyes saying her time with her husband had been less than pleasant.

Carrie pretended not to notice. "We gave both of them a hot bath, and then tucked them in with hot water bottles," she continued. "And Polly sliced onions for their feet."

Amanda stared at her. "Onions? For their feet?" She frowned. "I had heard you weren't a doctor like other ones, but I ain't never heard of anything like that."

Carrie smiled. "It's an old Indian cure for colds and fever. Polly sliced the onions about a quarter inch thick, and then placed them on the soles of their feet before she covered them with warm wool socks. You'll want to replace the onions around midnight tonight, and then again in the morning around seven o'clock. I will be in not long after that. You also want to make sure they drink plenty of water. I have put two pitchers beside the bed. Make sure they drink it all. They won't feel like eating until their fever goes away. We'll have something for them in the morning." She paused. "We also put a bowl with onions on either side of their bed. All of it will help draw out the fever. I suspect the children will need to stay here a couple days before they can return home."

"I ain't never heard of such a thing," Amanda said, but there was no resistance in her voice, just curiosity. "Who would have ever thought onions could make my babies better."

"I thought it was crazy when I first heard it," Carrie admitted, "but I've seen it work too many times to not believe in it." She waved her hand toward the back room. "We put the children in one bed, and made another for you so you can be close to them. There is plenty of firewood for you to keep the clinic warm. I'm afraid I'll have to count on you to do that."

"I'm grateful, Miss Carrie," Amanda replied quickly. "It will be real nice to have my children warm." She hesitated. "Me, too," she admitted. Then she met Carrie's eyes. "I told my husband that it's nothing but wrong for our children to be cold and sick. I told him I understood his pride was hurt, but that he was gonna have to let me cut the firewood from now on."

"What did he say?" Carrie asked, admiring the other woman's courage.

"I think he knew how sick our kids were when I brung them here. Like I said, he's a good man. He agreed to let me cut the wood," she said with relief. She smiled slightly. "I reckon he'll be happy to be warm, too."

"Wonderful!" Carrie exclaimed. "I'm sure the children will be well enough in a couple days to come home. They will stay healthy if they live in a warm house." Since the clinic was empty, and she had a little time before she needed to return to the plantation, she offered Amanda a cup of hot tea.

Amanda reached for it gratefully. "Thank you," she murmured.

"Polly will be back soon with some bread and chicken soup. If the children wake up hungry at any time, the soup will be perfect for them."

Amanda smiled. "And the bread?"

Carrie shrugged. "Annie makes the best bread in the world. I think you'll love it." Then she changed the subject because she knew how hard it must be for Amanda to accept what must feel like charity. "You said Silas and Violet are supposed to start school tomorrow. Where?"

Amanda cocked her head in the direction of the back wall. "Right next door."

Carrie smiled. "I'm glad to hear it." Of course she knew about Rose opening the school to all children in the area, but no one knew if any of the white children would actually be allowed to attend. At least there would be two – as soon as Silas and Violet were healthy enough to go. She wouldn't allow them to spread their cold to the other children.

Amanda hesitated, but then looked at her squarely. "I ain't sure it's such a good idea."

"Then why are you letting them come?" Carrie asked.

"Because my children need education," Amanda said fiercely. "There ain't nobody making schools for poor white children, but there sure does seem to be schools popping up for these nigger children all over the place."

Carrie watched her, deciding to let the word nigger slide for now, even though she hated it. "I know that must be hard," she said instead. She had learned the value of letting people talk through their feelings.

"You ain't got no idea," Amanda said hotly. "This war destroyed everything I ever knew. I've been poor all my life. So has my husband, but we made do before the war by doing some farming down in Georgia. I kept my kids going by growing my own food and tending a few animals. It wasn't much, but we didn't go hungry. Then Sherman came through and torched everything we owned. He destroyed our whole state! Me and my babies hid in the woods and watched those men ruin our life and farm. By the time they moved on, we didn't have nothing left. We had to sleep in those woods for five days."

Carrie shuddered. "I can imagine how terrified you were. What did you do?"

Amanda hesitated, but then obviously decided to just tell the truth. "My husband showed up a few days later. He deserted the Confederate Army when he found out what Sherman was doing," she said boldly, pride shining in her eyes. "All he cared about was making sure me and the kids were safe. I can't even imagine how he walked all that way on one wooden leg, but he did. He said the South was gonna lose anyway, and that he was tired of fighting a war he didn't understand in the first place."

"He's a good man," Carrie said softly.

"You don't think he's a good for nothing deserter?" Amanda demanded, her eyes burning. "I heard your husband was a captain in the army."

"He was," Carrie agreed, "but all the suffering his men had to endure was so hard for him. He almost died himself at the end of the war. There were so many times I wished he would just walk away from the army. I didn't believe in the war, and I didn't want to lose the man I loved to it." She saw no reason to not be truthful.

Amanda's eyes widened. "Honest?"

"Honest," Carrie said firmly. "How did you end up here?"

Amanda shrugged. "My mama was up here. I grew up around this area, but moved to Georgia when I met Tim. We came back here, hoping for a place to start over."

"It didn't work out?"

Amanda shrugged again. "In a way, but not the way I hoped. My mama died about a week after we arrived. The war done used her all up, I guess. Once she knew I would have a home, I think she just gave up. We're living in her house. I think about her every day."

Carrie's heart swelled with sympathy. "I'm so sorry. My mother died six months before the war started. I don't think she would have survived it, so maybe it was for the best."

"She couldn't have survived with her fancy way of life taken away from her?" Amanda asked bluntly.

Carrie stiffened, but saw no anger in the other woman's eyes. She was simply stating the way she saw things. "I believe that is true," she said quietly. "My mother only knew one way of living. She was not very adaptable," she said wryly.

Amanda sat back with an expression of surprise and apology. "I shouldn't have said that. I'm sorry."

Carrie shrugged. "It was the truth." She fixed Amanda with a steady gaze. "The only way any of us are going to survive the end of the war is to work together. I may have a different way of life than you do, but we are basically the same people."

Amanda stared at her for a moment. "You have children?"

Carrie smiled, and laid her hand on her stomach. "Not quite yet."

"You're pregnant?"

"Due in July," Carrie said happily. Then she frowned. "But I'm terrified every day of the kind of world I'm bringing my child into."

"I know just what you mean," Amanda replied.

Silence settled on the room as the two women sipped their tea companionably and listened to the crackle of the fire in the wood stove.

****

Carrie was so tired when she trudged up the steps to the house, that she didn't see Robert in one of the rocking chairs.

"I'm glad to see you took it easy today."

Carrie couldn't miss the sarcasm in her husband's voice, but she didn't detect anger. She settled down into the chair next to him, gratefully accepting the blanket he offered. It was cold, but the fresh air felt wonderful. She'd had a bowl of soup before she left the clinic, so she wasn't really hungry, though she was certain Annie was waiting to force feed her. "I feel much better," Carrie said, "but I get tired so easily. I really don't think I overdid it today, but my body seems to feel differently."

"You're late getting home," Robert pointed out.

Carrie explained about Amanda, and her two children. "We were having a nice time talking, and I didn't really have the energy to come out into the cold. A bowl of soup made me feel better."

"I'm worried," Robert said quietly.

Carrie felt a flare of impatience. "About me, or about our child?" Was she going to have to deal with everyone's worry for the whole pregnancy? Just because her mother had almost died during her birth didn't mean she would have trouble.

"Both of you," Robert replied, in just as quiet a voice.

Carrie felt a surge of remorse. "I'm sorry," she said quickly. "I just don't like people watching every single thing I do. The morning sickness is over. There is no reason to believe the rest of my pregnancy won't be completely normal. Rose taught school right up to the day she gave birth to John."

"And she almost died," Robert reminded her dryly, "because she had worn herself down so much."

Carrie sighed. She had been remembering Hope's easy birth. Quite honestly, she had forgotten about John's difficult delivery. "I won't do that," she insisted. "But I have to take care of my patients," she argued. "I can't just sit around the house like a piece of furniture!" Robert chuckled, but she could hear the strain.

"I know I can't tie you to the bed," he agreed.

"How wise of you," Carrie retorted. She tried to push away her irritation, but her emotions seemed to run rampant. She knew it was a normal part of being pregnant, but it didn't make it any easier to deal with. "I'm hungry," she announced, hoping it would distract her husband.

"Then let's do something about that," Robert said, pushing up from the chair.

Carrie knew he was letting her win for the moment, but she also knew he wouldn't give up on his campaign for her to take it easy. She rose to join him, but stopped when he handed her two envelopes. "Letters!" she cried with delight. She held them up, but couldn't distinguish the writing in the dark.

"They're from Abby and Janie."

Carrie opened the letter from Abby as soon as she was seated at the table in front of a plate full of fried chicken and sweet potatoes. She ignored the fork next to her plate as she began to read.

"That food ain't there just to look at!" Annie said with a scowl. "Don't you know pregnant women 'sposed to gain weight, not lose it?"

Carrie looked up with an absent-minded smile. "Don't worry, Annie, I'll eat it," she promised, and then she gave a cry of delight. "Abby has met with Dr. Hobson."

"That a doctor that can talk some sense into you?" Annie demanded, exchanging a look with Robert.

Carrie ignored her.   "He's the homeopathic physician in Richmond!" Her eyes scanned the letter. "He says he would love to meet with me, and help me continue my education until I can go back to school." She pushed aside the uneasy feelings she still had about returning to school with a young child, and just what that would mean for Robert on the plantation. She would worry about those details later.

"That's wonderful!" Robert said sincerely.   "Have you learned any more about him?"

"Yes," Carrie replied. "He's in one of my school books. He was born in Cumberland County in 1810. He graduated as a doctor from the University of Pennsylvania when he was twenty-two. He studied in Paris for a year, and worked as a traditional doctor for twenty-six. He was drawn into homeopathy in 1858 when several cases showed him how much more effective it was than the type of medicine he was using. He changed his practice after that, and moved it to Richmond."

"I'm surprised you heard nothing about him during the war," Robert responded.

"He left Richmond for his family home when the war started," Carrie explained. "He returned shortly after Richmond fell, and now has a growing practice. Dr. Strikener told me he is a wonderful doctor. I'm thrilled to have the opportunity to work with him."

"How do you plan on doing that?" Robert asked curiously.

Carrie smiled. "Don't worry, darling. I'm not moving to Richmond. I'm simply going there to meet him. He has some books for me that have been recommended by Dr. Strikener, and then he will consult with me through letters on any cases I need help with. It will be much faster than waiting for information from Philadelphia."

Robert nodded, the relief evident on his face. "I'm happy for you, Carrie. Is the letter from Janie information for you?"

"I have no idea," Carrie responded. "I will read it after supper. I'm afraid Annie will be quite upset if I don't eat first."

"As if you ever listen to a thing I say!"

Carrie and Robert grinned at each other as Annie's voice floated through the kitchen door. The woman seemed to be able to hear every single word spoken in the house.

"Quit listening at the door, and come sit down with us to eat," Carrie called. "We established quite a long time ago that you are not a servant – you are family. Now get in here."

Annie pushed through the door reluctantly. "Thank you, Miss Carrie, but it just don't feel right."

"Well, it doesn't feel right for me to eat when I'm not hungry, but I'm having to do it," Carrie said firmly. "Now sit down so I can eat my supper."

Annie's face was set with lines of disapproval, but laughter lurked in her eyes when she slid into a chair.

Robert filled a plate for her quickly. "Thank you for joining us."

"Didn't seem to me like I had no choice," Annie replied dryly, but pleasure was evident on her face.

****

Moses was already awake when Rose opened her eyes. She smiled when she saw him beside the fireplace, outlined by the flames. "Good morning."

Moses turned, smiling broadly. "Good morning. This is a big day. I thought I would surprise you by having the room warm when you had to crawl out from under the covers."

Rose smiled, snuggling deeper into the quilts because the darkness outside said she didn't have to get up yet. "It would be even nicer to have you here with me before I have to crawl out," she said invitingly.

Moses grinned, and then quickly joined her. "I'll be glad when spring comes," he said, pulling her warm body close.

Rose bit her lip to not cry out when his cold skin touched her. After all, she had invited him. They watched the flames silently for several minutes. The only sounds were the hissing of damp firewood, and crackling flames.

"Are you nervous?" Moses finally asked.

Rose thought about the question. They had talked about her decision at length in the weeks since she had made it. She had thought she felt good about it, but now that it was only hours away, she was surprised how nervous she felt. "Not really," she lied.

Moses looked down at her with raised eyebrows.

"Terrified," Rose quickly amended. "I just don't think I should be. No one is making me do this."

"Hardly a reason to not be nervous," Moses observed. "I've been doing a lot of things no one has made me do, but that doesn't necessarily make them any easier."

"What if none of the white children come?" Rose asked.

Moses hesitated. "I think I'm more concerned that they will," he admitted.

Rose pushed herself up against the headboard. "What?" Their conversations about her opening the school to all area children had never gone in this direction.

Moses hesitated. "I received a letter from Matthew yesterday. He couldn't give me any specifics, but he said the blacks getting the vote in Washington, DC..."

"Which is a wonderful thing," Rose said firmly.

"Of course it is," Moses agreed, "but Matthew also believes it will ignite more anger and violence," he said heavily. "He told me we should both be very careful."

Rose absorbed his words before she responded quietly. "We agreed we can't live our lives in fear."

"And I still feel that way," Moses said quickly. "I shouldn't have said what I did about the white children coming. I just don't want anything to happen to you," he said huskily.

Rose snuggled closer, thinking through what he had said. "The school is already a target," she said. "We've already had to rebuild it once, and we know there are men watching. I've done all I can to protect the children."

"It's going to be different now," Moses said. "Matthew told me that having white children at the school will make vigilantes even angrier because they absolutely don't believe there should be any mixing of the races."

"Then they should build schools for their children," Rose retorted. She turned to look into her husband's eyes. "I will be careful, but I won't miss this opportunity. Freed slaves aren't the only ones who are suffering. So many of the whites in this area are just as poor as the black families. Their husbands have come home from war, but many were horribly wounded, and there is no work. The children deserve a chance," she said in a scolding tone. "We talked about this already."

"I know," Moses said heavily.

"But Matthew told you to try again?" Rose observed keenly.

Moses shrugged. "He didn't have to. And, it's not that I don't want you to do it. I agree with all your reasons. But I also can't imagine something happening to you." He turned and pulled her tightly into his arms. "You have to promise to be extra careful. And..."

Rose looked up as his voice trailed off. "And?"

"You have to accept that two of my men will be watching the schoolhouse while you are teaching."

"I'll be happy for it," Rose said promptly, burrowing into Moses' solid body. She was amazed that he could give her so much freedom, and also make her feel so cherished.

"You don't mind?" Moses asked with surprise.

"I'm stubborn," Rose said tartly. "Not stupid."

Moses chuckled. "Don't I know that, dear wife."

Hope made whimpering sounds in the corner. Rose turned her eyes toward the crib, and listened. When only silence met her ears, she smiled. "Our little girl is dreaming."

Moses gazed at her tenderly. "She's dreaming that someday she will be as powerful a woman as her mother is."

Rose stroked his cheek softly, and then pulled the covers back. "This mother has to get her children taken care of before I head to school." She pulled her heavy robe on as she moved closer to the fire, savoring the warmth. "Are the men still cutting firewood?"

"Yes. The last snowstorm brought down a lot of trees. We have plenty for the house, but I have them building mountains of firewood for the tobacco drying barns. It's much more pleasant to cut it now, rather than in the heat of summer. We ran out last season. I'm making sure that won't happen again."

Rose gazed at him. "You'll miss all of this, won't you?"

Moses nodded, meeting her eyes steadily. "Every minute of the day," he admitted. "But," he hastened to add, "I'm also excited about becoming an attorney. As much as I love farming, I will be glad to be of more service to my people."

"You still don't have anyone to take over when we go to college," Rose reminded him.

"I know.   Simon is happy over at Blackwell Plantation. I just figure someone is going to show up when the time is right."

Rose returned his nod, knowing that most of the last six years had been lived with no real knowledge of what the future held. "We'll just keep walking," she replied easily.

"Always forward," Moses agreed. "We decided we'll just keep walking forward, and let time show what will come. It's all we can do."

"All we can do," Rose murmured. She turned to the crib when Hope made noises of being fully awake. "Hello, baby girl," she crooned as she lifted her sleepy daughter to settle in against her shoulder. She just had time to feed her before John would be awake, demanding food to fuel his rapidly growing body. At the rate he was growing, Annie declared he was going to be even bigger than his daddy.

All the worry about school faded from her heart when Hope grinned and gurgled up at her. She always woke happy and alert. A warm determination spread through her as her daughter gazed up at her with trusting eyes. It was up to her and Moses to make a better world for their children to live in. "I won't let you down, baby girl," she whispered. "I won't let you down."

****

Rose could feel the tension in the air even before she rounded the last curve leading to the schoolhouse. She had left the plantation early enough to get there before any of her students, but the sight that met her eyes told her it hadn't been early enough. She slowed the carriage, grateful for the presence of two of Moses' men riding alongside, and took several deep breaths to remain calm before she urged the horses forward to her school.

It was true she had reached the school before any of her normal students arrived, but the gaggle of white families milling around in the yard amazed her. They had fallen silent when her carriage approached, but all of them were watching her. Rose met each of their eyes before she stepped down, recognizing fear, suspicion, and a cautious hope. Some of the men had hostility written on their faces, but their wives standing beside them with staunch determinism revealed why they were there.

"Good morning," she called. "Won't you all please come into the schoolhouse?"

Jeb eased up next to her. "We'll light the fire, Miss Rose."

"Thank you," Rose murmured, glad to have Jeb and Andy there. Both of them were new at Cromwell, but were completely loyal to Moses after serving under him during the war. She knew they would do anything to protect her. She could only hope that would not become necessary. She hung her cape on the hook, taking time to pull her composure together before she turned to face the room.

"Won't you all please sit down?" she asked with a welcoming smile. She waited while families settled into chairs, keeping their children close as if they weren't sure they would be safe. She supposed she could understand. Bringing their children to a school for blacks went against everything they had ever learned – and the way they must have lived all their lives. The world was changing, but accepting that fact didn't necessarily make it easier.

"I'm very happy to see all of you here this morning," she began. She figured she might as well acknowledge the feelings in the room. Ignoring them would not make them any less real. "I can only imagine how difficult it must be for some of you to be here. And I can imagine you are concerned for your children." She paused. "I know I would be if I were sending my children off to a white school." She watched as faces twisted with surprise, some melting into a grudging appreciation.

"I have opened the school to all children because I believe every child needs an education. Public education has become fairly common in the North, but..."

"I don't see a need for my child to come to school," one man growled. "I don't see no reason for my boy to be forced to live like them Yankees do."

Rose opened her mouth to reply, but his wife beat her to it. "You hush up now, Seth. We talked about this already. Josiah is living in a new world, whether we want him to or not. Our boy needs to know how to read and write. This is the only way it is going to happen. Ain't nobody down here building schools for us, and hiring teachers. If we want our boy to learn, we got to bring him here."

Rose felt a rush of sympathy at the frustrated helplessness she saw raging in Seth's eyes. The limp dangle of his left arm spoke of his years of service. "Josiah is welcome here," she said warmly.

Seth eyed her. "I ain't got nothing against niggers," he said tightly.

"I'm glad to hear it," Rose returned.

Seth wasn't done. "I ain't never owned a slave. Never even wanted to own a slave. I didn't fight in the war to keep your people slaves. I fought because I was told to fight. And to protect my home," he added.

Rose nodded, but he pushed on.

"I want my boy to have a better life than me, but I ain't sure what is gonna happen if he comes to school here. I don't care that y'all ain't slaves no more, but white people are just better than niggers," he said flatly. "I ain't so sure what he can learn from a nigger teacher."

Rose took a deep breath, deciding it was best to do a preemptive strike. "I am happy to have Josiah here, but we do not use that word in this schoolhouse," she said firmly. "You may call me black or negro, but you will not call me a nigger." She was just angry enough for her fear to not show.

Chapter Five

Seth flushed and blinked, but remained silent. Rose was quite certain he had never been talked back to by a black person, and most certainly not a black woman. She turned to everyone else. "Let's all be honest. If any of you had another choice, you would not be putting your children in this school." Her eyes swept the room. "You don't have another choice. My regular students are going to be just as uncomfortable as your children. I hate the idea that my students will be treated as if they are inferior, because they are *not.* If you decide to have your child become a student here, it will be my requirement that everyone treat each other with respect." She allowed that thought to settle in before she continued. "I am a good teacher. I can teach your children to read and write. I believe the day is coming when Public Education will be available in the South, and you will have more choices about where your child gets an education. Until that time, this school is your only option."

Rose finished speaking, and gazed around the room. At that moment, she didn't care if every white family stood and walked out. She had known what she proposed was difficult, but she didn't want the students she had grown to love to have to pay the price for her decision. She rather hoped they all *would* leave.

Seth's wife was the first to speak. "Not all of us feel like my husband, Mrs. Samuels," she said bravely, turning long enough to fix her husband with a steely glare. "But we're also afraid of what will happen if our children come to school here." She hesitated as a murmur of agreement rose up from the other mothers. "There are white people who are going to be real angry that we are letting our children do this. They will say we are making the South weak. We're afraid of what they will do." She met Rose's eyes with a look of desperation.

Rose knew better than to take what she was saying lightly. Hadn't she and Moses been talking about the identical issue that morning? "I understand," she said softly. "I'm afraid of the same thing," she admitted, understanding when eyes widened with surprise. "Our little school has already been burned down once by vigilantes." She saw no reason not to tell them the truth. They needed real facts to make the best decision for their children. "We have vigilante groups that watch us sometimes, but so far nothing else has happened."

"That's why them two nig... black men are here?" Seth asked keenly.

"Yes," Rose agreed. "But they are also here to protect me from *you* if it is necessary," she added evenly.

Seth blinked again, and then looked away uncomfortably.

Rose was satisfied she had made her point. "Everyone in this room is here because we want the best for our children. You have brought them to the right place if you want them to learn how to read and write."

"Why are you doing this?" Seth demanded suspiciously. "What do you want?"

"I want to be the best teacher I can be," Rose replied, "but, yes, it is more than that. I have a four year old son, a one year old daughter, and a twelve year old daughter. They are the joys of my life. They are being forced to grow up in a very different world. The change that has come to the South is going to be difficult for everyone. The only way I can truly help my children is to try and help make life better for them. I believe that if blacks and whites can realize we are not really so different, that it will be easier for my children. Right now I can only change the things in my little school, but the day will come when I will do more." She gazed around the room. "It starts here."

The room fell silent, the only sounds coming from the new fire in the woodstove. The air was not warm yet, but the chill was rapidly disappearing.

A woman who had remained silent so far, stood up in the back of the room. "I thank you, Mrs. Samuels. I want my girl to know how to read and write. I'm willing to take the risk to have them come to school here."

Another woman stood. "Me too, Mrs. Samuels. My boy and girl ain't never been to school a day in their life. You are right about the South being different from here on out. I want my kids to have a chance at a better life. My husband tells me reading and writing won't help them none, but I don't reckon I see how it can hurt."

Rose watched as heads began to nod around the room. In spite of her misgivings, she felt a flash of triumph. "Let me tell you why education is so important. Slaves used to be able to learn how to read and write. It's true," she insisted when she saw the skeptical looks. "It's when the plantation owners became afraid of slave uprisings that they decided education was no longer allowed. They didn't want

them to be able to read the pamphlets being sent
down from the North about a different life."

"Why should I care about that?" Seth growled,
obviously angry again. "The North done destroyed my
whole life."

"You should care because the South has done the
same thing to you, Seth," Rose said flatly. "Wealthy
people know that education is power. They know that
the more knowledge you have, the less likely you are
to just go along with what they say. That's why the
South hasn't created public schools. They have been
content to just let privileged children learn.
Emancipation has freed the slaves to go to school, and
they are going in hordes. But why shouldn't all *white*
children have the same right? I know you hate that
the North won the war, but isn't it a good thing that
your child may have more opportunities?"

"Things were fine just the way they were," Seth
snapped, but his eyes were uncertain, and he was
beginning to look trapped.

Rose understood, but she knew now was not the
time to back down. "Whether things were fine or not
is not the issue," she said directly, letting her eyes
roam the room. "The North won. The South lost.
Now we all have to build a new life. Don't you want
your children to have the best chances?"

Seth's wife stood, her brown eyes flashing with
determination under her tan felt hat. "My Josiah is
staying right here," she announced. She looked down
at a boy who appeared to be ten, even though he was
thin and small for his age. "You gonna do whatever
Mrs. Samuels tells you to do, boy. If I hear anything
different, you're gonna have to answer to me. That
clear?"

"Yes, ma'am," Josiah said reluctantly. He looked to his father for help.

"You do what Mrs. Samuels says," Seth said curtly. "But you let me know if you have any trouble, you hear?"

****

By the time school started there were twenty white children who joined her forty regular students. Rose had to blink to believe the sea of black and white faces staring at her from the desks. In all her dreams of teaching, she had never once thought it would include white children. It was a completely surreal experience, but one that gave her a deep sense of satisfaction. She had no idea of the long-term results of her actions, but at least she had the knowledge she was trying to make the world better for her own children.

****

Felicia and Amber were silent for the first part of their walk back to the plantation through the woods. A deep cold had settled back in after a brief spring tease. Their frosty breaths rose up to meet the lowered clouds that promised more snow, and their footsteps snapped frozen twigs and limbs scattered on the trail. The only movement was from bushy-tailed squirrels leaping between the trees as if they were having their last playtime before the next storm hit.

Amber was the first to break the silence. "Do you believe this will work?"

Felicia rolled her eyes dramatically. "Having all those white kids in school with us?" She shook her head and sighed heavily, a thick plume heralding the words to follow. "I know my mama thinks it will."

"But you?" Amber persisted. "What do you think?"

"I think that whatever we think doesn't really matter," Felicia said flatly.

Amber stopped short, and stamped her foot impatiently. "You can just quit trying to dodge my question, Felicia. I'm only going to keep asking."

Felicia stopped as well, but she kept her eyes trained on the clouds. She was silent for a moment before she spoke. "I know things are changing," she said finally. "I read things every day that tells me it is true. But that doesn't mean people are changing along with the times," she added.

Amber waited quietly, knowing she had to give Felicia time to formulate her thoughts. When the silence finally stretched out too long for her patience, she said, "I heard him, you know."

Felicia quit staring up long enough to meet her eyes. "Heard him?"

Amber stamped her foot again. "Oh, you can quit trying to dance around every question like your mama does. You're my best friend in the world. I heard what that horrible Josiah said to you."

Felicia's mouth tightened. "He told me I would never be anything but an ignorant nigger."

"You should have told your mama," Amber snapped. "She would have taken care of it."

"Perhaps," Felicia said quietly, "but I have decided I prefer to do it another way."

"What way would that be?"

"Mama would only punish him. That would just make him angrier. I read in a book the other day that the only way to get someone to truly change how they believe is to give them a good enough reason to change." Felicia held out her hand to catch the first snow flake drifting down through the silvery limbs, a small smile softening her defiant look. "I will defend myself by being the opposite of what he believes I am."

"You're going to show him how smart you are."

"That's right," Felicia agreed. "I start teaching current affairs again tomorrow. He may not think I'm so ignorant after he hears me."

Amber nodded, but looked unconvinced. "My daddy told me that people don't change how they believe very easy. My mama told me that sometimes people can have all the evidence they need right in front of their face, but if they want to keep believing a lie, they will."

"Yep," Felicia said thoughtfully, "but I'm going to try. It's a real big thing my mama is doing – opening her school to white children. I've decided I'm going to help her as much as I can. I heard her talking to Daddy last night. She said that if we want white people to be tolerant of us, that we have to be tolerant of their stupidity if we want them to change. I'm trying to be tolerant."

Amber absorbed that for a minute. "Do you think there will be trouble?"

Felicia hesitated for a long moment this time before she finally turned and met Amber's eyes squarely. "I think we can count on it," she said somberly.

Amber stiffened. "Why?" She bit back her fear. She had counted on Felicia telling her they didn't have to worry; instead she had confirmed her worst fear. "What kind of trouble?"

Felicia shrugged, but her eyes remained dark with worry. "What does it matter, Amber? You and I have faced trouble our whole lives, just because we were born black. I don't see that changing for a long time."

She took a deep breath as the snowflakes fell faster and heavier. "It will get better," she announced with forced confidence. Then she summoned up a smile. "We've got to get home so you can play with All My Heart in the snow."

Amber stared at her for a moment, knowing Felicia was protecting her from whatever she suspected was coming, but the allure of getting home to All My Heart was more tempting than hearing about coming trouble she could do nothing about. She spun, and took off running down the trail. "I'll beat you!" she called tauntingly, knowing that Felicia wouldn't even try to catch her. Her best friend would continue to amble down the trail, busy with her thoughts and all the things she studied. All she cared about now was getting home to the dark bay filly that held all her heart.

****

Josiah's mother was waiting outside the school when Rose had released the children a little early. She was certain the thick clouds were going to produce a deep snow. She wanted to make sure everyone arrived home safely. Before she could acknowledge the other woman, she heard a small voice at her side.

"I had a real good time today, Mrs. Samuels."

Rose smiled down at the earnest little face. "I'm so glad, Violet. It was a pleasure having you. I'm happy both you and Silas were well enough to come."

Violet's head bobbed, her blond curls peeking out from her hat. "Mrs. Carrie made us well!" she announced.

"Come on Violet," Silas called. "Mama said we were to come right home!"

Rose patted the little girl on her head. "You go home, Violet. The snow has started. I'm glad you are feeling better, but you want to get home where it is warm."

"Yes, ma'am," Violet replied. "We got us a real warm house now," she said, lowering her voice to add one more statement. "I think even my papa be real glad about it!' She smiled gaily before she ran off to join her brother.

Rose watched her, happy there were at least two children glad to be at school. She took a deep breath before she turned to speak to the woman waiting off to the side for her. Trying to teach in a room that was as tense as a powder keg getting ready to explode had drained her. All she really wanted to do was go home before the snowstorm worsened, but she could tell by the look on the other woman's face that she needed to talk. She summoned up a warm smile, and turned to her. "Good afternoon. We didn't actually meet this morning. I know you are Josiah's mother, but I don't know your name."

"I'm Norma Whitely," the woman answered shyly. "Thank you for having my Josiah. I know Seth probably made you real angry this morning."

Rose chose to ignore the last part, taking stock of the red-faced woman with weary eyes. Her long dark hair was pulled back into a careful bun around her narrow face, but every line of her body radiated fatigue. She could only imagine what a hard life she must live. "It's nice to meet you, Norma. Why don't you come inside next to the fire?" She could see the woman trembling beneath her thin coat.

"Just for a minute," Norma said quickly.

Rose watched as Norma edged close to the wood stove, all the while maintaining a proud, erect posture. "How can I help you?" She suspected Norma had sent Josiah home before her to do more than just say thank you.

"I'm real sorry about them things Seth said this morning," Norma said earnestly.

Rose knew what she was really saying. "I know you are, Norma. You don't need to be worried. I will not count it against Josiah. I think your son is a fine boy." She had decided to not mention that she saw the same mean streak in the boy that she saw in the father. It was the job of a teacher to bring out the best in each student. She would strive to do just that.

Norma ducked her head before she looked back up with a small smile. "Thank you, Mrs. Samuels. I'm trying real hard to make sure he don't carry the same anger as his daddy. The war years were hard on all of us. Josiah had to do things no child should ever have had to do."

Rose's heart swelled with sympathy. "Too many children never had a chance to be children," she said gently. "All we can do is try and give that to them now."

Norma nodded, her face saying she was glad Rose understood. Then she arrived at the real reason she had waited. "Do you ever teach more than just children?"

"All the time," Rose said promptly. "We're waiting for it to warm up a little, but I teach adults how to read and write, too." She waited before she said more, not wanting to assume Norma was asking for herself.

Norma hesitated, and then looked into her eyes boldly. "Will you teach *me*? How to read and write? I ain't never learned how."

Rose nodded, pushing aside the thought of how much more challenging it would be to fill a school with black and white *adults.* "Absolutely," she said firmly, hoping she wasn't making a serious mistake. If she thought filling a room with black and white *children* created a tense situation, what would it be like to mix Confederate veterans and former slaves? It didn't matter, though. There was no handbook for living in this new world. Everyone, including her, would have to figure it out as they moved forward.

"Really?" Norma's face flooded with relief.

Rose nodded again. "You tell the other women they can come, too. We'll be starting up in March – after the snow melts." She glanced out the window, suddenly anxious to get home.

Norma's eyes followed hers. "Oh, my goodness! The snow is really coming down. I must be going."

"Can I give you a ride?" Rose asked. "I can drop you off closer to your home."

Norma's eyes looked wistful, but she shook her head immediately. "My Seth wouldn't like that."

Rose knew Seth wouldn't want his white wife riding in a black woman's carriage, flanked by two black horsemen. "Be safe," was all she said. "I'll look forward to seeing Josiah in the morning. If the snow is too deep you can keep him home."

"I'll have him here," Norma vowed. "After what we went through in the war, ain't just a little snow gonna keep him from school!"

Rose waved good-bye on the steps of the school, and then turned to her carriage; grateful Jeb and Andy had waited for her. She climbed into the carriage smoothly, eager to get home to Moses and her children. As she lifted the reins to urge the horses forward, she froze.

Barely visible through the thickening snow, she could see the shadowy forms of men on horseback advancing down the road. She felt, more than saw, both Jeb and Andy stiffen to full attention as they reached for their guns. "Wait," she said urgently, keeping her voice low.

She took a deep breath, trying to control her pounding heart as the men drew closer. Horsemen on a public road did not necessarily mean vigilantes. She would wait for them to pass, and then go home. It was wise to be cautious, but she didn't want to live in constant fear. She watched as the shadowy forms revealed themselves to be seven men dressed in bulky clothing, their faces covered by thick scarves. She tried to tell herself she still had no reason to be afraid. While it was true the vigilantes used many disguises to hide their identities, it was also true that any sane person would cover their face in blowing snow.

She remained silent as the group passed without a word, but she was fully conscious of the glaring eyes fixed on her. They were not threatening her, but they were surely communicating a message. The clarity of it made her blood run cold.

It was not until the entire group had passed that one man pulled his horse to a stop and turned back to her. "I would be very careful, Mrs. Samuels," he said quietly, his voice oddly apologetic. "They will not let you teach white children." Then he urged his horse forward and blended into the group.

Chapter Six

Thomas stepped into the warmth of his house, sniffing appreciatively as he hung his heavy cloak on the coat tree. "I'm home," he called.

"And just in time." Abby met him with a kiss. "I imagine you are as glad as I was to get out of the cold. It's not snowing, which I know I should be thankful for, but this winter seems as trying as Philadelphia winters are. That cold wind went right through me on the way home. Spencer piled blankets on me, but I still wasn't warm until I had been inside for a while."

Thomas smiled broadly as he reached forward to touch her cheek. "You've been in May's kitchen?"

"How did you guess?" Abby asked in surprise.

"You have flour on your cheek, my dear," he said fondly. "Still attempting to learn how to make biscuits like hers?"

Abby sighed. "I fear I might be a hopeless case. My mother used to tell me the same thing when I was growing up. I am fairly adept at cooking many things, but southern biscuits seem to be beyond my capability."

"Nonsense!" May said as she bustled into the dining room with a plate full of baked chicken and potatoes. "They get better every time."

Abby laughed. "Spoken like a woman who doesn't want to lose her paycheck."

"Well, there is that," May agreed with an easy smile.

"I notice you're not serving the biscuits I made," Abby continued, eyeing the plate May held in her other hand. "I could take that as an insult," she said with mock sternness.

"You could also take it as proof that your husband has a very intelligent housekeeper," Thomas added with a laugh. He reached forward and plucked a warm biscuit off the platter. "I know this is very improper," he said before he took a bite. "My only defense is that I'm starving."

Abby laughed, and reached for another of the biscuits. "Thank you for not serving those little rocks I pulled out of the oven."

"They weren't nearly that bad, Miss Abby," May protested, but then gave an impish smile. "Still, they for sure weren't meant to be ate."

Their banter was interrupted by a knock on the door. Thomas exchanged a look with Abby. "Are you expecting someone?"

"On a night like tonight? Hardly."

Thomas turned toward the door, but Micah beat him to it. He used the reprieve to take another bite of his biscuit, gazing longingly at the steaming plate of chicken on the table. He hoped whoever was at the door would not disrupt dinner for long. He had been so busy at the factory that lunch had slipped right past him.

"Why, Mr. Hobbs! Come in out of the cold." Micah's voice floated back through the house.

Thomas and Abby exchanged a stunned look before they hurried forward.

"Hobbs? Is that really you?" Thomas asked with amazement.

Warren Hobbs, his face almost as rusty colored as the hair that topped it, handed Micah his threadbare coat and scarf, and then turned. "It's really me," he agreed. "I know I have picked a terrible night to visit. I hope it's not too bad a time," he said hesitantly.

"Not at all," Thomas insisted as he stepped forward to shake his hand. "It's wonderful to see you again." He decided to not make mention that the young man seemed to have not gained an ounce since the end of the war. He had been pitifully thin, as had most soldiers and Richmond residents after the war, but almost two years had done nothing to change that.

"We're so glad to see you," Abby said sincerely. She didn't know Hobbs very well since he had left for West Virginia shortly after the end of the war, but she had heard all the stories of his relationship with Robert and Carrie. "Won't you please join us for dinner? We were just about to sit down."

Hobbs shook his head. "I couldn't. I'm real sorry to interrupt your meal."

Abby laughed. "You know that chicken smells as good to you as it does to me. Now you sit right down there and eat it. We won't allow you to do anything else."

"Well, since you put it that way, I guess it does smell right good," Hobbs admitted.

Thomas suspected it had been a while since Hobbs had enjoyed a good meal. He opened his mouth to ask May to set an extra place at the table, but she was already rushing forward with another plate and cutlery.

"Welcome back to Richmond, Mr. Hobbs," May said. "It's about time you got back down here to pay folks a visit."

"Hello, May," Hobbs said gratefully, though his eyes took on a shuttered look. He took a deep breath as he leaned back in his chair. "It's real good to be back."

"Are you here to stay?" Abby asked.

Hobbs shrugged. "I reckon that depends on whether I can get me a job."

Thomas frowned. "What happened to your farm in West Virginia? I thought you planned on being a farmer on your family's place after the war ended."

"The farm is gone," Hobbs said shortly, anger flaring in his eyes.

"I'm so sorry," Abby said gently. "What happened?"

Hobbs took a deep breath. "When I got home things were in terrible condition. It turns out mama lied just as much to me in her letters during the war as I did in the ones I wrote to her. They barely survived the war because troops kept coming through and taking what they needed. Didn't seem to matter much what side it was. They just took it. Being so close to the border weren't the best place to be. Both of them were skin and bones when I got there." His frown deepened. "So was Bridger, my old coonhound. He had hung on waiting for me, but he just didn't have nothing left. He died about a month after I got home."

Thomas ached at the grief in Hobbs' eyes. He knew how much the young man, not even twenty after four years of war, had dreamed of going back to the hills of West Virginia to go hunting and camping again with his dog. "I'm sorry," he said quietly, knowing there was more. "Your parents?"

Hobbs took a deep breath. "They died a few months back. Mama died first. The pneumonia took her. Daddy followed her a few weeks later. I figured he was only living for her. With mama gone..." His voice trailed away as he lifted his shoulders in a shrug.

Abby reached forward and took his hand.

Hobbs smiled slightly, and then forged ahead, obviously anxious to get it all said. "I tried to work the farm on my own, but this leg of mine makes it impossible to do it all." His face twisted with bitter helplessness. "I finally realized I was gonna starve and die up there just like my folks did, so I left. I heard it's real hard to get a job in Richmond, but I decided I would try." He lowered his eyes with embarrassment. "I planned on sleeping outside till I found a job, but..." His voice thickened with shame as he looked at them with a mute appeal in his eyes. "It's just real cold out there."

"You did the right thing, Hobbs," Thomas said firmly, thinking of the months Hobbs had survived in the trenches around Richmond during the last siege. "You saved my daughter's life, and you saved Robert's life, as well. You always have a place with us."

Hobbs lifted his eyes with gratitude. "Thank you. It's just until I find a job," he added quickly.

"Oh, you already have a job," Thomas said easily, "but you're going to stay here until you get back on your feet." He smiled at Hobbs' confused look. "Abby and I own a clothing factory here in Richmond now. We always have a place for someone like you."

Hobbs' eyes took on a shine. "I'll work hard, Mr. Cromwell. I'll learn whatever I have to learn."

"I'm sure you will," Thomas responded. "We have wonderful employees. I'm sure you will fit in well. Not everyone can."

Hobbs looked confused. "Why not?"

Thomas smiled, remembering the young man who had protected Carrie on her trips back and forth to the black hospital after he had injured his leg in battle, conspiring to keep it a secret from her father. "Cromwell Factory has an equal number of black and white employees," he explained, surprised by the sudden flash of anger in Hobbs' eyes.

"I see," Hobbs said tightly.

Thomas watched the flood of emotions on his face, wondering at the bitterness he saw there.   He remained silent, exchanging a look with Abby.

"I guess beggars can't be choosers," Hobbs finally muttered.

"You have a problem with black employees?" Thomas asked evenly, not willing to just let the comment remain unchallenged.

Hobbs hesitated, but then answered.   "I figure the jobs should go to the white men who fought to protect the South," he said flatly.   "The niggers shouldn't be getting the jobs."

"We don't use that word in our house," Abby said firmly.

Hobbs flushed, but he didn't back down.   "All the problems in the South are because of the *black* people."

"Is that right?" Thomas asked, deeply concerned with the changes he saw in the young man.   "How did you come to that conclusion?"

"I fought four years for the South.   I thought I was protecting my home, but now I realize I wasn't doing nothing but handing it over to the slaves.   I ain't got nothing, but the slaves are getting white people's jobs. They're getting education.   They got that Freedmen's Bureau to fight their battles for them.   Me? I ain't got nothing but myself.   How is that fair? The South is being forced to take care of all them slaves, but they ain't taking care of the ones who fought for it."

"So you think it is fair for millions of people that had their lives stolen by slavery for more than a hundred and fifty years to not get any help at all?" Abby asked.

Hobbs shrugged. "Seems things would be a whole lot better if they just went back to being slaves. Oh, I reckon that ain't gonna happen, but it means it's going to be up to us to keep things under control," he added harshly.

"Us?" Thomas asked, struggling to keep his temper under control. Only the knowledge that Hobbs had saved both Carrie's and Robert's lives kept him from throwing him out into the cold. He knew the war had changed everyone, but he never would have expected this cold bitterness from Hobbs.

"Why don't we just eat?" Abby asked, her voice breaking the tension. "I know Hobbs must be starving. We can finish this conversation after dinner."

Thomas wanted the answer to his question, but he knew his wife was right to interrupt. Surely Hobbs would be in a better place after he warmed up and had a hot meal. He tried to enjoy May's chicken, but all he could think about was that he had invited someone into his home who was a racist, and might actually be worse – a vigilante. His thoughts turned to Jeremy. He must be warned.

****

Dinner had ended up being mostly silent. Thomas could tell Abby didn't know what to say at this point any more than he did. Hobbs just seemed eager to eat everything he could – probably wondering if they would tell him to leave once he had finished.

A blast of cold air said Jeremy and Marietta had arrived home. Jeremy always left the factory, and then picked up his wife down at the school to make sure she was never alone on the dark Richmond streets. A whirl of frigid air rushed into the dining room when they strode in with bright eyes and rosy cheeks.

"It is cold out there!" Marietta exclaimed. "We could barely keep the school warm today." She stopped short when she saw Hobbs, and then gave him a welcoming smile. "Hello. I didn't know we were having company tonight."

"Hobbs was a surprise," Thomas replied, trying to keep his tone enthusiastic, though a quick glance from Jeremy told him he had failed. "Marietta, you have never met Hobbs. I owe Carrie's life to him. Robert's, as well."

Marietta grinned broadly. "Of course! Your reputation precedes you, Hobbs. I've heard many stories about you." She settled down in her chair just as May arrived with more hot chicken. "You live in West Virginia don't you? What brings you to Richmond?"

"Before he answers I get to tell him hello," Jeremy said cheerfully. He shook Hobbs' hand, and thumped him on the back. "It's good to see you. Be warned - my wife always has loads of questions."

Marietta tossed her head. "Curiosity is what makes me a great teacher," she retorted. Then she turned back to Hobbs.

Hobbs smiled at Jeremy. "Your wife? Congratulations."

"Thank you. She's the best thing that ever happened to me," Jeremy replied with a proud smile. "She's the most beautiful woman I know. The smartest, too."

"I think I heard you say that to Rose," Marietta said teasingly.

"Of course I did," Jeremy said easily. "She's my twin sister. But that was before you were smart enough to fall in love with me. Then you went to the top of the list."

Thomas stiffened when he saw Hobbs frown. He exchanged a glance with Abby. There was no hiding the truth, and he wouldn't want to anyway, but he didn't want trouble for his half-brother.

"You have a twin sister?" Hobbs asked.

"Yes," Jeremy answered. "Rose Samuels." He waited, seeming to realize from Hobbs' expression that more was coming.

Hobbs stared at him. "Carrie used to talk about a Rose. They didn't see each other again until after the war."

"Yes," Jeremy said cheerfully. "They are one in the same."

You could see the wheels turning in Hobbs' head. Finally he said, "Rose is black."

Jeremy continued to smile, though it was a little more forced now. "Well, half-black."

"She's black," Hobbs said flatly, and then continued with disbelief in his voice. "You're *black*?"

Jeremy quit smiling. "You have a problem with that?"

Everyone waited quietly while Hobbs stared at him, obviously searching for words. He opened his mouth, and then closed it again. His eyes darted around the room as if he were trying to find a way to escape.

Thomas tried to come up with a way to undo the invitation for Hobbs to live in their home. Everyone was already living with enough risk. They didn't need to invite more trouble. His mind raced to find the words that would send Hobbs on his way, yet still honor all he had done for Carrie and Robert.

Hobbs finally heaved a sigh. "I don't know what to think." He shook his head. "I know that everyone who has anything to do with this family are fine people, but there are a lot of folks who don't agree with me."

"That's true," Abby said quietly. "But the only thing that is important right now is what *you* think. Everyone else will not be living in our home." Her voice was gentle, but firm.

"Who is the everyone else?" Jeremy asked, sitting down at the table across from Hobbs.

The platter of chicken remained untouched. May stood in the corner of the room, her defiant eyes fixed on Hobbs. A brisk wind rattled the window panes, while a roaring fire fought to keep the cold at bay.

"I can't tell you that," Hobbs muttered; his face a mixture of embarrassment and anger.

"You came from West Virginia," Jeremy continued, his eyes locked on Hobbs' face. "I know there are vigilante groups everywhere, but I received word today that the Ku Klux Klan is spreading into that area."

Hobbs stiffened, and his face grew more rigid, but he didn't say anything.

Thomas decided to take the most direct route. "Hobbs, I invited you to stay here in our home. Are you going to put anyone here in danger?" he asked bluntly.

Hobbs shook his head immediately. "I wouldn't do that, sir."

"Why not?" Jeremy demanded. "The very fact you didn't deny association with the Ku Klux Klan tells me you have become part of them. I know what they are doing, Hobbs. They wouldn't take kindly to your living in a home where black and whites live equally, and especially to the fact that one is a mulatto."

Hobbs was already shaking his head. "I ain't part of the Klan," he said emphatically. "They..." He broke off abruptly.

Abby finished his thought. "They've been in your area talking to people, trying to recruit for the Klan."

Hobbs hesitated, but then nodded slowly. "That's true, but I ain't joined up with them."

"But you believe the way they do," Jeremy said angrily.

Hobbs shook his head again. "Truth be told, I ain't sure what I believe anymore." His eyes were desperate. "This country ain't nothing but a mess since the war ended. I don't see nothing good that came out of all those years of fighting. There's a whole lot of desperate people just trying to survive."

"It's hard for everyone to make sense of all the changes," Abby said calmly.

Jeremy was still angry. "It's only because the Congress let President Johnson have his way for too long. That's all changing now. Senator George Julian gave a brilliant speech last month that resulted in a bill being approved to impose military rule on the South. I believe it will become law, and then be put into action sometime in March. That's what it is going to take to change things."

Hobbs scowled defiantly, his supposed confusion evaporating into sudden renewed anger. "Oh, it will change things alright. They ain't gonna allow for that."

Thomas held his hand up to stop Jeremy from responding. Two angry men never really achieved more than flaming the fires that fueled their rage.

Obtaining information was far more important at this point. "Who won't allow for it?" he probed.

Hobbs hesitated, but then obviously decided he had already said too much to retreat now. "The Ku Klux Klan. But it ain't just them. There are vigilante groups all over the South that are going to make sure that don't happen."

Jeremy opened his mouth again, but Thomas silenced him with a quelling look. "They are willing to go to war again?"

Hobbs met his eyes squarely. "Most of them don't reckon the war is over," he revealed. "General Lee may have given up, but they figure they just got to keep fighting. They're just gonna do it in a different way."

"A different way?" Thomas asked, trying to keep the hard anger out of his voice when Hobbs all but revealed the Ku Klux Klan members were Confederate veterans. He knew he had failed, when Hobbs' eyes took on a shuttered appearance.

"It don't matter," Hobbs said. "Desperate men do what they have to do." He pushed back his chair and stood. "I'll be leaving now."

Thomas nodded, relieved beyond words that he didn't have to actually tell Hobbs to leave. He was dismayed when Abby reached out a hand, and put it on Hobbs' rigid arm.

"You're not going anywhere," Abby said firmly.

"I think it's best if he does," Jeremy said coldly, his eyes flashing anger and contempt.

Hobbs glanced down. "It's best, Mrs. Cromwell"

"Well, it would certainly be easier," Abby agreed, "but I don't think it would be best. If all any of us do is turn our backs on the people we disagree with, we're never going to create any real change." She smiled gently at Thomas and Jeremy. "I hate what you are talking about as much as my husband and Jeremy do, but I would think four years of war taught us the value of finding common ground and trying to work through issues."

"That may be," Hobbs said gruffly, "but thinking something, and actually *doing* it, are two different things." He met Abby's eyes squarely. "Just because you want me to stay here don't mean I'm gonna change what I believe."

"I know that," Abby said evenly. "But if we put you out on a cold night because you believe differently than we do, than we are no different than the Ku Klux Klan. Hate and intolerance are just that – no matter what side it is coming from."

Thomas, in spite of how much he wanted Hobbs to leave, knew Abby was right. His anger melted beneath the appreciation of her logic. "My wife is right, Hobbs. But," he added in a firm voice, "I need your word on something."

Hobbs met his eyes. "What would that be?"

"I have to know you are not going to bring trouble to this house. If you want to live here and work to rebuild your life, then you are welcome. If you are planning on alerting vigilantes to send them here, then you go now."

"And you would just believe my word?" Hobbs asked skeptically.

"Yes." Thomas took a deep breath, hoping with every fiber of his being that he was right. "You may be confused about what you believe, but I don't think the same young man who saved Carrie's life, and also kept Robert from dying, would do anything deliberately to hurt this family. If you give me your word, I will trust you."

Hobbs nodded quickly. "You have my word, Mr. Cromwell."

Thomas reached out his hand, relieved when Hobbs took it without hesitation. "Then you are welcome to stay here." Out of respect for Jeremy, he decided to not put Hobbs in the guest wing of the house where Jeremy and Marietta had their room. "May will prepare the green room two doors down from us." When he looked up at May, she gazed back at him with a stoic expression, but he knew the emotions bubbling beneath the surface. He had more than his fair share of them, so he certainly couldn't judge her for that.

Hobbs had come to them. Now they would just have to see what would develop.

Jeremy didn't argue the decision, but he obviously wanted Hobbs to have a clearer understanding of the situation. "I got a letter from Matthew today," he announced. He reached in his pocket and pulled it out. "He wrote to tell me more about Senator Julian's speech to Congress." He scanned the thick letter, and then began to read.

He told Congress that what the South needed was not President Johnson's "hasty restoration" or oaths that invited men to commit perjury, but **government***, the strong arm of power, outstretched from the central authority here in Washington. Only a prolonged period of federal control would enable loyal public opinion to sink deep roots and permit "Northern capital and labor... Northern energy and enterprise" to venture south to establish a Christian civilization and a living democracy. He believes the South should be governed directly from Washington and readmitted only at some indefinite future time when its political and social elements have been thoroughly transformed.*

Hobbs snorted, but didn't add anything to what Jeremy had read.

"You disagree?" Abby asked him calmly.

Hobbs stared at her, and then nodded his head curtly. "Why should the South want to become like the North?" he demanded. "We may have lost the war, but we didn't lose who we are."

"Until the war you were a farmer," Thomas reminded him. "Isn't that the same, no matter where you are?"

Hobbs shook his head. "President Davis made that clear."

"President Davis is still in prison at Fort Monroe," Abby reminded him.

"That may be," Hobbs said stubbornly, "but what he said was right."

"And what did he say?" Marietta asked curiously, her bright blue eyes glittering beneath her red hair.

Thomas knew how hard it must have been for her to remain silent until now. He could only imagine the thoughts and questions swirling through her mind, and blazing out through her eyes.

Hobbs shrugged. "He said the lower race of the human beings that made up the slave population of the South elevated every white man in our community. That it was a necessary part of our social order."

Marietta stared at him. "So white men need to enslave a whole people in order to feel good about themselves? That certainly doesn't say much for them."

Hobbs flushed. "There has to be an order of things," he insisted, refusing to back down. "I don't hate black people, but they shouldn't have the right to vote. They gonna take over the South and destroy it for the whites. I didn't fight the war for slavery – I fought it to protect my home. Now them Yankees aim to destroy it again by taking everything away from us, and giving it to the blacks. What are people like me supposed to do?"

"Work?" Marietta asked. Her simple question hung in the air for a long moment. "Why should anyone have to look down on someone else to create what they want for their own lives?" She looked at Hobbs' angry face thoughtfully. "I can understand why you are angry and afraid. It's only natural that everyone wants the best they can have for themselves. It just seems to me that if everyone was to focus on *everybody* getting what they need and want, that the combined energy of that would be more useful than trying to destroy another group's hopes and possibilities."

Hobbs stared at her, his face revealing he had absolutely no idea how to refute her simple logic.

****

Abby snuggled up close to Thomas as soon as they got into bed. "I'm very proud of you," she said tenderly.

"I might have just made a grave error," Thomas replied, wishing he could push away the dread of looming trouble.

"Perhaps," Abby replied thoughtfully, "but we can know we made the right choice. In times like this, sometimes that's the only thing that makes the rest of it bearable." She paused. "Besides, I believe it will actually be helpful. Once he realized we weren't telling him to leave, he seemed more willing to voice his opinions. I find I would much rather know what my enemy is thinking, rather than make mistakes because of ignorance. I don't believe Hobbs is our enemy, but I suspect he knows more about the Klan than he is telling us. The Ku Klux Klan seems to thrive on secrecy. Having Hobbs here might help us beat them at their own game."

Thomas grinned, his eyes filled with admiration. "You are as smart as you are beautiful."

"And, don't ever forget it," Abby said smugly before she kissed him, and then cuddled into his side and went to sleep.

Chapter Seven

Carrie was already on the porch when Rose stepped out the door to go to school.

"Eager?" Rose asked teasingly.

Carrie nodded, a glowing smile on her face. "I'm so excited to meet Dr. Hobson today, but I'm just as excited to see everyone else. It's hard to believe it's been almost two months. And Hobbs! I can't believe he is in Richmond. It will be so good to see him..." Her voice trailed off as she thought of the letter she had received a few days earlier from Abby.

Rose looked at her sharply. "What aren't you saying?"

Carrie sighed. "Sometimes I wish I could hide things from you."

"No, you don't," Rose replied confidently. "But don't try and change the subject. What *are* you trying to hide? Other than telling us Hobbs is there, you haven't seemed to have much more to say."

"How could I since I haven't even seen him?" Carrie protested.

Rose just looked at her, and waited quietly.

"I really don't know very much," Carrie finally said. "It seems Hobbs has changed a great deal. Abby didn't expound, but she did tell me I shouldn't expect him to be the same,"

"Lots of people changed from the war," Rose replied. "There is nothing odd about that."

"Perhaps," Carrie answered, and then shrugged. "Wondering won't accomplish anything. I'll know more when I see him today." She looked up as Jeb and Andy walked from the barn with their horses. "I'm glad there has been no more trouble at the school."

"It's been quiet," Rose answered with relief. "I wish I could say the tension between the students is better, but at least the vigilantes have not returned."

Carrie frowned. "No change at all?"

Rose shook her head with a sigh. "Oh, I'm sure there is some. I'm probably just not seeing it."

Carrie nodded. "Your mama told me one time that most changes take place like roots. You can't see them, but they are there, spreading out just beneath the surface. Then all of a sudden a plant pops up and surprises you." She smiled. "You're doing the right thing. I bet there are roots growing like wildfire right beneath the surface."

Rose smiled back. "I'm going to choose to believe you are right," she said cheerfully. She walked down the stairs, and then stepped into the carriage Clint had brought around earlier. "Have a wonderful time in Richmond. I'll see you in a few days."

****

Carrie leaned back against the carriage seat and drank in the fresh air. There was still a nip in the winter air, but she could feel the promise of spring in the soft breeze. Buds hung thick on the trees lining the road. Her favorite were the thick red buds of the maple trees, dangling their promise as if to tease her. In less than a month they would all break free into the verdant green that never ceased to thrill her. The red bud trees would bloom a vivid purple, and then the dogwoods dotting the woods would follow.

The first hour had passed with easy conversation between her and Delbert, one of the plantation hands Robert had asked to take her to Richmond. She knew he was excited about being in town for a few days, but now both of them were content to ride in silence with their thoughts.

Carrie was grateful for the quiet. Four and a half months pregnant, she could feel the changes happening in her body. The idea of being pregnant had finally settled within her, filling her with constant thoughts of the baby coming to life within her womb. She laid her hand on her stomach, awash with love for the child she and Robert had created. The morning sickness had completely abated, and now she felt more alive than she ever had. Awe consumed her every time she pondered the miracle growing within her. Birth happened every day, but the idea that it was happening to her made her truly aware of the sheer wonder of it for the first time.

A deer bounding across the road in front of them distracted her thoughts. She heard the shrill call of a red-tailed hawk as she watched the clouds dancing around the sun. She snuggled deeper beneath the blankets, and let the easy rock of the carriage lull her to sleep.

****

Carrie had spent a wonderful few hours with Abby, talking and laughing, before the men came in from the factory. She was thrilled her stepmother had come home early to be with her, but she had not been able to get her to say anything about Hobbs – except to reiterate that Carrie needed to talk to him and draw her own conclusions. It was the troubled look in

Abby's eyes that bothered her most, but once the older woman made up her mind about something, nothing could change it. She had quit asking questions about Hobbs, and focused on all the other things going on in their lives.

They were in the kitchen with May when they heard the men enter the house. Thomas had insisted Hobbs ride in the carriage with him and Jeremy when they went in to work. After dropping them off, Jeremy would be on his way to the Black Quarters to pick up Marietta from the school. Dinner would be served when they returned.

Carrie hurried out to the foyer, and caught Hobbs in a hug as soon as he hung his coat. "Hobbs! It is so wonderful to see you!"

Hobbs laughed and hugged her back. "You are a sight for sore eyes, Carrie Borden!"

Carrie saw nothing of the changed man Abby had warned her about. Hobbs' brown eyes snapped with life and joy as he gazed at her. "I wasn't sure I would ever see you again," she continued. "When you took off for the hills of West Virginia, I thought you would never come out of them."

The life and joy drained in seconds, replaced with a weary bitterness. "Life don't always go the way you think it should, Carrie."

Carrie gazed at her old friend, realizing she was looking into the eyes of someone far older than his years – someone who had known more pain than he should have. "I know you're right," she said gently. "I'm so sorry about your parents. And about Bridger," she added.

Hobbs looked down, his face a mask of defeat and grief.

"Come into the library with me," Carrie said in an effort to relieve his pain. "I have so much I want to talk to you about. Annie has put some hot tea and biscuits in there for us. She knew you would be starving when you came in."

Hobbs nodded, forcing a smile to his face. "That sounds real good, Carrie." He walked into the library, sank into a chair next to the fire, and then turned to her. "How is Robert?"

"Very disappointed he couldn't get away to come see you right now," Carrie answered. "He is thrilled you're in Richmond. He had planned on coming, but then one of his prize mares showed signs of foaling early. Clint is a very capable stable manager, but Robert wasn't willing to risk something going wrong."

"I would have done the same thing," Hobbs said, and then smiled. "I hear that horse is not the only thing going to give birth."

Carrie laughed. "That's true. I'm due in July. I can still hardly believe it."

"You'll make a great mother," Hobbs replied. "You got more caring in you than two other people combined."

"I hope so," Carrie answered wistfully, her thoughts focused for a moment on the reality that she had never been close to her mother. She didn't want that same kind of relationship with her own child. She pushed the thoughts away. "How are things going at the factory?"

Hobbs hesitated before he answered. "I'm real grateful to have a job, Carrie. And I'm real grateful for a warm place to live."

"But you would really rather be back in your mountains," Carrie finished for him, knowing he wouldn't give voice to his true feelings. "I felt that way every moment I was in Philadelphia. I was so happy to be at medical school, but I missed the plantation with every breath I took."

"Yep, it's that way," Hobbs agreed with relief, his eyes showing he appreciated the fact she understood. "I don't want to appear ungrateful."

"I know it must be hard to have to leave your home and come to the city," Carrie replied.

"There ain't many men in the South doing what they want to be doing," Hobbs said in a hard voice. "Ain't nothing ever gonna be the same again."

"I think you're right about that," Carrie agreed. "The South will never be the way it was before."

"And you're real glad about that," Hobbs said with an edge to his voice.

Carrie gazed at him, seeing again the man she had been warned about lurking in his eyes. "I can't be anything but glad that slavery is dead," she said evenly, "but my heart aches every day for the veterans who have returned from war to find everything they knew has been destroyed or changed. I treat many of them in my clinic. They are angry, but mostly they just seem confused. They have no idea how to live in the new South."

Anger flashed over Hobbs' face, and then he sighed. "I know how they feel," he said slowly. "I'm angry every single day, but mostly I just can't make sense of anything."

"Like what?" Carrie asked. She hoped getting him to talk would help him sort out some of his feelings.

Hobbs looked away from her probing eyes, and stared into the flames. He was silent for several minutes, only his tense shoulders revealing the struggle he was enduring.

Carrie waited, knowing she had to give him time to reveal what was churning in his mind.

"My mama taught me it was wrong to hate," he finally said, his voice halting and slow.

Carrie continued to remain silent. The years she had spent with Hobbs had taught her that pressing him would only cause him to shut down even more.

"I made it through the war without hating," he added, "even with all the killing. Maybe it was because it was war, and killing was just part of it." He clenched his fists. "But now? I got a lot of hate inside me," he admitted. He looked up at her with a mixture of rage and desperation, before he turned to stare back into the fire.

"Who do you hate?"

"Most everybody," Hobbs replied. "But mostly the blacks and the Yankees who have come down here to take control of my country."

Carrie decided to not point out that the South was not a country – the war had decided that. "Because you believe they have taken away everything that matters to you."

Hobbs glanced at her again. "They have," he stated simply.

"Was it them, or was it the consequences of the men who ignited the war?"

Hobbs opened his mouth to respond, and then hesitated. He finally shrugged. "I guess it was everyone," he admitted. "All I know is that one day I had a life."

"And then people made decisions that stole that life from you," Carrie said sympathetically.

"They did!" Hobbs insisted.

"I'm agreeing with you," Carrie said gently.

Hobbs took a deep breath. "So you understand why I got hate."

Carrie paused. "I understand there is much to be angry about, but the choice to hate is up to you."

"And you think you wouldn't?" Hobbs retorted. "Because you're the high and mighty Carrie Borden?" He looked ashamed for a moment, but then he plunged ahead, not able to stop the torrent of words once they were released. "You ain't never had nothing really bad happen to you, Carrie. Oh, you worked real hard during the war, and I know you were hungry sometimes, but nobody you loved died. Robert got real sick, but he's better now. You ain't never lost anyone during that war, Carrie. You don't know what it's like to suffer!"

Carrie thought about Sarah's comment that wisdom came from suffering. "You're right," she acknowledged.

Hobbs flushed. "I'm sorry. I shouldn't have said those things."

"Why not? They are true." Carrie thought about her next words. She knew the levels of suffering all around the country for those who had lost loved ones must be unbearable. She had also learned, however, that it wasn't always necessary to experience a particular situation in order to understand it. Suffering, no matter how it materialized in your life, could produce bitterness. She had fought that reality all during the war. Would she feel differently if Robert had actually died? She had no way of actually knowing that, but...

"The hate is eating me up," Hobbs added sadly. "One minute I'm so angry I think I will explode. Then, the next minute I'm so sad I reckon I'll never be able to breathe again."

Carrie finally found words. "It's true I haven't experienced all you have, Hobbs, but it's not true that I haven't suffered. And I certainly have people around me that have lost so much in the last six years. They have chosen to not hate simply because the hate ends up hurting them more than anyone. I've made the same choice. I may not like something that is going on, but I will not hate the people who I believe may be responsible, and I don't try and blame my life on someone who has absolutely nothing to do it with just to make myself feel better."

"Then what do you do?" Hobbs demanded impatiently, his words laced with a yearning to understand, even while his flashing eyes said he didn't want to hear it.

"I try to change things," Carrie said calmly.

Hobbs' face filled with triumph. "That's what they're gonna do."

Carrie took a deep breath. "The Ku Klux Klan?"

"Them and all the other groups," Hobbs declared belligerently. "They plan on changing things."

"With terror and violence?" Carrie demanded, not caring that contempt showed in her voice. "Is that the kind of country you want to live in? One where anything that is different is killed or terrorized? After years of white people enslaving black people, now you believe the best way to handle it is to kill them, rape them, and cause them to be afraid every moment of their lives?" She stared at him with disbelief. "You couldn't have changed that much, Hobbs!"

Hobbs flushed, but glared back at her. "You don't know the kind of country we're living in now, Carrie. Somebody has to do something."

"Somebody *is* doing something," Carrie snapped. "The Congress is enacting laws that will give equal rights to everyone – no matter their race. They are trying to help the South rebuild after the war. The vigilante groups are doing nothing but hurting the South!" Her anger built as she thought of all that was being done. "All they are doing is showing the rest of the country how truly ignorant Southerners are."

Carrie took a deep breath when she saw Hobbs' face tighten even more. She knew better than to fight anger with anger, but when she thought of the fear Rose and her students lived with every day, she could only feel contempt for the ones that caused it. Even though Hobbs insisted he wasn't a Klan member, he clearly supported them. In her eyes, that made him just as guilty. Groups like this were allowed to thrive by the masses of people simply turning away. She searched her mind for a way to free Hobbs from his bitterness. "Did Robert ever tell you how his father died?"

Hobbs' angry look turned to confusion. "What?"

"Did Robert ever tell you how his father died?" Carrie repeated.

"A nigger killed him," Hobbs growled.

"Do you remember me telling you about Moses?"

The look on Hobbs' face said he had no clue why she was asking him these questions. "The fella who got you off the plantation when the Yankees came through – before you got shot getting away?"

"That's the one," Carrie agreed. "His father was the one who killed Robert's father." Her words hung in the air as Hobbs' eyes widened. She had his full attention now. "He is also running Cromwell Plantation, and he and Robert have become like brothers."

"That ain't likely," Hobbs said dubiously. "Robert may have changed some about how he thinks of niggers, but he ain't changed that much. You don't forgive something like that."

"He forgave," Carrie said firmly. "Moses and Rose live in the main house with everyone else. My father made Moses half owner of the plantation."

Hobbs narrowed his eyes. "Your father didn't tell me that."

"Would it matter? They have given you a job and a place to live." When Hobb's eyes took on a calculating look, Carrie felt a surge of panic. What had she done? Had she put Moses and Rose in more danger by revealing the true state of affairs on the plantation? "Hobbs, Robert had the same hatred in his heart that you do. He finally realized there was a better way to live, and he understood it wasn't right to blame an entire race of people for something they weren't responsible for." Her voice gentled as she saw the confusion reappear in Hobbs' eyes. "The only way any of us can bring the South back to life is to take responsibility for making our own lives better – not by hatred and violence. You can spend all your life blaming someone else, or you can use your energy to *change* your life. Everybody in this country has lost something because of the war. It will take all of us working together to find a way to create a country that can rebuild everyone's lives."

Hobbs glared at her for a long moment before he seemed to deflate before her eyes. The anger melted away from his face, leaving behind an aching confusion that pulled at her heart. "I'm mad because I know you're right," Hobbs muttered. He turned back to stare into the flames for a long moment before he swung back to her. "It's gonna get real bad, Carrie."

Carrie felt her heart catch at what she saw on his face. "What do you mean?" she asked in an even voice, determined to stay calm.

"They're gearing up," Hobbs said flatly. He hesitated, reached into his pocket, and then handed her a folded sheet of paper.

Carrie's blood froze when she unfolded it and read the stark, bold print.

Negro women shall be employed only by white persons. Negroes meeting in cabins to themselves shall suffer the penalty. All white men found with negroes in secret places shall be dealt with... For the first offense is one-hundred lashes; the second is looking up a sapling. White man and negro, I am everywhere; I have friends in every place; do your duty and I will have little to do.

Carrie read it silently, and then read it again – her horror growing. "Where did you get this?" she asked hoarsely.

"I got it off a tree when I was on my way here."

Carrie knew he was lying, but she decided to not press the issue. Learning the source was far more important. "Who wrote this?"

"His name is Ellis Harper. He leads a group of men up in Tennessee and Kentucky," Hobbs said hesitantly, fear stamped on his face. He took a deep breath. "He's done some real bad things. He's killed a lot of people. Or had them killed," he added.

Carrie felt bile rise in her throat. "Why are you telling me this?"

Hobbs shrugged. "Because some of what you said makes sense. I still don't feel right about what is happening in our country, but ain't everybody like these men," he said in a more insistent voice. "There's lots of fellows who came home from the war who just want to go on with their lives. They ain't got nothing against black folks. They just want to rebuild their own lives and take care of their families, but there's a lot of other folks out there who want to stir things up."

"Who are the vigilantes?" Carrie asked, not able to take her eyes off the sheet of paper she was holding.

Hobbs seemed willing to talk now. "A lot of them are men who used to be part of the slave patrols. The rest of them are veterans."

Carrie closed her eyes for a moment. Her first thought was of Ike Adams, but she knew all the slave patrols were made up of ruthless, heartless men who killed easily. They had an engrained hatred and bitterness toward the blacks, and blamed them for their current circumstances. She also knew there were a lot of them who had been left adrift after the war. The idea of an army of such men should strike terror into the heart of any thinking, reasoning person.

"They don't just hate the blacks, Carrie," Hobbs warned. "They hate the whites who are helping them even more." He hesitated, his voice deepening with intensity as he continued. "They hate the Yankees, but they seem to have an even worse rage for Southern whites who help the blacks." His eyes met Carrie's squarely, his voice clearly imparting a warning. "They go after all of them."

Chapter Eight

Carrie, exhausted after a long night of conversation with her father and Abby following Hobbs' revelations, was up bright and early to meet Dr. Hobson.

"Looks like you could use some hot coffee, Miss Carrie."

Carrie reached gratefully for the steaming mug May held out to her. "Thank you," she breathed, hoping the hot liquid would melt her fatigue. She sank down in the rocking chair in front of the kitchen fireplace, thankful for the warmth that reached out to embrace her, but it still failed to relax her.

"That Hobbs fellow upset you," May muttered as she rolled biscuit dough on the floured cutting board. Her knowing eyes were locked on Carrie.

Carrie didn't see any reason to deny it. Everyone must feel the tension his presence brought to the house. She had shown her father and Abby the flyer Hobbs had given her. They had reacted, just as she had, with horror and grim anger. Carrie hesitated a moment, and then handed the flyer to the housekeeper. It was only fair that May and Micah were forewarned.

May gave her a curious look, dusted the flour from her hands, and then reached for the paper. Silence filled the kitchen as she read it, her face hardening with a mixture of anger and resignation. She finally handed it back to Carrie. "Nothing we didn't already know about."

"What do you know?" Carrie asked keenly.

"You don't need to hear the stories," May muttered, turning back to her biscuits.

"So you think hiding it from me will change things?" Carrie demanded. "Do you know who Ellis Harper is?"

"The man who wrote that paper?   We get stories from people passing through."

Carrie gazed at her stoic face. "You mean people running away?"

May sighed. "That would be the truth of it. Things ain't good anywhere, but there be places it's worse. Ellis Harper's territory be one of the worst.   Lots of folks leaving there, hoping that getting away will keep 'em alive."

"Running away is their only choice?"

May looked up, fury etched in the crevices of her face. "What else can they do?" she demanded. "All them soldiers spent years fighting the North.   Now they got nothing to do but terrorize and kill black folks. What's the use of trying to fight back? Leaving is better than windin' up dead!" Her rage dissolved as sadness filled her eyes.   "A woman came through Richmond a couple weeks back. Some friends of mine put her up for a few days before she kept goin'. She was up there in Ellis Harper's area. Her baby girl died of sickness.   While her husband was digging her grave, a bunch of Harper's men rode by..." her voice trailed off as she fought for control. "They done shot her husband to death while he was digging her child's grave. She tried to run to him, but they drove her off, saying they would be happy to kill her, too." May clenched her fists as she turned away. "She says now that she wishes she had let 'em. The pain done be eating her up."

Carrie remained silent, knowing there was simply nothing to say in response to such atrocity. When May finally looked at her, Carrie met her eyes levelly, trusting the sorrow she felt was radiating on her face.

May let out her breath and went back to rolling biscuits. "That woman went on down to family in Georgia. I don't know she be any safer there, but at least she won't be alone. Only time can heal that kind of misery."

Carrie gripped her coffee cup. "There must be something that can be done to stop this. It can't just be allowed to happen. The slaves are free now."

May shrugged but the tension radiating from her said there was nothing casual about her reaction. "We all gots to do the best we can. My Spencer tells me the best way to survive this is to work together." Her face softened as she thought of her new husband. "Ain't many bad things happening in Richmond right now— at least not as much as is happening other places. We got plans to fight for more rights here."

Carrie felt a flash of alarm. "What if it puts you in danger?"

May smiled slightly. "We in danger just because we be breathing, Miss Carrie. Oh, lots of us hope things will be better when the government sends more soldiers down here, but it might make those vigilantes so angry it will only make things worse. Only time gonna tell us that. Black folks done learned how to survive a long time ago. We'll keep right on doing that, hoping someday things will truly get better." She finished rolling the biscuits and then turned to take a tray of golden ones out of the oven. "Here, Miss Carrie. You gots to eat something so you can go meet that fancy homeopathic doctor Miss Abby told me about.

You ain't gonna solve any of this today, so you might as well get on with what you're here for."

****

Carrie stepped down from the carriage, steadied by Spencer's strong arm. He had wanted to turn back to the house when an icy rain started falling, but she had come too far not to fulfill her mission. Spencer had scowled his disapproval before handing her more blankets to provide protection, as well as giving her the umbrella he kept under the driver's seat. The sun had been peeking through the clouds when they left the house, but within moments the wind had started blowing, the sun had been gobbled by thick gray, and rain had turned into ice pellets.

"Don't you stay in there real long, Miss Carrie," Spencer ordered. "The last couple days of spring-like weather weren't nothing but a tease. Winter ain't done with Richmond yet." He cast a practiced eye on the clouds. "It's gonna spit ice for a while, but then it's gonna turn to snow. I'm going to get you back to your daddy's before the roads get real bad."

Before Carrie could answer, the door to the office building they had stopped in front of swung open. She looked up as a tall, vibrant man with thick brown hair and a flowing beard peppered with gray strode easily down the walkway.

"Mrs. Borden?"

Carrie smiled and stepped forward to accept his outstretched hand. "Dr. Hobson. It is so wonderful to meet you."

"And I feel the same. Your mother has many wonderful things to say about you."

"That's to be expected, don't you think?" Carrie asked with a laugh.

Dr. Hobson threw back his head as he joined in her laughter. His entire being radiated health and life. "Well, yes, but since the recommendation comes from someone with the reputation of Abigail Cromwell, it carries a bit more weight." He turned to Spencer. "I have a barn in the back. You can pull the carriage around, stable your horse, and then come into the office to escape this beastly weather."

"Thank you, sir," Spencer said gratefully. He leapt onto the wagon seat, picked up the reins, and urged the horse forward.

"Come, Mrs. Borden. We will be happier inside as well."

Carrie smiled when she entered his office. His waiting room looked like a comfortable living room, with a fire crackling within a brick hearth. A stunning picture of the Virginia countryside reigned over the room from its lofty perch above the fireplace. "This is wonderful," she exclaimed.

"Thank you. I want people to feel at home when they come here. I can best determine how to help them if they are relaxed and comfortable." Dr. Hobson led his way into his office. Other than an imposing desk stationed in front of the window, it looked much the same as the waiting room. Two high-backed chairs were pulled in front of another roaring fire, while lanterns filled the room with a glowing light.

Carrie sank down in one of the chairs, relieved when she heard Spencer come in the back door. She knew he would be comfortable while he waited.

"I have no patients coming until this afternoon, though I suspect the foul weather will keep them away. I adjusted my schedule so I could devote all my attention to you, Mrs. Borden."

Carrie flushed. "I'm honored."

Dr. Hobson smiled. "I suspect I should be the one honored," he replied. "Abigail's recommendation would have been quite enough for me, but then I received a letter from Dr. Strikener just a few days ago. He told me of your work with cholera patients last summer in Philadelphia. He assured me I would find a kindred spirit in my decision to put aside traditional medicine for homeopathic medicine."

"Oh, yes!" Carrie responded eagerly. "Once I understood how effective homeopathy truly is, I knew I could not, in good conscience, recommend any other course of treatment. Other than herbal medications," she added. "I find the combination of the two practices enables me to treat most patients."

"Yes," Dr. Hobson said thoughtfully. "I spoke with Dr. Wild this week, as well."

"Dr. Wild is still in Richmond? I thought he had left. Oh, how I would love to see him."

"I'm afraid he was only here for a few days on business. He and I attended a meeting together. I mentioned in passing that I was meeting a young lady named Carrie Borden. He filled my ears with stories of your exploits during the war."

Carrie blushed. "I would hardly call them exploits," she murmured.

"I don't know how else you could define it when your knowledge of herbal medicines and the teams of women you trained to go into the woods to collect much needed plants was the only thing that provided treatment for thousands of soldiers during the blockade."

Carrie smiled. "I owe my knowledge to one of my father's slaves. She taught me so much. I was grateful to have the information when it was needed."

"I suspect I could learn much about herbal remedies from you," Dr. Hobson replied, "but you are here today because you believe I can be of service. How can I best help you?"

"I would be honored if you would be my mentor," Carrie answered immediately. "I have begun my studies of homeopathy, but I have chosen to delay my formal education for a time."

"While you have a child," Dr. Hobson said, eyeing her astutely.

"Yes," Carrie said quickly, and then pressed on because she knew the weather had shortened her time with him. She was determined to learn what she had come for. "I am running a clinic near the plantation. I find the people out there are not overly concerned with whether I have a degree yet."

"They simply want to know you can help them," Dr. Hobson agreed, a knowing twinkle in his amber eyes.

"I'm able to treat most of them, but there are a few that my remedies don't help, and the homeopathic treatments I have with me don't seem to offer relief either."

"Such as?" Dr. Hobson asked.

Carrie felt a surge of relief and anticipation. It wasn't just the knowledge that she would be able to help her patients; she had missed the intense discussions with other students and homeopathic physicians. "I have several patients who are Confederate veterans. They lost limbs during the war."

Dr. Hobson listened carefully. "And they are experiencing severe pain, just as if the missing limb is still there."

"Yes!" Carrie exclaimed. "I have tried several different herbal remedies for pain, but since there is nothing actually there to create pain, I am at a loss. Putting the remedies on the stumps seems to have no effect." Her heart caught at the thought of the agony and pain the men were in.

Dr. Hobson nodded. "We call it phantom pain. It seems to affect sixty to seventy percent of all amputees. Some don't feel it right away. It can take as much as a year for it to develop."

"I have seen that to be true," Carrie agreed.

"Over time, it can become less frequent and severe," Dr. Hobson continued, "but as many as forty percent of those that suffer will continue to do so for a long time, or for the rest of their lives."

"Surely there must be a way to help them! All that is being done for most of these men is giving them doses of morphine and alcohol." She scowled. "It's doing nothing to ease the pain, but it's wreaking havoc in other areas of their life."

"Traditional medicine can certainly do nothing to help them," Dr. Hobson concurred. "I'm happy to tell you there are several homeopathic remedies that can produce relief."

Carrie leaned forward eagerly.

"*Belladonna* is the remedy to use if they are experiencing severe pain and have a lot of heat from the area."

"And a temperature?" Carrie asked, thinking of her patient who had lost a leg at the thigh during the battle at Gettysburg. When he had come in to see her because of the pain, he had also been running a high fever.

"Exactly," Dr. Hobson replied. "As long as there is intense pain, you will want to use the highest potency you can mix." He held up a hand when Carrie opened her mouth to interrupt. "And, yes, you can get the remedy from me," he added with a smile.

Carrie sank back in her chair, relieved beyond measure. She could hardly wait to get home and let her patients know she had a way to help them.

"*Hypericum* is another excellent remedy," Dr. Hobson continued. "It works well for any kind of nerve pain. For those patients who have extreme pain along the actual incision area, I use *Staphysagria*."

Carrie absorbed the information eagerly. "Two of my patients had bone damage with their amputation, Dr. Hobson."

The physician tightened his lips. "Mid-femur amputations?" he guessed. She nodded. "Give them *Symphytum.*" He stood and walked to his desk, selected a pamphlet, and handed it to her. "This information is just what you need. It has been created by the Union Army to help their veterans. It was added to by homeopathic physicians. Now, you make the best choice of a remedy based on your observations of the patient. If you do not see some improvement with the pain after four doses, you should consider a different remedy. Sometimes the only way to find the right solution is through trial and error."

Carrie flipped through the pamphlet, her elation growing. "Thank you," she said with heartfelt fervor. "It is so frustrating to have someone come to you for help but have no idea how to relieve their pain."

"Which gives you some idea of why I left traditional medicine," Dr. Hobson said with a chuckle. "I was frustrated all the time." His face grew serious. "Worse, I knew I was actually *hurting* my patients most of the time." He looked at Carrie. "How do you feel about surgery?"

"I believe there are surgeries that are unnecessary, but I also believe there is a place for it," Carrie answered honestly. "There are many soldiers who would have died during the war without it."

"Dr. Wild told me you worked right alongside him," Dr. Hobson said, admiration shining in his eyes.

"He went far against the norm to allow me to assist," Carrie replied. "I will always be grateful for what I learned, but I also hope I never live through another war that will require what we had to do." She pushed back the memories that could still rise to haunt her whenever anything reminded her of those times.

"I can echo a hardy amen to that," Dr. Hobson replied. He glanced out the window with a frown. "It's snowing now, and coming down heavy." He walked over to a door set into the wood-paneled wall. "Let me get you the remedies you will need. Anytime you run into a case you need advice on, you can send me a letter. I will respond to you immediately." He disappeared for several minutes. When he reappeared, he was carrying a cloth bag and an armful of books, which he placed into a wooden box next to his desk. "Dr. Strikencr asked me to give you these books when you visited. He is sending me more to replace them. The box will keep them dry, and you will find them invaluable."

"Thank you," Carrie said. "I had very high hopes for my meeting with you, but it has far exceeded even my lofty expectations."

Dr. Hobson smiled. "True medicine should only be concerned with helping people live in good health. We should all strive to do whatever we can to assist others in the same line of work. As you advance in your career, Mrs. Borden, you will help many people, but you will especially help women who are becoming homeopathic physicians. You have breadth of knowledge from all your experiences that most of them do not have."

"Yes, sir," Carrie replied. "I will do whatever I can to help anyone. I will consider it an honor."

There was a soft rap on the door, and Dr. Hobson opened it. "I suspected it was you, Spencer," he said warmly. "And you are right that you need to get Mrs. Borden home while the roads can still be safely traveled."

Buried under blankets again, Carrie waved goodbye to Dr. Hobson from the carriage. Within seconds, the blowing snow made it impossible to see him. She felt a surge of sympathy for Spencer before she pulled the blankets over her head and thought about all she had learned. The box of books was nestled securely in the floorboard of the carriage at her feet. The bag of remedies was clutched firmly in her hand.

****

Rose pulled the door of the school closed, relieved the long day had come to an end. She had sent the children home an hour earlier because of the snow, but she had wanted to finish up some lesson plans before she left. She knew Jeb and Andy were waiting for her, but when she turned, she didn't see them. Alarm radiated through her. There had been no more evidence of the vigilantes, but what if they had done something to her friends? Her pulse racing, she strained her eyes to see through the snow.

"Good evening, Mrs. Samuels."

Rose jumped as a voice sounded through the veil of whiteness. "Moses? Is that you?" She hated the fear she heard in her voice, but she couldn't stop it.

Moses materialized instantly. "What is it, Rose? Is something wrong?" He gripped her shoulders as he looked around.

Rose smiled, knowing he could see nothing but a curtain of snow. "I'm fine now. I was expecting Andy and Jeb to be here. Having you is a treat, but not one I expected. Is there a problem at the plantation?"

Moses let his hands drop to her waist before he pulled her in for a kiss. "Nothing is wrong. I decided I wanted some time with my wife. I reckon this is going to be the last snowfall of the year, so I wanted to enjoy it with you."

Rose stared at him. "It seems like it has snowed a hundred times this winter. It's cold and it's wet. What is there to enjoy?" She knew she sounded petulant, but she was so ready for spring that she could feel the longing about to explode in her chest. The sight of more snow had made her want to cry.

Moses cocked his head and lifted a brow. "Obviously, my wife has forgotten the magic of snow."

Rose sighed, simply not able to enter into the game. "I must have," she admitted.

Moses lowered his head closer as his voice dropped to a teasing whisper. "Is the schoolhouse still warm?"

Rose nodded, having no idea why it mattered. She had banked the fire, but even with the intense cold it would take time for the heat to dissipate. She gasped when Moses swept her up in his arms and produced the key that would unlock the door. "What are you doing?" she demanded, though as soon as the question escaped her mouth she had a very good idea of what he was doing. A smile pulled at her lips.

"Showing you the magic of snow," Moses said smugly. "I can promise you no one will bother us in the schoolhouse right now. I very seldom get my wife all to myself anymore." He lowered his head to claim her lips just as he pushed the door open with his foot, and carried her inside. "I don't want to talk about vigilante groups. I don't want to talk about teaching. I don't want to talk about the plantation. I don't even want to talk about our children."

Rose smiled softly. "That doesn't leave us much to talk about," she observed.

"Exactly," Moses murmured. "I don't want to talk at all." He held her easily with one arm while he locked the door behind them, then he carried her to the floor beside the stove and lowered her gently. "I figure our two coats are all the cushioning we need."

Rose laughed and pulled him close. "Absolutely all we will need," she promised.

Chapter Nine

March 1, 1867

Moses gazed at the packed schoolhouse. The first day of March had brought in the first truly warm day of the year. He could tell this wasn't the teasing spells of January and February. This was a heralding of the glories of spring just around the corner. The snowfall earlier in the week had completely melted. There was still a fire going in the woodstove, but only because night would bring cooler temperatures.

The first redbud trees were blooming in the woods, and crocuses lined every path with their dainty yellow, white and pink blooms. Wild daffodils waved their green leaves, their bulging buds promising a riot of yellow to follow soon. The robins had returned, their red breasts a sure sign that winter was done for another year.

As neighbors chatted and laughed, he thought about all that had been accomplished on the plantation. His men had prepared the seed beds for planting this year's crop of tobacco. They had burned away undergrowth to sterilize the ground and add ash. They had tilled and fertilized.

In early February, during a spate of several warm days, they had planted the minute tobacco seeds by first mixing them with soil and then spreading them over the beds. The beds had then been staked and covered with a linen cloth to protect the seedlings as they grew for six weeks. Moses had checked on them today. They were growing sturdy and strong, a green wave of seedlings stretching as far as the eye could see.

In one more month, as long as winter did not come roaring back, they would be ready to transplant into the fields that were being prepared. The days were full of breaking the soil with heavy plows pulled by an army of mules. Hundreds of acres of fields were being disked and fertilized with oyster marl. In another couple of weeks, his men would make furrows to transplant the seedlings into the fields—the beginning of another record-breaking Cromwell crop.

Moses pushed away thoughts of how much he would miss this when he went to school. Even after years of forced slavery in the fields, he had never lost the feeling of wonder that came from watching the seedlings grow and thrive. Now that the results were dependent upon him, it held even more wonder. The sheer joy of watching the crop grow was even more satisfying than the payment that would follow a good season. He bit back a chuckle as he had that thought. There was a time, not so very long ago, when the idea of receiving a cash payment for his labor would never have crossed his mind. Now, though he relished his growing bank account, he still found the greatest satisfaction in the process.

As he scanned the faces in the crowd, he hoped he would find equal satisfaction in the work he was preparing to do. He thought about the stack of law books beside his bed. He had made good progress through them during the winter months—Rose reading education books at the same time—but all that would cease when the crop started growing. It would claim every moment of his time.

Biting back a sigh, he stepped onto the makeshift platform and waved his hand for attention. The room quieted immediately.

Jeb spoke into the silence. "Why it be just men tonight, Moses? There be trouble you don't want the women folk to know about?"

"No," Moses said. "I'm hoping to keep all of you *out* of trouble." He kept his voice casual, but he hoped his words would impart just how important this evening was. The sixty men gathered in the schoolhouse gazed at him soberly. "I hope the day will come," he continued, "when we don't have to talk about things like this, but until that happens, I aim to make sure all of you are equipped to deal with it."

Moses paused, expecting someone to interrupt, but the room remained silent. He pushed down a twinge of alarm. "Every man in this room has to be extra careful around white women," he began, relieved when he saw Robert push in through the door at the back. Moses nodded silently when Robert mouthed 'sorry' before taking a seat. Something had made his friend late, but he had arrived in time. That was all that mattered.

"White people have a great fear of their women being raped by black men," he said bluntly, not surprised when resigned, disgusted looks showed on the men's faces. "It doesn't take much for someone to accuse a black man of rape." He waved Robert forward. "I'm going to give you some suggestions to keep yourselves safe, but first I want Robert Borden to explain why it is the way it is. I'm hoping that knowledge will help you appreciate how real the danger is."

He moved to the side when Robert stepped onto the stage. The room remained silent, every eye focused on Robert.

Moses, spurred by another jolt of alarm, raised his hand to stop his friend. "There is something more going on here that I don't know about," he said. "I've never heard all of you so quiet. Before Robert tells you what he has to say, I want to know what it is." He locked eyes with Jeb. "Jeb, I have a feeling you can tell me."

Jeb scowled and exchanged glances with several of the men in the room. "I reckon I can, Moses." He took a deep breath. "You know all of us think the world of your wife, but she done stirred up a hornet's nest by opening up her school to white kids."

"How?" Moses asked, though he had a sinking feeling he already knew.

"The kids been coming home with stories," Jeb replied. "Some of them white kids treating the other kids real bad and…"

Moses frowned when Jeb's voice trailed off, but his real concern came from the fear he saw in the other man's eyes. "And what?" he pressed.

"Some of them white kids be real good kids," Jeb said earnestly, "but other ones seem to carry the meanness of their folks in them. They's telling our kids that they gonna get their daddies thrown in jail." His face darkened. "Or worse…" he muttered. "It don't seem to matter none what we do, Moses. White folks got it out for us. They want to make sure we pay for whatever they figure is wrong down here since the war ended. You telling us we got to be careful ain't nothing we don't already know, but we don't reckon it's gonna do much good. Your wife done brought them white people right smack in the middle of our world. We can't do nothing about that."

Moses stared at him as he searched for words. He and Rose had already expected it would take time for the kids to learn how to accept each other, but neither of them had anticipated the decision to include white children in the school would also put the adults in danger.

Robert stepped forward. "All of you have reason to be concerned, but absolutely none of it is your fault," he said. "We've got to figure out answers for how to deal with it, but I've always found that understanding *why* something is happening is the first step to finding solutions." He stopped and glanced at Moses.

Moses nodded, relieved to have time to formulate his response.

"To tell the truth," Robert continued, "it makes me feel sick to have to tell you these things. I feel even worse that there was a time when I felt the same way, but I'm willing to tell you because I want you to know things can change. I changed. It means other people can too." He took a deep breath. "It's true that white men are scared that freed slaves are going to rape their women." He held up his hand as the room filled with scowls and angry mutterings. "Here me out," he pleaded.

Jeb stepped forward and turned to eye the men. "We got's to listen. We's been talking about why white men think like they do. This here be our chance to find out. You got to all hear Mr. Borden out."

Robert waited while the room grew silent again. "Slavery has created a set of beliefs that hurts everyone. Slavery is over, but that doesn't mean the beliefs have changed." He took a deep breath. "Southern white culture is a hard thing to understand. Slavery created a difficult relationship between white men and women. Many men put white women on a pedestal. They believed it made her inaccessible to blacks and was a guarantee of the purity of the white race."

Moses watched Robert. He knew how challenging it was for his friend to talk about this. While Robert's beliefs had completely changed, Moses knew it must be hard to talk against his own race. If their roles were reversed, he knew it would be hard for him as well.

"There were many white men who found they preferred to have sex with the slaves," Robert admitted.

"Cause they were so easy to rape?" one of the men called out angrily.

Robert grimaced but nodded. "I'm afraid that is true. Putting white women on a pedestal seemed to make them..." He paused as he groped for words, his face strained with the effort. "It made them less responsive in bed," he finally said.

"So the men came after our women?" another man asked. "My wife told me all her master's boys raped her when she was younger. There weren't nothing she could do because she was their property."

Robert met his eyes steadily. "I'm sorry that happened," he said. "It was wrong."

"You ever do that?" another man called out in a hard voice, his identity concealed by dark shadows beyond the reach of the flickering lantern lights.

"No," Robert said firmly. "I did many things I regret, but that was not one of them."

Moses raised his hand again. "Let him finish what he came to say," he commanded. "It's taking a lot of courage for Robert to stand up here like this. The least you can do is listen."

The room fell silent again, but the tension buzzed like an angry hive of hornets.

Robert glanced at Moses gratefully and then continued. "The more this went on, the more white women became like ornaments. They were a symbol of the Southern way of life." His voice grew more confident as he talked. "When the Southern way of life crumbled with the loss of the war, and when all the slaves were free, white men realized that black men were free to do to their women what they had done to yours."

"I don't want me no white woman," Jeb snorted. "Ain't a one of them as fine as my wife."

"That doesn't change what they believe," Robert replied. "Unfortunately, when a man believes something, his actions follow his belief. Too many white men feel helpless now because of all that happened. Their concerns have turned into a morbid fear that taints everything in their lives."

"How we gonna change that?" someone demanded. "This is all fine and good, but how do we fight something we didn't have nothing to do with?"

Moses stepped forward now. "Fear is never rational," he said. "White men are afraid of black men. So are white women. It's that simple. It also means that everything you do is something to fear. The men are so afraid, that they have made all the women afraid too. If you smile at their women, they think you are going to rape them. If you are friendly to them, they think you are going to rape them. There are areas where simple acts of kindness can have you accused of rape."

"That's crazy talkin'," Jeb muttered.

Moses locked eyes with him. "You're right, Jeb. But it doesn't change how things are."

Jeb's features hardened with anger. "So you stick all of us with a bunch of white people who bring their children to school with our children. I do my best to stay away from them people, but especially since I'm watching out for your wife, that puts me in a real bad position, Moses."

"I know," Moses said heavily. "I'm real sorry about that." He suddenly realized how vulnerable they were because of Rose opening the school to all children.

Robert laid his hand on Moses' arm. "We're not all like that, Jeb," he said. "And there is hope for change. There are white people who have been treated badly by the white aristocracy, too."

"Aristocracy?" a man snapped. "What kind of word is that?"

"He means all the rich plantation owners," Jeb answered. "Me and Rose talk about it sometimes going back and forth to school. Anyway, Robert is saying that not all white men think this way, but we still got to be careful."

"That's right," Robert agreed. "It's going to take time for things to change."

"A right long time," came a voice from the back.

Robert sighed. "I'm afraid you're right. The reason I told you all this is that if you understand why so many men are afraid, you'll realize how careful you need to be. You need to assume white people will take any sign of friendliness as a threat."

"Real hard to change how white folks see us if we can't never talk to them," Jeb observed.

"You're right," Moses said, "but as long as there are vigilante patrols roaming the countryside, we have to do everything we can to stay safe so that we're here for our wives and children. Getting yourself killed won't help anyone."

Silence gripped the room as his blunt words penetrated their anger.

Moses was convinced he had made his point, but he didn't want the men feeling hopeless. He decided to not share the letter Carrie had sent him about the Ellis Harper flyer. It was time to focus on something positive. "Now, there are also things to be excited about. I know things are bad, but the government will soon be sending down troops to help protect us."

"Ain't nothing we can't do ourselves," one of the men from his old unit growled. "I got me half a mind to go back into the army. I hear they sending black men out west to take care of things. It's bound to be a lot better out there than it is here. I got me forty acres of land and a house, but I got to spend every hour of the day wondering if some vigilante is coming after me. And, I gots to worry about my wife and children all the time." He scowled. "Something could be happening to them right this minute while I'm here at this meeting. Ain't none of us safe. Sometimes going back into the army sounds like a real good thing."

Moses nodded. "I heard about that. They started raising cavalry and army units back in September last year." That's all he said. He hated to lose any of his men off the plantation, but who could blame them for wanting to leave the South?

"You think I ought to do it?"

Moses was aware everyone else was listening closely. At least half the men in the room had served in the Union Army, many of them in his unit. "I think no one can make that decision for you," he said carefully, "but you have to ask yourself what life would be like here for your wife and children if you went back into the army. You can't take them with you."

The man looked thoughtful. "I couldn't leave them here to deal with things on their own," he finally said with a sigh. "I guess we gots to figure out how to live down here the best we can."

"I believe things will get better," Moses said as his gaze swept the room. "It's going to take time, but there is progress being made. New black schools are opening. New black colleges are being founded. There are a lot of people who are fighting to help improve our lives. But," he added, "we have to fight harder than anyone else. Slavery was a terrible thing, but what happens to us now is up to each of us. There are people who want to help, but we have to want it for ourselves even more." His voice rang through the room.

As he talked, he watched the men straighten their shoulders. He felt a deep sense of satisfaction as a determined shine came into their eyes. This is what he was meant to do. He would miss farming every single day when he left the plantation, but he could no more turn his back on his people than he could quit loving Rose. It was not up to him to understand why his words held such influence, but it *was* his responsibility not to walk away from the knowledge.

Chapter Ten

Carrie knew Annie was standing on the porch staring at her with disapproval stamped on her face, but she wasn't going to allow herself to care, and she wasn't going to acknowledge it. Truth be told, it was easy not to care—not when spring had descended on the Virginia countryside, complete with a soft, warm breeze to caress her face. Granite nickered as they walked down the road, his head bobbing joyfully. Carrie knew he wanted to run, but she held him in check.

She may be determined to ride today, but she was not forgetting she was almost five months pregnant. Though she had never felt better, that didn't mean she would be careless. Too many things could happen, and she knew a fall could be disastrous. The day was so beautiful that she was content to walk along and watch the winter-bound world come back to life.

Just a few days of warm weather had unlocked all the life waiting just below the surface for the signal to emerge. Yellow daffodils swayed in the breeze beneath trees bursting with buds taking on the tinge of green. Waves of white snowdrops nodded their heads over the carpet of lavender crocuses stretching out through the woods.

A doe, heavy with child, burst from the woods in front of her. Carrie gripped more tightly with her knees in case Granite shied, but he merely flicked an ear in the deer's direction. Squirrels leapt between trees in a riotous game of chase, while a flock of Canada geese, headed north, honked its way overhead.

Carrie waved when some of Moses' men spotted her, but she didn't stop. The winter fields of Cromwell now lay ready for a new crop. The land had all been plowed, tilled and furrowed in preparation for the seedlings that would be planted in a few days. She took a deep breath, inhaling the rich aroma of earth that held the promise of new growth. The thought sent a thrill through her as she laid her hand on her stomach. Her baby had kicked for the first time last night. She and Robert had waited eagerly for the next one, laughing with delight when their child seemed to kick right into his daddy's hand.

Carrie's face softened as she thought of the moment. She had never seen such pride and total joy on her husband's face. After coming so close to death twice during the years of the war, she knew he thought of their baby as proof of a brand new life for them as a family. As she thought about the look on his face, her peace dissolved, only to be replaced by a churning in the pit of her stomach.

Granite sensed the shift in her mood. He swung his head back to catch a glimpse of her as he nickered. Carrie rubbed his neck absently. "It's okay, boy," she murmured, but the tightness did not loosen.

When she emerged into her haven on the banks of the river, she finally felt the bands ease from around her chest. She breathed in the aromas of spring while she luxuriated in the sound of the gentle waves of the James River lapping against the shore. The water tinkled against the rocks while sunlit sparkles cavorted in the breeze.

Carrie dismounted carefully, unpacked the picnic bag Annie had handed her with a disapproving look, and then took off Granite's saddle and bridle so he could graze on the lush grass. She walked over to her favorite log, smiling at the carpet of snowdrops surrounding it. The large weeping willow tree stationed on the bank was already bright with green—always the first tree to burst into life each spring. She sank down on the log and lifted her face to the sun, forcing herself to take long, easy breaths.

Slowly, peace began to replace the churning in her soul. Her mind slowed enough to allow her to think about the urgency that had brought her to her special place. A sudden kick within her belly made her smile. She laid her hand on her stomach. "Hello, little one. I am going to choose to believe you're letting me know how much you love this spot. I promise I will share it with you when you are born. You'll grow to love it as much as I do."

Carrie pulled the letter from her pocket that had created her angst. Letters from Janie usually lifted her spirits, but this one had sent her into a tailspin—one she couldn't understand. She opened the letter and read it again. There was nothing within the letter to create the unrest she was feeling. Janie was simply telling about the classes she was taking, what she and Matthew were doing, and how much she missed her. Carrie closed her eyes and envisioned the crowded, noisy Philadelphia streets, and then reopened them to take in the shimmering blue waters of the James River. There was simply no comparison, but still...

She placed her hand on her stomach again. "Your mama is confused, little one. I made the choice to stay here. I don't regret it. The clinic is busy, and thanks to the remedies Dr. Hobson recommended, I'm helping veterans who are amputees in ways I couldn't before. Robert and I are happy, and it is wonderful to have so much time with Rose and Moses." The smile that had bloomed while she was talking faltered. "But what about after you are born, little one? How can I leave everything to go back to medical school and get my degree? How could I possibly take you away from your father for that long? How could I possibly leave you here when you are old enough?" The questions pounded in her brain as she gave voice to them. "How can I *not* get my degree after everything I have done? Will it be enough simply to work here at the clinic? My patients don't mind right now if I don't have a degree, but won't that change in the future as medicine advances?"

Carrie groaned, crumpled up the letter, and stuffed it back in her pocket as the questions pounded in her brain. No wonder every muscle in her body was tense. The love she felt for her unborn child grew with each kick, every tiny movement she felt flutter through her body. She could hardly wait until her baby was born, but she also acknowledged the birth would change everything. It would change her choices. It would change her routines. Quite simply, it would alter everything about her life. Rose assured her all the questions would melt away when she held her child in her arms for the first time, but she did not share the confidence.

Treating patients had taught her there were women who resented their children. They felt trapped, limited in what they could do. In a time when women were expected to have a large number of children, it was too easy for the *woman* to disappear into the *mother*. Carrie was used to going against the norm of what society expected of women, but the reality that her rebellion could impact another life was sobering beyond measure. She never wanted her son or daughter to feel anything but cherished and loved.

The world was changing, but societal shifts did not diminish the responsibility of being a good parent.

Carrie stood abruptly and began to walk around the clearing. The beauty and serenity faded as the roaring in her head took over. Granite lifted his head to stare at her, snorted, and then lowered his head to graze again. He seemed to know there was nothing he could do. Carrie jolted to a stop as she gazed at Granite calmly snatching at patches of fresh green.

That was it! Granite had felt her angst, had acknowledged he was aware of it, and then had gone back to eating because he knew there was nothing he could do about it. *Nothing he could do about it.* At least not at this moment in time... Just as there was nothing Carrie could do about it. She was pregnant. It was an irrefutable fact. In four more months, her child would be born. Her life would change. She could envision what that was going to be like as much as she wanted to, but it wouldn't be until she was holding her child that she would know how it truly felt, and how it would impact what she decided to do with the rest of her life. She could feel Sarah's voice echoing in her mind. *"Girl, you really figur' worryin' gonna do you any good? Ain't gonna do nothin' but stir up thin's inside. That be a recipe for misery, sho 'nuff. You just gots to keep walkin', Carrie girl. You gots to keep livin'. That old road of life will unfold before ya, just like it be meant to. You just gotta keep walkin'."*

Sarah had started telling her to stop worrying when she was just a little girl because she had always wanted to be steps ahead of wherever she was. Truth be told, she probably always would be. It was who she was.

Carrie walked over to the water, coming within inches of the river straining toward her. She stared east, seeing nothing but the endless ribbon of blue stretched before her. Someone following the James for the first time could never predict what was ahead. They would simply have to get in the water and follow the flow. Would it lead them to the ocean? Would it send them tumbling over a waterfall into jagged stones? Would it surge with muddy flood waters? They couldn't possibly know. *What would come would come.*

Carrie knelt down and scooped up a handful of cold water. She held it to her lips, tasting the mystery of life as she drank. As the liquid slid down her throat, she was amazed at the peace she felt. She was used to coming to her special place to receive answers. It felt odd, but somehow right, that the answer was the reality that there *was* no answer. She might still search for answers in the months to come, but she hoped she would hold tight to the truth that she must simply keep walking, letting the answers unfold as they came.

****

Thomas was smiling when he walked into the house. Everyone was already seated at the dinner table. The windows were open for the first time that year, letting in a soft breeze that fluttered the curtains and made the lantern light dance across the ceiling. As he entered the room, May pushed through the kitchen door holding a huge platter of beef surrounded by baby carrots and onions that he knew she had harvested from the winter garden that morning. The aroma almost made him forget his news, but the crinkle of paper in his pocket brought him back to the present.

"You look happy, dear," Abby said fondly. She patted the chair next to her that was at the head of the table. "You're here just in time." She eyed him keenly. "Are you going to tell us what put that smile on your face?"

"I know we had a successful report on earnings for the factory," Jeremy added, "but something tells me that isn't it."

Thomas smiled more broadly as he lifted his brow and remained silent.

"Did you hear about Opal finding her new restaurant?" Marietta guessed.

Thomas forgot about his own news for a minute. "She did? That's wonderful news." He turned to Abby. "Is it in a good location?"

"You doubt me?" Abby teased. "I met Opal and Eddie there when I left the factory. It is a small restaurant near downtown on a very busy street. She will do well there."

Thomas hoped so. "And you're not concerned about her being so close to downtown?"

Abby shook her head. "Opal and Eddie decided they were willing to take the risk of being outside the Black Quarters. I quite agree with them. Opal is a wonderful cook. White people will overlook her being black because of the food, and she will make much more money there."

Thomas nodded thoughtfully, his mind returning to the envelope in his pocket. "It is soon going to be safer in the South for everyone," he murmured as he pulled out the letter.

May hesitated at the door to the kitchen, and Micah stepped in from the library with an inquisitive look on his narrow ebony face.

"That what I think it is?" Micah asked, his eyes locked on the letter. "I done heard it might be real soon."

Thomas smiled more broadly. "Micah, you and May should hear this." He waved at two empty chairs and waited for them to sit down. He glanced around the table, his smile becoming a little more fixed when he encountered Hobbs' mutinous eyes. It amazed him that Hobbs continued to live with them. He and Abby talked nightly about whether it would create change in him. So far, they could only see the anger growing, not diminishing. He knew money was part of his reason for staying, but Hobbs was being paid well enough to rent a small room on his own. Was he saving money? Or was he gathering information for the vigilante groups? The latter option caused endless concern, but they both had decided they would not bow to fear in their own home. Hobbs was a guest. They would treat him with courtesy, but they would live true to their beliefs.

Thomas pulled the sheaf of papers out of his pocket. He wasn't going to read the entire thick letter, but there were portions he would refer to. "I received this from Matthew today. I am happy to report that Congress has passed the Reconstruction Bill."

"Glory be!" Micah and May yelled at the same time, their eyes wide with disbelief and joy.

"That's wonderful news," Abby exclaimed.

"Finally," Jeremy added. "This has been long overdue."

"Will it mean protection for the freed slaves?" Marietta asked. "The reports coming in are horrifying. I worry about my students and their families every single day."

Hobbs was the only one to remain silent, but no one anticipated anything different. The entire family treated Hobbs with respect, but they also acknowledged the hard wall he had put around himself. There were few efforts to breech it.

"It was quite a complicated and lengthy process to get this bill passed," Thomas began. He lifted the first sheet of the letter. "I think a quote from the *New York Herald*, once one of President Johnson's greatest supporters, says it best: '*The President forgets that we have passed through the fiery ordeal of a mighty revolution, and that the pre-existing order of things is gone, and can return no more—that a great work of reconstruction is before us, and that we cannot escape it.*' "

"We gonna get the vote, Mr. Cromwell?" Micah asked eagerly.

"Hush!" May snapped. "Let Mr. Cromwell tell it his way. We's gonna find out soon enough."

Micah shrugged, but his black eyes glittered with expectancy.

Thomas understood his impatience, but it was important to understand the process of what had happened. Less than two years ago, Micah would never have dreamed of interrupting his *master*. The fact that he now could spoke volumes of the progress since the end of slavery. "You know blacks in Washington, DC now have the right to vote. Just recently, Congress extended black suffrage to the western territories. The Radical Republicans in Congress were determined black suffrage would be part of this bill. Their insistence created quite a battle," he admitted. "The last few weeks have been full of political haggling that would bore anyone but the most committed politician."

"Which is why the letter from Matthew is so thick. Thank you for sparing us the details," Abby said. "I find I am much more interested in the bottom line." She smiled. "But I also know how much you love to tell a good story," she added fondly.

Thomas returned her smile with a nod. "That's true, my dear, but I have no problem getting to the bottom line this time because it is the *understanding* of the bottom line that will determine so much." He took a deep breath. "The actual title of the bill is *'An act to provide for the more efficient government of the Rebel States'*. It was passed yesterday, the second of March. Every former Confederate state will have to fulfill the requirements of the act in order to be readmitted to the Union."

"Which are?" Marietta burst out.

"First, the South is being broken into five territories that will be governed by the United States military. A majority of the Congress agrees that the only way to regain control of the violence in the South is to impose military rule."

"They's gonna stop them vigilantes?" Micah asked, carefully avoiding Hobbs' eyes as he focused on Thomas.

"That will be a top priority," Thomas assured him. He deliberately scanned the table, tensing when he saw the glassy-eyed rage on Hobbs' face. He locked eyes with him until Hobbs scowled and looked away. "Each state will be required to ratify the Fourteenth Amendment to the United States Constitution, and..." Thomas drew out his last word, biting back his smile as Micah and May leaned forward. "And, they will be required to grant voting rights to black men."

"Glory!" Micah burst out. "I been hoping I would live long enough to have the right to vote." His face was a mixture of stunned disbelief and joy. "I weren't too sure it would happen."

Marietta frowned. "What about the rest of the states? Don't they have to grant voting rights to black men? Only nineteen of the twenty-four northern states have the black vote. What good will it do to insist the southern states give the right to vote if they won't?"

Thomas hesitated. "Not at this point." He held up his hand to stop what he knew would be an angry outburst from his sister-in-law. "I feel exactly as you do." He picked the letter back up and searched for an area he had underlined. *"'Unfortunately, the Reconstruction Act reflects the circumstances of its creation. It was necessary to find a program two thirds of Congress could agree on, and also one that the Northern electorate would support.'"* He put the letter down. "We have taken a huge step in the right direction, but there is still more to accomplish," he admitted.

"Like just giving the whole South to the blacks?" Hobbs spat. He had obviously reached the limits of his ability to remain silent. "They gonna let blacks vote, but they ain't gonna let white men vote." He locked eyes with Thomas. "Don't it bother you that you can't even vote, Mr. Cromwell?" He didn't wait for an answer. "Ain't none of y'all see that it ain't just about giving the vote to the black man? It's about taking it *away* from the white man." His eyes burned. "How is that any kind of fair?"

"It's not," Thomas said quietly.

Hobbs swung back to stare at him. "You're agreeing with me?"

"I'm agreeing that I think everyone should have the right to vote," Thomas said. "Unfortunately, there are many men in the South who refuse equality. Until they can accept it, the consequences are the loss of the right to vote. Anyone who had a role in the Confederate government has been excluded from voting, but it is only temporary. Military rule is necessary, but it is only temporary."

"For how long?" Hobbs snapped.

"I suppose that will be determined by each state's actions."

"And you think it's okay for only the *South* to give the right to vote to black men?" Hobbs pressed.

"Certainly not," Thomas replied. "But I suspect that will be resolved rather quickly." He paused thoughtfully. "Have you ever seen a very large ship, Hobbs?"

Hobbs glared at him uncertainly. "Yeah," he said abruptly. "During the war. What's that got to do with anything?"

"There is a big difference between a very large ship and a tiny rowboat," Thomas continued. "If you want to change direction in a rowboat, you can do it very quickly. But if you want to turn a huge ship around it takes a while to shift course." He met Hobbs' eyes. "America is a very large ship, and this is very big change. It's not going to happen overnight, and it's not going to happen easily."

"It ain't even happening *right*," Hobbs retorted.

"What do you think should happen?" Abby asked gently.

Hobbs turned to look at her. "I don't figure blacks should vote," he snapped. "They ain't got the education and smarts to vote like white people."

"Is that right?" Marietta asked calmly. "How much education have you had, Hobbs? Do you believe you should vote?"

Hobbs stiffened even more. Everyone knew he had never attended school. "White men are smarter than black men," he parried. He stared at Thomas. "I heard you say many times that it was the role of white men to care for black people because they couldn't take care of themselves."

"I was wrong," Thomas replied. "So terribly wrong. As is every white person who still believes that." He held up his hand before Hobbs could reply. "I agree that education should be important for every person who votes. But not just for the black man," he added quickly. "It is important to educate every person in the United States. Men *and* women. Blacks will finally get the vote, but it is equally important for women to have the vote. And, it's important for white people to be educated. Race does not either qualify or disqualify you to vote, Hobbs." He held his eyes across the table. "Any person who wants to have a say in this country should be educated."

"It still ain't right for black people to vote," Hobbs said stubbornly.

Marietta broke into the tense silence. "Black men *used* to have the vote."

Hobbs jerked his head in her direction. "What are you talking about?"

Thomas watched her, just as curious to hear what she would have to say.

"It's true," Marietta said. "I received documents from some friends in the North recently. Many people don't want to acknowledge it."

"What did the documents say?" Abby pressed. "I'm intrigued to know."

"Back in 1856, the Dred Scott decision was passed," Marietta began.

Thomas was watching Hobbs and recognized the blank look in his eyes. "The Supreme Court decided that blacks, whether enslaved or free, could not be American citizens, and therefore had no standing to sue in federal court," he explained.

"That sounds right," Hobbs said gruffly.

"Except that it wasn't right," Marietta replied. "There were two justices that dissented. One of them was Justice Benjamin R. Curtis. He provided a lengthy documentary history to show that many blacks in America had often exercised the rights of citizens. During the time of the American Revolution, all free blacks had the vote on equal terms with all other voters."

"What happened?" Abby asked in an astonished voice.

"There were many state constitutions that protected black voter rights," Marietta answered. "Early American towns like Baltimore had more blacks than whites voting in elections. When the U.S. Constitution was placed before American citizens, it was ratified by both black and white voters in a number of states. It's true that slaves were not allowed to vote, but even in the South, with the exception of South Carolina, free blacks had the vote." She looked at Abby. "I'll answer your question, but first I want to make sure I tell you what I learned. Slaves were not allowed to vote, but during the Revolution, many worked to end slavery. It was actually Great Britain that prohibited the abolition of slavery in the colonies."

Abby frowned, remembering what she had learned from Carrie and Biddy. "Because they wanted to keep sending their own people from England and Ireland to America to be enslaved."

"Yes. Once Great Britain lost the Revolutionary War, most of the states in the North ended slavery. Many blacks had not only the right to vote, but they also held office."

Thomas shook his head in disbelief. "I never knew," he murmured.

"Most Americans don't know," Marietta replied, her eyes burning. "In the early years after the Revolutionary War, the Congress moved toward ending slavery and achieving voting rights for all blacks, not just free blacks. In 1789 they banned slavery in any federally held territory. Five years later they banned the exportation of slaves from any state, and then in 1808 they banned the *import* of slaves into any state. More progress was made to end slavery and achieve civil rights for blacks in America at that time than was made in any other nation in the world."

Micah shook his head. "I don't understand, Miss Marietta. How did things go so wrong?"

"Greed," Marietta said flatly. "By 1820 most of our founding fathers had died. A new generation of leaders, intent on money and power, began to reverse all the progress that had been made. They passed the Missouri Compromise that permitted the admission of new slave-holding states."

"And no one tried to stop them?" Abby asked incredulously.

"Oh, they tried," Marietta answered. "Elias Boudinot, who was a president of Congress during the Revolution warned this new direction would bring an end to the happiness of the United States. John Adams warned that lifting the slavery prohibition would destroy America." She let her eyes roam the table. "Thomas Jefferson was appalled at the proposal and also tried to stop it. Congress, of course, was no longer listening to these men. Their new attitude was reflected in the other states. In 1835, North Carolina reversed its policies and limited voting to white people. Maryland had already done it in 1809. The new Congress continued to pass laws that brought us to the Civil War that has just ended."

"And now we have a new Congress that is working to reduce the damage and turn things around," Thomas murmured, his mind spinning with the revelations. "Why does no one know this?"

Marietta smiled grimly. "Because our government knows that an uneducated public is easy to manipulate." She locked eyes with Hobbs. "That's why education is so important, Hobbs. Your vigilantes are fighting from pure ignorance and hatred. They are not trying to save America. They are fighting to continue the greed that has stripped equality from Americans that were once equal to you."

Hobbs opened his mouth to respond, but Marietta quelled him with a fierce look and continued. "As long as people are uneducated, groups like the Ku Klux Klan can feed off ignorance and fear. You are being used, Hobbs...you and the thousands of vigilantes who are out there terrorizing and killing black people, and the whites who are fighting for their rights. Blacks aren't out to get you, Hobbs. They aren't out to destroy your life. They are simply trying to live. They are trying to make something of the lives that have been stolen from them for so long. And you, and the people you support, are trying to stamp out their lives."

A thick silence filled the room when Marietta finished talking. Thomas watched Hobbs carefully, almost taking pity on the look of trapped rage he saw on his face. He saw something else, though. He saw confusion. He saw doubt stamped into the brown eyes that used to sparkle with life.

****

Carrie was smiling when she rounded the last curve and saw her white home glimmering pink in the setting rays of the sun. She was singing softly to herself when she approached the barn.

"Carrie Girl!"

Carrie stiffened, sure she was hallucinating. The familiar voice of her childhood reached out to fill her with memories. She strained her eyes to see through the glare of the sun, but all she could make out were shadows.

"Carrie Girl!"

A wild hope bloomed inside her. The hope burst into flower when Granite raised his head and released a joyful whinny. Heedless of her condition, Carrie released Granite into a gallop that swallowed the last hundred yards in seconds. Hands were there to lift her down as she slid to a stop.

"Miles!" Carrie cried, laughter mixing with her tears of disbelief.

Chapter Eleven

Carrie raised her hand and touched the leathery face peering down at her. "Miles?" she whispered. "Is it really you?"

Miles, his eyes sparkling with the vibrant life she had always known, had tears flowing down his cheeks, as well. "Carrie Girl," he said tenderly. "It's me, Carrie Girl."

Carrie stared at him. The man who had taught her to ride. The man who had given her the freedom her mother tried to hold from her. The man who had taught her how to jump. And the man who had been among the first slaves to escape from Cromwell Plantation. "I thought I would never see you again," she said tremulously. "It's really you."

Rose appeared from within the barn, her face wreathed in smiles. "He got here about an hour ago," she announced. "He surprised us all. I'm certainly glad you are back because he wouldn't tell us anything until you returned. He said he didn't want to have to repeat himself." Rose's voice was exasperated, but her eyes were full of love as she gazed at the elderly man who still stood erect and strong. "He's been inside all this time fiddling with the horse he brought with him."

Carrie shook her head, trying to clear the fog of shock. "You brought a horse?" she asked faintly.

"One of the finest horses I've ever seen," Robert confirmed as he strode from the barn.

Annie appeared on the porch of the house. "All right, Mr. Miles. You got what you want. Miss Carrie done be back. Now alls of you gots to come up on this porch. I'm bringing out some lemonade and cookies, and you's gonna tell everyone what you doing here."

Miles looked toward the porch and chuckled. "Looks like that Annie runs things around here."

"It's best to not cross her," Carrie agreed as she linked arms with her old friend.

Miles peered at her. "Says the woman who rode off on her horse even though she is pregnant."

Carrie laughed. "And I came back safe and sound, so obviously there was no need to worry."

Amber called from the barn. "Miss Carrie, you can't go up on the porch until you see the horse Mr. Miles brought with him!"

Carrie turned around to tell her they would be back soon, but the sight of the towering bay mare she was holding made her gasp and forget all about lemonade and cookies. "She's beautiful," she breathed, walking back to circle around the horse. She turned back to Miles. "How did you get her here?" She realized there were thousands of unanswered questions racing through her mind.

"All good questions," Robert agreed. "Miles wouldn't tell us a thing until you got back."

Miles laughed heartily as he walked up to the mare and laid a gentle hand on her neck. "Meet Chelsea," he said proudly. "Me and her rode down to Richmond on the train."

Carrie gaped at him. "The train?" she managed.

"That's right," Miles confirmed. "Mr. Carson paid our way to come down here."

"Mr. Carson?" Rose asked. "Where have you been?"

Carrie interrupted his answer. "I have a million questions as well, but first I want to know what kind of horse this is."

"It's a Cleveland Bay," Miles answered. "They are Great Britain's oldest breed of horse. The breed started up in an area northeast of England that used to be called Cleveland." His eyes shone as he talked. "The first one came over to North America about twenty-five years ago. The man I been workin' for raises them for carriage horses."

Carrie shook her head. "I simply don't know what to ask first." She smiled at Amber. "Put Chelsea back in her stall. Thank you for showing her to me." Then she turned and led Miles toward the porch. "Talk," she commanded.

Miles sank down into one of the rockers on the porch and accepted the glass of lemonade from Annie. "Things sure done changed around here," he commented. "I didn't never dream I would be drinking lemonade on the porch of Cromwell Plantation."

Carrie smiled. "It's been seven years since you left, Miles. You're right that a lot has changed."

Miles hesitated. "I'm real sorry about that, Miss Carrie. I've missed you something fierce since I been gone."

"Don't apologize," Carrie replied. "I would have done the same thing."

Miles eyed her. "Rose told me you set all the rest of the slaves free after your daddy left the plantation." He smiled at Rose. "I wouldn't say nothing, so she did a lot of talking to fill in the gaps."

"It was the right thing to do," Carrie said simply. "Where have you been, Miles?"

"Up in Canada. It took us about six months to get that far, but we made it."

"Did everyone make it?" Rose asked anxiously.

"*Everyone*," Miles assured her with a wide smile. "It was the happiest day of my life when we crossed over that Canadian border. Freedom felt just as good as I thought it would." His eyes darkened. "There were some real hard times in those six months, but we made it. That's what counts."

"I know what you mean," Rose murmured, reaching out to grasp his hand.

"I wouldn't have been able to do what I done if you hadn't taught me how to read, Rose," Miles said gruffly. "Folks up in Canada were used to black folks ending up in their country, but they was real surprised when we showed up being able to read and write. I got me a job almost right away because of that."

"Working with horses?" Carrie asked.

"Not at first. I worked in a factory for a couple years. The folks up in Canada were willing to have us, and I'll always be real grateful for that, but I can't say lots of them were really *happy* to have us. So many slaves coming up there made it real hard for the men up there to get jobs, so there was a lot of resentment."

Robert nodded thoughtfully. "I guess I can understand that."

"Me, too," Miles agreed. "I was just happy to have me any kind of job. The first day I got money for my work I just stared at it. I was afraid to spend it because I figured it would stop coming at any minute. Lots of us was like that."

"Did you ever get around to spendin' it?" Annie asked.

"Not much," Miles admitted. "I didn't need that much. But then I got me a real reason to save it." He smiled at Carrie. "I couldn't stay away from horses. I found out about a fella raising horses not too far from where I was living, so I went out there to take a look." His eyes took on a glow. "Carson Farms is quite a place." He seemed lost in memories for a moment. "Anyways," he continued, "we gots to talking about horses, and he found out I knew a bit."

"A bit!" Carrie snorted. "How long did it take him to find out how much you really knew?"

Miles grinned. "Not too long," he admitted. "By the end of the day, I had me a job working in the stables."

Carrie and Rose exchanged delighted looks.

"What did you do for Carson Farms?" Robert asked.

"Diff'rent things," Miles drawled, "but by the time I left I was runnin' their breeding program."

Robert eyed him thoughtfully. "That was an important job to leave."

"Yep." Miles nodded, not adding more to his simple agreement.

"Why did you leave?" Carrie pressed.

Miles gazed at her. "I missed home, Carrie Girl. Canada is a right nice place, but it sure gets cold in the winter. I missed the fireflies, and I sure missed the smell of honeysuckle on a warm summer evening. I kept watchin' how things were changin' down here. When I figured it was safe enough, I took all the money I saved and came home."

"With Chelsea?" Robert asked.

Miles looked at him. "Yep."

Annie snorted. "I know the look of a man who ain't tellin' everythin' he got inside him. You with friends now, Miles. You might as well tell ever'body the rest of the reason you're here."

Rose stared at her mother-in-law. "You know what it is?"

Annie snorted again. "Course not! But it don't take no special skills to know Miles ain't tellin' us ever'thing." She glared at Miles. "We ain't got time for games around here. You want any more of my lemonade and cookies, then you better start talkin'!"

Miles smiled widely, his eyes locked on Annie. "Well, I sure do want some more of those cookies," he replied. He looked back at Robert. "I spend a lot of time readin' breeding magazines."

"That so?" Robert asked, his eyes beginning to take on a gleam.

"Yep."

Carrie had seen Clint come over from the barn after training one of the mares during the afternoon.

Clint had been standing at the bottom of the stairs listening, but now he walked up onto the porch. "I reckon you read the article a few months ago about Eclipse coming here to Cromwell Plantation."

Miles nodded, his eyes shining with appreciation as he regarded Clint. "That's right. You be Clint?"

Clint nodded but remained silent.

"That article said you were the one responsible for bringing Eclipse here."

Clint shrugged. "I just picked him out. Mrs. Cromwell bought him for the plantation."

Miles eyed him shrewdly. "Then I reckon you know why I'm here."

Carrie stamped her foot. "There are other people listening," she said impatiently. "Would either of you care to tell the rest of us what you are talking about?"

Robert cleared his throat, his eyes locked on Miles, "I think I can clear up the mystery," he began. "The Cleveland Bay was long known as a powerful pack horse. They were used in northern England to carry the wares of traveling salesmen. Their type became known as the Chapman Horse. However, during the 1700s there was a lot of trade between the Barbary Coast of Africa and the northeast of England. The end result was that the Barb stallions were crossed with the Chapman mares."

Carrie listened closely. "I thought the Barb stallions of Africa were the foundation stock for Thoroughbreds? I remember reading about that when I got Granite."

Miles smiled his approval. "The Barbs *were* the breeding stock for the Thoroughbreds, but also the American Quarter Horse, and the Standardbred."

Robert took over again. "As carriages replaced pack horses, the Cleveland Bay evolved into an excellent carriage horse because of their strength, stamina, and sure-footedness." He paused, trying to remember everything he had learned. "I've read there is a very strong demand for upstanding carriage horses that are matched pairs."

"That's right," Miles agreed.

"The Cleveland Bays are being bred to Thoroughbreds to produce a taller, faster coach horse," Robert continued.

"That's right!" Clint said excitedly. "They are known as the Yorkshire Coach Horse." He stared at Miles as he put all the pieces together in his mind. "You brought Chelsea here to breed her with Eclipse."

"Well," Miles said, "I think that might be presuming a little much. Let's say I brought her here with the *hopes* of that happening, but..." He turned to gaze at Robert. "That ain't the main reason I'm here."

"You want a job," Robert said bluntly.

"That's right," Miles said, the first uncertainty showing in his eyes.

Carrie knew how far he had traveled and she couldn't imagine him not staying. She wanted to jump up and say that *of course* Robert was going to hire her old mentor and friend, but the stable was her husband's dream. He should be the one to decide who would work here.

Robert didn't make her squirm long. "I'd be a fool to not hire you," he said with an easy grin. "You obviously know horses. The operation is growing. I will welcome all experienced help I can get. But," he added, "Clint is my stable manager. You'll be working for him, as well."

Miles nodded. "That be just fine with me."

Carrie hid her smile as Clint's shoulders straightened even more and a look of deeper confidence came over his face.

Robert looked over toward the barn. "I think breeding Chelsea to Eclipse is a fine idea."

"I'll pay, of course," Miles said quickly, excitement shining in his eyes. "It will take me a little while to save up the money because buying Chelsea put a big bite into my savings."

Robert shook his head. "I have a better idea. The first foal from Eclipse will be yours. The next will be mine. I would like to see Cromwell Stables add a line of carriage horses. Even without researching Chelsea's lineage, I'm quite sure it is exemplary. You wouldn't have brought her all this way otherwise."

"Took most every penny I had saved to buy her," Miles confirmed. He stood, walked over to Robert, and shook his hand firmly. "You have a deal."

"And we can buy more from Mr. Carson if we decide to?"

Miles grinned. "He is expecting orders."

Robert threw back his head with a laugh and then looked at Carrie. "Miles was your mentor? I'm beginning to understand you better."

Carrie grinned and jumped up to throw her arms around Miles. "I can hardly believe you are back. You've only just begun to answer all the questions in my mind."

"And in mine," Rose added.

"I reckon we got's us lots of time now," Miles said, pleasure shining in his eyes. He looked at Rose. "Where that husband of yours be?"

Rose smiled. "He's out checking the new tobacco seedlings going in."

"He manage this place?"

"Not exactly," she murmured, her smile growing when Miles cocked an eyebrow. "He is half-owner of Cromwell Plantation."

Miles sank back in his chair, shock evident in his eyes. "What you say? Half-owner?"

"It's rather a long story," Rose replied.

"Sounds like it would be," Miles managed as he shook his head. He glanced at Annie. "And you be Moses' mama?"

"That's right."

"And you live here in the house, too?" Disbelief dripped from his voice.

Annie chuckled. "Ain't much of the South like it be here on Cromwell Plantation, but it works real well for us. It does take a mite gettin' used to, though," she admitted.

Miles continued to shake his head. "Seven years be a real long time, but it don't seem long enough for this kind of change."

Carrie thought it wise to warn him it wasn't this way everywhere. "Annie is right that most of the South is not like this, Miles. You'll have to be careful. The vigilantes don't like how we do things here."

Miles nodded easily. "I knows that. I kept up on things even though I was way up in Canada." His face was set in stern lines. "We done gave up too much for too many years. It's time that stopped. This is where I want to be. I want to work to make my own livin', and I want to start a fine line of horses. I ain't lettin' them vigilantes scare me away." He locked eyes with Robert. "The men around here carry guns?"

"They do. Most of the men working here on the plantation served in the Union Army. We've learned to be ready."

"I'm ready, too," Miles said.

Robert exchanged a long look with him. "I understand you used to live in the room over the barn."

"That's right."

"It's still available. It's yours if you want it to be."

Miles smiled. "I would like that just fine."

The evening wore on as they talked about all that had happened. It was too early for fireflies, but the smell of the first lilacs perfumed the air, and a southern breeze kept things warm. John, Felicia, and Amber played hide-and-go-seek out on the lawn, while Annie and Polly brought out platters of ham biscuits and raw vegetables from the gardens. Owls hooted as the crescent moon dangled over the treetops. Moses, in from a long day in the fields, held Hope close in his arms as he chatted with Miles.

In a world of great uncertainty, it was a perfect night.

****

Janie skirted the last remaining piles of gray slush, trying to ignore the prickly feeling between her shoulder blades. She chatted easily with her classmates about all they had learned that day, but try as she might, she couldn't dismiss the feeling of being watched. She hated the old familiar fear that clenched her gut. After all this time, had Clifford come after her to get his revenge? Had he sent someone to hurt her in retaliation for the humiliation their divorce had caused?

"Are you all right, Janie?" one of the women asked.

Janie summoned a bright smile, almost hating that she still knew how to cover her true feelings so easily. "I just have a lot on my mind," she responded. "School seems a little overwhelming right now." It was a blatant lie, but what did it matter? If someone was following her, she didn't want to put anyone else in danger. "I've just remembered something I left back at school. Y'all go ahead. I'll see you tomorrow."

"We'll wait for you," another woman replied.

"Nonsense," Janie said briskly. "I walk home from school by myself quite often. It is perfectly safe. Matthew will be waiting for me when I get there." She was determined not to put anyone else at risk, but neither was she willing to allow herself to be intimidated by fear. Those days were over. She was going to confront whoever it was that was watching her.

The woman who had wanted to wait nodded reluctantly. "I suppose it will be fine," she murmured. Her eyes were still doubtful, but she turned away and continued on with the rest.

Janie waited for several moments, concentrating on deep breaths to steady her nerves, before she turned around and scanned the crowds. Her eyes locked almost immediately on a slender man standing on the sidewalk about a hundred feet away. She frowned when she realized he was watching her. There was something very familiar about him, but she couldn't say she actually recognized him from that distance. Determined to not let her fears control her, Janie gathered all her courage and walked directly toward the man.

She was only a few feet away before her determination dissolved into disbelieving delight. Janie gasped and covered her mouth with one gloved hand. "Georgia?" She walked closer, shaking her head. "Is it really you?"

The slender man with short red hair and blue eyes broke into a broad smile. "I still go by George, but yes, Janie, it is me."

Janie continued to stare in disbelief. "But you are dead."

"Obviously not," George said calmly.

"But, how...?"

George took Janie's arm and led her to a quiet bench set back from the busy sidewalk. A tree blocked enough of the noise to make conversation possible. All Janie could do was stare.

Georgia smiled gently. "I realize this must be something of a shock."

"That would be putting it mildly," Janie managed. "Robert told us you died."

"Because that's what he was told," George replied. "Things were more than a little chaotic at the end of the war. I was with Robert at Appomattox. When the army was surrendered and released, I had no idea what I was going to do. My brother was dead, and I had no desire to return home to farm again."

"Why didn't you let us know?" Janie asked. "We were so heartbroken when we heard you had died."

Regret filled George's eyes. "I'm sorry," he said contritely. "I owe more to you and Carrie than I can ever repay. You hid my true identity and enabled me to pass as a man during the last year of the war. I had actually decided to go back to living as a woman, but then I saw a list of casualties from the last battles. My name was on there. I wanted so much to tell you and Carrie good-bye and thank you, but I thought it would be easier to start over if everyone believed I was dead."

Janie stared at him, reluctant understanding filtering in through the shock. "You died as a woman the day you saw the reports."

"Yes," George agreed. His eyes sparkled with gratitude. "As hard as it was to conceal my identity during the war, I really had no desire to go back to living as a woman. Being a man in America is, quite simply, much easier."

"Don't I know that," Janie murmured, delight replacing her shock. She reached out and grasped her friend's hands. As she did, she realized she had to let George come to life in her mind. He had made his choice, and she couldn't really blame him. "You are still quite a handsome man," she said.

George grinned. "I don't regret my decision. After the war years, I am quite comfortable living by myself. I have friends, and I like the people I work with. I have found that is quite enough for me. I have given up the option of marrying one day, but the trade-offs of living as a man in this country are worth it."

"How did you find me?" Janie asked.

"I wasn't looking for you," George responded. "I moved here to Philadelphia after the war to start my new life. I started as a line worker in a garment factory. The fact that I could read—thanks to you and Carrie—helped me get the job of the office manager within several months. The factory is just a few blocks from here. Last week I saw you walking down the street with some other women. I wanted to approach you then, but I was afraid it would have been too much of a shock, and..."

"You didn't want me to reveal your true identity," Janie finished his sentence for him. "Which I probably would have."

"And now?" George asked quietly.

"Now I am happy to have reconnected with my old friend, George, from Richmond," Janie answered evenly.

"Thank you," George said fervently. "I've watched you a couple afternoons. I still hadn't decided whether I was going to approach you. I was surprised when you turned around and saw me. How did you know?"

"I didn't," Janie answered. "I could feel someone watching me. I had to know who it was."

"I'm sorry I frightened you."

Janie shook her head. "I was afraid it was someone else."

"Clifford?"

Janie took a deep breath. "Yes, Clifford. How did you know?"

"It was something I sensed," George said, smiling slightly. "I may live as a man, but I still have the intuitions of a woman."

"I think I might actually be jealous," Janie said wistfully. She told George what had happened with Clifford. "It's over," she finished firmly. "Do you remember Matthew Justin?"

"Of course I do," George responded. "He was the journalist. I always liked him."

"So did I," Janie answered with a grin. "I liked him enough to marry him on Christmas Eve. We celebrated our three month anniversary a few days ago."

"That's wonderful," George exclaimed. "I'm so happy for you! And you live here in Philadelphia?"

Janie told him about going to the homeopathic college.

"What about Carrie?" George asked. "I thought she would be in medical school."

Janie laughed. "Carrie is having a baby in July!"

The two friends laughed and talked as they caught up on all that had happened. Janie suddenly realized it was getting late. Matthew would be frantic if she wasn't home soon. "I must go," she gasped.

"I will walk you home," George said. "You're safer with a male escort."

Janie smiled, knowing it would take more time to get completely comfortable with viewing Georgia as George. She also answered the question she saw lurking in George's eyes. "I won't tell anyone," she assured him. "Not even Matthew."

"And you don't mind? I hate to have you keep a secret from your husband."

"It's not my secret," Janie replied. "I'm happy to keep it for you."

"You may tell Carrie, of course," George said. "I do hope I will be able to see her again."

"Thank you," Janie breathed. "I was willing to keep your secret, but she might never have forgiven me if she ever found out."

The two friends strolled through the darkening streets. "Are you happy with your job?" Janie asked.

George shrugged. "It's a good job, and I am well-paid."

"But...?"

"Women's intuition?"

"Just answer the question," Janie replied with a smile.

"It really is a good job," George insisted, "but I do not like the working conditions in the factory. I am treated well because I'm in the office, but the people working on the garment lines are treated rather poorly, and I believe they are underpaid. People are so desperate for jobs they seem willing to accept any working conditions."

Janie had a sudden thought. "Would you consider working for another factory?"

George stared at her. "Garment factory jobs are hard to come by. Especially office manager jobs."

"Have you heard of Abigail Livingston?"

"Of course. Everyone in the garment industry knows who she is. Her reputation is impeccable. The things she has done as a woman makes me proud to be one, even if I'm not living as one."

Janie smiled. "Abigail Livingston is now Abigail Cromwell."

"As in Thomas Cromwell?" George managed through his obvious surprise.

"It's too long of a story for the rest of our walk home, but yes." Janie hurried on. "She and Thomas married and are opening a new factory here in a few weeks. I know she has not yet settled on an office manager." She smiled when she saw George's eyes widen. "There is only one thing that might be a problem for you. The factory is going to be in Moyamensing."

George shrugged. "The Irish area of Philadelphia? Why would that be a problem for me?"

Janie regarded him. "It is a problem for a lot of people."

George laughed. "I'm a woman living as a man, Janie. I would say I have learned not to judge anything. And," he added, "I would do almost anything for the opportunity to work for Abigail Livingston Cromwell."

"I'll contact her," Janie promised. She looked up as they neared the house, not surprised when Matthew stepped out onto the porch, warm light spilling out onto the steps.

"Janie!" Matthew called. "I was so worried."

Janie grabbed George's hand and pulled him forward. Now was as good a time as any. "I'm so sorry, dear. I ran into my old friend, George, on the way back from class. We got to talking, and I completely lost track of the time. I've invited him for dinner." She felt George stiffen with surprise, and then relax just as quickly.

"There is plenty," Matthew answered, reaching out to shake George's hand as they climbed the steps. "It's a pleasure to meet you, George." He paused as the light from the porch hit their guest's face.

Janie stiffened. Did her perceptive husband see right through the subterfuge?

"You are the wounded soldier who stayed at Thomas Cromwell's house in Richmond for a while, aren't you? I understood you had died."

"I'm happy to say the rumors were incorrect," George said and then quickly changed the subject. "I read all your articles, Matthew. I'm especially interested in learning more about the Reconstruction Acts."

"That's just the beginning of things to be talked about tonight," Matthew replied.

Janie glowed with happiness as they moved into the house, laughing and talking. She could hardly wait to write Carrie.

Chapter Twelve

Janie ladled thick stew into Wedgwood porcelain bowls as she listened to the wind whistling against the windows. A letter from Carrie had told her about spring descending on the plantation, but there were still only whispers in Philadelphia—whispers that were so quiet she had to strain to believe they were there. She knew warmer weather would come soon, but for now she was responsible for focusing on the good parts of a Philadelphia winter. Right now, the only thing she could come up with in her winter-weary mind was how grateful she was for a warm, cozy home.

Her and Matthew's home was not as luxurious as Abby's, which was just down the street, but it was more than adequate for their needs, and it kept her close to the women from the Homeopathic College who had moved in when Elizabeth, Alice, and Florence had moved out. In spite of the lingering hurt from the latter three cutting off their friendship because of her and Carrie's decision to practice homeopathic medicine, she still missed the easy friendship they had shared. There were many wonderful memories of long meals around the table while they laughed, talked, and argued about all they were learning, but they were tainted by the angry hardness of their faces when they had announced they were leaving.

Janie bit back a sigh as she turned away from the soup and sliced the warm bread she had pulled from the oven. She pushed aside any regrets as she heard

George's easy laughter ring through the house. She may have lost some old friendships, but she had also just miraculously gained an older one she thought was gone forever. Why was it so easy to focus on loss when she had so much to be grateful for?

George broke into her thoughts as he pushed open the door to the kitchen. "Do you need any help, Janie?"

Janie smiled at him as she began arranging the sliced bread on a platter. "I do believe you're the first man to come into my kitchen with an offer of help." Matthew pushed in just in time to hear her statement. She raised a hand to stop him before he could register a protest. "Other than my wonderful husband, of course," she said. "I am lucky to have two extraordinary men in my kitchen tonight." George's eyes glowed with gratitude. "But the answer is no. I have everything ready."

Silence reigned while the soup and bread were consumed. The wind continued to push hard against the windows, rattling the glass as the limbs of a nearby tree brushed against them. The warmth of the kitchen embraced them, wrapping them in a cocoon of coziness that pulled Janie's thoughts away from the challenges of the day.

"Better?" Matthew asked quietly.

Janie smiled, grateful he was able to read her emotions so easily. "Yes." She rose to start the tea kettle on the back of the stove. "Did the second Reconstruction Act pass?"

George pushed aside his bowl and leaned forward with a look of avid attention. "Did President Johnson veto this one, too?"

"Yes and yes," Matthew replied. "The second Reconstruction Act is really just a clarification of some things that were not made clear in the first one."

"Like a timetable for setting up the military districts?" George asked keenly.

Matthew nodded. "You read it?"

"Yes," George answered with a frown. "Not that it was easy to understand."

"I agree," Matthew responded. "Politicians and lawyers seem to enjoy communicating in such a way that the average person is left scratching their head."

"Perhaps to make certain no one can question their decisions," George said wryly. "When you're left guessing what they are trying to say, it is easy not to question it too hard."

"I'm afraid that might be true," Matthew agreed. "But back to your question, the military districts are being set up right away. The commanding generals have until September first of this year to register every male of voting age in their districts."

"Both white *and* black?" Janie asked.

"Yes, except for those whites who are disenfranchised by their involvement in the war." Matthew turned to George. "Once you wade through all the political jargon, it basically says that every state has to form a convention before the fall passes this year. They have to create a new state constitution that is approved by Congress. Each state has to ratify the Fourteenth Amendment and give blacks the vote if they want to be readmitted to the Union and have any political say in what happens."

George listened closely. "It's been three weeks since the first bill passed. How are people reacting in the South?"

Matthew shrugged. "I guess it depends on what people you are talking about. The blacks are ecstatic, as are the white Unionists who never wanted the war to happen in the first place. There are many other southerners who really have no understanding of what is happening at all because they are busy trying to create a new life after the war."

"And then there are the ones who are determined to fight it," George said.

Matthew looked at him thoughtfully. "What do you know about that?"

"For starters, I have read everything you have written," George answered. "I find your articles to be thoughtful and fair."

"Thank you," Matthew murmured. "You said 'for starters...'? "

George nodded. "I find I feel best about my decisions if I read everything I can get my hands on."

Janie smiled to herself, thinking of the days George had insisted there was no need for him to learn how to read. Obviously, the attainment of knowledge had given him the thirst to know more. She understood that. The more she learned, the more she wanted to know.

"And what have you learned?" Matthew pressed.

"The *Pulaski Citizen* carried an article about the Ku Klux Klan," George replied.

Matthew's eyes widened with surprise. "That article just came out yesterday."

George shrugged. "I find I have quite a bit of time to read."

Janie's heart swelled with both admiration and sympathy as she realized living an assumed identity must be quite lonely. She wondered how many dinner invitations George received, and how many he would actually accept. Her attention was pulled back to the conversation by her husband's angry response.

"The Ku Klux Klan is going to cause many problems," he said in a clipped voice.

George nodded. "There are many vigilante groups, but the Ku Klux Klan seems to have the ability to organize that the others lack." He changed the subject. "You said President Johnson vetoed this most recent Reconstruction Act?"

"I think we can safely assume he will veto everything this Congress has to put forward," Matthew dryly.

"Will they attempt to impeach him?"

Matthew looked surprised again. "I suspect it will come to that, but only time will tell if they succeed." He fixed his eyes on George. "I don't remember you being involved in discussions when you were living in Richmond."

George met his eyes squarely. "I had nothing to add because I knew nothing." He reached out and touched Janie's arm. "Your wife taught me how to read."

Matthew turned to stare at Janie. "You never told me."

Janie smiled. "George has taken his ability to read far beyond what I could have envisioned." Indeed, he had. She also knew his level of knowledge was directly related to how marginalized he had felt most of his life as a woman.

"There are too many people who let others make decisions for them," George said quietly. "Our country is where it is today because too many have abdicated responsibility, but then we complain because it's not the way we want it to be."

"How do you believe people should take responsibility?" Matthew probed.

Janie hid her smile as she watched her husband go into full journalistic mode.

"Knowledge," George said promptly. "No one is truly entitled to an opinion unless they have the knowledge to support it. It's easy to listen to someone and *say* you have knowledge, but it takes more than that. You have to dig to find the truth. You have to listen to more than one side before you can say you have an opinion." His blue eyes burned with passion, and now that he had an audience, he seemed eager to speak. "Too many people in this country still don't know how to read. That makes them easy targets for manipulation because they think they have to rely on someone else to discover the truth. There are also people who *can* read but decide it's easier to let someone tell them what to think or believe. I believe they are the worst ones because they don't have an excuse other than laziness."

"You know most people are lazy, don't you?" Matthew asked somberly.

George sighed heavily. "Unfortunately, I do. However, I would have to add that I believe the people who are *currently* voting are lazy. I don't believe blacks will be lazy because this is the chance they have been waiting for. I also don't believe women would be lazy."

"So you believe women should have the vote?"

"Absolutely. It's a complete travesty that women can't vote! I believe our whole country would be different if they could."

Matthew smiled. "No wonder my wife likes you so much. You are welcome at our dinner table any time."

Janie was glad when she saw George relax. He had stiffened when he had made his last comment, concerned, Janie was sure, that he was revealing too much. She decided to turn the attention away from him for a while.

"What article are you working on now, dear?"

Matthew smiled. "Something I find fascinating. The *Philadelphia Inquirer* has asked me to do an exposé on the role of women who passed as men during the war."

Janie felt George stiffen again, but she forced herself to remain relaxed. There was nothing in her husband's expression that said he suspected anything. She was quite sure Matthew would have no trouble with George's real identity, but it was not her secret to reveal. "I see," she said casually, wondering if there was a way to change the subject without it appearing obvious. She was surprised when George spoke up.

"Were there many?"

"Far more than I would have expected," Matthew answered. "They served in every area of the armies, even as soldiers."

"Fascinating," George murmured, his voice laced with shocked surprise. "How could they possibly have hidden something like that?"

Janie ducked her head to hide her smile. Perhaps George should go into the theater, instead of hiding his acting talents in a clothing factory.

"It doesn't seem to have been as hard as I would have suspected," Matthew mused. "Both the armies had strict rules about no women, but their inspection of recruits was far less stringent. They also accepted just about anyone who had teeth in their head once the war dragged on, especially in the South. They had young boys whose voices hadn't changed and who still had smooth faces, so females didn't stand out like you would expect. Women who wanted to join up did all kinds of things to find their place in battle. They bound their breasts, they wore loose, layered clothing, cut their hair short, and rubbed dirt on their faces. They claimed to be male, and the armies accepted them."

"They must have made poor soldiers," George said disdainfully.

"Far from it," Matthew responded. "It seems they performed admirably."

Janie couldn't believe the conversation had taken this turn, but there was nothing she could do to stop it, so she just sat back and listened.

"It's impossible to know how many there were, at least at this point in time," Matthew continued. "There were women soldiers who served during the Revolutionary War, too, but we didn't know about them until long after the war ended. I suspect it will be decades before we know enough to put a number on it."

"How were the women in the Revolutionary War discovered?" Janie asked. She had been completely unaware of this fact.

"They finally came forward and told their stories," Matthew replied. "Evidently, they didn't want to die without someone knowing the truth about what they had done. The women were quite proud of their contribution."

"As they should have been," Janie said firmly, wondering if George would ever reveal the truth about who he was.

"I read about a doctor in England who hid his identity," George added suddenly.

"Oh?" Matthew asked.

"It was discovered only two years ago," George replied. "A woman in London was asked to lay out the body of an eminent physician who had just died. His name was Doctor James Barry."

Matthew's eyes widened. "The Inspector General of Military Hospitals?"

It was George's turn to look surprised. "You know who he was?"

"He held the highest medical rank in the British Army. I understood he died of dysentery."

"That's true," George confirmed. "What they didn't reveal was that Dr. James Barry was actually a woman, and had even borne a child at some point."

Matthew sat back against his chair. "I had no idea." His eyes narrowed. "How do you know this?"

George smiled. "I'm glad you're suspicious," he said. "I could, of course, be making it all up. However, the woman who discovered his true identity is Sophia Bishop. She waited until after the funeral to reveal what she had discovered. It made the newspapers, but the government covered it up rather quickly because they were embarrassed."

"You could still be making this up," Matthew observed.

George was not offended. "Sophia Bishop is the sister of a woman I work with. I met her recently and did some research to learn more."

"Such as?"

"Dr. James Barry was actually Margaret Ann Bulkley. She always wanted to be a doctor, but females were barred from medical school."

"I know what that is like," Janie commented, fascinated by the story.

"Her family had influential friends who hatched a plan for her to enter medical school disguised as a man. Once she qualified, she discovered she could go to Venezuela and actually practice as a female doctor.

She was only fourteen when she entered medical school."

"Fourteen?" Janie echoed in disbelief.

"She was quite extraordinary," George agreed. "Anyway, one of the family friends who was going to open the doors to Venezuela died. At some point, she decided to continue living as a man, and she joined the British Army Medical Corps."

"Extraordinary," Matthew breathed. "He had no distinguishing qualities to make people suspicious?"

George smiled. "Actually, he had a rather high-pitched voice, and I learned he wore three-inch-high inserts in his shoes because he was only five feet tall. He wore oversized clothing and evidently was very difficult to get along with, especially if you mentioned his voice."

"He was definitely hard to get along with," Matthew said. "It was almost legendary." His forehead tightened in thought as he tried to remember what he had read. "He had extraordinary medical accomplishments, but I also read he had more than his fair share of arrests, demotions, and charges of insubordination that seemed to overshadow that."

"Or perhaps they are focusing on that because they don't want anyone to discover who he really was," George said blandly.

"Which is rather ridiculous," Matthew countered. "Man or woman, he was still quite a physician. He won great acclaim as a surgeon, and I remember reading that he performed the first Caesarean section in Africa in which both mother and baby survived."

George regarded Matthew for a long moment, appreciation shining in his eyes. "That's true," he finally said.

Matthew returned to the topic he had started with. "Hearing about Dr. Barry makes me want to learn about women passing as soldiers even more." He shook his head. "I wish I could sit down and talk with even one of them," he murmured.

George hesitated before he spoke. "What do you think you would learn?"

"What made them do it? What it was like? What are they doing now that the war is over?" Matthew shook his head. "Right now all I have to work on is speculations and rumor. I don't do that kind of journalism, even though there are plenty of reporters that do." He took a sip of the hot tea Janie set down in front of him.

George cocked his head. "Why do you believe their story should be told?"

Matthew considered the question as he took another sip of tea and nibbled on a cookie plucked from the platter Janie had placed on the table. "I suppose I believe that anything that reveals the equality of men and women should be revealed," he said. "As long as men's perception of women is not challenged, it will be difficult to force any kind of real change."

Janie felt a burst of pride so strong she thought it would surely swallow her. She knew how special Matthew was, but she loved that he continued to reveal it almost every day.

"As much as I want to tell the story," he continued, "I can also understand why no woman would want to come forward, especially right now. If they have gone back to living as a woman, it would be easy for people to simply not believe them, even if they did want to tell their story. If they have continued to live as men, like

Dr. Barry did, why would they want to jeopardize their identity?"

"You have a point," George conceded, his expression thoughtful.

Matthew abruptly changed the subject. "Why did you fight in the war, George?"

Janie was curious how George would answer. He certainly couldn't tell the truth; that he, as Georgia, had fought to be close to her brother because he was all she had.

"The same reason every man fought in the war," George replied easily. "We had to. Whether we believed in it or not, or whether we agreed with it or not, the South had gone to war. We were being invaded by the North, so we had to fight for our homes."

Janie watched him carefully. She was suddenly sure that was as equally important to George as his desire to be with his brother. They had never talked about it, though.

"My brother and I had our own farm. It was left to us by our parents. I was too young to fight when the war started, but I couldn't run the farm without my brother, so I went to war with him. I wasn't going to let the Yankees come down and destroy our home without fighting."

Janie gazed at George, realizing he was telling all but one piece of the truth.

"How do you feel about things now?" Matthew asked.

George considered the question for a long moment before he answered "If it were possible to know how things would end up when you make a decision, I'm sure I wouldn't have fought. But, since that isn't possible, I would have made the same decision again. It's easy to make a right decision when you have all the facts, but hardly anyone knew the facts back then. We just had to fight. I don't agree with what any of the vigilantes are doing, but I can understand some of what they are feeling." He hesitated. "*Most* of what they are feeling," he added. "They lost everything defending their homes. Now they're about to lose everything all over again." He shook his head sadly. "I wish there were a way to make things right for everyone, but there has been something put into motion that will probably be impossible to stop. Those men who started this war think it's over, but it's not." George's voice tightened. "I'm afraid of what is going to happen when all that hatred and rage are released." His voice trailed off, but his words lingered in the air as if they were trapped by the intensity of his voice. "It's going to be real bad..."

Silence held the kitchen for several minutes. The wind had died down some, creating an even deeper vacuum of quiet.

"Did Janie tell you about the book I am writing?" Matthew was the first to break the silence.

George shook his head. "I'm sure we have barely scratched the surface of things to catch up on."

"It's called *Glimmers of Change*. I am writing stories of positive change in the South. I'm also writing stories about people who have overcome challenges to make their lives better." He paused. "I don't believe I'm ready to write an article for the paper about women who passed as soldiers, but I would certainly love to interview one of them for the book."

Janie understood when she saw George's eyes darken with alarmed suspicion. Why had Matthew brought the subject back up again? He explained it in his next statement.

"I believe the North might handle things a little differently if they could truly understand how people in the South feel, especially now that the war is over. It would be fascinating for them to understand what a woman felt so passionately about that she was willing to fight as a man."

George cocked his head. "Anyone who might be willing to do that would surely not be willing to be exposed."

Matthew shrugged, but it was immediately evident to Janie that there was something in George's voice that had caught his attention. "Revealing someone's identity for this story would not be necessary. It would be entirely possible for them to remain anonymous." His eyes locked on George's face. "Do you actually know someone?"

"I might," George said noncommittally. "Suppose I did? How could they be sure they would remain anonymous?"

"I'm hoping you could assure them, from what you know, that my integrity would never allow me to betray them. You could also mention that my wife would probably kill me if I did anything to betray her relationship with a friend," Matthew added dryly.

George chuckled, but his eyes remained serious.

Janie watched closely, certain she recognized yearning in George's eyes. She fought to keep a naturally curious expression on her face. She knew Matthew would remain silent while George thought about his last comments.

"I do trust your integrity," George finally murmured, but caution still flared in his eyes.

Janie was watching Matthew now. She recognized the moment he realized the truth. His eyes widened slightly before he composed himself. A glance at

George's face revealed he had seen the same thing. George turned to Janie and gazed into her eyes, obviously looking for confirmation. She smiled sympathetically, and nodded slightly. "You can trust him," she said. She was certain it would be a huge relief for George to tell the truth, as long as he didn't have to give up the life he had so carefully crafted.

"I will do your interview," George said, his voice halting as he spoke around the fears clogging his throat.

****

Matthew pulled Janie close to his side when he finally came to bed. "You will never cease to amaze me," he said quietly.

Janie smiled, but merely cocked her head.

"I thought you were incapable of keeping a secret from me because your face always seems to give you away."

"There are secrets, and then there are critical life issues that deserve to remain hidden," Janie replied.

"Carrie discovered it at the hospital?"

Janie relaxed, realizing George had told the whole truth. Nothing she could say would reveal more than he wished to reveal. "Yes. That's why she brought Georgia home with her. It was the only way to keep the secret."

Matthew shook his head. "Amazing. Simply amazing."

"That we kept his secret?"

"All of it," Matthew answered. "Georgia deciding to fight as a man to be near her brother. Carrie and you keeping her—or *his*—secret. But mostly, I suppose, his decision to live as a man for the rest of his life."

"I don't find that amazing," Janie said. "Actually, I feel rather jealous."

Now it was Matthew's turn to cock his head. "Jealous?"

"It would be so freeing to live as a man," Janie said. "I would never do it because I couldn't live without you, but everything else..." Her voice trailed away as she allowed herself to envision it. "Being able to vote? Knowing I could own a business without anyone questioning it? Never having to fight through people's perception of women in order to become a doctor? If I were George, I feel certain I would have done the same thing."

Matthew listened carefully. "That would be a huge sacrifice," he responded after a long moment of thought.

"Not more than what every woman is sacrificing right now," Janie retorted. "I had someone tell me the other day that I shouldn't even be thinking about having the right to vote because it was far more important for blacks to have the vote now." She scowled as she thought of the conversation. "I told them that one wasn't more important than the other. Black men should have the vote, and *all* women should have the vote. This silly argument about blacks getting the vote first is simply another way for Congress to put off doing the right thing about woman suffrage. And not only have they put it off, they have actually changed the Constitution to say that only *men* are equal in this country." The more she thought about it, the angrier she got, until she looked up and saw Matthew's face. She managed a small laugh. "I know... I know... it's like preaching to the converts. I know you agree with me."

"It's going to take this much passion, from so many women, to ever turn the tide," Matthew observed. "I'm glad you are passionate. It's one of the things I love about you."

Janie looked up and saw the tender light in his eyes. And she saw something else that melted her anger and shifted her passion. She smiled softly and reached over to turn down the lantern light. "Come here," she invited.

Chapter Thirteen

Hobbs was already tired when he reported for work at the factory that morning. Living with the Cromwells was proving more difficult than he had anticipated, but working at the factory stretched him to his limits in every single area. He was enduring it, though. Somehow he had managed to swallow every angry comment that surged to his lips every time he had to engage with a black worker, but he could feel himself reaching the end of his tolerance. Some days it was impossible to even remember the young man who had so willingly driven Carrie to the black hospital to work. He frowned now as he thought about it. He wished he could pinpoint the exact time he had finally realized how dangerous black people were. As he approached the door of the factory, he acknowledged it wasn't really black people that were dangerous—it was black *equality*. The crazy people pushing for it were going to destroy the little that was left of anything good in the South.

Every day he spent in Richmond he felt a little more of himself dying. Being back in the city after returning home to the mountains seemed to suck a little more out of him each day. Things had been tough in the mountains, but at least he had fresh air to breathe and open spaces to explore. Richmond grew more crowded every day. He tried to appreciate the glowing dogwoods and the myriad colors of the azaleas that bloomed through the city now that spring had taken a firm hold, but every breath included smoke from the train station and fumes from the factories that now clogged the riverfront. Richmond was fighting to come back from the destruction of the war, and he had to admit they had come a long way, but evidence of the four-year struggle still remained almost everywhere you looked.

"Good morning, Hobbs."

Hobbs looked up, fighting to control his scowl, but he was sure his feelings blazed in his eyes. If he could get away with it, he would just ignore Marcus' greeting, but he knew the rules about getting along with each other in the Cromwell Factory. Somehow he managed to summon a pleasant look as he nodded at Marcus. Every black person bothered him, but Marcus bothered him more than most. His tall, muscular body made Hobbs feel diminutive in comparison. The fact that Marcus had been a free man who worked as a blacksmith before serving in the Union Army made Hobbs hate him. *And fear him...*

Hobbs watched Marcus disappear into the factory and then took a final breath of real air, however inadequate, before he followed him. He was making money for the first time in a long while, but that wasn't the real reason he stayed. The crinkle of the letter in his pocket reminded him of his true purpose. He set his lips and went inside to do his job.

****

Jeremy couldn't identify the reason for his uneasy feeling on a beautiful spring morning, but he had learned to not discount them. Grateful for the guard who rode with him every day, he was also comfortably aware of the pistol nestled against his side. He had quit having nightmares, but he doubted he would ever lose the memories of being beaten almost to death. He scanned the crowds in search of any signs of trouble, but the trip passed uneventfully.

Thomas and Abby were coming in after him. He had chosen to come in early, after dropping Marietta off at school, because they had an especially large shipment going out that day. He straightened with pride as he thought about how well the factory was doing. They were growing rapidly, and now were one of the largest employers in the city. They still received almost daily threats for their insistence on hiring equal numbers of black and white workers, but there had been no more overt action taken against them. Jeremy suspected the very people that threatened destruction were also hoping for work in the highest paying factory in Richmond. Shipments of clothing were going out every day to markets in both the South and the North, and also on boats bound for Europe.

When he arrived at the two-story brick factory, he climbed the steps to the windowed office overlooking the production area. As he did every morning, he took time to gaze out over the floor, watching the buzz of activity. He smiled and nodded when Marcus looked up and lifted a hand in greeting. Besides becoming a good friend, Marcus was now his production manager. He was also his ally in working to bring equality to blacks in the city, and had played an active role in establishing the black militias.

Jeremy turned away to hide his frown. He had received two threatening letters the day before that seemed to go beyond the usual dire predictions of what would happen if Cromwell Factory continued to employ equal numbers of blacks when so many white men needed jobs. The threats had been aimed toward him personally, and had explained in vivid language what happened to niggers who tried to pass as white. He knew that was the real reason for his uneasiness that morning, but he and Marietta had decided before they married that they would not let fear stop them from doing what they believed was right.

Jeremy pushed back his thick blond hair while he closed his vivid blue eyes for a long moment, and then pulled up the order form for the shipment going out that day. He wanted to be certain there were no mistakes because it was from an account that would increase their profits greatly if the first shipment met their satisfaction. He knew Marcus would assure the quality of the clothing, but he wanted to make sure there were no hiccups in the packing and shipping.

****

Hobbs knew he was distracted, but he couldn't keep his mind off the letter in his pocket. He wasn't sure how he was supposed to do what was detailed in the communication, but he was fairly certain what the consequences would be if he didn't succeed. He'd been carrying the letter around for more than a week, but he was no closer to knowing how to handle it.

"Hobbs, you're needed in the shipping department!"

Hobbs looked up and nodded absently. He knew there was a big delivery going out that day. His leg may not support plowing fields behind a team of mules, but he did fine lifting heavy boxes and crates. He wove his way through the narrow aisles clogged with whirring sewing machines until he broke out onto the shipping dock. Big wagons were already pulled up to the loading platform. Once they were full, they would be taken to the train station at Broad Street before beginning their journey north.

Hobbs eyed the towering stack of carefully sealed wooden crates full of police uniforms headed for New York City. He thought about the conversation around the table a few weeks earlier. Abby's connection with her old friend Nancy Stratford, whose son worked on the New York Police Department, had resulted in the huge order. That thought led to his discomfort with how much he liked Abigail Cromwell. She had been nothing but kind and welcoming to him since he had arrived. It made the feel of the thick letter in his pocket even more discomfiting. He sighed and moved toward the mountain of crates.

He was reaching up for the first container when he heard a warning shout.

****

Jeremy strode onto the shipping dock just in time to hear the shout. His head swiveled until he identified the cause. His stomach tightened as he watched the heavily laden trolley, full of additional crates, pull free from the hands of the two men guiding it into position. It picked up speed as it rolled down the slightly sloped loading platform straight toward the stack of crates waiting to be loaded.

Suddenly, Jeremy realized someone was standing on the other side of the crates, his arms already filled with a heavy box. The worker couldn't see the danger headed his way, and as Jeremy registered it was Hobbs, he realized Hobbs couldn't get out of the way in time to escape danger with his bum leg.

"Hobbs!" Jeremy broke into a run, knowing he wouldn't get there in time to stop the disaster he saw unfolding. "Hobbs!" he yelled more loudly, his voice almost swallowed by the cavernous room.

When he was still more than a hundred feet away, Jeremy spotted a blur of movement coming from the side. A form sprinted forward, scooped Hobbs over his shoulder, and dashed back to safety moments before the loading trolley careened into the mountain of crates, sending them crashing down to where Hobbs had been standing only moments before.

Jeremy rushed forward, praying as he ran that no one had been caught beneath the avalanche. As he neared, he saw Marcus lower Hobbs to the ground. "Is everyone all right?" he demanded.

Marcus nodded. "It was just him. I got him out in time."

Hobbs, obviously dazed, swiveled his head and stared at the boxes strewn across the loading platform. "What happened?" he managed to ask in a husky voice.

Jeremy explained briefly.

Hobbs stared at the mound of splintered crates, and then turned back to eye Marcus. "You saved my life," he muttered.

Marcus shrugged modestly.

"Why?" Hobbs demanded.

"Why?" Marcus looked confused.

"I don't get it," Hobbs sputtered, his mind spinning as he tried to absorb the reality of what had happened. "Why did you save my life?"

"It seemed like a life worth saving," Marcus responded.

Hobbs could think of nothing to say in response to that. If the roles had been reversed, he was quite sure he would not have put himself in danger to save Marcus' life.

Jeremy knew it was time for him to bow out. He shook Marcus' hand firmly. "Thank you."

Hobbs struggled to sort through his feelings. Somewhere in the midst of the shock over what had happened was gratitude that he had not died. It would have seemed somehow wrong to have survived four years of war only to die under a mountain of clothing crates.

"Did you figur' I would let you die?" Marcus asked quietly.

Hobbs considered the question, but he was too tired, too shocked, and too shaken from near-death to consider his answer. "I would have let you die," he said bluntly.

Marcus shrugged. "That don't surprise me none."

Hobbs blinked at him, trying to decide how to respond.

"Do you hate all of us?" Marcus asked.

"Niggers?" Hobbs shot back, somehow incensed by the fact he was being forced into a conversation just because this man saved his life. Somewhere in his mind he knew it didn't make sense, but he had been pushed to his limit. He scowled when all Marcus did was shrug in response to his angry question. "Yep. I reckon I do."

"Why?"

Hobbs' angry eyes caught the debris scattered all over the loading dock. The reality of how close he had come to death struck him again. It also seemed to deflate his anger. "I don't really hate you," he muttered. Speaking the words released something in him. He met Marcus' eyes squarely. "I hate what is happening in our country," he admitted. "I done lost everything I ever known. The way I see it, I'm only going to keep losing things. It ain't right."

Marcus nodded thoughtfully. "I reckon I know how you feel."

Hobbs was at a loss for words again. "You do?" he finally managed.

"Yep. You don't want to lose the only way of life you ever had, but the war sure seems to have taken care of that for you. The flip side of that is that I sho 'nuff don't want to *keep* living the only way of life I ever knew. I had it better than most, since I was free, but there be millions of freed slaves that don't ever want to go back to living that life."

Hobbs, even though everything inside him was fighting what he was hearing, realized coming so close to death had released something within him. He nodded reluctantly. "I guess I can understand that."

"Figuring out what to do is a problem, though," Marcus stated. "Seems like everyone wants something different. And they want it so badly, there's folks willing to kill for it."

Hobbs stiffened, remembering the letter in his pocket. There was no way Marcus could know about that. "What are you talking about?" he asked. He wondered how much Jeremy had told Marcus, and then decided Jeremy had probably told him everything and asked Marcus to keep an eye on him.

Marcus looked at him thoughtfully for a long moment, and then evidently decided to tell Hobbs what he was thinking. "I had someone come to my house last night," he said in a grim voice that matched his eyes. "They was running away from Tennessee." His voice hardened even more. "The Ku Klux Klan got them."

Hobbs didn't know what to say, so he remained silent.

"They weren't black folks," Marcus added.

Hobbs blinked. "They were white?" He had heard of the Klan going against white Unionists, but why would they have ended up at Marcus'?

"They *looked* white," Marcus replied.

Hobbs considered his words. It became clear in an instant. He tried to remember the word he had heard Jeremy and Marietta use. "They were mulatto." He couldn't think of anything to add, because he was too busy trying to figure out why Marcus was telling him about it.

"Yep. The man was a little darker, but he didn't have no trouble passing. The Klan found out and decided to teach them a lesson. They came out to their little farm about a week ago. First they broke their way in and raped the woman. Told her if she was gonna act like a white woman that she ought to know what it was like to be with a white man. Then they beat her till she was almost dead."

Hobbs battled with his feelings. Marcus' face held almost no expression, unless you counted the blazing fury in his eyes.

"They held the husband and made him watch," Marcus ground out in a flat voice. "Then they took him outside, tied him to a tree, and went after him with a whip."

Hobbs winced, but there was still a part of him that thought they had probably deserved it. It was time for everyone to understand whites were in charge, and that blacks who tried to pass as white were dangerous to the country. Those lessons had been drilled into him by his connections with the Klan.

Marcus' eyes narrowed in contempt, as if he could read his mind. "That could have been Jeremy and Marietta," he snapped. "Would you been okay with that, too?"

Hobbs caught sight of Jeremy watching from the door at the end of the loading area. He thought of Jeremy's courtesy toward him, in spite of his beliefs. He thought of Jeremy and Marietta's easy laughter and warm conversation during meals. He thought of the love the newlyweds shared. He thought of Thomas' relationship with his half-brother. As one thought after another spiraled through his mind, they collided with the new belief he carried. Collided, and then almost against his will, collapsed. His beliefs lay shattered at his feet like the remnants of the shipping crates scattered across the floor.

Hobbs took an unsteady breath. "No," he said huskily, his voice trying to catch up with the rapid changes in his mind. "I wouldn't have been okay with that." The simple statement released the last cords of hatred that had bound their way around his soul. He took another deep breath and held his hand out. "Thank you for saving my life, Marcus."

Marcus regarded him for a long moment and then reached out to shake his hand. "Like I said, I reckon it was a life worth saving."

"Not really," Hobbs muttered. He had done the right thing in thanking Marcus, but his problem was far larger than that.

****

Matthew and Peter had arrived, and dinner was on the table, when Hobbs finally returned home after a long, exhausting day. The work had been tiring, as always, but it was the turmoil in his mind that had sapped him of all his energy. He breathed in the aromas of May's fried chicken, more certain than ever before that he didn't deserve to eat at Thomas Cromwell's table.

"Hello, Hobbs," Jeremy called. "Come on in. We're just getting ready to start."

Hobbs searched his mind for an excuse not to join them, but his stomach kept him from verbalizing the few weak ones he came up with. He wondered what Marcus had told Jeremy about their conversation, and then remembered Jeremy had left the factory not long after the mishap to take care of some banking business. He didn't remember seeing Jeremy return, so he may not have had any conversation with his production manager. Hobbs wasn't sure if he was sorry or relieved.

Matthew smiled broadly when Hobbs pulled out his chair and sat down. "Good to see you, Hobbs."

"You too, Matthew," Hobbs said warmly, and then smiled at Peter. "Did y'all get into town today?" He sincerely liked both the men.

"We did. Both our newspapers sent us down to report on the reaction to the Reconstruction Acts."

Hobbs, even though something inside had changed, was still surprised when there was no immediate flash of anger. Instead, he felt the belt of worry tightening even more in his chest. He saw the surprised look on Thomas' face when he had no immediate response. "I see," he finally murmured because he knew everyone was watching him.

Matthew continued speaking as if there was no tension in the room. "We know the vigilante groups are gearing up to fight back, but we seem to be running into brick walls about what their plans are." He summoned a smile for May when she carried in a basket of hot biscuits. "No one in the world makes biscuits like you do, May."

"You better not be telling Miss Janie that!" May snorted.

Matthew chuckled. "Janie would tell you that just about anyone can make biscuits better than she can."

"I believe I would give her some competition," Abby murmured, her smile turning into a laugh when May nodded her agreement.

Thomas turned the conversation back to more serious matters. "I've been doing some reading on secret societies. It seems like the Klan, even though they are more organized than other vigilante groups, isn't really doing much that is original."

Marietta looked up from buttering her biscuit, her red hair gleaming in the lantern light. "What do you mean?"

"The Ku Klux Klan is working to have a hierarchy that thrives on secrecy and vague political aims, but they are far from the first," Thomas explained. "Back in 1849 there was the Order of the Star Spangled Banner. It was a secret society started in New York City to protest the rise of Irish, Roman Catholic, and German immigrants."

Peter nodded. "I've done some reading about them, too. My first mentor at the newspaper told me they were opposed to all immigration, but they were especially against Catholics, who they thought of as dangerous voters under the control of the Pope. They were convinced that allowing Catholics into the country would destroy America."

"That's absurd," Marietta sputtered. "Every single one of them was an immigrant themselves."

"Unfortunately," Abby said, "that doesn't stop people from wanting to look down on others. Too many people fear something simply because it is different from them, and they fight to find a way to feel superior."

"Yes," Thomas added. "They believed the Catholics would wipe out Protestantism."

"The English were equally afraid of Irish Catholics—the reason they tried to wipe them out," Matthew replied.

"Thanks to my ancestor, Lord Cromwell," Thomas said heavily. He raised his hand when he saw Abby open her lips to protest. "I realize I had nothing to do with it, but I also can't sit back and watch when something happens here just like it." He shook his head. "The Order of the Star Spangled Banner believed they were nativists, and based many of their beliefs and actions on that."

"Nativist? What is that?" Jeremy asked.

"They used the term Native American to refer to white people with a relatively established history here, especially those who were born here in the United States," Thomas explained.

"Even though they were all immigrants?" Abby asked in astonishment. "How could they call themselves nativists? At the most, the vast majority of them had only been here one generation."

"For the same reason you mentioned earlier, dear. So many people want someone to look down on or someone to persecute. They decided to go a step further than just a secret society, however, so they turned the religious differences between Catholics and Protestants into a political issue." Thomas' eyes darkened. "The Order was very active during elections in the fifties."

"When Catholic immigration reached a new high," Peter observed. "It was five times greater than a decade before. Most of them were poor immigrants from Ireland and Germany who crowded into tenements."

"Like Moyamensing," Abby contributed. "Until Biddy stepped in to help, crime rates soared."

"It happened in almost every large city," Thomas added. "The Order was determined to fight it. I don't agree with their methods, but I do recognize there was a serious problem and no one seemed to be stepping up to solve it."

"What happened to the Order of the Star Spangled Banner?" Jeremy asked.

"They developed a large organization revolving around secret codes, handclasps, and rituals. Whenever someone, especially a reporter, asked them a question they claimed they 'knew nothing'. Horace Greeley, the editor of the *New York Tribune*, heard this same thing so many times that he named them the 'Know Nothings.' "

Peter nodded. "The Order decided to push their agenda on a political platform. They formed their own party called the American Party, though they were known popularly as the Know Nothings. In 1854 they actually carried a lot of elections. They tapped into people's fears and bigoted ideas about Catholics. People were afraid the Catholic immigrants were going to take something away from them so they swarmed into the party. It grew from about fifty thousand to more than a million in just a few months."

"That was only thirteen years ago!" Marietta said. "I would wonder why I hadn't heard more about it, but I was just a child."

"I knew about it," Thomas said, "but it is only recently that I decided it was important to know more because I see so many similarities to what is happening now. The Know Nothings formed a chapter in San Francisco that opposed Chinese immigration and made life miserable for anyone of Chinese descent. They also elected a mayor of Chicago that barred all immigrants from city jobs. And that was only the beginning." His voice grew disdainful. "They used religion to pit immigrants against each other so they could strengthen their party. They were really quite successful in winning many elections," he said ruefully. "Nativism became a new American rage. They had Know-Nothing candy, Know-Nothing Tea, and Know-Nothing toothpicks. However dangerous their agenda, I can't deny they managed to tap into a deep emotional vein in the country."

Peter stepped in. "Most of the party's growth came from rapidly expanding industrial towns in the North because Yankee workers faced direct competition from the new Irish immigrants. The new members of the party looked down on wealth and elitism, and were focused on elevating the working man."

"I can understand how they felt," Jeremy said reluctantly. "Were all the voters native Americans?" His voice made it clear he found that difficult to believe.

Thomas snorted. "Hardly! The Know Nothings so castigated the Catholics that new German and British Protestants who had just immigrated joined the party in droves. They were looking for someone to hate, and for a way to appear more powerful in their new country." He paused. "However, in all fairness, the Know Nothings weren't all bad. If they had been, they wouldn't have gotten so much popular support. They opposed slavery, supported an expansion of women's rights, wanted to regulate industry more carefully, and they wanted to improve the status of working people."

"I can see why they were popular," Abby said.

"Don't be fooled," Thomas said sourly. "To make sure they got their way in cities where they weren't popular, they had no problem starting riots and rigging the ballots. Very few people saw the whole picture of who they were because they were masters at painting the picture they wanted to be seen." He paused. "They tried to get me to join their ranks, but there was something that didn't feel right, and I wasn't political at the time—I just wanted to run the plantation. I knew nothing about the secret society that had spawned much of it, but they didn't have as much of a hold in the South as they did in the North."

Marietta raised her eyebrows. "You never hear about them anymore, though. Thirteen years is not a long time. What happened?"

"There was a lot of infighting," Thomas said, "but I believe Abraham Lincoln put his finger on it. Even though he never openly fought them because he didn't want to lose their vote, I saw a portion of a letter he had written." He walked into the study for a moment and returned with a book. "You should hear this."

"*'I am not a Know-Nothing — that is certain. How could I be? How can anyone who abhors the oppression of Negroes be in favor of degrading classes of white people? Our progress in degeneracy appears to me to be pretty rapid. As a nation, we began by declaring that "all men are created equal." We now practically read it "all men are created equal, except Negroes." When the Know-Nothings get control, it will read "all men are created equal, except Negroes and foreigners and Catholics." When it comes to this I should prefer emigrating to some country where they make no pretense of loving liberty — to Russia, for instance, where despotism can be taken pure, and without the base alloy of hypocrisy.'"*

"I loved that man," Abby said quietly. "I still can't believe he's gone."

A long silence filled the room. Jeremy was the first to break it. "I fear what is happening in our country now that his voice has been silenced. President Johnson, with his commitment to white superiority over blacks, has allowed things to be set in motion that will most likely take generations to resolve. I believe our country would be completely different right now if President Lincoln had not been assassinated."

"I think you're right," Matthew said somberly. "Though our country is legislated by Congress, the presidency is a powerful thing. Congress, and the people of the country, can fight back against it, just as we are, but the things Johnson has put into motion can never be undone. I'm afraid our country will be paying the price for a long time to come."

When he finished speaking, the only thing that could be heard was an occasional owl hoot and the sound of barking dogs not yet let in for the night.

Thomas cleared his throat. "The Know-Nothings virtually disappeared as a party, but that doesn't mean the sentiments disappeared. One of their members from right here in Virginia, George Bickley, formed the Knights of the Golden Circle."

Abby raised her brows. "That's one I have never heard of."

"Thank God they didn't last long enough for more to know about them," Thomas retorted. "except that they seem to have resurfaced." He shook his head. "Their name came from Bickley's scheme for a South American filibustering expedition. The group drew a great circle on the globe that put Cuba as its center.

The circle encompassed Mexico, Central America, the northern part of South America, and the West Indies."

"For what purpose?" Marietta asked.

Thomas' smile was humorless. "Bickley proposed to lead private armies across the Rio Grande, conquer and annex these lands, and parcel them out as twenty-five new slave states so he could preserve the Southern balance of power with the North. He called it the Golden Circle."

"That's insane!" Marietta sputtered, her eyes wide with disbelief.

"He didn't stop there," Thomas continued. "He was adamant to preserve the rights of pro-slavery Southern whites. He proposed that the Circle could serve as a secret police force to identify abolitionist traitors so they could preserve the orderly operations of slavery. The goal was to increase the power of the Southern slave-holding upper class to such a degree that it could never be dislodged."

"I've never heard of an invasion into Mexico," Marietta observed. "What happened?"

Thomas shrugged. "The Golden Circle managed to establish chapters and enroll members in every Southern state, as well as in California and portions of the Midwest. They actually mustered up two expeditions of the Knights to the Mexican border, but they never managed to cross the Rio Grande." He paused. "Then the war started. Bickley decided to turn the order into a secret instrument of Confederate support."

"And now?" Marietta demanded. "Obviously you think all of this ties into the present. These people didn't simply disappear."

"No," Thomas agreed. "I don't believe they did."

"You believe the Golden Circle has evolved into the Ku Klux Klan," Matthew guessed, his brow furrowed with intense concentration.

Thomas shrugged, though his expression was far from casual. "I believe they have been given a natural political and military framework for the Klan to emulate. The question is just how that is going to happen. Even though the Klan is active in their violence, their plans seem to remain secret. I am quite certain there is a master plan, though."

Matthew scowled. "It's hard to fight something when you don't know what they are doing, or what they are *going* to do. Surely there must be something they are planning on doing to press their agenda forward. I would give anything to know what that is!"

****

Hobbs had been listening carefully, the band of worry growing tighter with each revelation. His hatred had dissolved, but the fear instilled in him had grown ever bigger as the conversation flowed around the table. He wanted to stand and walk out of the room. He wanted to believe this had nothing to do with him. And he wanted to believe he had no responsibility for any of it.

The weight of the letter in his pocket told him differently. It seemed to grow thicker and heavier with each passing moment. And then it seemed to get hot, the searing heat pressing through his leg and traveling up to his brain. For a moment, he thought he was going to pass out.

"Hobbs?" Abby's voice broke into his befuddled mind. "Hobbs, you look ill. Are you all right?"

Hobbs latched onto Abby's kind voice, using it to pull him back to reality like a drowning man would reach for a buoy in rough waters. His heart rate slowed a little as he forced himself to gaze into her eyes, relieved when he saw nothing but kindness and compassion. There were times he was certain she could read his mind, but this time she simply looked worried.

Abby reached out to take his hand. "Are you all right?" she repeated.

Hobbs drank in the sight of her caring eyes and then used every bit of his strength to reach into his pocket and pull out the letter burning his leg. "I know what they are going to do," he said weakly, surprised when his voice actually worked.

Chapter Fourteen

"What?" Thomas asked sharply. "What are you talking about?"

"The Klan." Hobbs had to force every word past the fear lodged in his throat. He knew what happened to people who betrayed the secrecy of the Ku Klux Klan. He lifted the letter he was holding. "It's in here."

Tense silence gripped the room.

Jeremy was the first to speak. "Are you going to tell us?"

Hobbs nodded, feeling his first sense of rightness since he had arrived on their doorstep. "They are... having a convention... in Nashville... in April." Every word was halting, coated with the thick terror clogging his throat.

"During the Nashville Convention for the selection of Democratic candidates for the fall election. They know the masses of people will hide their meeting," Matthew murmured, his eyes locked on Hobbs. "Where is it going to be?"

Hobbs, now that he had decided to reveal what he knew, felt the fear ebbing away with every word he spoke. Evidently, the hold the Klan had on him only worked if he was too frightened to take action to combat it. "The Maxwell House," he replied, his voice stronger.

"I wonder who is heading it up," Peter asked, obviously not expecting Hobbs to know.

"George Gordon," Hobbs answered.

Thomas narrowed his eyes. "The brigadier general for the Confederacy?"

"Yes, sir. He is from Pulaski. He's been involved with the Klan almost from the start."

Abby was the first to ask the question on everyone's mind. "Why are you telling us this, Hobbs?" Her voice was one of gentle probing, not harsh judgement.

Hobbs turned to look into her eyes, drawing even greater strength from the compassion he saw shining there. He could not believe she was not full of revulsion. "It's the right thing to do," he said, not sure he was willing to say more.

Matthew filled in the blank for him. "The Klan doesn't take kindly to betrayal," he said soberly.

"Secret societies have strict rules about no one revealing their actions," Thomas agreed. "There must be a very important reason you are telling us this."

Hobbs sighed heavily and nodded. "The hate was eating me up," he finally admitted. "I didn't even recognize who I was anymore. Blacks never did nothing to hurt me, but I let others convince me I should hate them, and that they were out to destroy me."

"What changed?" Abby pressed.

Hobbs looked to Jeremy for help, not certain he could force more words from his mouth.

"Marcus saved his life this morning," Jeremy said. He explained what had happened while watching Hobbs carefully. "I suspect there was something more, though."

Hobbs sighed again. He had been willing to tell them what he knew, but that didn't mean he wanted to tell them everything. However, with every eye in the room fixed on him, he didn't know how to evade the truth. He looked at Jeremy. "It was you and Marietta," he said.

Everyone waited quietly for him to continue. May, coming in from the kitchen with dessert, moved to stand against the wall so she could listen.

"Marcus told me about that couple who came to him last night." Hobbs saw mostly blank expressions and realized the news hadn't spread yet.

Jeremy recognized the same thing and filled them in quickly.

Hobbs understood the grim looks plastered on every face. "It could have been you," he muttered, and then looked up to meet both Jeremy and Marietta in the eye. "That couple could have been you. And you ain't been nothing but kind to me ever since I got here. I didn't deserve it." He paused for a long moment. "The idea of it happening to you suddenly made it all seem real. It wasn't just a bunch of ranting and raging about people I don't know. It was about you and Marietta. People I care about. When I realized that, I reckon it made all the hate disappear." He wasn't ashamed of the tears that filled his eyes. "I was real wrong." His gaze swung around the table, resting the longest on Thomas and Abby. "I wish I had words to say how sorry I am."

Abby's response was to reach forward and take his hand. "We forgive you, Hobbs. Thank you for doing the right thing."

"I'm proud of you, son," Thomas said, reaching out to shake his free hand. "Thank you."

Affirmations came from everyone around the table. Hobbs could hardly believe they were so quick to forgive him. Even May and Micah were regarding him with warm eyes. The rest of the band tightening his chest dropped away. He took his first easy breath since he had knocked on the front door that frigid night. "Thank you."

"Now that you're forgiven," Matthew said quietly, "will you tell us the real truth about why you are here?"

Hobbs stiffened, but he couldn't say he hadn't expected this.

Matthew, eyeing the letter Hobbs held, continued. "I suspect there is more than what you have told us in that letter, but I also suspect only certain people received information about the Nashville convention. Why you?"

Hobbs took a deep breath, trying to calm the rapid pounding of his heart. He should have known the renowned journalist would see through him and realize he wasn't telling everything he knew. He had given them the information they needed, but he certainly hadn't told them everything, and he still wasn't sure it was necessary. He struggled to control his thoughts and decide what to do.

"The truth is usually easiest," Abby said gently.

Hobbs looked at her and realized she was right. He would simply tell the truth and deal with whatever consequences came from it. "I was sent here," he said bluntly, realizing he didn't have the energy to figure out the best way to word what he had to say, so he was simply going to say it.

"Why?" Thomas asked.

"To report back to the Klan on what you have been doing." Hobbs fixed his eyes on Thomas. "The Klan hates you because of what you are doing. They know about the factory, and they know about what is going on at the plantation." He swung his eyes to Jeremy. "They know you are mulatto, and they know you are fighting to bring equality to blacks in Richmond." He looked at Abby next, his voice growing even more apologetic. "They know about what you are doing up in Philadelphia." He took a deep breath. "They know you were an abolitionist, and they blame you equally for what is happening in the factory here in Richmond."

"Because you told them?" Peter snapped angrily.

"No," Hobbs insisted. "They already knew all of it. They got people everywhere who are telling them about folks. They done sent me down here to report back on how the Klan could hurt you. I was desperate...and I believed what they told me—that all of you were destroying the country and destroying my life. Once I got here, though, I couldn't do it. I hated what was going on, but all of you were good to me, and I couldn't forget all Carrie and me went through." His voice faltered. "How could I hurt her family?" He held up the letter, hating that he couldn't stop the trembling in his hand. "The rest of the letter is about what is going to happen to me if I don't tell them what they sent me down here to find out."

"What will they do?" Abby pressed, reaching out to enfold his hand again.

Hobbs looked down at their linked hands and managed a weak smile. "Let's just say it ain't good." He fought to push away the images crowding his mind as he remembered the detailed description of how they were going to hurt him if he didn't fulfill his mission.

"Thank you for telling us," Matthew said, his eyes matching his voice's intensity.

"What are you going to do with what I told you?" Hobbs asked. "Does it help at all?" He realized he was desperate to believe his betrayal would result in something positive. If he was going to die at the hands of the Klan, who had eyes everywhere, he wanted to at least believe it had been worth it.

"More than you can imagine," Matthew assured him. He exchanged a long look with Peter, and then looked back at Hobbs. "Peter and I will be at the convention."

Hobbs managed a bitter smile. "You don't really think they're just gonna let you in, do you? They know exactly who you are."

"No," Matthew responded, "but we have our ways of listening in when we want to."

Hobbs remembered something Matthew had told him many years ago. "Like you and Robert listened in on the secessionist meeting before the war started?"

"Just like that," Matthew agreed grimly. "I thought *that* meeting was important, but it means practically nothing compared with the one you have told us about."

Hobbs wanted to believe it could make a difference, but he had heard too much. "You ain't gonna be able to stop them," he stated. "They are getting real powerful."

For a moment, Matthew's gaze faltered, but then his face filled with resolve. "It's not up to me to know the results of our being there. All I know is that I could never live with myself if I didn't at least try to reveal what is going on with the Klan. The power they have is within their secrecy, and in the fear they instill. If we can shine the light on some of those secret plans, perhaps it will give people courage to stand against them."

"And if you get killed in the process?" Hobbs asked.

Matthew's smile was sad. "Then at least I'll know I wasn't one of those who turned their backs and let them have their way."

Hobbs stared at him as the truth of his statement penetrated the remaining fear gripping his mind and heart. It cut through the fog and allowed him to see more clearly. "You any good at disguises?" he asked.

Matthew blinked. "Disguises? Why?"

Hobbs shrugged, his determination solidifying as his mind came up with a solution. "I reckon I don't want to turn my back neither. If you gonna go to that convention, I reckon I ought to go, too. You can come with me, but you can't come looking like you do. I guarantee the Klan knows exactly who you and Peter are. You can't look nothing like what you look like now."

Matthew's face was still troubled. "Disguises can be created, but you won't be safe there, Hobbs. You haven't given the Klan what they wanted. You can't just waltz in there."

Thomas had been silent for a long while. "Then let's give them what they want," he said. "You and I both know you might not find a secret entrance into the Maxwell House in Nashville. If Hobbs can get you in, you'll find out what you need to know." He nodded, his eyes filled with certainty. "It's the perfect solution."

Hobbs' mind was spinning. "How am I gonna give the Klan what they want? I ain't gonna do nothing to hurt you and the rest. That's the only thing that will satisfy them." He shook his head firmly. "I ain't gonna do it!"

"We'll figure it out," Thomas said. "When something is right, there is always a way to accomplish it. I don't know the answer just now, but I'm sure there *is* an answer. We'll find it."

The confidence in Thomas' voice broke through Hobbs' fear again. He nodded slowly. "It will have to be good," he warned. "They got eyes everywhere."

"We'll make it good," Thomas promised. He smiled suddenly. "It feels wonderful to actually be *doing* something—not just waiting for something else to happen." He turned to everyone at the table. "Let's come up with a plan."

****

Spring had spread upward from the South and taken a firm hold on Philadelphia by the last week of April. Maple trees were bright with green, oak leaves were unfurling to cast gentle shade on the sidewalks, and window boxes were full of vivid colors celebrating the demise of another brutal winter. Heavy winter coats had been exchanged for light sweaters that acknowledged a lingering chill in the evening air. Hordes of people strolled the streets or settled on porch chairs to chat with neighbors. Stars competed with lanterns just being lit to combat the evening dark, and a crescent moon hovered on the horizon.

Carrie took a deep breath as she joined Abby and her father in the carriage at the train station. "It's so good to be here!" she exclaimed, excitement radiating through her as she gazed around. Making the decision to be home on the plantation with Robert, rather than the forced confinement of the city, had freed her to enjoy all the things Philadelphia had to offer. She felt a small twinge of regret that she was not arriving to start school, but the joy of her life on the plantation was so much greater. She had accepted the fact that answers would come at the right time.

"You're sure you feel well?" Thomas asked anxiously.

"I'm fine," Carrie assured him. She had been a little concerned about how she would handle the long train ride, but the private room her father had secured was comfortable and surprisingly spacious for a train car. She had been fatigued by the carriage ride in from the plantation the day before, but the gentle sway of the train had lulled her to sleep almost immediately. "I can't believe I slept almost the whole way!"

The anxiety in her father's eyes didn't diminish. She knew he had probably been alarmed when she had slept for so long. "Have you ever been pregnant?" she demanded. She didn't bother to wait for an answer to her rhetorical question. "You have no idea how exhausting it can be to live and sleep for two."

Thomas managed a laugh. "That is an argument I can't refute," he said wryly. His face relaxed and his eyes slowly followed. "You'll have to forgive a father for worrying about his only daughter."

Carrie leaned forward to kiss him on his cheek, satisfied she had alleviated his concern for at least a little while. Abby had warned her he would be especially vigilant because he still had such vivid memories of her mother almost dying when she gave birth. She supposed she could understand his fear, but nothing would have stopped her from taking part in the opening of the Moyamensing factory.

She turned to her stepmother. "Will it be strange not to stay in your home?"

"Not a bit," Abby assured her. "I was so glad when they gave my room to another student from the College of Homeopathy. It seemed such a waste for my room to merely sit there empty. And besides, it will be wonderful to stay with Janie while Matthew is gone."

Carrie frowned, thinking again of what her father had revealed about Hobbs last night. She was grateful Hobbs had told the truth, but was also horrified by how much he must have changed to even contemplate hurting her family. The betrayal would take time to dissipate. She also understood he was trying to make up for it by taking Matthew and Peter to the Ku Klux Klan convention in Nashville, but all the knowledge did was bring up a whole new host of worries.

Carrie forced her thoughts in a different direction. "Speaking of Janie, I received a letter from her a few weeks ago. She mentioned she had a very special surprise waiting for me, but she refused to divulge any details. I've written her twice to get more information, but for once she seems capable of keeping a secret."

Abby smiled, but didn't respond.

Carrie narrowed her eyes, glad to have something else to pursue. "You know the secret," she accused. "Out with it."

Abby merely smiled more brightly, her gray eyes dancing with fun. "Janie may have trouble keeping secrets, but I am perfectly comfortable with it."

"Can you at least tell me if I will like it?" Carrie demanded, her curiosity and anticipation growing.

"You will *love* it," Abby replied, and then turned to talk to Thomas.

Carrie knew she would say nothing more. Her mind played with all the possibilities as they rolled along the city streets, but she kept drawing a blank.

****

Carrie shivered with anticipation as the cluttered skyline of Moyamensing appeared on the horizon. She wasn't sure what she was most looking forward to. She could hardly wait to see Biddy and Faith. They had exchanged letters through the long winter, but it wasn't the same as being with the two women she had grown to love so much. She also suspected word had gotten out of their arrival. The street would be lined with children waiting to see Carrie. Many of them had been her patients, or they knew her because she had saved their parents from cholera the summer before.

Thank goodness for the long, cold winter that had beaten the cholera back, stamping out the last cases as it withdrew before the brutal temperatures. She knew there were areas of the country—especially in the South—still battling the disease, but she had heard of no more new cases in Philadelphia.

As the carriage rolled along, her mind turned to Janie's secret. Her friend had still refused to reveal anything, in spite of her most persuasive attempts. Janie had just laughed and told her this day was going to be even more exciting than she anticipated. Since Carrie found that impossible to believe, she was just going to have to wait.

"How much further to the factory?" Thomas asked.

"Just another couple blocks," Abby answered. "You're going to be quite proud of it."

Carrie understood the look on her father's face; an odd mixture of hope and anticipation. The new factory would create additional profits, but that was not the reason for its existence. Her parents had decided to invest in the new clothing factory to provide jobs for the people of Moyamensing. It was her father's way of helping redeem the horrible things his ancestor, Oliver Cromwell, had done to the Irish. She was quite sure he couldn't fully understand what this was going to mean to people who had been caught in a quagmire of hopelessness and despair for so long. The factory couldn't offer jobs to everyone, of course, but Biddy had planned the employment carefully, making sure that as many households as possible had at least one person with a good job at the factory.

"I know anything you have done I will be proud of," Thomas said quietly, the look on his face revealing how much he loved his wife.

Carrie watched them, so grateful each of them had the other. It was evidence that the darkest times could emerge into brilliant light.

"Biddy has been a tremendous help," Abby said. "I've been here twice, but her years of business experience made it possible for the factory manager to get everything done so quickly." She shook her head. "I have to remind myself constantly that she is ninety-eight years old. She is so full of life, it just doesn't seem possible she has lived almost a century! And Faith is just like her. She is twenty years younger than Biddy, but she is still elderly. I hope I am just like both of them when I reach their ages."

Carrie nodded her agreement, but didn't speak because excitement was pounding in her chest. There had been many difficult aspects to her decision to not return to Philadelphia. Leaving Biddy had been one of them. She had never known her grandmother, and her grandfather was nothing more than a vague memory—a reality she had been glad of when she discovered how he had violated Sarah to create Rose and Jeremy. Biddy had become her grandmother in the months they had shared.

"Miss Carrie!"

Carrie was jolted out of her reverie when Paddy dashed up to the carriage, his blue eyes snapping with excitement beneath his thatch of red hair. She had been so lost in thought she hadn't realized they were only a block from Biddy's house. The little boy peering up at her was one of her favorites. His father had died of cholera eighteen months earlier, but she had been able to save his little brother the summer before. He had become like her shadow when she had been treating people in Moyamensing.

"I been waiting for you all morning!" Paddy proclaimed in his rich Irish brogue as he ran beside the carriage, keeping pace easily because the street had grown more crowded.

Now that Carrie was paying attention, she realized there was a throng of children clustered behind him. She laughed with delight. "Stop the carriage," she called. When the carriage had pulled to a halt, she stepped down carefully and turned to give Paddy a big hug. "It's wonderful to see you," she said, letting her gaze sweep the thirty or so barefoot children staring up at her. "All of you."

Paddy jumped back and stared at her. "You gonna have a baby, Miss Carrie?" His eyes widened as his eyes fixed on her expanded stomach. "Are you gonna be a ma?"

"That I am," Carrie confirmed with a smile. The warm rush of love she felt for the little boy in front of her made her realize just how much she would love her own child.

"When is it gonna be born?" Paddy demanded, eyeing her appraisingly. "My mama has had four more babies since I was born. My birthday is July eighth. Looks to me like your baby is going to come close to that."

"Pretty close," Carrie agreed. She thought about Paddy's mother raising five children under the age of eight without a husband. She hoped they had made it through the winter with no illness. She had left them some homeopathic remedies because Paddy's mother,

Celia, had helped her with some of the cholera patients. "How is everyone in your family?"

"They're all fine!" Paddy announced. "My ma got her a job in that new factory."

Carrie felt a surge of relief. "That's wonderful!" She reached down to give him another hug and then made sure she hugged each child. When the last child had been embraced, she looked up and realized they were standing in front of Biddy's house.

Biddy was watching her with a warm smile, her blue eyes radiating with warm love. Faith, her dark eyes flashing a glad welcome, stood beside her.

"Biddy! Faith!" Carrie left her father and Abby in the wagon as she dashed forward. Her concession to her pregnancy was to take the steps more slowly, but it was only seconds before she was engulfed in a hug with both women.

Biddy finally stepped back and took Carrie's face between her hands, peering deeply into her eyes for several moments. Carrie gazed back, almost swallowed in the deep wisdom that radiated from the old woman's eyes set in wrinkled porcelain skin.

"You look fine," Biddy announced. "Janie had me worried, but you look like being with child becomes you."

Carrie smiled as the rich brogue rolled over her. "Janie likes to worry," she said lightly. She took Biddy's hand, grabbed Faith's, and turned them toward the road. "I'd like you to meet my father, Thomas Cromwell."

Biddy's smile was a bright beam of sunshine. "Welcome to my home, Mr. Cromwell. It is a pleasure to be meeting you, for sure!" She stepped forward to clasp the hand Thomas held out with both of her own. "I'll be thanking you with all my heart that you and your lovely wife have brought your clothing factory to Moyamensing."

"Please call me Thomas. And it's I that should be thanking you," Thomas proclaimed. "It seems like such a little thing, but it is a start."

"More of a start than you can imagine," Faith said fervently as she moved forward to clasp his hand next. "A job in Moyamensing means hope. The people here haven't had much of that. Watching that factory come to life this winter gave people what they needed to make it through the cold, dark nights. Now that spring is here, it's all they talk about."

Both women turned next to draw Abby into their embrace. The children remained clustered around the porch, laughing and smiling as they watched the reunion.

****

Carrie leaned forward with anticipation as the carriage rounded the last corner. The last two hours had been filled with conversation, as well as a plate of Faith's famous Irish oatmeal cookies, but she was eager to see the factory. It had been nothing more than an empty, cavernous shell pocketed with broken window panes when she had last seen it in the fall. It was difficult to believe it could actually be ready for operation. She understood the look of skeptical expectancy on her father's face, but she couldn't miss the calm confidence on Abby's. Her stepmother had been here twice during the long winter to oversee the preparations, and she knew Abby was too astute a businesswoman to let the factory open if it wasn't ready.

Carrie gasped when the factory came into view as they rounded the last corner. "Oh my!" she breathed, clasping a hand to her mouth. She whipped her head around to look at Abby. "I can't believe it's the same place!"

"They have done amazing work," Abby agreed proudly. "And all the work was done by people here in Moyamensing."

Carrie grinned with delight. She knew Abby's manager, brought in from another factory, had wanted to hire outside workers, but Abby had been adamant that the factory was to belong to the people of Moyamensing. They should be the ones to do the labor to bring it to life. "It's wonderful. It's absolutely wonderful."

"I couldn't agree more," Thomas said warmly, reaching over to take his wife's hand. "Thank you."

Carrie was struck by the tone of her father's voice. More than anything, those two simple words told her how much the factory really did mean to him. He had not wanted to believe the horrors his ancestor had inflicted on the Irish, but once he had accepted the truth, it had become his mission to do something, no matter how small, to make a difference. She knew her father, so she suspected this would be just the first of many things that would turn Moyamensing into a place of hope for many wanting to create a better life.

Carrie continued to gaze at the three-story factory. Smoke from boilers put in place to operate the machinery poured into the sky. Window panes gleamed in the sunlight. Masons had repaired all the damaged brickwork, and solid doors had replaced ramshackle ones. Green grass was growing in the area next to the building that was full of picnic tables and benches for meal breaks. The loading platform

door was open, with two wagons already unloading
supplies. They were still two hours away from the
opening ceremony, but people were starting to gather
outside, their faces bright with happiness.

"Here they come!"

Carrie smiled when a woman's voice broke through
the noise of wagons and carriages. "Celia!"

A slight woman with flaming red hair broke free
from the group clustered in front of the building.
"Hello, Carrie!" she called gladly. "Paddy came to tell
me you were on the way."

Carrie could easily envision the little boy dashing
through alleys between a maze of buildings to
announce their arrival to his ma. She had learned the
summer before that even though he was not yet eight
years old, he knew the streets of Moyamensing like
the back of his hand. She had never met a lad more
resourceful. "Your son is a marvel."

"That he is," Celia agreed. "This your ma and da?"

Carrie quickly introduced her father and Abby.

Celia stared deeply into her father's eyes. "I want to
thank you from the bottom of my heart for what you
have done here, Mr. Cromwell. Carrie and I have
talked about Lord Cromwell. Sure enough, he was an
evil man, but you and your daughter are proof it
doesn't carry through the generations." She turned
quickly, before he could respond, and waved to
everyone watching. "Folks, this is Mr. Thomas
Cromwell. He and his beautiful wife are the ones who
have created this miracle for us!"

The watching group broke into applause as Thomas
stepped from the carriage and moved into the crowd
to meet some of the onlookers. Carrie was prepared to
do the same thing, but Abby stopped her with a hand

on her arm. "There is a folder in the office that I need. Would you be so kind as to get it for me?"

Carrie nodded, but couldn't help wondering about the look on Abby's face. Something about her request didn't quite ring true, but her stepmother didn't give her time to press. Carrie pushed down her sense of disappointment over not getting to talk to everyone and headed into the building.

The office location was evident as soon as she walked into the three-story brick building. The door stood open, with a wide glass window looking out onto the factory. Just as in all Abby's other factories, she had wanted employees to feel the office was always available to them for either questions or problems.

Carrie stopped long enough to gaze out over the huge open area filled with tables, chairs, and machinery. She knew people had been coming in for training during the last two months, but this was the first day the entire factory would be open. It was to be a celebration the likes of which Moyamensing had probably never seen. Every worker's entire family was coming, neighbors had been invited, and anyone who carried any title of importance would be there to celebrate the first factory to open in their impoverished area.

Finally, she turned away and entered the office. The desks were well-spaced and clear. She frowned when she didn't see a folder on any of them. She moved forward to look more closely, and then jolted to a stop as she stared in disbelief at the young man who had appeared around the corner from the back.

"Hello, Carrie."

Chapter Fifteen

"Georgia!" Carrie screamed. Her mind raced as she struggled to absorb the impossible. "How?" She stammered as she continued to stare. Thoughts swirled through her brain, but she seemed incapable of movement. "You're my surprise," she whispered.

George smiled. "Janie insisted on keeping it a secret."

Carrie surged forward and wrapped him in a hug. "You can explain later. Right now I just want to feel you and actually know you are alive."

George laughed gladly. "It's so good to see you, Carrie!" He returned the hug and then stepped back. "The rumors of my death were exaggerated," he said lightly.

"Obviously," Carrie said ruefully, still trying to make sense out of what she was seeing. "Explain." As George complied, she completely understood why Abby had sent her in alone. Except that... "Does Abby know?" she asked.

George looked uncomfortable. "Only that you cared for me during the war and believed me to be dead. The fewer people who know, the better..." His voice trailed off apologetically.

"I understand," Carrie said. "You could completely trust Abby, but I understand why you are being so careful. I imagine I would be in your case, as well."

"Thank you," George said fervently.

Carrie looked around, realizing how far George had come from being an illiterate girl on a small farm who went to war with her brother. "Are you enjoying the factory?"

George nodded vigorously. "More than I can possibly say. I enjoy the work, but it's knowing the impact the factory is having on Moyamensing that means so much. My mother came over from Ireland with nothing but the clothes on her back. She told me so many stories about how bad things were in the Old Country, but that things weren't really that much better here. She would be so happy to know what I'm doing now."

"As a man?" Carrie couldn't resist asking as she raised an eyebrow playfully.

George grinned. "There are some things it is better that a mother never know." His eyes settled on Carrie's stomach. "If your child ends up anything like you, there will probably be *many* things you would be better off not knowing."

Carrie laughed. "I'm sure that is very true. I constantly horrified my mother, but she knew only a fragment of all the things I did. God help her if she had known it all!"

George nodded. "My point exactly."

The two friends laughed and chatted until Thomas and Abby appeared at the door.

"George!" Thomas said warmly. "Abby just told me who the new office manager is. I can't tell you how glad I am that you are still alive, and she tells me you are quite talented in your job."

George shook Thomas' hand firmly. "Thank you, sir. It is an honor to have this privilege."

Carrie watched while George talked to her father. It was impossible to see any remnants of the frightened young man who was desperately hiding his true identity as a woman. George was obviously comfortable living as a man. Confidence radiated from him as he discussed office management with her father. It felt more than a little surreal to see him this way. She wondered if Janie had felt the same envy she was feeling now. She was somehow certain she had.

****

It was later that afternoon before Carrie had an opportunity to talk to Janie. The ribbon had been cut. Speeches had been made. The first shipment of clothing created during the two months of training had been placed on the waiting wagons for its trip to the train station. The mountains of food that Moyamensing residents had loaded onto the tables had disappeared like fog before a blazing sun.

"Did you enjoy your surprise?"

Carrie spun around when she heard Janie's voice behind her. "How in the world did you keep from telling me? I didn't think it was possible for you to keep a secret that long."

"Matthew helped," Janie admitted. "I wanted to write you so badly, but he convinced me you would love the surprise."

Carrie's eyes widened as she interpreted the look in Janie's eyes. "Matthew *knows*? All of it?"

Janie explained George's decision to be interviewed anonymously for Matthew's book. "It was quite a brave thing to do," she finished.

"George has become an amazing man," Carrie replied. "I'm so glad to know he is alive. I know Robert will be as well. He always had a soft spot for him."

"Actually, he had a soft spot for *her*," Janie said wryly. "He just didn't realize the truth."

Carrie decided to ask the question she had been thinking all day. The crowd had dispersed so they could talk quietly without the risk of being overheard. "Are you as jealous as I am?"

Janie laughed, her face showing her obvious relief that Carrie was voicing her own thoughts. "Green with envy? Every day!"

"During the war, all I could think about was hiding George's identity." Carrie had decided to only call him George. She was determined she would not be the one to betray his trust with a thoughtless statement during an unguarded moment. "Now I suddenly realize, in spite of all he has to hide, that his life is so much easier than ours. He can freely own a business. He can *vote*."

Janie nodded. "I think about that all the time. I long to have a voice in what happens in our country. I believe things would be so different in America right now if women had been part of the process," she said fiercely. "And he doesn't have to wear these ridiculous dresses. I think it would be so marvelous to wear pants every day!"

Carrie laughed and gave Janie a tight hug. "Someday we will have the vote," she proclaimed. "Someday we will own businesses, and someday we will all walk around in pants."

Janie looked doubtful. "Are all men going to disappear off the face of the earth?"

Carrie shook her head. "No. I know it seems impossible right now, but I have to believe it's true. Look how far we have come, Janie. You're in medical school. You're married to a man who gladly supports your right to vote. Black men are going to soon have the vote. Things are changing."

"You're right," Janie agreed. "They just aren't changing fast enough," she proclaimed. "We didn't really have time to talk last night. Are you still all right with not being in medical school?"

Carrie took a deep breath and laid her hand on her stomach. "I am," she replied, happy to know she meant it. "I don't know what the future holds, and I have far more questions than answers, but I'm all right with that for now. All I can think about is meeting the little one kicking me right now." She smiled brightly. "It should only be about two and a half more months."

Janie reached out and touched Carrie's stomach. "I can hardly wait to meet your baby," she said softly.

Carrie understood the wistful look on her face, but she didn't feel comfortable asking. She knew Janie and Matthew wanted children. She also knew the pain of waiting.

****

Matthew looked at himself in the mirror. "I think I look rather dashing with black hair," he said cheerfully.

Peter smirked. "Does that mean you have gotten used to how you look without that red beard?"

Matthew sighed heavily. "I haven't been without a beard in years." He frowned at himself in the mirror, trying to accept that his hair was also far shorter than it had ever been. "I don't even recognize myself," he said plaintively as he ran a hand down his smooth cheeks. Wire spectacles, combined with the plain clothing of a Tennessee mountain man completed his disguise.

"Which is the whole point," Peter reminded him.

"So you're telling me you're happy as a redhead?" Matthew demanded, trying not to laugh at Peter's transformation. Even the beard growing on his friend's face since they had devised their plan was a rusty red.

"Well... I think I look better than you do," Peter taunted as he pulled his fingers through his short red hair. "As long as it doesn't rain and wash out the mineral dye May created for us, we should be all right."

Matthew nodded, hoping for fair skies. "The whole reason we have umbrellas."

"As soon as this masquerade is over, however, I'm dunking my head in a barrel of water. Somehow, you manage to look decent with all that red hair. I look like an idiot."

Matthew bit back his easy agreement with a smile, but was still disgruntled. "At least you can just dunk your head in water. It will take time for my hair and beard to grow back."

"Ah, the costs of journalism," Peter retorted. "We do whatever it takes to get the story."

Matthew felt a tad better when he saw the gleam of admiration in his friend's eyes. His hair *would* grow back. He could only hope they would discover something at the convention that would make the elaborate disguises worthwhile. "Where is Hobbs?" He was still concerned about his safety, even though the plan they had developed seemed to be foolproof.

"He went out to meet with one of his Klan buddies," Peter said gravely.

Matthew took a deep breath as he saw the unspoken message in his friend's eyes. They were having to go on faith that Hobbs wouldn't cave under the pressure and betray their real identities. He had seemed sincere enough during his revelations and during the planning sessions, but what if it was all part of the ruse?

Peter read his thoughts. "We have to trust him."

Matthew nodded. "I know. Most of the time I do, but now that we're two blocks from the Maxwell House, it all seems a little more risky." He thought about his and Robert's adventure spying on the secession convention in the months before the war started. If they had been discovered, they would have been thrown out, but he was confident they would not have been harmed. He felt none of that confidence now. The stories coming in about the actions of the Klan were growing ever more violent.

"Are you having second thoughts?"

Matthew considered the question, hearing something in Peter's voice that indicated he almost wished he was. He had not forced Peter into this scheme, but he could feel his misgivings. "I wish I thought we could afford to have second thoughts," he said honestly. "I'm scared, too." He watched Peter's eyes carefully, recognizing the relief that came with realizing he wasn't the only one frightened. "But I'm more afraid of what will happen if the Klan continues to grow without any resistance at all. I figure if we can survive Libby Prison, then we can handle a surveillance mission into a Klan convention." He forced confidence into his voice, hoping he could trick his mind to believe what he was saying.

Peter nodded, but the look on his face said he was well aware of what Matthew was trying to do. "We can't really prepare for this one," he said ruefully. "We're just going to have to move forward and see what transpires. At least we'll know we didn't sit back and allow it to happen without trying to make a difference."

"Always forward," Matthew agreed. A rap at the door made him stiffen, but he forced himself to relax. It could only be Hobbs. He refused to allow himself fantasies of who it could be if Hobbs had betrayed them. He strode to the door and swung it open.

Hobbs stepped through. "You shouldn't open the door unless you know who it is," he scolded.

"Like not opening the door would stop someone," Matthew said dryly. "Is everything all right?" He searched Hobbs' face for signs of trouble.

"They believed me," Hobbs said quietly. He walked over and sank down in the chair pulled in front of the empty fireplace.

"Thank God," Matthew murmured.

"No suspicion?" Peter probed.

Hobbs shrugged. "They are suspicious of anything that breathes, but I think they believed me."

"You gave them the letter?" Matthew asked. He thought of the long hours of scheming before Thomas had actually written it.

Hobbs nodded. "They believe I gave them enough information to make my time in Richmond worthwhile." He sagged against the back of the chair. "They believed my story that I stole the letter when Thomas asked me to mail it."

Matthew sighed with relief. The letter was full of false information concerning a large shipment of clothing being transported north for the military. The shipment was actually happening, but it wasn't going to happen the way the letter detailed. They hoped the Klan wouldn't hold Hobbs responsible for the factory changing the shipment agenda. If the Klan believed they could inflict harm on Thomas, Abby, and Jeremy at one time by destroying a shipment worth thousands of dollars, they would continue to believe Hobbs was doing as they requested.

"And they are agreeable with you bringing us to the meeting?" Peter asked.

"Once I convinced them how much you hate the Cromwells and everything that is happening in the South, they said you could come," Hobbs answered. "I vouched for you. Right now, my word still means something."

Matthew understood when his eyes darkened. Now that the Reconstruction Acts had passed, the Klan was even more determined to fight back—meaning they would be more diligent than ever. They might forgive Hobbs when the information about the shipment proved wrong, but they would also be watching him more closely, and they would expect more concrete results. The only way to protect him was to remove him from the situation. When the convention was over, Hobbs had accepted Thomas' offer to head west to Oregon. He was leaving from Nashville.

Hobbs read Matthew's thoughts. "It's better this way," he said quietly. "I can't never go back home to West Virginia, even if I thought I could make a living there. They wouldn't let me live real long," he said matter-of-factly. "I done some reading about Oregon. It seems like a mighty fine place to live if you like to hunt and fish. Thomas gave me enough money to get started, and I'll get a job quick as I can."

Matthew gazed at him. "You sound as if you're looking forward to it."

Hobbs considered his words for a moment, and then met his eyes steadily. "I reckon I am. I don't like what the Klan is doing, but I don't like what is happening in the South much better. I reckon I think everybody is wrong, and I think it's gonna get a lot worse before it ever has a chance to get better. I figure Oregon is far enough away that things won't be like they are here. From everything I can tell, it's a different world out there. After the war, and after watching my folks and Bridger die, there ain't nothing left here for me. I'm going to help you do this, and then I'm going to be glad to leave and never look back."

Matthew thought about his words, realizing how much truth there was in them. "You deserve better things," is all he finally said.

****

Matthew tried to relax as he joined the throng of men entering the Maxwell House, but every cell in his body screamed at him to run the other direction. He could almost feel the hatred and animosity pouring from the men surrounding him. Hard eyes and harder faces revealed these were men with an agenda who had no intention of being denied what they were after. He realized every man he was looking at was probably a Confederate veteran. They had lost the war, but they didn't intend to go down without a fight to preserve the life they believed was being ripped away from them. He forced himself to keep his face and eyes expressionless, but soon realized even that would make him suspect. He allowed a glance at Peter, and then overheard Hobbs engaged in conversation with a man next to him.

"Things are getting out of control." The statement came from a rail-thin man who looked to be in his late twenties. His icy blue eyes glared from beneath shaggy blond hair. "The Klan is growing as big as a blood-thirsty tick, but ain't nobody really know what is going on."

Hobbs nodded. "It's time for someone to do something," he declared. "I sure hope that's why we're here. It's time for someone to take charge before things get totally out of hand."

"Someone needs to take charge, I reckon," the blond man growled, "but men are only doing what the federal government has forced on them."

Matthew decided to join the conversation. "The South shouldn't have to take any more abuse," he said firmly, sifting everything he had learned through his mind. "It isn't right that the slaves should get to vote while the brightest minds we have are kept from having a say."

"That's right," another man growled as he pulled his hat down over dark hair.

Matthew couldn't miss the fact that the new speaker only had one arm. "Which battle?" he asked.

"Wasn't a battle," the man growled. "I was a guest of Camp Douglas up in Chicago for the last two years of the war. I got in a fight, my arm got gangrene, and they cut it off."

Matthew winced, but he also understood the bitterness and anger in the man's eyes. Just as Andersonville had become notorious as a Confederate prison camp, Camp Douglas had shared the same reputation of poor conditions and high death rates. Now that the war was over, though, no one wanted to acknowledge it. As terrible as Andersonville had been, he couldn't imagine living through a Chicago winter. Richmond winters couldn't compare to an Illinois winter, but Matthew had still barely survived Libby

Prison; not that he could reveal his being a guest there to *this* man.

"At least I lived," the man growled as he read the sympathy in Matthew's eyes. "I watched too many men die there, but sometimes I think it ain't as bad as what is happening now."

Matthew wanted to ask him what he meant, but he was sure he was supposed to know. "They're still trying to kill us off," he snarled. "They're just doing it a different way."

"I reckon they're finishing what General Grant didn't. Those poor bastards at Appomattox would have been slaughtered if General Lee hadn't surrendered. I know the government wishes he had just killed all the Rebels there. There would have been less of us to deal with."

Matthew tried to follow the reasoning, but even if Grant had fought at Appomattox, there still would have been far more Confederates alive today than would have died in that battle. Grant had shown compassion in letting the men return home instead of sending them to prisoner-of-war camps in the North. He swallowed a sigh of relief when the blond man responded, saving him from having to say anything.

"The government is too busy making sure all them niggers get taken care of. They figure it's all right if the rest of us white men just die off. Them Yankee soldiers are getting all kinds of care from the government, but we ain't getting much of nothing. Since there ain't no Confederate government to help us out, we ain't got nothing. Now they're trying to take away the little we got left."

"That's right, boys."

Matthew looked up when a cultured voice broke into the conversation. He eyed the well-dressed man who had stepped up. His portly body said he had either never fought in the war, or had rapidly regained the weight lost by most soldiers. He also had a sharp intelligence radiating from his eyes that the others lacked.

"Mitchell Cummins," he said quietly, extending his hand to Matthew.

Matthew hesitated, not sure why he was being singled out, but realized a refusal to shake hands would be dangerous. "Conrad Pickens," he answered.

The man didn't bother to acknowledge anyone else in the little group that was talking. "Right now the Klan is having to operate in secrecy," Cummins said. "In some regard, it always will, but this meeting today is essential in laying the groundwork for how we will operate in the future."

Matthew had a thousand questions that sprang to mind, but he knew none of them were appropriate, so he forced himself to listen.

"Are they going to help us make things right down here again?" Peter asked. Matthew knew his voice would make it obvious he wasn't from the hills of Tennessee. He had managed to mask the northern accent, but there was no mistaking he was educated and articulate.

Mitchell eyed him keenly. "And you are?"

"Darrell Davidson," Peter said as he extended his hand.

Mitchell shook it and then answered his question. "We are going to make things right again," he promised.

Once again, Matthew longed to know exactly who he was. Mitchell's next comment answered some of his question.

"We're growing fast down in North Carolina. Some of our men spent some time in Tennessee to learn methods, and then we started recruiting. The response has been eager."

Matthew was sure it had been. North Carolina had suffered greatly during the war. He was certain there were thousands of bitter veterans eager to fight back.

The blond spoke next. "All we want is the right to take care of our wives and children," he said. "When the Yankees came through my area, it wasn't good enough for them to win the battle. They had to destroy everything they found. They burnt all the houses, tore down all the fences, and mangled just about every piece of machinery they found." His face twisted with a mixture of anger and pain. "I lived through the war, but now I'm watching my children starve because I can't feed them off my land. It's gonna take years before my farm gonna produce like it did before the war. I kept hoping for the war to end, but things seem like they're worse than they was before."

The dark man nodded vigorously. "You got that right. I'm from a group down in Georgia. That General Sherman just about wiped out most of our state. I had one of them carpetbagger fellas tell me they were sorry about that, but it was the only way to break the spirit of the South." His eyes blazed with fury. "He said it just like that. *They had to break the spirit of the South.* I guess they sure enough did that. Two of my buddies killed themselves last week because they couldn't find a way to start their life again. I thought about it, but then I found out about the Klan. I owned a general store before the war started. Sherman came through and burnt it to the ground. I don't have a way to make a living anymore, so I figure I'll do everything I can to make things better for the South."

"We're the only ones who will do it," Mitchell said solemnly. "The Freedmen's Bureau is dedicated to helping the niggers, but they don't have the same concern for the white man who has been disenfranchised in their own country."

Matthew knew better than to protest, but he also knew plenty of money was going to poor whites through the Freedmen's Bureau. He was quite certain no one was open to reason, and he didn't want anyone to look at him and Peter with suspicion, so he just nodded along.

Mitchell locked his eyes on Matthew. "What are you doing here?"

Matthew forced himself to remain relaxed and meet Mitchell's probing eyes. "I'm here with Hobbs," he said simply.

"What for?" Mitchell snapped.

Suddenly Matthew understood. Hobbs was still being watched carefully, which meant that anyone who appeared with him would be suspect. He had to perform well to make sure Hobbs was in no greater danger. "It's time we stood up and said enough is enough," he said firmly. "I used to be a bank manager in Richmond. The bank was rebuilt after the fires, but there are nothing but Yankees working there now because they brought all the money in to bring it back to life. I have yet to find a new job." He knew that wasn't true of all banks, but he was counting on Mitchell not knowing that. Abby had carefully prepped him on his story. When he didn't see a spark of suspicion, he felt confident his tale had been accepted.

"How do we do that?" Mitchell asked.

"In whatever way it takes," Matthew answered. "I understand the Klan uses some methods that some may look down upon, but I'm beyond caring what anyone else thinks. If the South is going to survive, it will be because Southerners stand up and fight for what is theirs. No one seems to care about the Southern white man anymore, so we have to care about ourselves."

Mitchell had watched him carefully while he spoke, and suddenly his face cleared. He slapped Matthew on the shoulder. "Hobbs said you could be trusted. I guess he was right."

Matthew knew he needed to take it further. He nodded toward Peter. "Darrell and I are here to help in whatever way we can. There are a lot of men who feel the same way we do in Richmond. We want to find out how we can start a group of our own." He reached over and put a hand on Hobbs' shoulder. "We had heard some vague rumors about the Klan, but Hobbs let us know what was happening after he overheard us talking in a restaurant one day. When he was confident we could be trusted, he told us he knew how we could become involved. That's why we are here," Matthew added eagerly, almost gagging at the sound of his own voice.

Mitchell smiled at Hobbs with a bright light of approval in his eyes. "Well done, Hobbs."

Matthew forced himself to not reveal his relief, and prayed the meeting would be called to order quickly. He wasn't sure how much longer he could play this charade. His prayer was granted almost immediately.

"Everyone inside," a man shouted.

Matthew stepped in place beside Peter and Hobbs as they joined the mass of men moving toward the large room.

****

As Matthew waited for all the men to enter the room and for the meeting to start, he thought about all he had heard. In spite of his horror at what the Ku Klux Klan was doing, he also had to reluctantly admit he understood the bitter anger fueling it. No one would ever know how the country would have been rebuilt if President Lincoln had not been assassinated, but Matthew was confident it would have been handled differently than President Johnson had done it. Johnson's short-sightedness, and his own bigotry toward the blacks, had put things into motion that might take generations to heal. If the steps toward reunion had been done thoughtfully, with every single person taken into account, the rebuilding of a destroyed nation might have gone differently. As it was, a fire had been ignited that would take a long time to extinguish.

The questions kept pounding through his brain... Did Lincoln have a plan to make things right in areas like the Shenandoah Valley and Georgia that had been completely destroyed? Had he intended that northerners would come down and snap up Southern properties and businesses at ridiculously low prices? Did he have a plan to help restore Southern dignity, while at the same time holding them responsible for a war that had ripped the country apart? Did he have a strategy for introducing citizenry to the black population, while also assuring that all white men maintained their voice?

Matthew sighed, knowing he would never have answers to his questions. One thing he was certain of though—President Johnson's actions had made the

Reconstruction Acts absolutely necessary. He was equally certain that the acts, and the reality of Southern military occupation, had ignited the inferno that resulted in the very meeting he was sitting in. He could not excuse one thing the Klan was doing, but he also understood that men pushed to the brink of hopelessness would not hesitate to attack.

As the meeting was called to order, he knew he had to discern just how much they were willing to fight back.

Chapter Sixteen

Matthew was exhausted by the time the convention was called to a close. A look at Peter's face revealed his friend felt the same way. All he wanted to do was go back to their boarding room and settle in, but they had decided to put Hobbs on the train leaving town that night. He would attract far less attention that way because it seemed everyone else was leaving Nashville the next morning. They didn't want anyone to know which train Hobbs had caught, just in case he was being watched.

Hobbs looked up from the schedule he was examining. The plans had already been explained to him, but Matthew knew he was nervous. "I'm going as far as North Platte, Nebraska on the train."

"That's right," Matthew told him. "That's as far west as the train goes right now. They are working to build the tracks further west, and there are other crews working to build track east from California across the Sierra Nevada, but it is hard work that is taking a lot of time."

"Do you think they will ever join together?" Hobbs asked skeptically.

"Absolutely," Peter said. "Things came to a standstill during the war, but there has been a lot accomplished in the last two years."

"Didn't they start working on it in Omaha?" Hobbs asked, revealing he knew far more than he was letting on. "Laying track as far as North Platte doesn't seem like much for two years work."

"It moved slowly in the beginning," Matthew agreed. "Finding men to do the labor has been difficult, but when the war ended, veterans moved west to find work on the railroad. It took time to train them, but now things are moving fairly smoothly." He knew his words didn't convey the reality of the backbreaking, dangerous work in the middle of Indian country.

"I heard they were mostly Irish."

"On this end," Matthew confirmed. "The railroad coming east from California is mostly being built by the Chinese, and they have recently added Chinese to the crews that are heading west."

"Taking soldiers' jobs?" Hobbs asked with a frown.

"Only because there aren't enough veterans willing to work on it," Matthew answered, though he also knew it was because the Chinese were willing to work for far less than the Irish veterans were, even though they were underpaid as well. Like usual, profit was ruling the decisions made, and the railroad barons were taking advantage of a population desperate for work. Matthew was quite certain that if the war hadn't freed the slaves, the railroads would have figured out a way to build it for free with slave labor. He was glad it hadn't come to that.

"And there are Indian attacks," Hobbs commented casually, though his eyes revealed how concerned he was now that the time for him to leave had actually arrived.

"You'll be safe on the train," Matthew said confidently.

Hobbs shrugged. "That's not what I'm worried about. I still have to cross Wyoming, Idaho and Oregon in a wagon train. The odds of an Indian attack seem pretty high, I reckon."

Matthew didn't bother to deny it. Indian attacks were a regular occurrence on the trails that led through their sacred grounds. Hobbs should be over the mountains and into Oregon before winter hit, but you never knew what could happen with one of the wagon trains. "You don't have to do this, Hobbs," he said instead. "We can come up with another place to send you."

Hobbs shook his head. "I've thought about this. If I can't live in West Virginia, there ain't no place on this side of the country I want to live in. Even though I might die on my way out there, I reckon my odds are better than staying here. Folks are making it through, or they wouldn't keep going. I reckon I'll take my chances."

Matthew heard a train whistle in the distance. "That's your train," he said somberly.

Hobbs nodded and straightened his shoulders. "I reckon it is."

Peter shook his hand warmly. "Thank you for what you did, Hobbs."

Hobbs looked uncomfortable. "It was the least I could do after how I lied to the Cromwells."

Peter shrugged. "You made it right in the end. That's what counts."

"You reckon it did any good?" Hobbs asked seriously. "Going to the convention?"

Matthew nodded even though he wasn't at all sure it had. He would send Hobbs off with the belief he had contributed to the effort to stop the Ku Klux Klan. "Absolutely," Matthew said heartily as he avoided Peter's eyes.

Hobbs' face showed glad relief. He grabbed his single satchel close as the train pulled to a stop. The men waited quietly, relieved they didn't see any faces of the men they had met at the convention. When the conductor called for everyone to board, Matthew and Peter shook hands with Hobbs one last time and watched him step onto the train. They stayed in their spot until the train pulled out, understanding the resolved wistfulness on the young man's face as he waved good-bye to the only life he had ever known.

****

Matthew and Peter were too tired to talk during their dinner at the hotel, but when they had settled into their room, Matthew asked the question he knew was on Peter's mind, as well. "Do you think the convention was worth everything we did to attend?" He was almost embarrassed to say what he was really thinking.

Peter said it for him. "You mean was it worth shaving your beard to be there?"

Matthew chuckled as he nodded. "Yes, I suppose that's what I mean."

Peter shrugged. "I think it's obvious they are gearing up for impressive growth. The Ku Klux Klan *Prescript* that Gordon laid out made that clear. The passing of the Reconstruction Acts has galvanized the action that seems to have been planned all along."

Matthew fingered the copy of the *Prescript* that he had bought at the convention. He remembered most of what Gordon had said, but he was glad to have a copy of the Klan rules. "Gordon seemed eager to establish some order."

"He's a military man," Peter replied. "He knows a large organization has to have order if it is going to be successful."

Matthew thought about the carefully laid out plans for the Klan. Every group within the Klan was called a den. Dens within a county would be overseen by a Grand Giant and his four assisting Goblins. Counties within a congressional district (Dominion) would be headed by a Grand Titan and his six Furies. Dominions within a state (Realm) would be governed by a Grand Dragon, assisted by his eight Hydras. And in charge of all states within the Klan's "Invisible Empire" was the supreme commander, the Grand Wizard, who would be assisted by ten Genii. The chain of command was clear.

"Do you think Gordon will be the Grand Wizard?" Peter asked. "Take command of the entire Klan?"

Matthew shook his head. "I don't think so. He seemed content with his election as the Grand Dragon of the Realm of Tennessee." It would have been hard to take all the jargon seriously if he hadn't seen so much evidence of how deadly the Klan was. "I think he has someone else in mind, but he was careful not to talk about it."

"He was careful not to talk about a lot of things," Peter said ruefully. "He laid out some political aims, like securing the rights of the oppressed, but he seemed to be deliberately vague."

Matthew was troubled by that as well. He had hoped to gain more concrete information that would help him foil the agenda of the Klan. He couldn't help feeling he was walking away empty handed. "He was quite clear about the dire oath of secrecy."

"I can see why they will sell many copies of the *Prescript*," Peter agreed. "It's the only way possible to know all the secret passwords and hand grips."

"That he didn't even spell out in detail," Matthew lamented, feeling once again that attending the convention had been in vain.

"I believe Gordon achieved his agenda," Peter commented. "He knew he had to create some type of political and military structure because the Klan is growing too quickly and becoming reckless. And now everyone at the convention has to go back to their dens and sell the organizational structure to everyone else. You do realize they will be waiting for a report from *us* on how things are going in Virginia."

Matthew felt marginally better as he thought about that. "We will at least be able to foil *that* expectation," he said. Suddenly, he was anxious to rid himself of all connections to the Klan. Even being close to it had made him feel sullied. "I was going to wait until morning to wash out this dye, but I would rather do it now."

"Let's do it!" Peter agreed emphatically.

Thirty minutes later, not even minding the cold water they had not taken time to heat, they had their heads rinsed clean of the dye. It took several jugs of water, but it was deeply satisfying to see the basins fill with black and red liquid, washing away their connection to the Klan. Tomorrow morning they would be on trains bound for Philadelphia and Boston.

They had done what they could, and they would have accurate information to feed to the public about the Klan's organizational structure. Only time would tell if it would make any difference. As Matthew towel-dried his red hair, he had a sick feeling it wouldn't matter.

****

Rose breathed in the spring air that already carried a hint of summer humidity. She didn't mind. The heat brought out the fragrant aromas of the honeysuckle lining the fences along the road, and the heady perfume of the wisteria hanging in great purple clumps from trees. The glorious blooms of the redbud trees had withered and dropped to the ground, but the pearly white of the dogwoods glistened in the woods as the soft breeze rustled new leaves that danced in a myriad of green shades.

Rose had left for school early, hoping the beauty of the countryside during a slow carriage ride would ease her concern, but it wasn't working. What made it worse was that she couldn't put a finger on any reason for her worry. Perhaps that was it. Things were going well, which usually meant trouble was on the way. She hated feeling that way, but too many negative experiences had made her both cautious and careful. She wondered if she would live long enough to see that reality change, but somehow she doubted it. America was changing, but too many mistakes had been made after the end of the war. She was sure it was blacks and women who would pay the highest price for people's decisions and actions. A heavy sigh escaped her lips as she pondered what could be coming. Her greatest wish was that Felicia and Hope would live to see a better country, and live a life full of freedom and opportunities. She fully intended to press forward in becoming an educator, but her heart told her there were many dark times ahead.

Things had been so quiet she had insisted Jeb and Andy be relieved of guarding her. She knew they were needed in the tobacco fields. Moses had resisted but finally agreed there seemed to be no danger. Why then was her heart catching with every movement in the woods?

Scolding herself that she was simply being pessimistic didn't do any good. Yes, slaves were free and black men were about to get the vote, but the letter they had received yesterday from Matthew about the expansion of the Ku Klux Klan revealed that while things were getting better in some areas, they were going to get worse in others. She knew the reality of the black vote was going to galvanize hatred and violence more than anything had to date.

As her carriage rolled down the road, Rose thought about what her mama would have said. Surely, she would have told her she was just borrowing trouble, but she could also hear Sarah's voice telling her to be wise in the midst of difficulty. *Ain't no good to pretend trouble might not be comin', Rose girl. Trouble seems to always be followin' black folks. You got to believe the best, but you's got to be smart about livin'.*

"I'm trying to be smart, Mama," Rose whispered. She only hoped she could be smart enough to protect all the people she loved.

A deer burst out of the woods, startling her horse. "Easy girl," Rose murmured soothingly. The mare flicked an ear in her direction and relaxed back into the harness. Rose was glad Carrie was coming home tomorrow. She had missed her terribly, but Carrie's glowing letter about the factory opening had soothed any concerns over difficulties with her pregnancy. Now she was just glad to have her best friend coming home. She had learned to never take a moment of their time together for granted, and she was quite sure a long conversation would release the tension that seemed to be wrapped around her heart and mind.

Her concerns evaporated when she rounded the last curve leading to the schoolhouse. The yard was full of children laughing and playing. It seemed almost surreal that she had both black and white students. There were still some tensions, but most of them seemed to have worked out their issues. She knew it was because all the white students were reading now, and their hunger to learn matched all her other students. No one had anything to feel inferior about, so most of the children seemed happy to just act like children. She wished all of America would follow the lead of her tiny school.

She watched as four of the children broke free from the group and raced down the road toward her.

"Mrs. Samuels! Mrs. Samuels!"

The fear in their voices put her on immediate alert. Rose pulled the carriage to a stop and jumped down to meet them. Two of them were black students, two were white. "Good morning, children. How are you?" She kept her voice calm, hoping it was just her own baseless fears that she was reflecting onto them. Their next words destroyed her feeble hope.

"There were men watching us this morning!" Sally said, her blue eyes wide with fear.

"Where were they?" Rose asked, trying to keep her voice even so she wouldn't amplify their fears.

"In the woods about five minutes from here," Sally answered, her voice quivering as she relived it. "At first I didn't think much about it, but then I realized there were a bunch of them. I waved at them, but they just stared at me. I got a real bad feeling, so I ran all the way here to school."

Rose hid her frown. "You did the right thing, Sally." Fourteen-year-old Sally was the daughter of a Confederate war veteran. Her father had been reluctant for her to attend school, but the girl's mother had been adamant. She knew most of the students were here because the mother's insisted they have schooling.

Seven-year-old Bunny crowded closer, her dark eyes even more frightened than Sally's. "We gonna be all right, Mrs. Samuels? Them men coming after us?"

"Are we going to be all right, Mrs. Samuels? Are those men coming after us?" Rose automatically corrected the girl's speech, while her mind spun with the possibilities. The vigilantes had threatened to return. Perhaps planting had kept them too busy to carry out their agenda, but now that all the crops were in, perhaps they had turned their attention back to her school.

Bunny stared up at her, her breath coming in short gasps. "They gonna burn our school like last time?"

Rose knelt down and gathered the little girl close, realizing now was not the time to correct grammar. "Everything is going to be fine," she said confidently. "Did you see the men, too?"

"Yessum!" Bunny replied, her black braids bouncing on her back as she nodded vigorously. "Me and Paul be coming through the woods alone today 'cause Mama ain't feeling good. Them men were staring at us real fierce like." She shot a look at Sally. "We ran all the way to school, too.

Rose's heart sank, but she knew she couldn't let the children sense her fear...or her anger that the men hiding in the woods had so frightened the children. She controlled her sudden urge to peer into the surrounding trees. Instead, she hugged Bunny closer to her side. "You were very brave to run," she complimented her. "Now, I believe it's time to start school."

"We're still going to have school?" Sally asked as she eyed the woods fearfully.

Rose realized Sally had something else on her mind besides scary men in the forest. "What is it, Sally?"

"Why are they watching *us*?" Sally burst out. "We're *white*, just like they are."

Rose wondered if she should tell the girl the truth—that white children attending a black school might be seen as *more* of a threat to the vigilantes. The stories pouring in about the Ku Klux Klan revealed their atrocities were often more horrible when directed toward whites who were seen to be supporting blacks, but that was not something to put into the mind of a fourteen-year-old child. Rose would protect Sally from the truth for as long as possible.

"We don't know what they were doing," Rose responded. She allowed herself to look around, not letting her eyes do more than skim the woods. "I don't see anyone now, though. We are at school to learn. That is what we are going to do."

Bunny shrank even closer. "But what if they come to the school?"

Rose didn't have an answer for that, so she raised her voice and called for all the children to enter the building. It was still fifteen minutes before school was scheduled to start, but she didn't want the children outside if the men returned. Sally was watching her with a knowing look, but the girl didn't say anything. Instead, she put an arm around Bunny and led her inside. Rose hated that she hoped there weren't vigilantes watching Sally's kindness. It would surely make her more of a target.

Rose took a deep breath, wavering somewhere between fury and terror. She was determined not to let terror win, but she wasn't sure what to do with the fury.

Felicia sidled up next to her before Rose stepped into the school. "You want me to go get Daddy?"

Rose realized Sally must have told her daughter what happened. She thought about it quickly, and then shook her head. If there were vigilantes out there, she wasn't going to allow Felicia to go back through the woods alone. The clinic was closed for the days Carrie was in Philadelphia, so there was no one to send for help. She longed for Jeb and Andy at that moment, but she was on her own. Rose swallowed hard before she put an arm around Felicia. "Thank you, but no. Everything is fine." She kept her voice confident, but the look on her daughter's face said she wasn't fooled.

"We're going to do school as planned," Rose said quietly, deciding she could at least let Felicia draw courage from her refusal to give into fear. Truth be told, she was more scared to let all the children go home alone through the woods. Perhaps by the time school was done, the vigilantes would have left. "I believe you are teaching first," she said firmly.

Felicia nodded her head slowly, and then allowed herself one long look into the woods. "Yes, Mama." She drew herself up as tall as she could, straightened her narrow shoulders, and lifted her head high before she walked regally into the school.

Rose felt her heart swell with pride and admiration as she followed her daughter. She would deal with how to get the students home when the time came. And if the vigilantes attacked the school? She refused to let herself think that way because it would do no good.

****

Amber stuck her head out the barn door again, but the drive was as empty as it had been the last dozen times she looked. "When are they going to get here?" she asked impatiently.

"Don't you know a watched pot never boils?" Miles asked indulgently.

"That's not true," Amber retorted. "My mama used to tell me that, too, so I tested it. It boils every single time. It feels like it won't ever happen, but it does every time."

Robert chuckled as he exchanged a glance with Miles. "I told you she is too smart for the likes of us."

"That you did," Miles said fondly, his eyes glowing with love as he looked at the little girl.

Robert could hardly believe Miles had been here such a short time. He had fit into their operation so seamlessly it seemed as if he must have always been part of it. The old man was both wise and patient. He carried a wealth of horse knowledge so vast that Robert only hoped he could learn it all before Miles died. The man was in excellent shape, but his true age was just a guess—somewhere in his seventies most likely.

Clint was comfortable managing the stables, but he was also smart enough to give needed jobs to Miles, and then just stay out of his way. Robert often found the two of them talking late into the night, Clint plying Miles with question after question. Miles treated each question with serious attention.

"You still haven't answered my question," Amber reminded Miles.

"They'll get here when they get here," Miles replied, his eyes twinkling with fun.

Amber glared at him and stamped her foot. "You're playing with me. You know when they are getting here!"

Robert decided to step in. "Captain Jones and Susan will be here soon. The best they could tell me was that they would arrive before lunch. It's a long ride out from Richmond, and there could be a lot of things to delay them."

"But I want to show them how far all their babies have come!"

Robert bit back a smile. One of the things he loved about Amber was that she had very little patience. She was always eager for things to happen quickly, except when it came to the fillies and colts she had been training all winter. She was a paragon of patience when it came to training, never asking for more than the yearlings were able to give. They had bloomed under her and Clint's careful tutelage. In truth, Robert was just as eager for Mark and Susan to arrive. The siblings had trusted Robert last fall when they had purchased every one of the foals. He was eager to show them their confidence had not been misguided.

Robert stepped outside the barn to look at the carefully groomed yearlings waiting for their new owners to arrive. Their coats gleamed in the sunshine as they cavorted in the green grass. Most of them carried the dark bay coloring of their sire, but there were sorrels, chestnuts, and even one gray. The picture they made almost took his breath away.

His attention was caught by a faint cloud of dust in the distance. He grinned and waved to Amber. "I believe I see them coming now."

Amber gave a shout of excitement as she raced toward him. Robert scooped her up and set her on the top rail of the fence. She was lithe as a monkey, and hardly needed his help, but he loved to feel her in his arms. He could hardly wait for his and Carrie's child to be born, but no one would feel any more like a daughter than Amber did. His love for her seemed to grow every day.

Miles strolled out to lean against the fence.

"They're almost here, Miles," Amber yelled.

"Sure seems like it," Miles replied easily.

"They're gonna be here a whole week!"

Robert had been thrilled when Mark and Susan said they planned on staying a full seven days. They were eager to work with all the yearlings alongside Amber and Clint, but they also wanted to spend time with Carrie, who was due back the next day. Robert forgot his visitors for a moment as he thought about his wife arriving home. He had missed her dreadfully, and he was willing to admit he had worried about her every single moment she had been gone. He had tried not to, and there was no way he would have prevented her from attending the factory opening, but he also would have been happier if she had stayed on the plantation where he could watch over her, as much as she would have hated knowing that.

"That's what I hear," Miles agreed. "A week is a right long time."

Amber stopped bouncing up and down on the fence long enough to stare down at him. "Do you ever get excited about anything?" she demanded.

"I reckon I be excited right now," Miles protested good-naturedly.

Amber stared at him. "Well, you sure do hide it good," she retorted.

Miles smiled. "Not sure that fence would hold me bouncing up and down on it."

Amber thought about that for a moment, and then laughed loudly. "I reckon not."

"Would you be happier if I did a little jig?"

Amber, a wide smile filling her face, nodded eagerly. "Yes!"

Miles bowed low at the waist and then shuffled a jig in the dirt next to the fence. After a few steps he stopped.

"Don't stop!" Amber commanded.

"Dancing ain't no fun without a partner," Miles explained as he held out his hand.

Amber laughed, jumped from the fence, and danced around him as Miles went back to doing his slow jig.

Robert watched them, their antics clearing his mind of worry about his beautiful wife. Just then, the wagon rounded the curve. "We have company."

Amber stopped dancing and raced toward the wagon. "You're here! You're here!"

Susan Jones, her blue eyes flashing with excitement, leapt from the wagon and swept Amber up into a hug. "And here is the little girl who beat me in the Tournament last year."

"This year, too, if you're brave enough to ride again," Amber said smugly as she returned the hug. "I'm real glad you're here."

"And we're glad to be here," Mark said as he climbed down from the wagon, shook hands with Robert, and leaned down to hug Amber.

"I want you to meet Miles," Robert said. "He was the brains behind the Cromwell horses for decades. Now that the war is over, he is back here to work."

Mark and Susan greeted him warmly and then walked over to lean against the pasture fence.

"Look at them," Susan said softly. "They are stunningly beautiful." Her face filled with something like awe.

Mark nodded, not able to look away. "Every one of them is special," he agreed. "I knew we had purchased some fine horseflesh, but I have to admit I didn't think I would be *this* impressed."

Amber climbed up on the fence so she could look Mark in the eye. "Just wait until you see them in action, Mr. Mark. Every one of them will make you proud!"

Before Mark could answer, a sharp whinny split the air.

A dark bay filly, the sun gleaming off the heart shape on her forehead, came racing toward the fence. Amber laughed as she slipped down and ran to meet her filly. All My Heart skidded to a stop and did a half rear before she lowered her head to gently nudge the little girl. Amber laughed harder and slipped her arms around the filly's neck. "Hey, little one," she said gently.

Susan climbed the fence nimbly and jumped down to join them in the field. "Still as spoiled as ever, I see."

Amber shook her head vigorously. "All My Heart is not spoiled," she protested. "She is well-loved." As laughter rang out through the air, she stepped back and raised her right hand. All My Heart came to immediate attention, her head held alert as she stared at Amber's hand. She remained a frozen statue until Amber suddenly swirled her hand in a circle. The filly settled back on her haunches and then spun easily in a circle of her own. When she was facing Amber again, the little girl bowed low toward her filly. All My Heart bent one leg close to the ground and dipped her head deeply.

Mark and Susan applauded as Amber leapt forward to hug her filly again. "See," she boasted, "All My Heart is well-loved."

"That she is," Susan agreed, gazing at Amber with unabashed admiration. "Did you teach her how to do all that?"

Amber shrugged. "She's smart."

Robert watched the exchange, his heart full of emotion. He understood the expressions on his friends' faces. He had never known a ten-year-old with such horse training skills either. Of course, he knew the total love the two shared made the training even easier. It was not really training—it was simple communication between friends.

"Have you done that with all our horses?" Mark asked.

Amber smiled. "I said they were all real smart, but I didn't say they were as smart as *my* filly," she said coyly. Laughter rang out in the morning air as Amber grinned. "They are all real smart," she said. "They are just waiting to show you what they can do."

"Not until you folks get up here for some tea and biscuits," Annie called from the porch.

Robert chuckled. He didn't know how Annie seemed to hear everything that went on at the plantation, but she surely didn't miss much.

"Ham biscuits?" Mark called hopefully.

"Only one way to find out," Annie yelled before she disappeared into the house, the screen door slapping shut behind her.

"That woman is a marvel," Miles muttered.

Robert thought Miles' eyes were bright with something more than hunger, but right now all he could focus on was how loudly his own stomach was rumbling.

****

Robert was content to lean back in his rocking chair while he munched his ham biscuits and drank his cold tea. He had gotten up extra early that morning so he could help Clint, Amber and Miles groom all the yearlings. He hadn't realized just how hungry he was until Annie had demanded they eat. He took a deep breath as the soft spring air washed over him, carrying birdsong and whinnying horses.

"You look like a happy man," Mark said quietly.

Robert turned his eyes to him, aware Susan and Amber were chatting. Miles had gone into the house to check on something with Annie. "I've never been happier," he admitted.

"Do you miss Oak Meadows?"

Robert considered the question and then shook his head firmly. "Not even for a minute. There were times during the war that the thought of going home was the only thing that kept me going, but Cromwell Plantation has become my home now. Everything that matters to me is right here." His mind swirled with images of Carrie, Amber, the horses, Moses and Rose. "Cromwell Plantation is home now," he repeated, awash with something akin to awe when he realized how completely he meant it.

"And Carrie is doing well?" Mark asked.

Robert nodded, praying the trip home from Philadelphia wouldn't be too much for her. "Carrie is strong."

Mark leaned forward to look at him more closely. "But...? I sense there is something you are not telling me."

Robert frowned. "I shouldn't worry so much," he insisted. He told Mark about Carrie's mother almost losing her at birth. "Carrie is healthy, though. And she has taken good care of herself." He pushed aside thoughts of how hard she still insisted on working at the clinic. "There is no reason to think she will have anything but an easy birth."

"But you are still worried," Mark observed.

Robert sighed. "I'm terrified of losing her," he said softly. "We've had so little true time together. Between the war and my illnesses, it seems like there has always been something to keep us apart. The last few months have been like heaven to me." He stopped talking as he stared out over the pasture, trying to push down the sudden foreboding he felt.

"None of us who went through the war takes anything for granted," Mark said. "Susan and I love being at Oak Meadows, but there are so many nights when I dream of the entire Shenandoah Valley going up in flames again. I wake up hearing the screams of horses." He shook his head. "None of it is real, of course, but I suspect the memories will be with me forever. I always have to step outside to make sure everything is all right."

For a moment, Robert wanted to point out that it was *Mark's* army that had destroyed the Shenandoah Valley, but he knew the destruction had sickened his friend almost as much as it had the Virginians who had endured it. The war was over, and the country was struggling to rebuild. They had to let the other fighting go...let the past be the past. "I suspect those memories will always be with both of us," was all he said. He knew he would never forget the horror of watching the Shenandoah Valley burn. Oak Meadows—only because of Matthew's intervention—was one of the few plantations that had been unharmed.

"Where are the mares and the new crop of foals?" Mark asked suddenly.

Robert was happy to let him change the subject. He could not explain the feeling of foreboding that had come over him, but he was determined to push it away. "They are all in a back pasture. Clint moved them this morning so we could bring the yearlings up front for you and Susan. He is working with the new foals right now."

"Are the new ones as wonderful as the yearlings?"

"Just as wonderful, and more of them," Robert confirmed happily. He had used the money from Mark and Susan's purchase of the yearlings last fall to buy additional mares. There had just been enough time to breed them. Nothing gave him more joy than watching the new foals playing in the fields. He had increased his herd size by fifty percent in just one year.

"I told some of my friends about my purchase," Mark revealed.

Robert nodded. "I know. I've heard from several of them." He smiled broadly. "Thank you. All of them will be here in the next few months. If we're lucky, they will buy all this year's foals." It still stunned him to realize how true his projection might actually turn out to be. He was years ahead of where he thought he would be at this point in his business.

"All of them?" Mark asked, seeming to sense there was something he wasn't saying.

"Not all of them," Robert replied. "There are a few that carry every attribute Eclipse could possibly pass on to his offspring. I am keeping those here to deepen the quality of the stock." He also told Mark about Miles bringing Chelsea down from Canada to breed with Eclipse to create a new breed of carriage horse.

Mark listened closely. "I've heard of the Cleveland Bay breed. In fact, my ancestors raised them in northern England. I remember reading journals about their experiences, and about the results of their breeding. They are fine animals."

"Chelsea is special," Robert agreed. "I can hardly wait to see her offspring next year. Miles will own the first one, but I will keep the next one."

A long silence fell on the porch as the men looked out over the plantation. Susan and Amber had disappeared into the barn sometime during their discussion.

"You're living your dream," Mark finally said.

"I am," Robert agreed. "This is all I ever wanted to do with my life. I can still hardly believe I've been lucky enough to do it." He paused. "Sometimes I feel guilty. Most of the South is struggling so hard. Men can't find work. People are hopeless. And here I am, doing what I always dreamed of doing because Abby and Thomas had the money to make it happen."

"She had the money, but you have made it happen with your hard work," Mark replied. "And yes, there are many people suffering, but you have found a way to make this plantation an example of what life can be like in the South if people will learn to let go of their hatred and prejudices. That is something to be proud of."

Robert nodded thoughtfully, thinking of Moses and Rose. Annie. Amber. Clint. Miles. He supposed it should bother him that he was the only white person on the plantation when everyone else was gone, but he no longer saw it that way. He wasn't sure when he had stopped seeing color; he just knew that now he only saw friends. "I am indeed a lucky man," he said warmly. He pushed up from his chair. "I say it's time we see exactly what these young'uns of yours can do."

Chapter Seventeen

Rose breathed a sigh of relief when school ended. There had been no evidence of vigilantes through the long day that had seemed at times as if it would never end. There had been random carriages, wagons, and men on horseback who had passed the school, but that was no different than any other day, and no one had appeared to be threatening. She tried to tell herself it was safe to relax, but every fiber of her being remained on high alert.

When school ended she didn't want to alarm the children, but neither did she want them to be careless. "I don't want any of you going home alone," she said firmly. "There is no reason to think you won't be safe, but I want you all to be extra careful." She allowed her face to express her concern because she wanted to be sure her message was taken seriously. "I want all of you to go in groups of at least five." She thought that was a number that would make anyone hesitate because it would be too easy for one of the kids to break free and sound the alert. Rose wished she could take every single one of them home herself, but it wasn't possible.

As she watched all the students leave, she was glad Amber had talked her into letting her miss school so she could present the yearlings to Mark and Susan, because it meant Felicia could sit with her in the carriage. There was no way Rose would allow her to walk back through the woods alone.

"Mama?"

Rose could hear the fear in Felicia's voice as she stepped close. She knew the little girl would never lose the image of watching her mother and father be murdered during the Memphis riot. She reached down and gripped her hand. "It's going to be fine," she said confidently, praying that this time Felicia wouldn't see through her charade. She longed to give the brave child the feeling of security she deserved.

"I was hoping Daddy would come today," Felicia said in a small voice.

Rose had, too, but she also knew Moses was swamped with work in the tobacco fields, and he had no reason to anticipate trouble. "We'll be home soon, honey," Rose replied. She forced herself to not look nervously toward the woods when she stepped into the carriage and picked up the reins. She also forced herself to not urge the horses into a mad gallop to get home sooner. It would only frighten her daughter and draw attention to them. Swallowing her own trepidations, she managed to chat normally about the school day as the carriage rumbled down the road.

Moses was waiting on the porch when they arrived. "You're home early," Rose called, glad her voice was steady. She had seldom been so glad to see her towering husband. Just looking at him bolstered her courage.

Moses took one look at her face and jumped off the porch, completely ignoring the steps. "What is it?" he asked.

"Vigilantes," Felicia burst out, tears following her trembling words.

Moses gathered his daughter close as he looked at Rose. "What happened?" His voice was calm, but his eyes were burning.

"Nothing," Rose assured him. "That I am aware of," she corrected, because she didn't really know if all the students were safely home. She explained that several of her pupils had reported being watched by threatening groups of men in the woods on the way to school.

"Nothing more?" Moses asked keenly.

"Nothing more," Rose assured him.

"But you believe something more is going to happen," Moses observed, his eyes locked on her face.

Rose shrugged. "It's just a feeling." She knew, just as Moses did, however, that her feelings were usually right. "Something is going to happen."

"I've been feeling it all day," Moses revealed. "I couldn't put my finger on what I was feeling, but it was like a warning sound going off inside. I just didn't know where to look for the trouble." His voice was disgusted. "I should have sent Jeb and Andy as soon as I suspected something."

"You had no way of knowing anything was happening," Rose protested. "And, in fact, nothing *did* happen."

"Yet," Moses added grimly.

Rose agreed with him, so she didn't bother to correct him. She just moved closer so he could pull her in with the free arm that wasn't holding Felicia.

****

From his position on the porch, Moses looked down at the group of men he had pulled together. Robert, Mark, Clint, Miles and Gabe stared back up at him. All the plantation hands who had served with him in the war met his eyes grimly. All together there were thirty men. All were armed, and all had determined expressions.

"We don't know where the trouble is going to be," Moses said again. He didn't add that there may not be any trouble at all. He had learned to trust his intuition, and if he had any doubts about his own, he had absolutely no doubt about his wife's.

"Should we split up?" Mark asked.

Moses felt a moment of amazement that his commanding officer from the war was asking him for direction, but he accepted the responsibility as he shook his head. "I don't want to weaken us," he replied. "I want everyone to spread out along the perimeter of the property so we can anticipate trouble from any direction."

Robert glanced up at the house.

Mark interpreted his look. "The women are all inside. The children are safe in your room."

Robert read the question in his eyes. "You're wondering why we put everyone in there."

Mark nodded. "Your window looks out on the front. It seems they would be safer if they were deeper in the house."

Robert hesitated, but decided to tell him the truth. Mark and Susan had become family, and Susan might also have to use the Cromwell secret. "There is a tunnel," he said very quietly, making certain no one else could overhear him.

Mark's eyes widened. "From your bedroom?"

"It's behind a mirror brought over by Cromwell ancestors."

Mark's voice was full of admiration. "It's how Carrie escaped during the war."

Robert grinned, glad to release some of the tension that had drawn him tight as a bow. "It's been quite useful in the last five years," he replied. "We won't have to worry about anyone in the house coming to harm."

Mark drew himself up more erectly. "Good. That means we can put all our focus on whatever is going to happen out here." His voice was full of easy confidence.

Robert wished he felt the same confidence, but there was something gnawing at him.

Mark narrowed his eyes. "You're worried."

Robert wanted to deny it, but the best he could manage was a shrug. "We've had trouble before. We've always dealt with it."

Silence settled onto the night as all the men spread out about a hundred yards apart, their positions concealed by the dense foliage. The only sounds were hooting owls and the crickets tuning up their orchestra for the evening. It would have been peaceful if the air wasn't also fraught with tense expectancy.

Robert listened carefully, not wanting to miss any sounds that would identify trouble closing in on them. He knew most of the vigilantes were veterans who were also experienced in nighttime combat. Just the knowledge that he could be awaiting attack by some of the men he had once commanded set every nerve on edge.

Two hours passed. The sun had long set, but a thin layer of clouds had obscured all but a tiny glow from the half-moon riding low on the tree line. Robert tried to relax, but in spite of there being no sign of trouble, every muscle in his body remained tight. He forced himself to breathe slowly, but he recognized the feeling as one he had experienced before every battle.

The first sign of trouble was a wild thrashing in the woods near the barn. Robert watched closely, but doubted the noise was a harbinger of an attack. Whoever it was had no concern for a quiet approach. He knew Moses was close behind the barn.

"Halt!" Moses' voice split the night with harsh command.

"Mr. Samuels!" A badly frightened voice lifted into the night air. "Is that you?"

Moses stepped out just as a young white boy, about eleven years old, burst from the woods. "What is it?"

The young boy plowed to a stop, struggling to breathe as he stared up with frightened eyes at the towering man before him. "My daddy said not to talk to anyone but Roses' husband, Mr. Samuels. Is that you?"

"It is," Moses said grimly. "What is going on?" He laid a hand on the boy's shoulder to let him know he was safe now.

"It's the school," the boy gasped, leaning over to catch his breath. "Men are after it with fire sticks. My daddy said to come get you right away. We was coming home from supper at my grandma's house when we saw them turn into the schoolyard."

Robert wondered why the father had sent a young boy on a mission through the dark woods, but there was no time to get answers. The man must have felt like he had no other options.

"You did well, son," Moses said. He raised his voice. "Robert, I want you to stay here with Mark, Gabe, Miles and Clint. We don't know for certain that they won't come here," he added. "My men? Follow me."

Moses swung onto his gelding, Champ, and raced down the trail that led to the school.

Robert watched them go and then turned to the young boy. "What's your name, son?"

"Harvey." The little boy glanced at the woods. "I should go help my papa."

Robert admired his courage, but shook his head. "We'll take care of it," he promised. "I want you to go into the house where you'll be safe."

Harvey looked up at the house, admiration shining through his fear. "In there?"

"Yes." Robert took his hand and led him up onto the porch. The door opened immediately, and Rose stepped out.

"Mrs. Samuels!"

Rose caught Harvey into a hug, holding him while Robert explained the situation. "Come inside," Rose said warmly. "Thank you for coming to warn us. My husband will make sure your father is all right. I believe there are some warm cookies coming out of the oven right now," she said enticingly.

Harvey hesitated, looking back at the menacing, dark woods, and then followed Rose into the house with an expression of relief.

Robert watched him go, glad the boy would be safe, and then he waved the other men toward him so they could calculate the best way to protect the plantation now that there were just five of them.

****

Moses wasn't overly concerned with noise because he knew the crackling of flames would cover the sound of them approaching. His fury was tempered by a sorrow that Rose's school was most likely being destroyed again. He didn't know how many times they would have to rebuild, but he was certain they would. The only way to keep the vigilantes from winning their battle of terror was to refuse to bow down to the fear.

He was realistic enough to know there might be someone who would lose their life during the long night ahead, but he also knew all his men were as equally determined to protect their new freedoms as he was.

When they were a couple hundred yards from the schoolhouse, Moses slid Champ to a halt and looped his reins loosely around a tree so the horse could escape if he didn't return. Holding his hand up for silence, he ran quickly down the remainder of the trail, and slowed to a stop when he reached the edge of the clearing. When he was close enough to see the school, his mouth gaped open with astonishment.

"What is going on, Moses?"

Moses looked over and realized Jeb had materialized next to him. "I reckon we're going to listen and find out," he muttered, almost speechless as he watched the drama being played out in front of them. He held up his hand to keep his men in place. Right now they weren't needed, and their appearance might make things worse.

The school was indeed surrounded by a gang of vigilantes with bandanas covering everything but their eyes, but the inner circle surrounding the school was a small army of white men who he quickly identified as parents of Rose's students.

As the vigilantes pressed closer, the parents lifted their rifles and took careful aim. Moses heard the lead vigilante curse as he jerked his horse to a standstill.

"What do y'all think you are doing?" the lead man called. "You're protecting a nigger school."

"Nope. I'm protecting my children's school," one of the parents yelled back defiantly. "All of you need to leave now."

"Are you crazy?" one of the vigilantes called in a voice filled with rage.

"They're crazy all right," another man yelled. "They're crazy if they think we are going to let them get away with having their kids in a nigger school. It makes all of us look bad. We're not going to get things under control if things like that are going on!"

As Moses watched the scene unfold before him, he motioned his men forward and gave them quiet instructions. "If a single one of those vigilantes throws a fire stick or discharges their gun, I want you to shoot every one of them," he said grimly. He could only imagine the repercussions if they were to kill the vigilantes threatening their school, but he didn't imagine it would be much worse than what was happening now. It was time to make a stand. He watched with grim satisfaction as his men took position behind sheltering trees and cocked their triggers.

The white parents must have been put on alert when their children arrived home from school with reports of being watched in the woods. What the veterans had feared was indeed happening, but instead of siding with the vigilantes, they had decided to fight back. Moses felt a swell of admiration rush through him. Right on the heels of the admiration came a tidal wave of hope. He had never dreamed he would see a group of white veterans come to the defense of their school – perhaps there was hope for their country afterall.

"What are you doing this for?" the lead vigilante hollered.

As Moses watched, he realized the band of men was not keen on attacking a group of white army veterans.

The work of vigilantes was usually done in secret, without true identities being revealed.

"You think I don't know that is you, Granger? You can hide like a coward behind that bandana, but you ain't fooling anyone!"

Moses saw the lead man stiffen in shocked surprise. The vigilante's biggest weapon was covertness. That had just been destroyed.

"And you too, Chad Hawkins," the parent yelled. "You should be ashamed of yourself!"

Moses narrowed his eyes and focused in on the parent defying the threatening band. He was only a little surprised when he realized it was Amanda's husband, Alvin. He had resisted Silas and Violet coming to school, but he had evidently changed his mind somewhere along the way. Rose brought home glowing stories of how well the two children were doing.

"We got to take back control of the South!" The man who had been identified as Chad yelled back as he lifted his burning pine stick higher into the air.

"You move that stick even one inch closer to this school, Chad, and I will shoot your arm off," Alvin promised in a cold voice. He was evidently the self-appointed leader. "Now look, we don't want to have to shoot any of you, but don't think we won't. I may only have one arm left, but it's my shooting arm. It works just fine."

"You're destroying the South for your children!" Chad hollered. "The only way to make things right again is to run all them niggers out."

"And where do you think they're going?" Alvin asked calmly, as he kept careful aim on the gang facing them. "Even if they wanted to leave, which they don't, they ain't got nowhere to go. Nope. We all gots to live here together now."

Granger raised his hand in an attempt to regain control. "You're only making it harder on yourself, Alvin. You shouldn't let your kids come to school here." His voice was low and menacing.

"That so?" Alvin asked.

Moses was impressed with Alvin's self-control, but he could also hear the fury lacing each word. It wouldn't take much to push the man over the edge. Moses knew the feeling of fear and anger that fine-tuned every nerve in your body until you thought you would explode.

Alvin wasn't done talking. "I don't see any of the fancy plantation owners around here setting up schools for my children," he said bluntly. "Y'all don't care nothing about my kids. Mrs. Samuels has them all reading," he boasted.

"That Mrs. Samuels is going to get what's coming to her," Granger growled. "That giant nigger man of hers won't be able to protect her."

Jeb's hand appearing on Moses' arm was the only thing that kept him from launching forward into the clearing.

"Be smart," Jeb whispered. "They probably suspect we're out here. They're trying to make us show ourselves."

Moses shook his head to clear the burning in his eyes. He knew Jeb was right. He had to be smart. No one would hurt Rose as long as he had anything to do about it. Right now, she and the children were safe in the house, with the tunnel available if it was needed. He took several deep breaths to steady himself so that his shooting would be on target if the need arose.

"Your children don't need schooling, Alvin," Granger replied in a cold, taunting voice. "Y'all aren't anything but white trash. It's what you have always been, and what you always will be."

Moses' fury was replaced by renewed admiration for the parents guarding the school. He saw every man there tense with fresh anger, but no one shifted their position. The whole school was encircled, making it impossible for any of the vigilantes to sneak up without being seen.

"I don't reckon I care what you rich boys think," Alvin said dispassionately. "You may think you're better than us, but I happen to know you ain't got any more than I do. You lost it all during that war you were so all-fired determined we would fight for you. You think my kids aren't good enough for schooling, but you didn't have no trouble letting me and my friends fight your war for you."

"If you men had won the war, we wouldn't be having the problems we're having right now, would we, Alvin?" Moses could hear the smirk in Granger's voice when he replied, even though his face was hidden.

Moses could sense the fury pouring off of Alvin like steam rising from a kettle.

"I think that stupid white man went further than he should have," Jeb muttered.

Before Moses could reply, he saw Alvin raise his pistol higher and fire.

Granger squealed like a stuck pig as he ducked down into his saddle. "You fool! Do you think you can got away with trying to shoot me?"

Moses grinned as the entire group of vigilantes started to raise their rifles, but paused when the parents raised their rifles in immediate response. They looked treacherous in their concealing garb, but they were really nothing but cowards.

"If I had been trying to shoot you, you would be dead," Alvin said in an icy voice. "I'm real close to losing my patience. That was a warning shot. The next one I fire will be the real thing, and all the men around me will follow suit. You might get a couple of us," he said casually, "but I can guarantee all of you will be dead. It's up to you whether you want to take the chance."

Alvin, clearly done with the game he was being forced to play, took a steady step forward. "I'm going to give you about ten seconds to get out of here. And don't bother to come back. If even one thing happens to my kid's school I'm going to know who to come after. You might burn our school down, but I don't figure you'll want your fancy homes burned down," he said harshly.

Granger flinched. "We're leaving," he muttered, "but you're going to be real sorry for this, Alvin. And not just because of what *we're* going to do. A new order is being established in the South. Pretty soon, it's not going to be safe to be black, and it's surely not going to be safe to be a white man who protects the niggers. You might stop us, but you sure can't stop the entire Ku Klux Klan."

Moses saw Alvin tighten again, but this time he knew the reaction was fear, not anger.

Alvin still stood his ground. "That might be, but I stopped you," he taunted.

"You just think you did!" The yell came from a man on horseback who was almost hidden in the shadows. He waved his hand toward the woods. "I figure them niggers from Cromwell Plantation are hiding there in the woods right now, letting you do their work for them. They're going to be sorry when they get back to their precious plantation!"

****

Robert strained his ears to hear through the dense forest separating the plantation from the school, but he could hear nothing. He supposed he should be glad because the sound of gunfire would have filtered through, but every part of him was still tense.

"Something is coming," Mark said quietly.

Robert nodded. "I'm afraid you're right, but there is nothing we can do until something actually happens."

"That was what I most hated about battle. There were too many long nights when all you could do was wait for the next day, wondering if you would live through it."

Robert remained silent, although he agreed. Taking action was always preferable to waiting, but there was no action to take right now. All he could do was peer into the darkness and speculate about what might be waiting out there. He cast a look at the house, glad all the women and children were safe inside, close to the tunnel that would take them to the river if the need arose. As he had many times, he gave silent thanks to the Cromwell ancestor who had built it.

"I would feel a lot better if Moses and his men returned," Mark said.

"You and me both," Miles agreed. "I done me a little shooting, but I ain't sure how much I will help you two."

"I've been practicing," Clint said grimly.

"So have I," Gabe added. "The stories coming down from around Tennessee should make any black man keep his gun oiled up and ready."

Robert nodded, trying not to think about the danger Matthew had warned him waited for white men who were deemed to be disloyal to the Southern cause. His friend's letter that had arrived earlier that day had been fairly blunt about the agenda of the Ku Klux Klan and other vigilante groups. For a moment, he almost wished the country was back at war. At least he had known what enemy he was fighting. He glanced toward the barn, wishing they had turned all the horses out. If there were attempts to burn the plantation, he didn't want any of the animals to be trapped.

"We need to let the horses out," he announced.

Clint sprang forward to join him when he headed toward the barn, but they had not gone more than a dozen feet before a band of men burst forth from the woods.

As the men on horseback raced toward the house, Robert saw them expertly light the fire sticks they had tied to their saddles. The long pine sticks, wrapped in kerosene-soaked cloth, caught quickly, turning into flaming torches that split the night with their brightness. "Get them!" he yelled, pulling his rifle up to his shoulder and taking aim.

When he heard the men yell in surprise, he understood they thought everyone from the plantation had raced to the schoolhouse to thwart the attack there. Robert felt a surge of triumph when he realized they had the element of surprise. The vigilantes would have no idea what kind of force they were facing. "Fire, men! Fire!" He would make them believe they faced a much stronger force than was actually there. Right now the odds were fifteen to five, but the dark shrouded the truth. If they attacked quickly, they might drive the vigilantes off before any harm could be done.

Mark gave a yell of triumph as one of his shots propelled a man forward in his saddle. The fire stick tumbled to the ground, illuminating the man's surprised face as he pulled his horse to a stop and gasped for breath. The jolt had made his face covering slip down.

Robert felt sick when he realized it was a man who had come by the plantation two weeks earlier under the guise of examining his new crop of foals. Had he merely been planning this attack? His fury surged even higher as he took aim and shot again, yelling loudly to create chaos that would make their numbers seem higher. "I got another one," he hollered. It wasn't true, but he knew his yells would add to the confusion. It was a tactic the Rebel soldiers had used successfully through a war fought against superior numbers. He knew he was fighting fellow Rebels, but the tactic would still be effective.

He spotted Gabe and Clint hastily reloading their guns as they prepared to renew the attack. He grabbed another pistol and continued to fire. Mark was doing the same thing, but Miles seemed to be struggling with a jammed rifle.

Robert saw the band of men veer away from the house. He was surprised, until he heard the sound of gunshots coming from inside. Flashes of muzzle fire appeared in three different windows. He managed a grin of relief when he realized Rose, Susan and Polly were not going down without a fight. He was sure they had put Annie and the children into the tunnel when the men had attacked, and then returned to join the battle.

Encouraged, he raced toward the house, shooting as he ran. It almost didn't matter if they hit anyone right now. The show of force would most likely scare the vigilantes away. Men who attacked in the night with covered faces were nothing more than cowardly bullies. A strong show of force would send them running.

"Robert!"

Robert ground to a stop, trying to figure out where Mark's voice was coming from. When he swiveled his head, he realized five of the men had broken off from the group attacking the house and were now headed directly toward the barn with their fire sticks raised high. "No!" he hollered, turning to race back toward the barn. The women would keep the group away from the house. Now, he had to save the horses.

Chaos reigned around him as gunfire filled the air, a terrifying glow rising from the burning sticks as the men bore down on the barn. Robert fired and breathed a sigh of relief when he saw Clint and Gabe raise their rifles to their shoulders, take careful aim, and fire. Two of the men lurched forward in their saddles, dropping their fire sticks, but the other three were not to be deterred. It was obvious they were determined to inflict destruction, even if it wasn't all they had hoped to do that night.

Robert ran even harder, determined to reach the barn before the men did. Even if they set fire to it, he was going to find a way to release all the horses. He would have to trust Mark and the rest to provide cover for him. The yearlings were in the pasture, whinnying their terror, and the mares and foals were safe in the back pasture, but there were horses still in the barn. Granite. Eclipse. Chelsea. All My Heart. Pegasus. He couldn't let anything happen to them. He felt like his heart would explode from his chest, but he refused to slow down.

When he was less than one hundred feet from the barn, he saw something that almost made his knees buckle. Amber, sleepily rubbing her eyes, appeared at the door of the barn. Robert faltered, his brain racing. How had the little girl gotten away from the house? He answered his own question as quickly as it had come to his mind. He was quite sure she had entered the house with everyone else, and then found a way to sneak out under cover of darkness, determined to be with her beloved filly if there was going to be danger. He could imagine the panic in the house when they realized she was missing, but it couldn't compare to the panic he was feeling right that moment.

"Amber!" Robert pushed his legs even harder. "Get back in the barn!"

Amber, terrified by the chaos swirling around her, seemed paralyzed. She stared at him uncertainly and then turned to look at the men racing toward the barn on horseback. Her eyes filled with terror that tore at Robert's heart.

"I got me an open shot at the nigger girl!"

Robert heard the yell just as he reached the barn. He flung himself forward, grabbing Amber in his arms, and threw her to the ground, landing on her heavily.

He barely even felt the shot that pierced his back.

Chapter Eighteen

Carrie leaned forward eagerly when the train neared the Richmond Broad Street station. She had loved every minute of her time in Philadelphia, especially the time with her father and Abby, but her mind was already back on the plantation. She had missed Robert greatly and could hardly wait to hear how excited Mark and Susan were about the yearlings they were there to pick up. If she had harbored any doubts about her decision to remain on the plantation, they were put to rest by her elation to be home. She had picked up valuable information from Janie and the other students, which would help her tremendously with a few of her patients. She held herself back from bouncing on the upholstered leather seat in anticipation, but she made no attempt to hide the grin on her face as she leaned forward to admire the hills of the city as they came into view.

"It doesn't seem possible that we've been gone over a week," Abby said.

"It's the longest I've been away from the factory," Thomas responded.

"Only the one here in Richmond," Carrie observed, forcing her thoughts back to the train. "I do believe you and Abby own that factory we just left."

"That's true," Thomas conceded. "I suppose I'm realizing this is the longest time I've been out of Richmond since the war began. I know I was in Danville for a while, but somehow that doesn't count."

Carrie sobered at that thought. Her father had always loved to travel whenever he had the chance. He and her mother had taken many trips north when she was growing up, but then the secession fever had started, and her father had become afraid to leave the plantation because of what might happen with the slaves. The war had followed quickly. Her father had fled to Danville when Richmond fell with the rest of the Confederate government, but she knew every minute had been spent wondering if he would be arrested for war crimes. For the first time, she had a deeper understanding of how the years that had so transformed her, had also changed her father.

"Was it hard to leave Philadelphia?" Abby asked.

Carrie considered the question. She knew Abby had been wanting to ask it ever since the train had pulled out of the Pennsylvania station. Finally, she shook her head. "Oh, there is certainly still a part of me that wishes I could do everything all at one time, but the idea of being home with Robert and enjoying the plantation while we wait for our child to appear in the next few months makes the allure of Philadelphia completely disappear."

"I'm glad to hear it," Abby murmured.

"The foals that were born this spring are truly special," Carrie continued. "I can't really ride much anymore until the baby is born, but I can certainly help with the foals' early training. Amber has agreed to let me help her," she added wryly.

"That little girl is amazing," Thomas said. "She treats every one of those foals like they are her own."

"As far as she is concerned, they are," Carrie confirmed. "She loves them all, but more importantly, she wants Robert to have the very best horse operation in the world. The two of them are so close it constantly amazes me. I can hardly wait to see my husband with children of his own. Amber has completely taught him how to be a father," she added with a grin. She looked up and caught an odd expression on her father's face. "What is it?"

Thomas looked at her fondly. "I'm just glad to know you feel this way. I supported your decision to stay on the plantation, but I've been concerned you would regret not continuing your education. One thing after another has kept you from achieving your dream of being a doctor. Staying here in Virginia and becoming a mother only delays it more."

"Yes," Carrie agreed calmly. "I had some times down by the river when I was struggling with that reality, but I wouldn't have missed this time for anything. It's not only that I'm about to become a mother, it's more about the time I've had to spend with my husband. We've really had so little time together. The war...Robert's trip to Europe...and then his long illness." She paused for a moment. "I finally feel married," she admitted. "In so many ways, I didn't know what that meant. I certainly loved my husband, but I didn't really know what it meant to be married." She smiled brilliantly. "I do now."

"From the look on your face, you highly recommend it," Abby replied.

"Oh, yes, I highly recommend it." Carrie agreed. She looked out the window as the screech of wheels against the metal tracks said they had arrived in Richmond. "If I thought it wouldn't be too much of a strain, I would leave for the plantation today."

"You'll survive until tomorrow," Thomas said hastily.

Carrie laughed. "Don't worry, Father. I've grown up enough not to be totally foolish. My baby and I will wait until tomorrow, and then let Spencer take us home."

****

Thomas was laughing at something Abby had said when Carrie saw Mark Jones straining his head above the crowd. Her first thought was joy to see him again, but she quickly realized he was in the wrong place. He and Susan should already be on the plantation. She pushed down the flash of panic that seized her, telling herself there were a dozen reasons he could be at the station. Perhaps he and Susan had been delayed, or Jeremy had sent him to the station because there was trouble at the factory... The sick feeling tightening her gut told her it was something completely different.

"Carrie?" Abby's voice broke through her thoughts. "What is it?"

Carrie pointed above the crowd. "Mark Jones is here."

Thomas turned his head quickly. "Where?"

Mark pushed through the crowd just then. The look on his face when he caught Carrie's eyes almost made her knees buckle. She felt Abby's hand grip her elbow, but she managed to hold herself erect. "What's wrong?" she asked.

Mark stepped up close to her and grasped both her hands. "There has been an accident," he said.

"Robert?"

Mark nodded soberly.

"Is he dead?" Carrie forced the question out through almost frozen lips. The look in Mark's eyes said something terrible had happened.

"No," Mark said quickly.

Carrie read the truth in his eyes. He didn't really know if Robert was alive or not. "How bad is it?"

Mark avoided her question by turning to Abby and Thomas. "I have a wagon waiting to take all of you to the plantation."

"Jeremy knows?" Thomas asked. He seemed to know that now was not the time to press for more information.

"He knows," Mark confirmed. "He will be joining us. Marcus will handle things at the factory."

That statement, more than anything else, told Carrie how bad it must be. Why else would Jeremy be leaving the city? It made sense for her father and Abby to come if there had been an accident, but if Jeremy was coming... This time when her knees buckled, it was only her father and Abby holding her elbows that kept her from collapsing. "Tell me what happened," she snapped, her panic morphing into anger, before sliding back into abject fear.

Mark turned to her again. "Robert was shot."

Carrie felt sick. "How?"

"Vigilantes attacked the plantation," he explained. "I'll tell you more on the way, Carrie, but we need to go."

Carrie was completely oblivious of being led through the throng of arriving passengers. The noises were drowned out by the roaring in her head. When they reached the road, she saw that Granite was tied to the wagon. Mark must have ridden him into town. She could hardly stand to see the sympathy radiating from Spencer's eyes as he stepped down to take their luggage.

Carrie grabbed Mark's arm. "Is my husband dying?"

Mark took a deep breath. "I don't know," he admitted. "Dr. Wild is on his way out to the plantation." He looked quickly at his pocket watch. "He is probably there by now."

Carrie's head spun. "Dr. Wild?"

Mark nodded. "I saw him at the station when Susan and I arrived two days ago. He was here in town for a meeting. Thankfully, he told me where he was staying. I rode in last night after Robert was shot. He left as soon as I found him this morning."

Carrie tried to absorb what she was hearing. "So he might live?" she demanded. When Mark hesitated, she turned away from what she didn't want to see in his eyes. Her mind filled with images of surgeries she and Dr. Wild had performed during the war. There were many times when it had taken both of them to save badly damaged soldiers. She thought of how badly Moses had been wounded. Together, they had saved him. "I'm riding Granite home," she announced.

"Carrie!"

Carrie ignored her father's response. "I have to get to my husband," she said frantically. "Dr. Wild and I might be able to save him together."

"You can't ride to the plantation," Thomas replied, fighting to keep his voice even. "You are too pregnant."

Carrie shook her head, certain of only one thing. "I have to get to Robert," she repeated. "He needs me." She shook her arm free of her father's hand. "I can get home two hours sooner if I ride Granite," she said stubbornly.

"And if you can't make it?" Abby asked quietly. "What then?"

Carrie had a vision of the hard ride causing her to go into labor, but she pushed it aside. All she could think about was Robert lying in a bed with a bullet in his body. She whirled to stare at Mark. "Is he waiting for me to get home?" Mark's face couldn't hide the reality of the situation. Carrie grabbed his hand and squeezed it tightly. "Thank you for not lying to me," she choked.

Ignoring the expression on Thomas and Abby's faces, she untied Granite, accepted the hand up from Mark, and started down the road. She couldn't race through the streets of Richmond, but as soon as she was on the outskirts of town she would make far better time than the wagon. She fought to breathe evenly, knowing that her fear would make it even harder on her baby. Now that she had decided on a course of action, she felt calmer. She and Robert had lived through one trauma after another since they had met. He had almost died twice during the war, but he had been saved both times. Her mind filled with the memories. This time would be no different. He was strong, and they were about to have a baby.

She shook off the memory of the stark sorrow in Mark's eyes as she left Richmond behind and moved Granite into a smooth canter.

****

Carrie was exhausted when she rode up to the house, but she had made it.

"Carrie!" Rose rushed onto the porch, her face a mixture of sorrow and concern. "You rode here?"

Carrie chose to ignore her question since the answer was rather obvious. "Robert?" she asked.

Rose hesitated as if she was searching for the right words. "He's in your room." Her voice was laced with a deep sadness.

Carrie pushed aside what she saw in her best friend's face. None of them had seen the wounded soldiers she and Dr. Wild had saved. She ignored the others filing onto the porch and ran up the stairs, also ignoring the sudden cramps that gripped her stomach. Robert was waiting for her.

She stopped at the door to the room, suddenly afraid to walk inside. She could feel the darkness that belied the warm sunshine streaming in the window. Her vision blurred as she caught sight of Robert's pasty face outlined on the pillow. *Was he...?*

"I'm glad you're here." Dr. Wild's voice broke through her fog.

"Is he...?" She couldn't bring herself to finish the question, and she also couldn't make herself move forward. She seemed paralyzed in place. Even without stepping into the room, her mind was telling her the truth she refused to believe. She could feel the darkness pushing aside the light.

"He's still alive," Dr. Wild said, taking her arm to help her walk forward.

Still. Carrie's heart almost failed her as she heard the word. Suddenly her spirit rose up in defiance. "What do you mean *still* alive?" she asked fiercely. "We are going to save him just like we did Moses and so many others."

A sheen of tears appeared in Dr. Wild's eyes. "I'm sorry, Carrie."

"No!" Carrie almost shouted as she gasped for the breath that seemed to allude her. "You thought we couldn't save Moses either. We will save him." Dr. Wild stepped aside, allowing her to draw close to the bed. One look and Carrie knew the truth. She had seen too many soldiers on the brink of death not to recognize what she was seeing.

She would find out what had happened later. All that mattered now was being there for her husband.

"Robert," she said softly as she laid her hand on his cold cheek. "I'm here, Robert."

Her husband took a quivering breath as he forced his eyes open. "Carrie," he croaked in a whisper.

"Yes, my love. I'm here." She moved her hand and began to run it through his wavy, dark hair. "I love you," she said tenderly.

"Love you," Robert mouthed, his eyes filled with a regret that shattered her heart.

Carrie knew what he needed. She pulled the covers back and slid into the bed, pressing her body close as Robert's breath came in shallow gasps. "You're not alone," she crooned. "You're not alone." She could barely speak around the pressure of her heart breaking into pieces.

Robert lay quietly for a long moment, and then his eyes opened with a look of urgency. "Tell our baby... I love her." His voice strengthened. "Make sure she knows I loved her...even before she was born."

Carrie barely registered his belief that their baby was a girl. All that mattered was easing his last few moments. "I promise," she said, fighting to keep her voice from cracking. "I promise, Robert. Our baby will know you loved her completely. Just like I do." Her voice dissolved into tears as Robert's eyes caressed her face.

"Tell Amber...I would do it again. I want her to have a great life." His eyes burned with fever and intensity. "You tell her I loved her just like she was my own." His eyes closed, and his breath became even more ragged.

Carrie thought he was gone, but he forced his eyes open one more time.

"I love you, Carrie," he whispered, his voice growing fainter even as it steadied. "You are the single best thing in my life. I'm sorry I'm leaving you. I'll always be watching you." His voice faded as his eyes closed, but he forced them open again. "Always love you..."

Carrie was sobbing even before he drew his final breath, and then lay still in her arms, his face filled with peace. "Robert..." Her broken heart shattered into a million pieces as she felt his vibrant spirit depart. "No... Robert." She cradled his face in her hands and pressed her warm lips to his cold ones, wildly wishing she could breathe her own life into him. A deep groan of agony ripped through her.

She was completely unaware of Rose entering the room as she stayed snuggled into her husband's body. Carrie felt all the life depart as his skin grew colder under her touch.

Finally she became aware of Rose sitting next to the bed. Carrie turned to stare at her, unable to process anything of what was happening. Taking the next breath seemed all she was capable of doing. "Rose." She stared up at her best friend as a sudden vicious spasm shot through her body. "Oh..." She fought for the next breath and then doubled over as another spasm gripped her. She couldn't hold back the scream as pain ripped through her.

"Carrie!" Rose jumped up from the chair and grabbed her hand.

Carrie, caught somewhere in the thick blackness of grief and pain, barely heard Dr. Wild's voice.

"She's in labor."

The thick blackness swallowed her as another explosion tore through her abdomen.

✦✦✦✦✦✦✦ A

Moses could do nothing but pace and pray as he waited on the porch for someone to come down and give him an update. The grief over Robert's death, relayed briefly by Rose before she grabbed Polly and raced back upstairs, would have been enough to immobilize him. Knowing Carrie was in labor two months early and was fighting for her life was more than he could comprehend. He watched blindly as John raced around the front yard, oblivious to the life and death battle being played out behind the window staring down upon him. When he heard the sound of a wagon approaching, he prayed for a way to break the news.

Annie appeared on the porch beside him. She laid a weathered hand on his arm. "Just tell them the truth, son. There ain't no easy way to do this, and there ain't no way to make it easier for them to hear it."

Moses took a deep breath. He looked over at the barn and spotted Clint and Susan taking feed and water to the horses. Amber had not returned to the stables since Gabe and Clint had taken her home the night before, a tiny huddled form tucked between them on the wagon seat. Polly had stayed behind to help care for Robert, and Mark had ridden off as soon as they had Robert in the house. Carrie's arrival was the evidence he had not been killed by vigilantes as he went for help.

Spencer pulled up to the house, his grim eyes locked on Moses' face, but he remained silent.

Thomas and Abby didn't move either. Their eyes said they were already aware the news was bad. They obviously were scared to receive confirmation.

It was Jeremy who finally stepped out of the wagon, holding Marietta's hand. "Tell us," he commanded quietly.

"Robert is gone," Moses managed to say around the lump in his throat. "Dr. Wild couldn't save him."

Abby gasped.

Thomas muttered a curse, climbed out of the wagon, and snapped, "What happened?"

Moses met his eyes but ignored his question for the moment. "Carrie got here before he died, but..." His voice broke off as the pain pressed down harder, making it impossible for him to form the words.

"But what?" Thomas asked, his voice harsh and composed as his eyes blazed with fear. "Tell me."

Moses took another deep breath. "She went into labor right after Robert died, Thomas."

Thomas' eyes took on a wild gleam. "And...?" he whispered.

Abby appeared at his side. "Moses, is Carrie...?" She couldn't finish her sentence.

"She's not dead," Moses said, praying he was right. There had been no report for the last two hours, just Polly and Rose running up and down the stairs with a frantic look in their eyes. "But, it's real bad." He knew he couldn't hold the truth from them. "Dr. Wild is with her. So are Polly and Rose."

Abby threw open the front door. Moses could hear her running up the stairs moments later.

Thomas stared after her blindly, his face a mask of confusion and pain. "Again?" he murmured faintly. "It's happening again?"

Moses didn't want to give him false hope, but he also didn't want him to believe something they didn't know was true. "We don't know what is happening, Thomas," he said gently.

Thomas turned burning eyes to him. "Carrie's child isn't due for months," he said bitterly. "There is no way the child will survive." He gritted his teeth and slammed his fist into the railing. "Robert. My grandchild. I can't lose Carrie, too."

Moses wanted to assure him that wouldn't happen, but the continued silence from upstairs said they were fighting to keep her alive. The best he could do was reach out and grip his brother-in-law's shoulder so that he would not feel so alone.

Thomas turned to stare out over the fields, but Moses was quite sure he wasn't seeing anything. He finally swung around to look at him. "Tell me what happened. I know part of it from Mark, but I will admit I didn't hear a lot of what he had to say because I was too worried."

"The vigilantes paid us a visit last night," Moses began. He told him about the attack on the schoolhouse, and about the revelation that the plantation was also under attack. Mark didn't know any of that because he had left so soon after. He didn't communicate the raw terror and rage he had felt as he had ridden through the black woods. "We raced back here, but we arrived too late," he said, anger shaking his voice as he relived the moment. "When I broke out of the woods, I heard the gunshot. I heard Amber scream, and I saw Robert go down on top of her. I thought they had shot Amber, but Robert..." His voice trembled with the memory. "Robert saved her life. He took the bullet meant for her."

"What was Amber doing in the barn?" Thomas demanded. "Why...?"

Mark appeared on the porch. "Amber was concerned about All My Heart, Thomas. She snuck out of the house and made her way to the barn. We didn't see her because we were all looking for someone to come toward the house, not *out* of it. Robert saved her life. When he heard one of the men yell that they had a good shot at her, he dove forward and took her to the ground. The bullet entered his back."

"And pierced his lungs and heart," Thomas said hollowly.

"Yes," Moses said hoarsely, remembering all the blood flowing from Robert's limp body when he picked him up. "He lost too much blood."

"Dr. Wild?" Thomas asked.

"He tried to save him, but it was too late," Moses said as grief constricted his throat. He couldn't believe the man who had become like a brother to him had died in his front yard, taken down by a fellow veteran after surviving four years of war. "Surgery wouldn't have done any good, but he gave him morphine to deal with the pain, and he kept talking to him while we waited for Carrie." His eyes glazed with hot tears. "He wouldn't let go until Carrie arrived."

"He had to tell her good-bye," Thomas whispered. "Did he?"

Moses was glad he at least knew that much. "Yes," he said. "He told her good-bye."

"And then he died," Thomas said in a flat, disbelieving voice. "Robert is dead," he said numbly. "He survived the war, and now he's dead?" His voice vibrated with rage as he whipped around to stare at Moses. "Who did this?" he snapped. "Who killed Robert? Who is responsible for the death of my grandchild, and for..." His voice trailed off before he finished his thought, but then it hardened again. "Who did this?"

"The man who shot him disappeared in the chaos," Moses answered. "All of them did. We shot some of them, but somehow they stayed on their horses. We let them go because we were focused on saving Robert."

Thomas nodded. "Of course, but..." His voice was thick with frustration.

"But I know who was at the school," Moses added. "The lead vigilante was Granger. Another man with him was named Chad."

Thomas whirled around to stare at him. "Granger Southerlin?" he ground out. "Granger Southerlin from a few miles west of here?"

Moses shrugged. "Alvin can tell you who they are. He recognized their voices."

Thomas turned back around to stare into the afternoon brightness. "They will pay for this," he said grimly. "They will not get away with this. Not this time."

Moses prayed he was right. Retribution would not bring Robert back, nor the grandchild that most surely had not survived, but at least there was a target for their rage. It would have to do for now. At least it gave Thomas something else to focus on.

****

Abby didn't bother to knock at the door, but pushed her way in. Rose's face filled with relief when she saw her, but Dr. Wild didn't even notice her entry. Polly was stationed at Carrie's side, her eyes locked on Dr. Wild as she waited for instructions. Pails of hot water had been brought up, and there was a mound of clean cloths next to the bed.

Carrie's face was white and still as she lay beside her dead husband. Two hours into labor, and the baby had still not been born. "Has she been conscious at all?" Abby whispered, sickened by the sight of Robert's slack body, but knowing that for now she had to focus on her daughter.

Rose shook her head. "She was with Robert when he died," she whispered, "and then she went into labor almost immediately. The pain made her pass out quickly. She hasn't woken up since."

Abby swayed slightly before she set her lips. They must move Robert before Carrie woke up and found herself in bed with her husband's corpse. She shot a quick look at Dr. Wild, relieved to find his eyes on her. "I want to have Moses come up and take Robert to another room."

"That will be best," Dr. Wild agreed. He held up his hand when he saw the rest of the questions in her eyes. "I don't have anything else to tell you right now. Carrie is alive, but we're going to have to get the baby out quickly."

"You're going to operate?" Abby asked.

"Yes," Dr. Wild said. "I need the entire bed, and I need a sterile environment." His eyes narrowed. "Quickly." He turned away, but then whipped back around. "Only Moses and Mark can come in here. I don't want Carrie's father to see her like this."

Abby could not have agreed more. She flew back down the stairs, returning moments later with Moses and Mark. The room remained silent as the two men picked up Robert carefully and carried him from the room, taking him to the bed next door.

****

Thomas, barely able to breathe, grabbed Moses' arm as soon as he stepped back out onto the porch. "What is going on up there?"

"We moved Robert's body," Moses said, knowing the feeling of his dead friend's body in his arms would remain with him for the rest of his life. He took a deep breath. "They are getting ready to perform surgery on Carrie right now."

Thomas stared at him blankly. "Surgery?"

Moses reported the little Dr. Wild had told him. "He is going to perform a Cesarean Section on Carrie. He has recently learned how to do the procedure." He tried to infuse confidence in his voice, but he was quite sure he had failed. The sight of Carrie's face had almost brought him to his knees.

"They're going to cut Carrie's baby out of her?" Thomas had read something recently in a medical journal left behind in an office he had visited. "Can it possibly live?" His voice grew harsher. "Will Carrie live?"

"I don't know," Moses answered honestly. Obviously, Thomas knew more than he did about the procedure Dr. Wild was about to execute. He gave him the only hope he could offer. "Dr. Wild seemed confident he could help."

"And that's all you can tell me?"

"I'm sorry, Thomas," Moses said faintly.

Annie appeared beside him and took control as she grasped Thomas' arm. "You come sit down right over here, Mr. Thomas. Standin' up here ain't gonna make nothin' happen any sooner. Whatever is happenin' up there is gonna happen for a while."

Thomas said nothing but allowed her to settle him into a rocking chair.

"Now you drink some of this hot tea and eat one of these biscuits," she commanded. "I already know you feel like you can't eat nothin', but Carrie is gonna need you when she wakes up. It won't do at all for you to be weak and sick." She plunked a loaded tray down on the table beside the chair. "You eat every bite of this or I'm gonna shove it down your throat myself," she threatened as she blinked back tears.

Thomas stared at her wordlessly for a long moment before he reached for the tea. Annie watched him take several swallows before she turned and stepped back into the house, her face a mask of raw pain.

****

Abby watched as Dr. Wild unstrapped his black medical bag and began to lay out surgical instruments. She had a thousand questions swarming through her mind, but she didn't want to disturb his concentration. Carrie's breathing was becoming more labored, and other than occasional spasms, she had not moved.

"I know all of you are scared," Dr. Wild said calmly.

Now that he had made the decision to perform surgery, his tension seemed to have disappeared. Abby took comfort from the look of steady confidence gleaming in his eyes.

Dr. Wild grabbed a sheet of paper and began to write rapidly. When he was finished, he thrust the paper at Polly. "Have someone ride to the clinic and bring me back these treatments."

Polly scanned the list. "We got all this right here," she revealed. "Miss Carrie said we had to be as ready here at home as we are at the clinic."

"Wonderful!" Dr. Wild responded.

"I'll be right back," Polly announced. "And I'll have more hot water brought up."

Dr. Wild managed an almost natural smile and then turned to Rose. "This is going to be hard for you because the two of you are so close."

"Don't you worry about that," Rose snapped, her face tense with worry as her eyes bored into his. "I'll do whatever needs to be done."

"As will I," Abby added. "You just have to tell us what you need."

Dr. Wild eyed them both for a moment and then nodded. "I'm going to explain what I'm doing as I do it," he said conversationally. "It used to be the only way to deliver a baby from someone in Carrie's condition was a craniotomy."

"It sounds barbaric," Abby replied, her eyes fastened on Carrie's face.

"It is," Dr. Wild agreed, "but it was often the only way to keep the mother and baby alive." His hands moved smoothly as he made preparations. "Carrie was born this way. She was removed from her mother by forceps, but she was an on-time delivery, so she survived."

"Her mother almost died," Abby whispered.

"Yes. The procedure can often cause internal tearing. From what Thomas told me, Carrie's mother almost bled to death from the hemorrhage. They were lucky to save her."

Abby understood now why the memories of Carrie's birth had so traumatized her husband. "And now? With Carrie's baby coming so early?"

Dr. Wild hesitated. "A craniotomy would certainly kill the child. With a baby this young, it would require removal of the baby from the vagina a little at a time." He didn't elaborate, but the grimness in his eyes told the rest of the story.

Abby absorbed that, her insides threatening to rebel as she envisioned Carrie's baby being torn apart in the womb piece by piece. She couldn't stop the shudder that wracked her body. "And you're not going to do that?" Her question came out in a squeak.

"No. I'm going to perform a Cesarean section. The procedure has progressed greatly in the last decade," Dr. Wild said. "Once I make the incision, I will be able to remove Carrie's baby easily. It used to be quite a dangerous operation, but many women survive it now."

Abby sucked in her breath, knowing by his statement that there were a number of women who did *not*. She refused to allow herself to focus on that possibility.

"It's really becoming much more common now," Dr. Wild continued. "The first recorded successful cesarean was actually done in South Africa by a woman masquerading as a man serving as a physician to the British Army."

Abby tucked that morsel of knowledge into her mind so she could tell Carrie about it when she was awake again. *You are going to be fine, Carrie!* Her mind screamed it, even though she remained silent.

Dr. Wild looked up when Annie pushed into the room with fresh pots of hot water. Polly followed close behind her with a basket full of carefully labeled bottles. "Thank you," he said. He motioned to Polly. "Please put those right over there. We will use them to ensure there is no infection when I have finished sewing her up." He went back to explaining what he was doing, knowing the sound of his voice was helping everyone. "I have anesthesia with me. Carrie will not feel a thing." He pulled out a bottle of chloroform, wet a cloth, and handed it to Polly. "You know what to do with this?"

Polly nodded. "I help Miss Carrie all the time."

"Good. She is unconscious now, but we don't want her to wake up during the operation."

Abby pushed the image of that possibility from her mind as Dr. Wild stepped over to one of the buckets of hot water and began to carefully wash his hands and arms. He pulled out a loose fitting gown from his bag and pulled it over his clothes. She knew he was ensuring the operation would be as sterile as possible. Carrie had explained to her once that it had been only recently that physicians had come to understand the importance of a sterile environment for surgery. It relieved her to know Dr. Wild was making sure there was as little chance for infection as possible.

Dr. Wild turned to Abby. "When I have delivered the baby, I am going to pass her off to you and Rose. If she is alive, I want the two of you to clean her up and cut the umbilical cord. Can you do that?"

"I can," Rose assured him. "I helped my mama many times when Carrie or her mother weren't around for a birth down in the quarters."

"Good." Dr. Wild stepped closer to the bed, his face and eyes intense with concentration. "I'm ready."

Chapter Nineteen

A thick silence fell on the room as Dr. Wild picked up his scalpel. He lowered the covers, pulled away the gown Rose had put on Carrie after her collapse, and set his lips. He closed his eyes for a brief moment, obviously praying, and then opened them again. "It's time for this baby to be born," he murmured. He looked up long enough to meet Abby's eyes, an expression of sorrow telling her the truth.

There was little chance it would be a live birth. Whatever had happened in Carrie's womb had almost certainly killed her baby. Abby held her breath as she kept her gaze locked on Carrie's face. She longed to hold her daughter close in her arms, but all she could do was watch, and pray that Dr. Wild could save her life. Was it really only hours earlier that Carrie had been laughing and chatting on the way home on the train? How could life change so drastically in such a short period of time? Abby knew the answer of course—all their lives had been shattered time after time in the last six years.

She forced herself to push away the reality of Robert's death, and just how Carrie was going to respond when she gained consciousness. Right now all she could do was pray she would live. Somewhere in the corner of her mind, she was also aware that if Robert's murder had not brought Dr. Wild to the plantation, Carrie would most certainly be hovering at death's door right now, if not already dead. There was no one here at the plantation that could have handled a birth this complicated. The knowledge floated through her mind, but everything was still too raw to form gratitude for any of the nightmare unfolding before them.

It seemed like only seconds before Dr. Wild pulled a still, tiny form from Carrie, and thrust it at Rose. "Take care of her daughter," he said tightly before he turned back to his work.

Abby's heart sank. In spite of the message he had communicated before the surgery began, she had held on to hope that the baby would somehow survive. From the sound of his voice, she already knew what he hadn't said. She watched as Rose's face crumpled with renewed grief, and then she stepped forward to take the baby. "I would like to hold my granddaughter," she said softly, forcing her voice to remain composed. She stared down at the fully-formed little face with its rosebud lips, dark lashes, and a surprising amount of black hair. "Oh, little one," Abby whispered, her heart breaking anew.

Rose laid a hand on Abby's shoulder. "Carrie was going to name her Abigail Bridget," she said quietly. "Abigail, for both her mothers." Her voice caught. "And Bridget, which is a Celtic Irish name that means power and strength, as a tribute to Biddy, whose real name is Bridget. They were going to call her Bridget."

Abby let her tears fall on the baby, washing her with a grandmother's love. "Abigail Bridget," she murmured. "It's wonderful to meet you. I wish..." Her voice choked and trailed away as she thought of all the hopes and dreams they had all carried for this fragile bundle in her arms. "You are loved," she said tenderly as she accepted the soft blanket Rose handed to her. She wrapped it around the baby carefully and held her against her chest. She would clean her later, but if there was any part of the child that could feel her love, she wanted her to know how cherished she was.

Rose turned to help Polly hand items to Dr. Wild as he barked out orders.

Abby watched, her heart both numb and shattered, as Dr. Wild cleaned out the cavity left behind by the baby's birth, and then carefully sutured the incision. When he had sewn Carrie closed, he asked for the natural remedies that would sterilize the area to make sure there was no infection. When he was satisfied every part of the wound was clean and sterilized, he covered the incision with bandaging and secured it.

Abby continued to rock quietly while he finished the operation, softly stroking Bridget's fine hair and feathery soft skin. She wondered if the baby had Robert's blue eyes, or Carrie's green ones. Just that simple question made the silent tears turn into choking sobs. There was so much that none of them would ever know about the little girl that lay in her arms. The realization made her heart ache even more for Carrie. When she woke up, her entire world was going to have splintered into irreparable fragments. It was going to take all of the people who loved her to help her put it back together again.

Dr. Wild took a deep breath and stepped back from the bed. "The procedure went well," he said, his face lined with grief as he looked at the child in Abby's arms. "I wish we could have saved her baby, but she was already gone. It was probably..."

"Stop," Abby said firmly. "I don't want any of us to know, especially not Carrie, what might have killed Bridget." She knew every one of them would always wonder if Bridget would have lived if Carrie had not ridden home to be with Robert, but no one needed confirmation. "The reason is not important. All we can do now is help Carrie recover from losing both Robert and her daughter."

Dr. Wild nodded, his eyes filled with something like relief. "Robert was not alone when he died," he murmured. "It was the greatest gift Carrie could have given him at the end."

"I'm glad," Abby replied, surprised that she felt so calm. No one could change what had already happened. Somehow they would all deal with the grief and move forward. She had such vivid memories of the day her husband had died and the months of black grief that had almost destroyed her. She would help her daughter navigate the darkness. That was all that mattered now. "How long will Carrie be asleep?"

Dr. Wild frowned. "I don't know," he admitted. "The chloroform will keep her asleep for at least three hours, but when she wakes up is anyone's guess. She has undergone a tremendous shock, and now her body is going to have to fight off any possible infection."

Abby tried not to finish the rest of what he didn't say. *I hope she sleeps a long time because the world is going to be a terrible place when she wakes up.* "But she will wake up?" she pressed. It was the only thing Thomas was going to want to know.

"I believe she will, but only time will tell for certain. Carrie is strong and healthy. I don't believe there will be any infection from the surgery. She has experienced a tremendous shock, though," he said cautiously.

"Carrie will wake up," Rose snapped. "She just needs time."

Abby gazed at Rose's face, seeing the complete devastation. "Of course she will," she said soothingly.

She was sure Rose had not slept a wink for the last two days. As she glanced at the window, the orange glow told her the sun was setting. "Would you like to hold Bridget?" she offered softly.

Rose stiffened and stepped back. "I can't," she breathed, tears forming as she gazed at the still body. "I just can't..."

Then she turned and fled.

****

It was completely dark when Rose heard snapping branches on the path to the river. She had not moved since she had run all the way to the rock she and Carrie had welcomed each New Year since they had been children. Her tears had dried, but her heart still felt destroyed. The peace she had come in search of was nowhere to be found. She knew the identity of the approaching person long before he stepped out onto the river bank and held open his arms. Rose flew into them, her tears starting anew.

Moses let her cry. The rigidity of his body said he was fighting his own emotions. When she finally quieted, Moses led her back to the rock she had been sitting on for the last two hours.

"Carrie is still asleep," Moses said somberly.

Rose had expected that—it had been the only reason she had been willing to leave—but it released something in her to have it confirmed that Carrie was still alive. "I'm sorry I ran away."

"Don't be," Moses replied. "You needed to take some time by yourself." He lifted her chin as he peered into her eyes. "Did it help?"

"No," Rose answered. "I don't think this could hurt anymore if it were you and Hope who had both died in the same day. Even though Carrie hasn't woken up yet, I am already feeling what she will feel." She leaned back in her husband's arms. "I'm almost afraid for her to wake up," she admitted. "I have no idea what to say to her." Tears formed in her eyes again. "How can words ever mean anything?"

"They will mean something," Moses promised, "but mostly she is just going to need you to be with her." His words were full of certainty.

"And you know this how?" Rose asked. "Is it because of the men you lost in the war?"

"No, that was different. The only reason I know is because Abby told me."

Rose drew in a quick breath as she remembered. "Abby lost her husband."

Moses nodded. "Charles died of cholera ten years ago. Abby had no family there, but she had a good friend who simply let her be with her grief. She told me she doesn't remember a thing the friend said, but she does remember her being there, holding her hand, and letting her feel whatever she was feeling."

Rose listened closely, knowing she was receiving the secret of how to help Carrie through her grief. "How could this have happened?" she finally murmured.

Moses scowled. "Ignorant men with a vendetta murdered Robert."

"I don't even know what happened," she said as she realized it was the truth. "You disappeared, men attacked the plantation, I was shooting at them from our bedroom window, and then I saw Robert racing toward Amber. I remember hearing him yell, and then I saw him throw himself forward." Her voice trailed away as she shuddered. "I saw Amber crawl out from under him, but he didn't move again. And then suddenly you were standing in the house with Robert in your arms."

Moses held her tightly as he told her the whole story.

"The school is all right?" Rose asked vaguely, realizing she didn't really care. If they had gone ahead and burned the school, maybe Robert would still be alive, and Bridget would still be waiting to be born.

"It is," Moses said. "I know this is little comfort right now, but the reality that it was the white parents who saved the school should tell you how much your decision to educate their children impacted them."

Rose felt a surge of fury, followed closely by a crushing guilt. "And it also made us more of a target," she said bitterly. She gasped for air as the reality hit her. "If I hadn't opened the school to white children, the vigilantes would have stayed away." She swayed in Moses' arms. "Robert would still be alive."

"Nonsense," Moses said hoarsely. "Don't think I haven't felt everything you are feeling right now. If we hadn't moved into the main house... If I had said no to the white students... If I wasn't holding meetings in the school..." His voice choked. "Maybe Robert would still be alive." He clenched his fists. "But none of that is true," he said. "Robert is dead because so much hatred has been released into this country. He's dead because he cared enough to save a little black girl that he loved with every fiber of his being. He's dead because some ignorant white man thought it was okay to shoot a defenseless child standing in the door of a barn he was trying to burn down."

Rose shrank closer to his body as she envisioned the scene from the night before. "If you hadn't gotten here in time, they would have burned the barn," she muttered. "They didn't care that they had shot Robert.

They were still racing straight for the barn until you and everyone else burst out of the woods. You stopped them."

"Not in time," Moses said, pain dripping from every word. "If I had gotten here even a minute earlier, Robert would still be alive."

"You can't blame yourself," Rose cried.

"Any more than you can," Moses muttered, pulling her so close she thought his body might swallow hers.

Rose listened to the frogs and crickets filling the night air. Fireflies lined the foliage along the bank and danced through the oak tree hanging over the rock. The waves lapped against the pebbles lining the shore. All the things that had once given her peace were now nothing but a reminder of her best friend who was right now fighting for her life. "She can't die," she whimpered. "Carrie can't die."

She was grateful Moses didn't try to convince her of something he couldn't possibly know was true. He simply pulled her closer and held her.

Rose finally leaned back to stare up at him. "We're not going anywhere," she said quietly.

Moses gazed down at her. "No, we're not. Neither one of us will leave Carrie now. Besides the fact that we love her, I owe my life to her, and both of us owe our freedom to her." He managed a tight smile. "At least we know why I haven't found anyone else to run the plantation. *I'm* going to continue running it."

Rose shook her head. "You could still go on to college."

"Stop," Moses said, an edge of anger in his words. "I will never leave until I know Carrie is alright and rebuilding her life. I don't know how long that will be, but it doesn't matter. We are simply here. And we will be together. That's all that matters."

His simple statement filled Rose with the stark truth that it could just as easily have been Moses who had been killed by the vigilante's bullet. Another thought broke through the fog. "Thomas?"

Moses sighed heavily. "About as you would expect," he replied. "He is devastated but hanging on to the hope that Carrie will live. Everyone is together on the porch, trying to make sense out of all this. I don't think any of us can focus on our grief over Robert and Bridget because we're too afraid Carrie will die."

"There is no making sense of this," Rose cried, a fresh rush of pain threatening to crush her. "Bridget was so beautiful, Moses. She looked like a perfect combination of Carrie and Robert. Even over two months early, she still looked perfect." Her voice crumpled. "Perfect...but so tiny." Another thought crowded through her pain. "If Carrie had been here...when Robert was shot"—she gazed up at her husband—"could she have saved him?"

"I'm sure Carrie will want to know that, too," Moses said. "Dr. Wild says there is no way anyone could have saved him. The bullet went through his back at an angle that collapsed both his lungs and nicked his heart—the reason there was so much blood. No one could have saved him. The fact that he stayed alive long enough for Carrie to get here was a miracle."

"He loved her so much," Rose managed to say. "He couldn't leave until he told her good-bye, and until she promised she would tell their baby how much he loved her." A fresh stab of pain speared her as she spoke the words. "She never got to do that."

Both of them retreated into silence again. Rose finally stood. "We should go back. I want to be sure I am there when Carrie wakes up."

"You need some sleep," Moses protested. "You won't be any good to her unless you get some rest."

"I'll sleep in the chair next to her," Rose replied. "I am going to be there when she wakes up."

Moses nodded. "Abby said you would say that. She pulled up two chairs next to the bed so that you would have one."

****

Rose felt terrible the next morning, but she knew Carrie felt far worse. She thought she had slept a little in the uncomfortable wingback chair, but she wasn't really certain. There had been no movement at all from the bed.

"Go get some breakfast and fresh air," Abby urged her.

"You need some, too," Rose protested as she bit back a yawn and stretched her cramped limbs.

"You're right," Abby agreed. "Annie will bring me some food. When you come back, I will take my turn."

Rose nodded hesitantly. She knew Abby was right, but she hated the idea of Carrie regaining consciousness without her there.

Abby read her thoughts. "I promise I will have someone come find you if Carrie wakes up."

Rose planted a warm kiss on Abby's cheek and left the room. The house was unnaturally quiet. She was puzzled until she realized the sun had not yet topped the horizon. Everyone must be asleep. She knew they all had stayed up very late the night before, hoping against hope that Carrie would wake up. They had finally all given up and gone to bed.

Rose was suddenly hungry for air that didn't smell like death and herbal ointments. She pushed through the front door, stopping on the porch to breathe in the fresh morning air full of lilacs and honeysuckle. Part of her felt guilty for even noticing the sweet aroma; part of her was grateful for the reminder that there was still beauty in the world. She glanced up at the room where Carrie lay fighting for her life, and then strode out into the dawn. She had heard Moses leave a little earlier, heading out into the fields to give his men an update and get them started on a new day's work. In spite of all that had happened, the tobacco was not going to quit growing, and work still needed to be done.

Rose pushed aside the image of Robert's dead body. Moses' final act last night had been to carry his friend's corpse out to the wooden casket that Miles and Clint had built. They were hoping to wait until Carrie woke up before they had the funeral, but she didn't know if it was possible. She glanced back up at the window. "Wake up, Carrie..." she whispered. "Wake up"

As she walked toward the barn, unsure why she was heading toward the spot Robert had died, she heard the muffled sound of sobbing. She stopped, listened carefully, and then walked behind the structure. She found the source of the crying beneath the towering oak tree that shaded the southern corner of the barn during the long summer months. Rose rushed forward and sank down onto her knees. "Amber," she said gently as she pulled the grief-stricken child into her arms.

Amber cried even harder when she felt Rose's arms, sinking deep into her body. Rose held her tightly, remaining silent as she let her cry it out. Polly had told her the little girl had cried all the way home after Robert had been shot, but that she had been stoically silent since she had found out he died. Now, huddled against the tree, Amber was releasing her pain and grief.

"Robert!" Amber wailed, her little body clenching in a spasm as agony poured through her.

Rose stroked her hair but remained silent. There were no words that could ease this kind of pain. After what seemed like an eternity, Amber finally fell quiet, but her little body was still tight and tense.

"I'm real sorry I killed Robert," she whispered.

Rose leaned back so she could tilt Amber's face to meet hers. "You didn't kill Robert, honey," she said.

Amber shook her head, her eyes full of a devastated knowing. "If I hadn't snuck out to the barn to be with All My Heart, he wouldn't have had to save me," she whimpered. "I'm the reason Robert is dead." Her face twisted with another fresh pain. "And I'm the reason Carrie's baby is dead." She looked at the house fearfully. "And now Carrie might die. All because of me."

Rose understood her feelings all too well. "That's not true, Amber, but I know how you feel. I told Moses last night that it was my fault."

"Weren't your fault," Amber said flatly.

"I'm the one who let white children come to the school," Rose said. "I'm the one who made the vigilantes so angry. If I hadn't done that, Robert would still be alive." Sometime during the long night, she had reached the realization that she wasn't responsible. Now she had to help Amber understand the same thing.

"Weren't your fault," Amber repeated. "Them were real bad men."

"Yes, they were," Rose agreed, "but they wouldn't have been here if I had left things alone."

Amber shook her head again. "My mama and daddy said they were just bad men who would have come here no matter what because they got so much hate inside."

"I think your mama and daddy were right," Rose said softly, continuing to stroke her head. "Honey, what made you come out of the barn?"

Amber thought for a moment. "I heard shots," she said. "I reckon I fell asleep with All My Heart once I snuck out there. Then something woke me up."

"That's right," Rose said. "Shots woke you up. Were there a lot of them?"

"Sure sounded like a lot," Amber replied in a frightened voice. "When I came out there was still a lot of shots."

"So Robert could have been shot before," Rose prompted.

Amber thought about that for a moment and then shook her head, her face wilting under the memory. "He weren't killed by them other shots."

"That's right," Rose said gently, "but he could have been." She took a deep breath. "Robert was shot saving the little girl he loved like a daughter." She gripped Amber even closer. "Robert would have done anything for you, Amber. I already know he is glad he saved your life."

"How do you know?" Amber demanded. "Did he tell you?"

"He told Carrie."

Amber leaned back and stared up at her. "What did he say?" she asked in a trembling voice.

Rose repeated it just as Robert had said it. *"Tell Amber... I would do it again. I want her to have a great life. You tell her I loved her just like she was my own."*

Amber's eyes bored into her. "He said it just like that?"

"Just like that," Rose promised.

"He wasn't mad at me?" Amber's voice was filled with disbelief.

"He had nothing to be mad at, honey. Robert was killed by some very bad men with evil and hatred in their hearts. He was so glad he saved your life. He loved you very much."

Amber dissolved into fresh tears, but Rose knew they were a different kind of tears that would begin the slow healing her heart would need. Once again, she held the little girl and let her cry, thinking of all the times her mama had held her just like this. The grief would take a long time to heal, but it was better that she wouldn't carry the belief she had been responsible for Robert's death.

A long time passed before Amber lifted her head again. "What do we do now, Rose?"

Rose took a deep breath. It was the same question she was asking herself almost every moment. "We keep moving forward," she murmured as she thought about the moments she and Moses had shared with Carrie and Robert on the porch on Christmas Eve. Her heart constricted as she remembered Robert's laughing eyes and vibrant energy. "We keep moving forward, honey."

"How?"

Rose stared out at the pasture full of playful yearlings. She watched as two bay colts twirled on their back legs as they batted at each other. Suddenly, she remembered what her mama had said when her husband had died so soon after returning. "We remember all the good times," Rose said firmly. "We have to be grateful for all the times we had with

Robert while he was alive." She took courage from her own words, knowing her mama was reaching through her grief to help her yet again. "Robert would want you to be happy," she whispered. "He would want to know you were doing everything you ever dreamed of doing."

Amber listened with a frown. "I dreamed of doing everything with Robert."

Rose's heart constricted. "I know, honey. It always hurts to lose someone you love, but you never really lose them."

"He ain't coming back," Amber said. "Clint told me that."

"No," Rose agreed, "he's not coming back, but he is never going to leave your heart. You are always going to have the things he taught you. You are always going to have the memories of the things you did together." A shrill whinny cut the air. Rose looked up with the first smile she had smiled since the gunfire had split the night. "And you are always going to have All My Heart," she added softly. "Robert gave her to you because he loved you so much. Every time you look at her you can remember that."

Amber stared out at the pasture, her little face puckered in thought.

"Do you remember the day Robert gave you All My Heart?" Rose asked.

Amber nodded vigorously. "Of course I do! I remember every minute of that day."

"Do you remember the love in Robert's eyes? Do you remember how happy he was that he could give you All My Heart?"

Amber's eyes filled with tears again, but a slight smile twitched at her lips. "I remember. It was the best day of my life."

"That is how Robert would want you to remember him," Rose said.

Amber thought about those words for a long time. "It's still gonna hurt," she finally said.

"Yes," Rose agreed hoarsely. "It's going to hurt for a very long time." She stared up at the sky barely visible through the leafy green canopy covering them. "It's going to hurt all of us who loved him." As the leaves rustled in the breeze, she remembered something else her mama had told her. "And someday we'll even be glad."

"Glad Robert was killed?" Amber asked in a horrified voice.

"No," Rose assured her quickly. "We'll never be glad of that, but someday the hurt will disappear enough for us to be glad we had Robert in our life."

Amber considered that for a long time before she slowly nodded. "I remember everything about my time with Robert," she said slowly. "We been real close ever since he woke up in our house after that bad battle in the war."

"He told me about that," Rose replied. "You saved his life." She took a deep breath. "And you saved it again when you gave him a reason to live after the war ended and he was so sick."

Amber stared at her. "And now he saved my life," she whispered. "I wish he wouldn't have had to die to save me. I'm going to miss him every day for the rest of my life."

"Me too, honey," Rose managed to say as fresh tears clogged her throat. She pulled Amber close again. "But I'm sure glad he saved you."

****

Matthew was exhausted when the train finally pulled into the Philadelphia station. There had been one delay after another since he had left Nashville, but he was finally home, three days later than he had planned. He could hardly wait to take Janie in his arms and enjoy a night alone with her. She had wanted to meet him at the station, but he had insisted she wait for him since he wasn't sure if the train would be on time.

When he disembarked from his car, he grabbed his bag from the luggage rack and began to look around for a carriage to hire.

"Matthew!"

Matthew whipped his head around, surprised to see Janie pushing her way through the crowd. His immediate reaction of delighted pleasure faded as soon as she was close enough to see her face. He steeled himself for whatever news she had for him. "What is it?" he asked quietly. "What happened?"

"Robert has been shot by vigilantes."

Matthew stared at her, the words barely penetrating the fog that had suddenly obscured his mind. "What?" His mind spun. "Robert?"

"Yes," Janie said, her voice breaking now that she had delivered the news.

"What happened?"

"I told you all I know," Janie replied. "Thomas sent a telegraph when they arrived in Richmond and received the news. They were headed right out to the plantation, of course. I've not heard anything since."

Matthew nodded. "They wouldn't have been able to got another telegraph off." Now that the initial shock was over, he began to process the news. "We have to get there," he said urgently.

Janie held up a bag he hadn't noticed before. "I'm ready," she said evenly. "I have a collection of homeopathic remedies that Dr. Strikener suggested I take."

"Carrie will be glad to have them," Matthew said. He narrowed his eyes when Janie hesitated. "What else?"

Janie took a deep breath. "Carrie refused to ride out in the wagon. She rode Granite so she would get there sooner. Captain Jones seemed to believe it was that urgent. They couldn't stop her."

Matthew fought to comprehend what her last words meant. He pushed aside what it could indicate about Robert's condition and focused instead on Carrie. "She's six months pregnant," he protested.

Janie's only response was to hold up her bag, her eyes filled with unspoken fears. 'I have remedies. Our train leaves in twenty minutes."

Chapter Twenty

Carrie could barely hear the sound of rushing water in the distance. As she pushed through the dense fog that threatened to smother her, the sound pulled her forward. She couldn't identify why it was so important to reach the water...she simply knew she must.

As prickly limbs reached out to grab her, she pushed them aside, vaguely aware that the thorns piercing her flesh resulted in no pain. She paused for a moment, wondering why that was something she wondered about, and then kept on. The water was the only thing she cared about. She must find the water...

"Carrie!"

Carrie paused, impatient when she heard her voice called in the distance. She shook her head and kept moving. Without being able to explain why, she knew the water represented peace. She had to reach the water. A dim glow began to illuminate the fog, allowing her to proceed at a faster pace. As the rushing sound increased to a roar, her heart pounded in response. Everything would be all right if she could only reach the water. She hesitated as she wondered what had to be made right, but she had no answer, just the compulsion to reach the roaring sound in the distance.

The air began to glow a soft blue as the fog continued to dissipate. The beauty of it wrapped around her, giving her the courage to keep moving.

"Carrie!"

This time she stopped, certain she recognized the voice. "Leave me alone," she called. "I have to get to the water."

"Carrie!"

Carrie sucked in her breath as she identified the one calling her. "Robert?" She didn't understand why her voice was trembling with disbelief. She also couldn't fathom why Robert was trying to keep her from the water. "Come with me," she called, turning back to plunge toward what awaited her.

"Carrie! No!"

Carrie plunged to a stop again, certain she could now see Robert's form in the glowing blue light. Why didn't he come join her? Why was he holding her back? "I'm going to the water," she yelled, every particle of her frantic to reach what she suddenly realized was a gushing waterfall catching every ray of sun beaming through the fog—splitting the light into every color of the rainbow. She stared in awe as the colors danced in the spray of the waterfalls. Calling her... Calling her...

She stepped forward, knowing what she had to do. She had to join in the dance of the colors. She had to merge with the spray of the waterfall.

"Carrie, no!"

Robert's voice became more urgent, his desperation cutting through her intense longing. Once again she stopped, just short of the final step that would send her into the dance of the waterfall. "Why are you stopping me?" she screamed with frustration. Everything would be all right if she simply entered the dance.

The form materialized into the man she loved, but it made no sense because Robert was floating over the waterfall. She stared at him, wondering how her husband could float in the glowing air. "I want to come dance with you," she whispered, realizing that was *what had pulled her forward. She had known Robert was here...here in the waterfall...here...waiting to dance.*

"No," Robert said, his voice quiet now. "It's not time, my love."

"I want to be with you," Carrie breathed. Never had she wanted anything more. "I want to dance with you in the waterfall."

"You will," Robert replied softly, in a voice full of more sorrow than she had ever heard. "But not now, my love. Not now."

"Why?" Carrie whispered, her heart shattering when she realized Robert was denying her wish. It would take only one step to join the dance.

"It's not time," Robert responded, both hands reaching out to her in a gesture of love. "I love you, Carrie. I always will. Never forget it."

"Robert..."Carrie swayed on the edge of the waterfall.

"There are others who need you," Robert continued. "You can't join me now." His voice increased in its urgency. "You must not join me."

The love in Robert's voice, and the intensity in his eyes, caused Carrie to take a step back from the edge. As she did, the glow began to fade, and Robert's form was barely visible.

Another step, though everything in her screamed for her to join the dance. Robert's love was forcing her back.

The rainbow colors evaporated, leaving nothing but cold spray that buffeted her fatigued body. Robert was gone.

Carrie sobbed as she took another step.

The roar of the waterfall dissolved into a vague murmur as the fog settled back in, threatening to once again consume her.

Carrie began to thrash her arms to beat away the fog. Desperate to return to the dance of the waterfall, no longer caring what Robert had said, she had to find her way again.

"Carrie!"

Carrie spun around to identify the voice coming from another direction.

"Carrie!"

Her confusion grew. This was not Robert's voice. It was a new one calling her loudly. Insistently. Lovingly.

"Carrie! Come back! Please come back!"

Carrie glanced over her shoulder once more, knowing the dance of the waterfall was only steps away, and then she followed the sound of the new voice. Without another sound coming from the fog, she could feel Robert smiling his approval.

The smile broke her heart.

****

Abby jolted awake when she realized movement was coming from the bed. She jumped up and rushed forward, Rose close behind her. It had been almost three days since Carrie had lost consciousness. She and Rose had only left her side for brief moments. Her daughter had not once been alone.

A groan burst forth from Carrie's lips as she began to thrash her arms wildly, but her eyes remained closed.

Abby reached down to hold her arms, knowing sudden movement could burst the sutures holding the incision together. "Carrie," she murmured. "Carrie, come back to us."

Carrie groaned again. "Robert!" she suddenly cried, her reedy voice cracked with pain. "Robert! No...don't leave." She shuddered and fell silent.

Rose reached out to grab Carrie's hand. "Come back, Carrie. Come back to us!"

Carrie jerked again and then lay still. Her harsh breathing slowed.

Abby stiffened. Was Carrie dying? Had she gone to be with Robert? "Carrie," she whispered. "We love you. Please come back to us."

Dr. Wild opened the door and rushed in, alerted by Annie who had stationed herself just outside the door. He reached down and felt her pulse, nodding his encouragement to Abby. "She's coming around," he said reassuringly. "When someone has been unconscious for so long, it sometimes takes time for them to wake up."

Abby took hope from his words, but the harsh pain in Carrie's voice had pierced her heart. What was life going to be like for her if she returned? On the heels of her question came the reality of how wonderful her own world had become. She had thought her husband's death was the end of her life, but she had survived, grown their business, and now had a loving husband and daughter. She grabbed Carrie's hand and squeezed it tightly. "Come back, Carrie," she said, her voice now infused with hope and belief. "We love you. Come back!" Her final words were more of a command than a plea.

Carrie took a long shuddering breath and opened her eyes. For lengthy moments there was a blank expression of unseeing, but she slowly focused on

Abby's face. She stared at her intensely, and then shifted her eyes toward Rose. Then Dr. Wild.

Abby watched the confusion with an aching heart, but she knew the confusion was better than the reality that was about to sink in. It took only minutes before it happened, raw pain filling her daughter's beautiful green eyes.

"Robert..."

Abby reached out to stroke her hair. "Robert is gone," she said tenderly, knowing it was best to let her deal with the truth.

Carrie's eyes shifted back to her. "Yes," she agreed. "He sent me back to you." Her voice was faint, but certain.

Abby's heart filled with gratitude for whatever had happened during the long days they had waited for her to wake up. "I'm glad," she whispered.

Carrie's eyes grew confused again. She slid her hand out from Abby's and reached down to touch her stomach. "My baby?" Her face filled with a wild hope. "My baby. I want to see my baby."

Abby's eyes filled with tears as she took Carrie's hand again. "Your daughter didn't make it," she said. "I'm so sorry, Carrie."

Carrie's stare was blank and uncomprehending. "My baby? My baby is dead, too?"

Abby couldn't speak around the vise on her throat. Tears continued to pour down her face.

Rose stepped forward. "I'm so sorry, Carrie. Bridget didn't make it."

Carrie's eyes sought Rose's face. What she saw there told her the truth. She gasped and seemed to shrink inside herself. "Bridget is dead? My daughter? I killed them both?"

She closed her eyes and slid back into the welcoming darkness.

****

Thomas squeezed his eyes tight with gratitude when Abby brought news of Carrie's waking, but his heart filled with fresh grief and rage when she told him what his daughter had said. He stood and strode to the edge of the porch, staring out at the offending sunset that somehow seemed to mock his agony with its beauty. "I've waited long enough," he growled.

Moses, Mark, and Jeremy rose to stand beside him. No one had to say a thing. They had talked through their plan during the long hours of waiting.

Thomas turned to look at Abby. The steady look of love in her eyes filled him with courage and resolve. "Your men are ready?" he asked Moses.

"They are," Moses assured him.

The sun had long set when the twenty men needed for Thomas' plan were mounted and ready for action. The sound of a lone approaching horseman told Thomas the final piece of the puzzle was just arriving.

The new arrival looked at Thomas when he pulled his horse to a stop. "You're sure about this, Cromwell?"

"Without a doubt, Sheriff Horn," Thomas snapped. "It's been confirmed by several veterans." He knew it was necessary to emphasize the fact that white war veterans had confirmed his report. In spite of the fact that Moses and his men had seen all the same things, he wasn't taking any chances on them not being believed—or worse, simply not listened to.

"Let's go," the sheriff said, his face indicating he was not excited about the night's activity.

Thomas tensed with anger, almost certain the sheriff was sympathetic with the vigilantes, but Thomas Cromwell was too important in the area for him to simply be ignored. He raised his hand and led his men down the road in an easy trot. While it was dark, he preferred it be closer to midnight before they made their move. It would be more effective that way.

When they were a few hundred yards from the columned entrance to Granger Southerlin's plantation, he raised his hand to bring all of them to a halt. It took only a few minutes for them to don the costumes Polly and Annie had created during the interminable wait for Carrie to regain consciousness.

Sheriff Horn scowled when Thomas handed him one. "I don't want to put this on," he protested.

Thomas stared at him with a hard gaze. "You said you wanted to know the truth. Do you, or do you not?"

Sheriff Horn hesitated and then pulled on the long white cloak over his uniform. "This is a bunch of nonsense," he muttered.

"How about telling that to my daughter who just had her husband murdered," Thomas growled. He took a deep breath, knowing his anger would not make things right. The only way he could begin to deal with Robert's death, and the death of his granddaughter, was to at least make certain he had justice.

"Let's go," Sheriff Horn replied, his face saying he knew he didn't have a choice.

"The hood, too," Thomas reminded him as he pulled his own over his head, glad Annie had cut extra-large eye holes in all of them.

****

The Southerlin plantation was shrouded in darkness as the horsemen galloped down the road, making no attempt at secrecy. When they were less than a hundred feet away, all of them began to yell loudly as they lit the fire sticks they were holding. Jeremy jumped off his gelding, raced up the stairs, pounded on the door, and then ran back to mount again. It took only a few minutes before they saw the door open. The yard was illuminated with an eerie glow.

Granger Southerlin stepped out onto the porch, his face a mask of confusion and fear as he stared at the white-cloaked men gathered in his yard, forming a semi-circle around his porch. "What is going on here?" he called, failing at his attempt to sound commanding.

Jeremy had been appointed the spokesperson because Southerlin would not recognize his voice. "Me and some of the boys from the Ku Klux Klan thought we would pay you a visit," he said in a menacing tone.

"Why?" Southerlin sputtered.

"We've been hearing some rather disturbing things," Jeremy continued in a conversational tone.

Thomas almost smiled when he saw Southerlin stiffen with terror. His smile faded into a scowl as he thought of the fear Robert must have felt when he saw that Amber was about to be shot.

"What kind of things?" Southerlin demanded.

"Well, I suppose you should be the one to tell us," Jeremy continued. "We had heard you were a loyal patriot of the South, but recent activities reveal that is not true."

"How can you say that?" Southerlin asked indignantly. "I've been doing the work of a true patriot." He pulled himself erect as he fought to regain control of the situation. "You should be here to thank me." He had gained an authoritative ring to his voice.

"And just what would we be thanking you for?" Jeremy asked.

Right on cue, Mark said in a stern voice, "We hear you support the black school down the road that has white students. And we hear you are paying black laborers more than the rest of your neighbors do. We're not pleased." His ringing accusation echoed off the woods pressing in against the darkness.

"We've been sent to warn you of what happens to people who do that," Jeremy intoned in a somber voice. "We have an agenda for the South. We won't let anyone stand in the way of accomplishing it."

Southerlin, confident he was on solid footing, stepped forward to the edge of the porch. "I don't know who has been telling you those lies, but they are nothing but nonsense," he said. "Why, I was the one who put together the group that went down and tried to burn that school." His voice grew more arrogant. "And I also made sure the traitors on Cromwell Plantation paid for what they are doing to destroy the glory of the South."

"And just how did you do that?" Jeremy snapped in an even more menacing tone.

Thomas smiled grimly as it had its intended effect.

"Robert Borden let the niggers live in his house like they were family, and blacks on that plantation are paid far more than everyone else around here. I sent a group of men over there when I realized we couldn't burn the school." Southerlin gave an evil grin.

"Borden is dead now. James Stowe put a bullet right through him. I thanked him myself, just yesterday."

"Is that right?" Jeremy asked, rough anger deepening his voice.

"It's God's truth," Southerlin boasted. He stepped back in shocked surprise as twenty rifles and pistols were lifted and aimed at him. "What...?"

Sheriff Horn lifted the hood off his head. His voice was almost apologetic as he said, "You are under arrest, Southerlin, for aiding a murder and for attacking the school. I will arrest James Stowe in the morning."

Southerlin's face froze in furious disbelief. "Why, Sheriff Horn, I thought..."

Thomas decided not to allow him to finish his statement because he didn't want Sheriff Horn to feel more trapped than he already was. Perhaps the reality that so many had heard Southerlin's confession would guarantee his punishment. He urged Granite forward and whipped off his own hood. "You're lucky we don't shoot you where you stand right now, Granger," he said, sudden aching pain mixed with his fury. "That was my son-in-law you killed. And my daughter, Carrie, who played with your daughter when they were children, is right now fighting for her life after losing the baby she wasn't due to deliver until July. The shock of Robert's death sent her into labor." His voice deepened. "That's what your stupid hatred is doing to the South, Granger. It's destroying what you say you love so much."

Jeremy whipped off his hood next. "We came in disguise tonight to show you how ridiculous the Ku Klux Klan is. You say you are fighting for the South. All you are doing is ensuring its destruction. Your crazy vendetta is going to bring the military might of the North down on you once again if you don't change your ways."

Thomas was suddenly very, very fatigued. "We were friends once," he said heavily. "I can hardly believe you have allowed yourself to come to this." He turned Granite and rode back into the night. He would let Sheriff Horn do his job, though he harbored doubts the man would do anything more than issue warnings to Southerlin and Stowe to be more careful.

Thomas was anxious to get home to be with his family. He longed to feel Abby's body pressed to his. He needed to know Carrie was still alive. He wanted *home*. He had fulfilled the mission that had given him a sense of purpose during the long days of waiting, but it had done nothing to fill the void in his heart.

He stopped long enough at the gates to pull off the offending cloak and wait for everyone to do the same. He watched with grim satisfaction as Moses set fire to the white mound, and then he urged Granite into a gallop.

It was time to bury his son-in-law and granddaughter.

Chapter Twenty-One

June 1, 1867

Carrie stepped out onto the porch, barely aware of the early summer heat causing a misty fog to hover over the plantation. The morning air was still cool, but it would be in the mid-eighties by the middle of the afternoon. She took long walks every day—anything to get away from the house—but she had been banned from riding until her incision healed.

Her incision. Every time Polly cleaned it or put new ointment on, it was like she was losing her daughter all over again. Over and over again. When she was awake. In her dreams. She felt an empty void where life had once kicked and demanded to be acknowledged.

Carrie walked slowly down the porch steps, refusing to glance up at the window to her and Robert's room. Abby had cleaned out their bedroom and placed her in another room at the back of the house. There was part of her that felt grateful to be separated from the memories, but another part felt she was being ripped further away from the man she loved. Instead of resisting, however, she simply acquiesced. She didn't deserve to feel close to the only man she had ever loved—the one she had allowed to die.

She looked up, startled, when Miles suddenly appeared before her holding Granite. She had no energy to do more than stare at him as he smiled brightly.

"It's been a month, Miss Carrie," Miles said. "Dr. Wild said you could ride again after a month if you take it easy."

Carrie absorbed this new information. "Oh." *A month.* It had been a month since Robert had died from a bullet in the back. A month since Bridget had died within the supposed safety of her womb. A wild pain ripped through her, but she had become somewhat accustomed to it. It was the way it would be for the rest of her life.

Miles continued in an easy voice. "I figured you and Granite could go on down to the river for a while." He pointed to a bag tied to the saddle. "Miss Annie put together a picnic for you. It's all your favorite foods."

"I don't think so," Carrie said vaguely. Granite nickered and moved forward to nudge her with his head. She reached up, more out of habit than anything else, and put her hand on his neck, welcoming the soft warmth. Her horse had not seen her since she had ridden him home that fateful day. The memory almost caused her to double over in pain, but she held herself erect. It had been her choice. Her *fault.*

"Your horse needs to be ridden," Miles said in a firmer voice.

Carrie scowled. "I'm not a little girl anymore," she snapped, anger surging through the painful deadness filling her.

"No, Miss Carrie, you're a grown woman," Miles replied steadily, holding her in place with his eyes. "A grown woman with a grown horse that needs to be ridden. He calls for you every day."

Carrie's knees almost buckled. In her dreams she could hear Robert calling to her. She could hear her little girl calling to her. She willed back the tears she had no right to. The life she was living was all her own doing. No one was responsible but herself. She sucked in her breath when Granite nudged her again, his dark eyes staring into hers like they always had. Carrie trembled and touched his neck again, feeling the longing that coursed through him, just as she had always been able to. She nodded slowly and reached for the reins.

Miles didn't smile, but his eyes lit with deep pleasure. "Dr. Wild said to take it real easy for a while."

Carrie nodded. It seemed more than she was capable of to simply mount her horse. Her days of riding as a carefree young woman were long gone. Miles gave her a leg-up into the saddle and then stepped back.

"Have a good time, Miss Carrie."

Carrie stared at him for a long moment, but could think of absolutely nothing to say that would not sound rude. She turned Granite and walked slowly down the road. Her usually energetic, prancing horse seemed to know there was no place for antics today. He settled into a ground-swallowing walk, his head bobbing happily in the morning air.

Carrie fought to hold back the memories of her last ride and the frantic fear that had driven her to reach the plantation before Robert died. She remembered almost nothing of that journey, just the fear that had propelled her forward. Her first memories were when she walked in the bedroom, took one look at Robert, and knew she was about to lose her husband forever. The vivid recollection of his slack face caused her to almost double over in pain. "Robert..." she whispered, certain her pain and guilt would never ease.

Carrie pushed back the darkness, forcing herself to look around at where she was riding. Only then did she realize she was on the road in between two of the tobacco fields. When she had left for Philadelphia, the seedlings were less than a foot high. Now, tall stalks of tobacco swayed in the breeze, their blossoms filling the air with their sweet, smoky aroma. Carrie inhaled out of habit, her thoughts turning to the long rides she and her father had taken when she was a child, and he had been so eager to teach her everything he knew. The blooms would not be left on the plants long. Her practiced eye said they would soon be broken off, and the plants topped in order to stop the growth of suckers, forcing the remaining leaves to grow thick and broad.

The sight of men in the distance caused her to jerk her eyes away. She saw one raise his hand in greeting, but she ignored it and pressed on. All she could think about was getting away from everyone and everything. She had been forced to stay close to the house while she was healing. She knew she should appreciate everyone's solicitousness, but every kind word only made her guilt and grief more impossible to bear. She could tell people were thinking carefully about every word they said. It made her tired. She could only imagine how they truly felt.

Amber came every day to invite her out to the barn to work with the foals. Every day, she fastened a polite smile to her lips and said no. It took every ounce of energy she had to not lash out at the child. She had no intention of ever entering the barn again. How could she ever walk over the spot where her husband had lain, his blood pooling on the ground as his life ebbed away?

The vision she attempted to push down every day caused her to urge Granite into a trot. He tossed his head joyfully as she carefully posted, relieved when there was no pain in her stomach. The feeling of relief made her scowl. Who was she to feel relief? She longed for the pain that reminded her every minute of the tiny casket that had been placed into the ground next to Robert's. She had never been able to hold her baby. Never seen her sweet face. Never been able to keep her promise to Robert to make sure his daughter knew how much he loved her.

"No!" Carrie screamed. Granite tossed his head as she leaned forward, giving him the signal to run. It was the only way she knew to escape the pain threatening to swallow her. Much to her amazement, her horse, who loved to run more than anything, only sped up to an easy canter. "Run!" she screamed. "Run!" She didn't care who saw her. She didn't care who heard her. She simply had to alleviate the pain that was ripping her up from the inside.

Granite continued to canter smoothly as Carrie cried and gasped for breath.

She lost track of time, but she knew the minute they reached the trail that would lead down to the river. The sky disappeared, and the woods swallowed them. The embrace of the forest calmed her, allowing her to regain control. She took several deep breaths as she patted Granite on the neck to express her reluctant gratitude, though a very large part of her still wanted to run wildly. She made herself continue to take deep breaths. As her heart rate slowed, she noticed the violet-blue monkey flowers that grew beside the bubbling stream. Soapwort blooms added their faint pink glow to the early morning, while small daisies nodded at her. There was a time when the sight of them would have filled her with joy, but now there was nothing but regret that she would never share their magic with Robert and Bridget.

When Granite followed the familiar path to the river, Carrie swung off him, removed his saddle and bridle, and turned him loose to graze. A part of her felt at home. Another part of her was consumed with memories that stole her breath. Her and Robert's first kiss. The lovemaking that had produced Bridget. She groaned with agony and moved over to sit on a boulder as close to the river as possible. It had probably been a mistake to come here, but then, there was no place on the plantation that did not taunt her with recollections that produced searing pain and regret. There was not a day that passed when she didn't dream of escaping the plantation, but she could also not imagine leaving the home she had shared with the man she loved. More than that, though, she could not fathom leaving the tiny grave that held the daughter she had never had a chance to know.

Carrie gritted her teeth, clenched her fists, and stared out at the sparkling waters of the James River. As the breeze picked up, the ripples were teased into dancing waves crowned with glowing white caps. A large fish broke the surface, the water droplets falling as diamonds back into the river. The beauty nearly took her breath away, but suddenly, with no warning, a dark rage consumed her.

Robert would never see this again. Bridget would never experience what she had experienced as a child. The dancing waves turned into a taunting melody of all she had lost. *Never again... Never again... Never again...*

Carrie, hardly able to breathe, bent over, rage darkening her vision until the river disappeared entirely. She was completely unaware of the screams that ripped from her throat. She could feel rocks cutting into her hands as she grabbed them frantically and threw them in great clumps into the river. "Robert! Bridget! No! No!"

Carrie spun around, vaguely aware of Granite standing at attention as he stared at her, but the fury in her still demanded release. She grabbed more handfuls of rocks, smashing them into the closest tree, ignoring the pain as several ricocheted back at her, cutting her arms and face. She continued to scream and heave rocks until there was no breath in her lungs. Only then did she collapse to the ground and let the tears come.

Moments later, she felt arms enclose her.

"Carrie," Abby murmured, pulling her close. "Let it out, my dear, let it out."

Carrie didn't question her sudden appearance. She grabbed Abby like the lifeline she needed to keep from drowning, and let the sobs rack her body. She had no idea how long she cried, but finally she was spent. She sagged against Abby, comforted by the steady stroking of her hand against her hair. There was a part of her that resisted, her consuming guilt telling her she wasn't worthy of this kind of comfort, but she didn't have the energy to push away. She needed it too badly.

Abby remained silent, stroking her hair as she held her close.

Carrie looked up. There was no peace in her heart, but the violent rage had been appeased. "What are you doing here?"

"When Miles told me you took Granite, I knew where you were coming. I thought you might need me."

Carrie hesitated. "How long have you been here?" She couldn't remember much of the rage, but she was certain it must have been ugly.

"Just long enough," Abby murmured.

Carrie thought about that for a moment and decided it didn't matter if Abby had seen her. *Nothing* mattered anymore. Another long silence passed. She almost wished Abby would say something, but her stepmother had spoken very little to her since the funerals—she had simply sat with Carrie for long periods of time, letting her know she wasn't alone. Carrie appreciated it, but it was also another layer of guilt because she knew she was keeping Abby away from Thomas, and away from the factory. Her father had stayed for three weeks, but had finally been forced to return to Richmond.

The breeze died away as heat settled the day. Carrie was gradually aware of buzzing bees and the call of birds. "How did you do it?" she finally asked.

"Survive Charles' death?" Abby responded. "Much like you are. My world was full of pain and loss."

Carrie thought about it and shook her head. "You didn't kill your husband and daughter," she said.

"And neither did you," Abby responded steadily. "But I know you're not ready to believe that yet, so I'll just tell you I thought my grief would swallow me for the first months after Charles died."

"It's been one month," Carrie whispered. "It seems like yesterday."

"It will seem like yesterday for a very long time," Abby said sadly.

Carrie wished that wasn't true, but she appreciated Abby telling her the truth. She wasn't going to ask if things got better. She could look at Abby's life and know she was happy now, but she hadn't carried the burden of knowing she had been responsible for her husband's death. Abby couldn't possibly understand how she felt.

Still, Carrie couldn't hold all the pain locked away inside her any longer. Even if the future was nothing but a stark mockery of what she had dreamed life would be, hurling the rocks had at least eased the band around her heart. "None of this seems real," she admitted. "I hear Robert and Bridget calling me in my dreams. I can't save them..." She paused as her voice cracked. "When I wake up, I realize it's a dream, but I forget it's real—that they are really gone. And then..."

"And then you remember," Abby said tenderly.

Carrie decided to be honest. "I wish Robert hadn't told me to return." The words hung in the air, but she had no desire to take them back. It was the truth.

"I know," Abby replied. There was no judgement in her voice, just soft understanding shining from her eyes.

Carrie wanted to ask if she would stop feeling that way, but her burning guilt kept the words lodged in her throat. She had stolen the lives of the two people she loved most so it was only right that she would suffer for the rest of her time on Earth. "Why?" she whispered, the words forced from her throat by a power greater than herself.

"Why did Robert tell you to come back?"

Carrie nodded, desperate to understand. She didn't know why she thought Abby would know the answer, but the question haunted her every waking minute. She had such vivid memories of the rainbow colors in the waterfall. She could feel the pull to take the final step and join the dance that would have reunited her with Robert and Bridget. Mixed with her grief, was anger that Robert had not let her join them—that he had sent her back to suffer. "Did he want me to suffer for killing him and Bridget?" she asked. "Is that it?" Voicing the question ripped an even larger gaping hole in her heart.

"No." Abby's voice was firm and certain.

"How do you know?" Carrie pleaded. "How can you possibly know?"

"Because Robert loved you," Abby stated as she lifted Carrie's face so she could peer in her eyes. "What were his final words to you, Carrie?"

Carrie frowned, not because she didn't remember her husband's final words, but because she was certain he wouldn't have said them if he knew she had killed their daughter.

"What you're thinking is not true," Abby said tenderly.

"How do you know what I'm thinking?" Carrie asked, though she already knew Abby had always been able to read her heart and mind.

"Tell me what Robert said," Abby repeated.

Carrie's voice cracked with pain as she spoke the words that played over and over in her mind. "*I'm sorry I'm leaving you. I'll always be watching you.*" As if he were right there, she listened to his voice fade as his eyes closed and reopened. "*Always love you...*" she finished, tears clogging her throat.

"And that is why he told you to come back," Abby whispered. "Robert loved you so much. He wanted you to continue to live."

"Without him and Bridget?" Carrie cried. "Why?"

"I know you will not believe me when I tell you a day is coming when the pain will not be so crushing, but it is true. Right now every time you think of Robert and Bridget it is nothing but a dark blanket that smothers your soul."

Carrie listened, knowing that Abby understood at some level.

"Honey, it is not just Robert and Bridget's death that has sucked the life from you. It is an accumulation of everything during the last six years. You have had to be strong for so many people. You have had to care for so many. You have finally run into a grief and tragedy so terrible that you have nothing left." Abby's hand rested on Carrie's cheek. "That's why I'm here. You don't have to be strong. You don't even have to feel like living. I'm here."

Carrie absorbed the words, but they couldn't touch the pain. She thought of all the women in the country who had lost loved ones during the war. Husbands... Sons... Brothers... Many had lost more than one. She had been spared all that. If she was honest, at some level she had hoped it meant she was somehow special enough to be spared that pain. She knew now that she wasn't special at all. Death had come to perch on the threshold of her life, never to leave.

"May I ask you a question?"

Carrie nodded, certain before Abby opened her mouth that it was a question she wouldn't want to answer.

"Would you have wanted Robert to die alone?"

"Of course not!" Carrie cried. She remembered the look of stark relief on his face when he had opened his eyes and seen her. She could still hear his sigh of gratitude when she had climbed into bed with him and took him in her arms. "I couldn't let Robert die alone," she whimpered.

"Did he have two more hours to live?" Abby pressed.

Carrie knew what she was doing. She wanted to ignore the questioning, preferring the searing pain that almost made the guilt comfortable. Dr. Wild had explained everything to her after she regained consciousness—the miracle of Robert living long after he should have succumbed to his injuries. Her mind had heard it, but her heart had kept it locked away. "No," she whispered.

"Then you didn't really have a choice," Abby said quietly.

Fresh rage rose in Carrie. She pushed away and stood, moving over to stare at the river defiantly. "Why did I have to choose? Why did my choice to be with Robert mean that Bridget had to die?" The questions continued to rampage through her mind. *Would she have still ridden home if she had known the price she would pay? Would her love for Robert have overridden her concern for a child she had never seen?* The very questions made bile rise to her throat. "Why did I have to choose?" she almost screamed.

Abby stepped up to her side but didn't reach out to touch her, seeming to know Carrie needed to stand alone in her agony. "You'll never know the answer to that question," she said regretfully. "All of us may want to know, but we'll never have an answer."

"So I just accept it?" Carrie asked bitterly. "Accept that *God* knows best?" Even speaking the words made her angry. "That's not fair!" She clenched her fists. "Does God hate me so much? Am I such a horrible person?" The rage evaporated into a fresh surge of grief that stole her breath. "Oh..." She groaned as she leaned over. Abby reached out now. She wrapped her arms around Carrie, holding her close while a fresh spate of tears filled her eyes.

Carrie blinked them back, preferring to focus on the anger that at least made her feel alive. "I hate God!" she cried.

Abby nodded. "He knows."

Carrie gasped and waited for Abby to say more. The only sound was the wind through the trees. "That's all you are going to say?" she managed. The guilt she already felt was only amplified by her stark pronouncement.

"That's all," Abby replied, a trace of amusement easing the sorrow in her voice. "Do you think God doesn't know how you feel?"

Carrie considered the question. Merely screaming the words had eased some of her pain. "I think some things are better not said," she finally replied.

Abby shrugged. "I used to feel that way," she admitted. "Then I decided that as long as God knows what I'm feeling anyway, I might as well be honest about it. Saying it can't possibly be worse than feeling it. I figure if God can't take a little honesty, then he shouldn't be God."

Carrie stared at her stepmother, completely taken aback.

"Carrie, I know you are not ready to believe this, but I'm going to keep telling you what I'm about to say because one day you will be ready to hear it."

Carrie looked at her, certain she knew what Abby was going to say. She wasn't going to believe it for a minute, but the moment's reprieve the words might provide, even though her heart knew they weren't true, made it worth listening to.

"You are not responsible for Robert's death," Abby said. "Dr. Wild has explained it to you, but right now the guilt you are feeling somehow makes the pain a little more bearable."

Carrie blinked and looked at her more closely. There was something more in her voice...

Abby sighed. "When cholera struck Philadelphia almost eleven years ago, Charles wanted to leave the city. He insisted it was the only way to stay healthy. Some friends had invited us to their mountain home for the summer." She paused, staring out over the churning waves. "I didn't want to go," she said. "I can't even remember why now. I just didn't want to go. Charles always let me have my way, so we stayed in the city. And he died," she finished in a flat voice. "Because I wouldn't leave."

Carrie reached down and took Abby's hand, somehow able to move past her own pain to understand what a terrible burden this was. She also finally realized that Abby understood the weight of the grief and guilt that was destroying her. That knowledge helped in some small way. "I'm sorry," she whispered.

"Me, too," Abby said quietly. "You see, while Robert's death is truly not your fault, it was most assuredly *my* fault that Charles died."

"He could have gotten sick in the mountains, too," Carrie protested, though her mind told her it wouldn't have been likely.

Abby's look revealed she knew the truth. "Charles forgave me," she said. "Before he became too sick to speak, he told me he loved me, that he was sorry to leave me, and that he would always be watching me."

Carrie gasped. That was what Robert had told her, too.

"Our husbands loved us, Carrie," Abby said. "And they knew we loved them."

Carrie's mind said Abby was speaking the truth, but her heart told her it was too soon to even hear the message. There was a small part of her that could accept the reality that she had not been responsible for Robert's death, but there was little doubt she was guilty of Bridget's death. "I wish I could do it over again," she admitted.

Abby pulled her around to face her. "Do you really?" Her gray eyes probed her heart. "Would you have made a different choice?"

Carrie stared back, wishing she could run away from this conversation. They had already discussed this, but the horror of her impossible choice was also impossible to loose. She swung around and looked out at the water. *Would* she have let Robert die alone if she had known Bridget would die? She forced herself to face the question honestly, certain either answer would be devastating, but at least she would be facing it head on.

"If God had come to stand before you, and told you that you had to choose between Bridget dying, or making sure Robert did not die alone, what would you have chosen?" Abby's voice was more insistent.

"How can you ask me that question?" Carrie implored with a bitter taste in her mouth.

"Because you need to answer it."

"Why?" Carrie knew she was stalling, but she couldn't bring herself to put her thoughts into words.

Abby remained silent.

Carrie scowled, but now that the question had been put to her so plainly, she knew what choice she would have made. Memories flooded through her as she thought about Robert... *His laughing eyes. The tender look on his face when he was watching her. The pride he expressed in who she was. The warmth of his kisses. The joy of his lovemaking. The courage to change his beliefs when reality showed him a different truth. His closeness with Amber. His easy camaraderie with her father, and with Moses and Rose.* She sucked in her breath as she thought of their riding through the snow on New Year's Day and returning home to discover she was pregnant.

"I would never have let Robert die alone," she said, tears filling her eyes as she accepted the truth. "No matter what price I had to pay, I had to be there to tell my husband good-bye."

Abby nodded. "Then you made the right choice, my dear."

Carrie wished there was something about those words that made her feel better. Something about the realization that made losing Bridget bearable. Each emotion was equally powerful. As glad as she was that she had been with her husband at the end, the pain of losing him and Bridget made the gladness so miniscule it could hardly be taken into consideration.

Abby read her thoughts and gripped her hands tightly. "I know none of this makes you feel better...at least not now. The time will come, though, when your heart will be ready to accept what you have discovered today. In the meantime, you must focus on getting through each day in a world that is dark and full of pain."

Abby's final words gave Carrie what she needed. The pain still took her breath away; she knew it would for a long time. She knew everything she saw on the plantation was going to cause hurt. Someday, perhaps, that would change, but she couldn't see it now.

"Your father had to leave the plantation," Abby murmured. "He had to get away."

Now, for the first time, Carrie understood her father's need to flee the plantation when her mother died, but she shook her head fiercely. "I won't leave." Leaving would be like casting aside her heart, her memories, and the graves of the ones she loved. "I'm staying," she said in a voice that she knew held desperation.

Abby nodded. "I understand."

****

Nothing more was said for a very long time.

Abby laid out the food Annie had prepared. Carrie forced herself to eat some of it, but she didn't taste a single bite. She gazed idly at Granite and Maple as they munched on the lush grass, and then she turned to stare out at the water again. She knew Abby was willing to sit in silence with her. For that, she was grateful.

When they finally left, after watching the sunset over the river, she felt no peace, but at least she felt she had been granted a brief reprieve.

Chapter Twenty-Two

Rose was still not certain she should leave the plantation. She knew Abby felt the same way, but she had said she still intended on going to New York City after she had returned from her time with Carrie the day before. Neither woman had said anything when they returned from the river, but Rose had felt what seemed like a slight release in her best friend. Still, all Rose could do was stare at the pile of clothing on the bed waiting for her to pack.

"Them clothes ain't gonna jump in that satchel all by themselves."

Rose managed a brief smile when her mother-in-law's voice sounded from the open doorway. "I know," she admitted. "I want to go to the ERA Convention, but I can't imagine leaving Carrie."

"You reckon you can do any more than you been doin'? Annie asked.

"I suppose not," Rose replied, wondering if she had accomplished anything at all since Robert and Bridget's death. Carrie was like a walking corpse. She was breathing, but it was the only real evidence of life. She never talked, and she avoided everyone in the house as much as she could. There were times Rose had been able to sit with her on the porch, just watching the day or listening to the crickets, but silence seemed to be the only thing Carrie wanted. Rose was happy to give it to her, but there were times she felt...

"Miss Carrie needs the two of you to leave," Annie said bluntly.

Rose's head shot up. How had Annie read her thoughts?

"That girl needs time to be alone with her grief," Annie said, her gruff voice softening. "This house been so full of people, I 'magine she feels like she has to put up some kind of front all the time. She loves you and Miss Abby, but she also knows how concerned you are about her. The two of you need to skedaddle so she ain't got to do nothin' more than she wants to do."

Rose listened closely. Annie had suffered the death of her husband and one of her daughters before having the rest of her children ripped away from her on the auction block. Then Sadie had been killed in the Philadelphia fire. More than anyone in the house, Annie knew the burden of grief.

Annie walked forward to take one of her hands. "I'm here for Miss Carrie," she said firmly. "If she needs anything, I'm right here."

Rose took comfort from her words, but another thought made her frown.

"What you thinkin', Rose?"

"Back when Carrie first found out she was pregnant we were talking about something my mama said." Rose hesitated, but Annie remained silent, waiting for her to finish. "Mama said it took great suffering to be a great woman."

Annie nodded as she eyed her keenly.

"Do you believe that's true, Annie?"

"Don't matter none what I believe," Annie retorted. "What do *you* believe?"

"I believe I wish it weren't true," Rose admitted, determined to keep the whine out of her voice.

"Don't we all?" Annie muttered. "I don't care to be any greater a woman than I am right now."

Rose felt a warm rush of affection. She couldn't have agreed more. "I love you, Annie."

Annie gazed at her, a surprised pleasure shining in her eyes. "And I love you, Rose. I reckon my son made a real good choice when he done chose you."

Rose smiled, realizing that was the most complimentary sentence that had ever come out of her mother-in-law's mouth. She knew Annie loved her, but the older woman was not comfortable expressing her feelings. Rose decided now was a good time to bring up a subject she and Moses had been discussing just the night before. "It seems to me like someone is wanting to choose *you*."

Annie scowled. "What nonsense you be talkin' now?"

Rose smiled. She hadn't missed the flash in Annie's eyes. "Unless Miles eats enough for ten men, he seems to spend a lot more time in the kitchen than he needs to," she observed.

"That man do like to eat," Annie replied with a chuckle.

"I think he prefers to watch the cook," Rose retorted.

Annie ducked her head. "It's pure nonsense. We both be too old for nonsense."

"Now *that* is nonsense," Rose replied. She would never forget the shine in her mama's eyes when John returned to the plantation after eighteen years of their being apart. "You're never too old to love," she added quietly. "Miles doesn't seem to think *he's* too old."

Annie started to scowl again, but the look in her eyes softened. "That Mr. Miles be a real fine man," she said.

"I agree," Rose said firmly. "And not that it matters," she added, "but Moses happens to think so, too."

Annie peered at her. "That so?"

"That's so." Rose began to stuff clothing in her satchel. She would let Annie ponder what to do about Miles. She had a trip to get ready for. "Thank you for taking care of Carrie."

"You just go up there and make somethin' happen toward women gettin' the vote," Annie commanded. "I be real tired of livin' in a country that men made such a mess of!"

Rose laughed. "We'll do our best, because I happen to totally agree with you!"

****

Rose smiled when the spires of the Richmond churches, thrusting up from the hills of the city, came into view. "I haven't been into the city in such a long time," she said brightly, before her smile fell.

"Don't," Abby said. "You are not going to feel guilty for feeling happiness when Carrie is in so much pain."

Rose narrowed her eyes as she turned to stare at Abby. "Carrie told me you can read minds."

"I'm not reading your mind," Abby said with a soft laugh. "I'm telling myself the exact same thing. I could see it in your eyes. I would give up my own happiness if I thought it would make Carrie feel better, but it won't. I have to focus on living my own life, and I have to love her as hard as I can to give her the courage to live hers." She took a deep breath. "I love Richmond, and I'm about to see my husband for the first time in two weeks. What's not to be happy about?"

Rose agreed, but she still couldn't shake the image of Carrie's haunted eyes as she had watched them leave early that morning from the window of her room. "At least I know she will be safe," she murmured.

"You can count on that," Jeb said firmly as he turned back to look at them from the driver's seat of the carriage. "Moses would have brought you, but he refuses to leave the plantation."

"I know," Rose agreed, relieved to know there was a constant guard of men around the house at all times. It made the long days in the fields even longer for those who were pulling guard duty, but not one man had complained. A contingent of white parents was doing the same thing, both day and night, for the school. The fateful night of Robert's death had strengthened the bond between the white families and black families that formed her school, and most especially with the students. She had feared the attack by the vigilantes would have the opposite result, but the reality had planted hope in her for the future.

"Are Southerlin and Stowe still in jail?" Jeb asked.

"They are," Abby assured him. "The letter that came from Thomas yesterday said that even though Sheriff Horn is sympathetic to the vigilantes, he couldn't very well ignore a clear confession while he was listening. They were brought to the jail here in Richmond the day after all of you visited Southerlin."

"That was a real good plan Mr. Cromwell came up with," Jeb said enthusiastically. "I was real glad I got to be a part of it."

"He couldn't have done it without all of you," Abby said warmly.

"You reckon they'll be in jail a long time?"

"Long enough to make the vigilantes think more than once before they do something again," Abby said, "but no one is going to take anything for granted."

Rose wished Abby's confident statement made her feel better, but all it did was bring the horror of that night back into stark relief in her mind. She could hear the yells, the sound of gunfire, and the pounding hoof beats. She saw Amber stumble from the door of the barn in confusion, and then she could see Robert flying through the air to protect the little girl he loved so much. She shuddered, grateful when she felt Abby grip her hand. The older woman remained silent, but the simple connection enabled her to focus again on the vivid sunshine of the day.

****

They were on the train to Philadelphia when Abby brought up the subject Rose was trying her hardest to avoid.

"How are *you* doing with Robert's death?"

Rose remained silent for long moments, watching the trees flash by, before she looked back at Abby. She searched for words, but all she could muster was a helpless shrug.

Abby smiled gently. "You think your feelings can't possibly be as important as Carrie's."

Rose shrugged again. "They aren't."

"That's not true," Abby protested in the same gentle tone. "You lost someone you grew to love a great deal. You lost the little child you saw growing in Carrie's womb. And," she added tenderly, "in many ways you have lost your best friend to the grief that has consumed her."

Rose blinked back the tears burning her eyes. She couldn't deny that any of that was true, but her grief still seemed miniscule compared to what Carrie was suffering.

"Grief is grief, Rose."

Rose gazed at Abby. She was almost used to the woman reading her mind, but there were still times it surprised her. "I can push down my own grief to help Carrie through hers."

"Can you?" Abby asked keenly. "Can you truly help Carrie if you are swallowed by a grief you refuse to acknowledge?"

Rose looked down. She didn't have an answer to the question. "It's not just that," she admitted.

Abby cocked her head and waited.

Rose took a deep breath. "It could so easily have been Moses," she whispered, images of the night once again rampaging through her mind. "He told me if he had gotten back sooner he might have been able to stop it..." Her voice faltered.

"And he might have been the one to take the bullet," Abby finished softly. "And so you feel guilty because as much as you hate the grief Carrie is feeling, you are still grateful Moses didn't die that night."

Rose could do nothing more than stare, searching for judgment in Abby's eyes. She was relieved when she saw nothing but warm compassion. "Yes," she murmured.

"You would be less than human if you didn't feel that way," Abby said. "Your heart can be filled with grief over Robert's death, and at the same time be grateful it wasn't Moses. Your gratitude does not negate your sadness."

Rose pondered Abby's words, recognizing truth, but Abby continued on with what was really the crux of what was bothering her.

"And you're glad to be going to New York for the ERA Convention, but you're scared to death because you have left Moses and your babies back on the plantation when there are still vigilantes loose in our country."

Rose momentarily closed her eyes to block out the images of what could be happening. "That's true."

"Do you think your being there will change what might or might not happen?"

Rose considered the question carefully, knowing that Abby was offering her a lifeline. "I think that if something happens, my children will need me there to love them and help them through it," she murmured. Images of baby Hope gazing up at her with complete trust filled her mind. She knew Annie and Polly would take excellent care of the children, but what if something bad was to happen? They would need their mother.

"I believe that is true," Abby agreed, "but if you had chosen to stay would you have given power to the vigilantes to let them control your life and your decisions?"

"Yes," Rose admitted. "That's why I finally decided to come. Moses and I talked it through, and we decided once again that we couldn't let fear control our lives." She sighed. "I just wish I felt better about it."

Abby gazed at her for a long minute. "I'm sorry," she said contritely.

Rose raised a brow. "Sorry for what?"

Abby's eyes were full of sadness. "I'm sorry it is so very difficult for you to live in America. I hate that you have to worry every moment about your family's safety. I mostly hate that there is so much hatred in people's hearts." She shook her head heavily. "There are times I am ashamed to be an American. What we have done to black people is truly horrific."

Rose's heart swelled with gratitude. She reached out and clasped Abby's hand. "It is true that white people are making our lives difficult, but it is also true that white people were responsible for our finally gaining our freedom. It was white people who set up the Underground Railroad. White people who changed the laws that held us enslaved." She paused as she let her thoughts come together. "It is not race that makes people good or bad—it's what is in their minds and hearts. I'm reminded by something almost every day...that I have to see each person as an individual, not as a color. It would be too easy for black people to be angry at the entire white race, but if we do that, then we are really no better than the people who hate us. I agree we have to be careful, but complete fear will do nothing but close our minds and hearts to the good waiting to be discovered."

Abby smiled with admiration. "You have become a very wise woman, Rose Samuels."

Rose returned the smile. "Thank you." She hesitated, and then frowned. "I'm hoping I don't become wiser, though."

"Excuse me?" Abby asked with bemusement in her eyes.

Rose could not rid her mind of the conversation between her and Carrie by her mama's grave. "My mama told Carrie that great wisdom comes from great suffering."

"And you're watching Carrie suffer right now, and don't feel the wisdom gained is worth the price," Abby observed astutely.

Rose didn't see any reason to deny it. "If I have a choice, I would rather not be any wiser, but I have a feeling I don't really have a say in the matter."

"I wish I could disagree with you," Abby murmured, "but evidently we don't, because I remember wishing the same thing once."

Rose considered that and sighed. "I wish I didn't have to go through any more suffering, but I also long to be as wise as you and my mama, so I guess I just have to walk out whatever comes."

"I believe that's the only way to get through living," Abby agreed somberly. "The only thing I would add is that we have to choose almost every day to not become bitter and angry. Life will always be a mix. There will be wonderful times that will fill us with joy, and then there will be seasons of darkness that threaten to rip our souls from us." Her eyes darkened with painful memories. "We just have to keep walking forward through the darkness until we reach the next season of light."

"Do they always come?" Rose asked, more for Carrie than for herself. "Do the seasons of light always return?"

"I believe so," Abby said. "But only if we keep bitterness and anger from our hearts. I have discovered that if I accept the dark times as a part of life, I can release them and be ready for the next season of joy. If I flounder in bitterness over what I am having to deal with in my life, I find it makes it impossible to move forward."

Rose thought about this carefully, but a question rose to taunt her. "Don't you ever feel angry, though?"

"Of course," Abby said quickly. "I feel sad. I feel angry. I feel hurt. It's only natural for you to feel those things, Rose, but it's when we hold on to those feelings and let them take on a life of their own that we become trapped in the bitterness that robs us of the joy of living."

Rose listened with all her heart. She could feel her mama's spirit reaching out to her in Abby's eyes and voice. She had a sudden urge to know something. "Do you get lonely, Abby?"

Abby blinked, obviously surprised by the change in subject. "Lonely?"

Rose nodded. "I have felt lonely so many times during the last years. It seems I want things that many other women don't want—that I care about things many other women don't care about. I seem to always be defending why I do what I do."

Abby's eyes cleared of confusion. "Now I understand. And, yes, there are many times I feel very lonely. When I made the decision to run my husband's business after he died, I was attacked by equal numbers of both men *and* women." Her eyes clouded. "There were so few people who supported me."

"How did you do it?" Rose pressed, almost desperate to know.

"Matilda Greenwold," Abby said quietly, a tender smile on her lips. "She came to my door in Philadelphia one day and introduced herself to me. She was one of a handful of businesswomen in the city. She offered her friendship that day, and she also became a mentor. She explained to me that most women would criticize my decision because they felt it threatened their own decisions to be satisfied with their lives as they were. Instead of either choosing peace about their decision, or deciding to change it, they would attack me because they believed it made them look better." Abby took a deep breath. "She explained that powerful women would always find each other and be there as a support. Matilda was my lifeline through those first years. She encouraged me to be all I could be, and she held me when all of it was too much for me to endure. She was the reason I made it through that time." Her eyes filled with sadness.

"What happened to her?" Rose asked.

"She died from pneumonia three years after we met," Abby replied. "I've missed her every day since."

Rose nodded with complete understanding. "You were very lucky to have her."

"Yes," Abby murmured. "I was very lucky indeed. She introduced me to a world of powerful women who wanted more for their lives than what society offers. I met other women who were pushing the boundaries and demanding more. They became my source of strength, and their presence in my life kept me from being lonely." She paused. "It's why I go to these conferences. I truly want women to have the vote, but I also long to be around women who refuse to accept less than everything they believe they should have."

Rose was surprised when she heard a snort come from the row behind their seat on the train. She glanced back over her shoulder, right into the furiously indignant eyes of a well-dressed woman. She might have imagined the snorting sound, but there was no mistaking the anger directed at her and Abby. Before she could think of anything to say, the strange woman filled in the gap of silence.

"Both of you should be ashamed of yourselves!" The woman's cultured voice was full of disdain.

"Excuse me?" Rose asked pleasantly. She thought about what she and Abby had been talking about. Certainly there had been nothing said to promote this kind of ire.

The woman looked away from her, almost as if she didn't exist, and fixed her eyes on Abby. "I know who you are," she said accusingly.

"I'm so pleased," Abby responded graciously, her eyes dancing with fun. "Who do I have the pleasure of meeting?"

Rose bit back a smile, suspecting it would cause even more irritation, but the fun lurking in Abby's eyes made her relax. It was obvious Abby had faced many women like this.

"I wish I could say it was a pleasure," the woman said in a biting tone, "but I feel it's my duty to tell you that you are destroying womanhood in America."

"My, I had no idea I have that kind of power," Abby replied.

"Oh, you and your kind are determined to wield all the power you have to destroy my life," the woman shot back. "Mine, and the lives of millions of other women who want nothing to do with your agenda."

"The right to vote?" Abby asked. Her voice was still pleasant, but her eyes had narrowed with the last accusation.

"That's correct," the woman snapped. "It is quite unnatural for women to have a say in the political process in America. It will destroy the family, and it will also destroy the place of women."

Rose watched her in astonishment, wondering how she could possibly mean what she was saying. "I don't understand," she interjected. The woman turned her attention from Abby to stare at her. She could tell from her expression that the woman believed Rose's lack of understanding came from her being black, but Rose refused to look away from the woman's piercing brown eyes surrounded by lined skin.

"It's really quite simple," the woman sniffed as her voice took on a patronizing tone that made it clear she believed she was communicating with someone of lesser intelligence. "Suffrage does not make political sense. Not for women, and not for the nation as a whole. It is a blessing that women are exempted from political and legal responsibilities like serving in the army or sitting on juries." Her eyes widened as she suppressed a shudder. "Why would women want to have to shoulder male responsibilities like providing for the family, paying debts, and going to jail for minor crimes? I find the possibility horrifying."

"And if the wife engages in illegal business, the law will hold your *husband* responsible, not you. I can certainly understand why you would find that preferable," Abby said dryly.

Rose was glad Abby had responded to the woman because she was still too shocked to find words.

The woman turned back to glare at Abby. "That is scarcely the point," she retorted.

"I would say it is exactly the point," Abby answered. "There are far too many women who want to be exempt from any responsibility for their lives. If they can blame everything on men, because they have no *choice* in the matter, then they believe that to be a better way to live their life." She held up a hand when the stranger opened her lips in protest. "I've heard women like you say that the right to vote simply makes women aggressive." Her lips tightened as her voice took on an aristocratic tone that matched their attacker's. "You say that it makes us unlovely or less pleasant. You say it makes women bitter, aggressive, and antagonistic, and that it takes them away from caring about their family."

The woman lifted her head arrogantly, her eyes blazing. "And all that is certainly true," she said stiffly.

Rose could no longer stay silent. "That's ridiculous," she snapped, certain pleasant tones were not being appreciated in this conversation, so there was no need to make the effort. "I have three children I adore and care for. I also happen to be a teacher who is educating over fifty children. I have a husband who supports my desire to have the vote because he believes in the intelligence and value of women. How can you possibly believe that is a bad thing?"

The woman's eyes narrowed until they were little more than slits. "I hardly think you are capable of understanding the intricacies of politics." All pretense of pleasantry disappeared from her voice. "It's bad enough that black men are going to receive the vote." Her voice hardened. "It's simply inconceivable that black *women* will vote. What will happen to this country when so many ignorant people have a say? Thank goodness there are women who realize how ludicrous the idea is." She turned away from Rose and stared at Abby. "You must be intelligent enough to know Congress is not going to give suffrage to women. And just in case they consider it, there will be plenty of women telling them to block it."

Abby met her eyes evenly. "It will be a battle," she agreed, "but in the end we will win. Then this country will simply have to figure out what it means to have women voters." She smiled pleasantly, but her eyes were sharp. "Women voters, and then women in Congress. And someday?" She paused dramatically. "We will have a woman president."

The woman barked a disbelieving laugh before she turned away to stare out the window.

Rose gazed at Abby for several moments before she felt a smile twitch her lips. "Seriously?" she murmured. She was careful to keep her voice low so she wouldn't be overheard. "That woman is serious?"

Abby smiled, though the gravity in her eyes revealed just how often she had faced situations like this. "She is serious," she whispered with a wink. "Don't be surprised if she doesn't vote in the future."

Rose swallowed a laugh and settled back against the bench for the rest of the journey. As she let her mind roam, she realized that hearing the woman's ignorant response to female suffrage had released something inside her. She found it almost inconceivable that there were women who truly wished to have no say in their country, or in their lives, but it had taught her something very valuable. No matter what she would choose to do with her life in the future, someone was not going to like it. There would be people who would fight against her efforts and the things she believed in. There would be people who would belittle her opinions and actions. She would never be able to please everyone.

As she let the realizations fill her mind, she felt a strength and confidence she had never known pour through her. She could hardly wait to reach the ERA Convention and meet other women courageous enough to take a stand.

Chapter Twenty-Three

Rose felt it as soon as they entered the large meeting room in the Church of the Puritans, closing out the noise and chaos of New York City. Tension buzzed through the rooms like the hum of millions of honeybees swarming on a dark, summer night. A casual look revealed nothing more than determined-faced women talking in little groups, but a closer examination showed the tight lines of tension, and the suspicion radiating from eyes as they gazed around the room. The air crackled with the expectancy of a late summer thunderstorm right before the lightning struck with ferocious intensity.

Rose took hold of Abby's arm. "What's going on?"

Abby frowned. "I've been rather out of the loop because of the factories, and most recently the situation with Carrie, but I didn't realize things had gotten so strained." She gazed around the room, smiling when her eyes settled on who she was looking for. "Nancy Stratford is here. She will fill us in. Let's go."

Rose followed Abby through the crowd, increasingly aware of the tense atmosphere. She had heard many stories about Abby's friend Nancy Stratford, from New York City. Her husband was a real estate mogul, and her son was a New York policeman.

A petite blonde looked up as they approached. A wide smile bloomed on her face. "Abby Cromwell!" she cried, rushing forward with outstretched hands. "I was afraid you would not be able to come."

Abby hugged her friend and introduced Rose.

Nancy greeted Rose warmly. "Carrie has told me so much about you. I'm thrilled you could be here." She turned to Abby. "How is your daughter?"

"Grieving," Abby said. "I wasn't sure if I could attend this year, but I believe Carrie needs some time alone on the plantation without her mother and best friend hovering over her." She changed the subject quickly as her eyes swept the room. "Have things really gotten this bad? I can feel the angst pulsating in here."

Nancy frowned and pulled them to the side of the room where they could talk privately, but she cast a hesitant look at Rose.

Rose interpreted her thoughts, certain she knew the reason for the hesitancy in her eyes. "Please talk freely, Mrs. Stratford. I'm aware there are many mixed feelings about black men getting the vote before, or in lieu of, women getting the vote."

"Please call me Nancy, and I will talk freely."

Rose smiled. "Nancy," she agreed.

Nancy took a deep breath. "There is not a woman in this room who does not want black men to have the vote, but there are many determined to fight it if the vote for women is not also granted. We are still reeling from the fact that if the Fourteenth Amendment is passed, it will put the word *'male'* into the Constitution for the first time ever."

Rose nodded. "The women here are demanding voting rights for black men based on the broad principle of natural rights that is in the Constitution, but the logical result of that action must be the enfranchisement of all ostracized classes, which includes women of all colors."

Nancy cocked her head. "You are well informed."

Rose smiled. "My daughter keeps me up-to-date on current affairs. Without her, I'm afraid life on the plantation would be rather isolating."

Nancy raised her eyebrows. "You do not look old enough to have a daughter who would keep you so well informed."

Rose chuckled. "My brilliant daughter is only twelve." She smiled proudly. "She is also my teacher's aide at school, making sure all the students know what is going on in the country."

Nancy's eyes widened with surprise.

Abby laughed. "She amazes all of us, too," she confided. "Thomas sends her every magazine, newspaper and journal he receives because she is so hungry for information and knowledge. She is quite extraordinary."

"Obviously," Nancy murmured.

Rose decided to enlighten her further. "Felicia is my adopted daughter. She saw both her parents murdered during the Memphis riots last year. Moses brought her home to be part of our family."

Nancy's eyes filled with sympathy. "The poor child."

"She is quite resilient," Rose replied. "She has come a long way."

"And she is also a direct part of one of the historic occasions that led to the passage of the Fourteenth Amendment," Nancy observed. "It was the riots in Memphis and New Orleans that spurred the North to vote the Republicans into office last year, giving them the power to make the Fourteenth Amendment happen, and also to begin Radical Reconstruction." She swung around to look at Abby. "How do you feel about all this?"

Abby sighed. "Politics are messy," she said ruefully, "and they are seldom simple." She gazed around the room while she formulated her thoughts. "It is easy to understand why the motivations and goals of those who have been working so closely together for the last several years are beginning to unravel. It is rather a slap in the face to realize that women stepped back from fighting for suffrage in order to support the abolitionist movement, and now we are being cast aside as not important."

"So you agree with those who want to block the Fourteenth Amendment?" Nancy pressed.

Abby hesitated. "I'm not sure I would go that far," she objected. "Yet," she finished in a firm voice.

"I believe it is going to split the ERA," Nancy predicted. "If the Fourteenth Amendment is passed, and we allow the word '*male*' to be included in the Constitution, it might well set suffrage for women back for generations to come."

Abby frowned. "I realize that is true."

"And you're all right with that?" Nancy asked sharply.

"Not at all," Abby protested. "I read something recently that indicated that if they attempt to pass the amendment without introducing the word '*male*,' it will certainly be defeated. There seems to be wide political support for protecting the freed slaves, but not for giving women the right to vote."

"So we just give up all we have fought for in order to let black men have the right to vote?" Nancy sputtered. "I can't believe you think that."

"I *don't* think that," Abby retorted. "I'm simply telling you what I read."

Rose chuckled, hoping to alleviate the tension she felt building between the two friends. "Well, I certainly understand why the room feels like a bomb getting ready to explode," she said. "I understood you two were good friends."

Abby took a deep breath. "We are," she said quickly.

"We are," Nancy agreed. "I think what I hate the most is that political decisions made by men have had the power to turn women who have worked as allies, almost into enemies."

Abby nodded sadly. "There must be a way to come to a point of agreement on this."

Nancy shook her head. "I'm afraid it is too late for that. I fear each woman here is going to have to make a decision about what side they stand on if the Fourteenth Amendment passes as it is written."

Rose was very much afraid Nancy was right, but she had doubts that granting black men citizenship would automatically grant them the right to vote, because she knew how hard the southern states would fight to keep that from happening. They might pass the amendment in order to gain their voice in the country's government, but that didn't mean they wouldn't find ways to exclude blacks from voting. Whatever happened with the Fourteenth Amendment, it was still going to be a long, difficult battle to achieve equality—for blacks *and* for women.

****

Rose's head was spinning by the time Sojourner Truth took the stage during the second day of the convention. There had been many excellent speakers who had given her much to think about. They didn't all agree about the right course of action, but they were all equally passionate. No matter what decisions were made, it was clear not everyone would agree.

Rose took a deep breath of admiration as she gazed at the elderly woman who held her head proudly as she looked out over the audience. Felicia had made sure she was well educated on who Sojourner Truth was before she came. Sojourner had been born into slavery in 1797 and endured great cruelty and tragedy before escaping the year before New York State banned slavery in 1827. She changed her name to Sojourner Truth in the 1840s and began her life as an abolition activist. The calm strength shining from her eyes made Rose long to be just like her.

Almost as if her thoughts had called Sojourner, the woman turned her head and stared deeply into Rose's eyes. Rose shivered, her heart absorbing the wisdom she saw there. Sojourner's gaze was searching and intense. She felt a jolt as she realized it felt as if the old woman was passing a baton to her. Rose chided herself for thinking something so ludicrous, but she couldn't shake the feeling as the dark eyes penetrated her soul. Sojourner Truth had fought what most certainly must have seemed like a losing battle for decades, simply refusing to give up. Rose was certain the battle she would fight in the decades to come would seem just as hopeless at times. Yet here Sojourner was, the scourge of slavery abolished, now fighting for women's rights. Rose straightened her shoulders, lifted her head even higher, and with a nod accepted the challenge Sojourner was passing on to her.

Sojourner smiled slightly, her eyes shining bright approval, before she turned to gaze out at the rest of the crowd applauding her and began to speak...

"My friends, I am rejoiced that you are glad, but I don't know how you will feel when I get through. I

come from another field—the country of the slave. They have got their liberty—so much good luck to have slavery partly destroyed; not entirely. I want it root and branch destroyed. Then we will all be free indeed. I feel that if I have to answer for the deeds done in my body just as much as a man, I have a right to have just as much as a man. There is a great stir about colored men getting their rights, but not a word about the colored women, and if colored men get their rights, and not colored women theirs, you see the colored men will be masters over the women, and it will be just as bad as it was before."

Rose stiffened, realizing how true her words were. She had already seen the results of black men being told they were the heads of their households. The abuse that had been heaped on them was too often now being heaped on the women in their homes.

"So I am for keeping the thing going while things are stirring; because if we wait till it is still, it will take a great while to get it going again. White women are a great deal smarter, and know more than colored women, while colored women do not know scarcely anything. They go out washing, which is about as high as a colored woman gets, and their men go about idle, strutting up and down; and when the women come home, they ask for their money and take it all, and then scold because there is no food. I want you to consider on that, chil'n. I call you chil'n; you are somebody's chil'n and I am old enough to be mother of all that is here. I want women to have their rights. In the courts women have no right, no voice; nobody speaks for them. I wish woman to have her voice there among the pettifoggers. If it is not a fit place for women, it is unfit for men to be there".

Sojourner paused and let her keen eyes sweep the crowds for a long moment. When they met Rose's eyes, once again she felt a silent message being passed on. Rose shivered, but this time she didn't question it.

"I am above eighty years old; it is about time for me to be going. I have been forty years a slave and forty years free, and would be here forty years more to have equal rights for all. I suppose I am kept here because something remains for me to do, I suppose I am yet to help to break the chain. I have done a great deal of work; as much as a man, but did not get so much pay. I used to work in the field and bind grain, keeping up with the cradler, but men doing no more, got twice as much pay; so with the German women. They work in the field and do as much work, but do not get the pay. We do as much, we eat as much, we want as much. I suppose I am about the only colored woman that goes about to speak for the rights of the colored women. I want to keep the thing stirring now that the ice is cracked."

Rose laughed along with everyone else, but everything inside her was responding with fierce agreement as Sojourner's words rolled through the room with equal parts passion and ferocity.

"What we want is a little money. You men know that you get as much again as women when you write, or for what you do. When we get our rights we shall not have to come to you for money, for then we shall have money enough in our own pockets; and maybe you will ask us for money. But help for us now until we get it. It is a good consolation to know that when we have got this battle once fought we shall not be coming to you anymore. You have been having our rights so long, that you think, like a slave-holder, that you own us. I know

that it is hard for one who has held the reins for so long to give it up; it cuts like a knife."

Rose looked around the room filled with a majority of white women. Until Sojourner's speech, she had never considered that white women were also held in slavery to the men who were determined to control all aspects of their lives. It was a jolt to realize she had been released from one kind of slavery, only to have to fight against another kind, while also fighting the prejudice inflaming the South with so much hatred. It was jarring to understand the free women surrounding her were, in many ways, as much a slave as she had ever been.

Sojourner, seeming to hear her thoughts, once again swung her piercing eyes to gaze at her before she continued. *"It will feel all the better when it closes up again. I have been in Washington about three years, seeing about these colored people. Now colored men have the right to vote. There ought to be equal rights now more than ever, since colored people have got their freedom."*

Rose took a deep breath when Sojourner finished speaking and moved away from the podium. Without being able to define it, she knew she had been radically transformed. Not so much by the words, which had been powerful, but by the unspoken communication that had passed between the two of them.

In the lull between speakers, Abby turned to her with a searching gaze.

Rose met her eyes, but said nothing. She was still too much under the spell of what had just happened.

Abby gave a satisfied nod. "You got it," she stated.

Rose didn't even bother to ask her what she meant. Abby would have been well aware of what had just transpired. Rose knew it would take time for the true meaning of the last hour to settle into her heart, but she knew that in the span of sixty minutes she had become a changed woman who was ready to do whatever it took to make things better for her people, and for all women in general. She had no idea how it was going to play out in her life, and she had no idea what it would require of her, but she was determined to live with the same passion, dedication and perseverance as Sojourner Truth.

****

Moses would be alarmed if he knew what Carrie was doing, but she simply had to be outside. She was quite certain if she spent one more minute in the house she would suffocate. Thankfully, she had the perfect way to disappear without being detected. She had reclaimed her and Robert's room when Rose and Abby had left. There were moments it was sheer agony to be in the room where Robert had died, and to sleep in the bed where she had lost Bridget, but it also connected her with them in a way that comforted her heart. She could feel Robert's presence in the room. She could almost see him poking the fire to make sure the air was warm when she finally crawled out of bed. She could hear the echo of his laughter and see the brightness of his eyes.

Carrie reached for the handle hidden within the mirror. The tunnel had been built for escape from Indian attacks when Virginia was first being settled. Now it was going to help her escape the memories that were attacking her sanity. She could hear the sound of John and Moses playing out on the lawn beneath her window—John's high shrieks mixing with Moses' deep laugh. Hope's gurgling chortle as Annie played with her was simply more than Carrie could stand. She stepped into the tunnel, welcoming the black cocoon that enveloped her, and shut out the sounds that taunted her.

It took only a moment for the candle she carried to illuminate the tunnel. At least here there were not as many memories of Robert. There were plenty of memories, but they were ones that distracted her from her grief. It might only be for a moment, but at this point she would take whatever she could get. She walked slowly down the corridor, running her hand idly along the sturdy brick walls that held more secrets than she would ever know. As she thought through the war years, the memories all became about Robert again—memories of him leaving her for battle, declared missing in battle for almost a year, coming home sick, and then...

Carrie tightened her lips as she lengthened her strides, once again desperate for air. The tunnel seemed to close in on her, compressing her chest and making her want to scream. She took deep gasps as her vision narrowed and blurred. Desperate to breathe, she broke into a run for the last hundred yards, pushing through the door at the end before she collapsed on the ground, tears streaming down her face.

She lay still for several minutes, letting the darkness of the night wrap around her. Stars glimmered down as the placid waters of the James reflected them back as little points of light. She could hear the hoot of owls in the distance, but it was the raucous chorus of frogs lining the bank that finally broke through her trance. Carrie sat up and gazed around, relieved to discover she was breathing normally again. She was a little startled to realize she truly was concerned about breathing. Most of her waking moments since Robert's and Bridget's death had been spent wishing she *wasn't* breathing. When had that shifted? She didn't know the answer, but was certain the shift was not warranted.

She stood, walked over to a boulder not far from the tunnel entrance, and sat down. The dark silence, broken only by animal calls, embraced her. She listened to the gentle lap of waves, and watched as fish leapt out of the river in pursuit of the bugs hovering over the surface. As the beauty lulled her, she was startled by a fresh wave of grief. She wanted to share this with Robert. She wanted to experience it with the man she loved. The brief reprieve fled before a fresh torrent of tears that coursed down her face.

"I miss you," she whispered into the night. She knew it was ridiculous, but she still found herself listening with all her heart, hoping she would hear the whisper of his voice on the wind. Silence mocked her, causing anger to mix with the grief. She was so tired of the torrent of feelings that ripped through her heart every single day, but she also knew they would never end. She did not deserve to feel better. She had killed her daughter. Whether or not she would have made a different choice about riding home to be with Robert didn't really matter. She had pondered the conversation with Abby, but in the end it had been her choice that had killed Bridget. Nothing could justify or change that simple fact.

Devoid of peace but not willing to go back into the stifling confines of a house filled with children's laughter, Carrie sat on the boulder until the moon had risen to perch on the treetops in the distance. She watched it silently, wondering how such beauty could exist when her heart was completely shattered. Beauty that had once given her joy now seemed nothing more than a mocking cruelty.

Slowly... slowly... she discovered a feeling that at least *resembled* peace. The quiet and beauty entwined its way into her heart and mind as she watched the moon glide across the sky. The night noises were like whispers of comfort to her battered soul. There were no children, no one wanting to know how she was doing, and nobody she had to pretend on any level with. Tears flowed... stopped... and then flowed again as she faced the stark reality of life without her husband.

The moon had long set and the eastern horizon was starting to glow before Carrie rose stiffly from the boulder and made her way back down the tunnel to her room. She still had no answers, but for at least this moment in time, it didn't seem to matter. And she already knew how she was going to spend the night to come.

Once again, the tunnel was going to save her life.

Chapter Twenty-Four

Eddie looked up sharply when he heard a knock on the door. He opened it, listened for several minutes, nodded an affirmation, and then closed it again.

"You going out, Daddy?" Amber asked in a worried voice, her fourteen-year-old eyes much too knowing.

"Is there trouble, Daddy?" Eleven-year-old Carl asked, his voice more curious than concerned.

Eddie glanced over at Opal who was helping the children with their homework. He didn't want to talk in front of the children.

"You might as well tell it straight out," Opal said as she rose to stand beside him, her stout form seeming diminutive beside his towering thin frame. "Doesn't do any good to keep secrets about the troubles for black folks in Richmond. It's best the children know what to expect."

Eddie knew she was right, but it still infuriated him that his children could never seem to know peace. All they had ever known was loss, grief and fear. Yes, they were in school now and learning faster than either of them could keep up with, but Richmond was still a hotbed of uncertainty and sporadic violence for its black residents. Not for the first time, he regretted his decision to move the family back from Philadelphia after the fire that destroyed their restaurant and killed his two oldest daughters, but they were here now and would have to make the best of it.

"Clark has been arrested." He strove to keep the anger out of his voice, but he knew it was flashing from his eyes and radiating from every part of him.

"Arrested?" Opal gasped with terror. "Arrested for what?"

Amber leapt up, pushing her books aside. "Why was Uncle Clark arrested?"

"My brother was part of the latest streetcar strike," Eddie responded, proud in spite of his concern. "I'll tell you more when I get back. I have to go." Opal's eyes filled with even greater fear. He knew she was remembering his being thrown into Castle Thunder during the war. He reached out and grabbed her hand. "It's not like before, Opal. We got rights now."

His words did nothing to appease the fear on Opal's face. He could understand. Freedom in Richmond did not always look like freedom.

"What are you gonna do, Eddie?" she asked, her voice quiet as she struggled to maintain composure for the children.

"We're going to get him out," Eddie said, before he turned and pushed his way out of the house. He ran to meet up with the group who had gathered at the end of the road and were already moving toward streetcar tracks. The group of determined men walked faster when he joined them. Clumps of people gathered on the sides of the road watched them. The expressions on the watcher's faces said they knew the men were headed toward trouble.

"God be with you!" one elderly lady called out as she brandished her cane in the air.

"Go get us our rights!" called out a narrow-faced woman holding two small children by the hands.

Eddie thought through what he knew as they walked quickly down the dusty roads that bisected the black quarters. The first streetcar strike had been about a month ago. The action had been inspired by a lecture from Reverend William Brown of Baltimore. Eddie had been there for the meeting at the First African Church. His powerful speech had called for the social equality of all the races, and he also told them of the successful efforts of Charleston blacks to gain access to the city streetcars in late March. There had been much talk in the quarters since then about doing the same thing.

The first action had been taken by four men, all friends of his, who had filed on to a car designated "whites only" and refused to leave. The four had been arrested but released soon thereafter with a stern warning not to repeat their actions. Their bravery had not resulted in any kind of action from the streetcar company.

The lack of change had prompted a more complex strategy. Eddie had thought the plan wasn't going to go into effect for a few more nights, but Clark and two more of his militia unit had thought this afternoon offered the perfect opportunity, so they had acted. The three of them, proudly sporting militia uniforms festooned with ribbons from their military service, had paid their fare and climbed into a "whites only" car, sat down, and refused to leave. Other blacks had run back to the quarters, summoning the support needed for the plan to have the impact they wanted.

As they rounded the last corner, Eddie saw hordes of people coming from every direction. There were women and children in the crowd, but the vast majority were men with angry faces and determined expressions. His heart pounded harder when he realized there were several hundred of them converging on the streetcar platform. He watched as white onlookers broke and ran, obviously terrified of what might happen. Eddie set his lips grimly and continued to press forward. He would have been a part of the crowd regardless, but the fact that it was his brother made him even more determined. He had learned the only way to effect change was to demand it.

Just as they reached the platform, he saw a group of uniformed and armed policemen emerge from the horse-drawn streetcar. Two of the policemen were holding Clark tightly by his arms. The other policemen had the same grip on Jubal and Ernst. As soon as they appeared, a roar rose up from the crowd. The policemen stood their ground, but you could tell by the look in their eyes that they were frightened.

"Give us our rights!" a man hollered as he raised his fist in fierce defiance.

"We will teach these Rebels how to treat us!" another shouted angrily.

"It's up to us to take matters into our own hands," another yelled. "We will have our rights!"

"We will ride in the city streetcars!" a nearby woman screamed. "It's our right!"

The policemen exchanged nervous glances as the throng grew louder, but they turned and began to march their prisoners to the station house.

Eddie joined the mob pushing forward to follow the prisoners. Clark somehow found him in the crowd. Eddie was proud of his brother, who was walking calmly down the street, his head held high with pride. They exchanged a long look, and then Clark swept his gaze over the rest of the crowd. His courage seemed to inspire them even more.

"Don't think we can't take these men back if we decide to," a man yelled.

"Y'all can't stop all of us!" another called belligerently.

"You can't take our men like this," an elderly gentleman hollered. "We got rights!'

Eddie watched Clark carefully. The initial plan had been to press forward and free them, proving the power of the black community, but the gazes of the three men said they didn't want that to happen. He quickly began to pass the message through the crowd not to rescue the prisoners. He could only hope Clark and the rest knew what they were doing. He hated to go back and report to his wife, Jewel, and their two children that Clark was in jail for his part of the protest.

Eddie remained with the crowd long after the police had disappeared into the station house with their prisoners, but finally broke away and headed home because he knew Opal and Jewel would be frantic. He had to take information to them, even if he knew it was news that was going to fill their sleep with nightmares.

****

Eddie made his way down the street, his mind filled with worry about what might be happening to Clark and the others.

"Eddie!"

Eddie looked up as the yell broke through his concentration, relieved to see Jeremy and Marietta pushing their way toward him. He stopped and edged over to join them on the sidewalk.

"What's going on?" Jeremy asked, his eyes scanning the crowd that was now moving back toward the black quarters, their faces filled with frustration and anger.

Eddie filled him in quickly.

"I thought that was happening in a few days," Jeremy muttered.

"I thought so, too, but Clark and the others must have felt different." Eddie paused. "Is there anything you can do?"

Jeremy took a deep breath. "I don't know," he admitted.

Eddie decided to push. "I don't know what they gonna do in jail to my brother and the others. Them policemen looked pretty scared." His gut tightened. "Scared men tend to do some bad things." He couldn't stop the swarm of memories that filled his mind.

Jeremy saw through it. "This isn't Castle Thunder."

"Nope, it ain't, but men pushed up against the wall are all the same," Eddie insisted. "The more we fight for our rights, the more pressure they gonna feel."

"Do you think they were wrong to refuse to leave the streetcar?" Jeremy asked keenly.

"No," Eddie said, "but that don't mean I don't want to take care of my brother. Ain't there nothing you can do to get them out of that jail?" If anyone had a chance it was Jeremy, but he also knew his friend was under increasing suspicion for his support of black activities.

Jeremy spread his hands as he shook his head. "I just don't know."

"But we'll try," Marietta said firmly. "All of those men have children in my school." She laid a hand on Eddie's arm. "We'll do everything we can."

A burly white man stopped beside them, a leer on his broad, whiskered face. "I got things you can do for me, darlin'. I figure if you're willing to be with a nigger, that you'll be way happier with me."

Marietta gasped with surprise, and she shrank away, fear glimmering in her eyes.

Jeremy knocked the man's beefy hand off Marietta's arm. "Take your hands off my wife," he snarled as he stepped in between them.

The man laughed, encouraged by the mutters of disgust from the other men he was with. "You let your wife touch a nigger, and I figure she is asking for whatever she gets."

Eddie knew the look of a man ready to attack. He laid a heavy hand on Jeremy's shoulder. "Don't give them what they want," he said quietly. "There are too many of them." He knew he was right. Even if he joined in the fight, Marietta was certain to be harmed. Twelve to two were not good odds. Jeremy glanced back at him, but the rage did not leave his face. Eddie sighed as he prepared for the brawl. He would not let his friend fight alone, but both of them were going to be badly hurt.

"I don't reckon this fight is going to go very well," a deep voice said.

Eddie spun around, relieved beyond words to find at least twenty of his militia unit forming a semi-circle around them. One reached forward and pulled Marietta beyond the circle to safety.

"You black boys are making a big mistake," the burly man snarled.

Jeremy stood his ground, confident now that he knew Marietta was safe. "I believe it will be you boys who will be making the mistake," he said calmly. "You've got about five seconds to move on. If you don't, then I suppose you'll find out just what my friends can do."

"Your *friends?*" the man taunted. His eyes narrowed. "You're that Jeremy Anthony," he spat, anger turning to cold fury.

"That's right," Jeremy confirmed.

"We expect niggers to be ignorant, but white boys who don't know their place are nothing but stupid," the man snapped.

Eddie and the rest took two steps closer and stopped.

"Let's get out of here, Brian," one of the white men facing them muttered. "I have no desire to be in a fight."

"That's right," another man added, his voice nervous as he stared at the militia unit clearly ready to do battle. "I'm getting out of here." Not waiting to see if anyone would join him, he turned and walked away.

Eddie breathed a sigh of relief as four more of the man's friends departed. The rest didn't leave, but they took several steps back to communicate to the agitator that he was on his own.

Brian cursed under his breath but edged backward. "Your day will come, Anthony," he warned. "Plans are being made to take care of people like you." His eyes narrowed with disgust. "Watch your back," he snarled before he turned and stalked away.

Eddie watched until the group disappeared around a distant corner. Only then did he relax, but he was still concerned for his friend. "Go home, Jeremy."

Jeremy locked eyes with Marietta, saw what he was looking for, and then shook his head. "We're going to the police station," he said. "This is our fight, too."

"Not that anyone knows," Eddie said under his breath, but Jeremy's sharp glance said he had heard him.

"Just because I look white doesn't mean I don't also know I am half black," Jeremy stated. "Marietta and I can sit back and do nothing, or we can fight to make things right."

"Why do you care so much?" one of Eddie's unit demanded. "You could just pass and live in peace like a lot of folks are doing."

Jeremy met his eyes evenly. "I could say that it's because it's the right thing to do, and that would be true, but it's more than that," he replied. "My mother was a slave. My wife and I could have a child that looks black. What kind of father would I be if I didn't try to give my child a world that is better than the one y'all are living in right now?"

The man who had challenged him eyed him for a long moment, and gave a satisfied nod. "We'll walk with you to the police station."

Jeremy smiled, tucked Marietta's hand through his arm, and began to stride down the street.

****

Jeremy and Marietta stood together in front of the gray, metal desk in the front lobby of the police station. Peeling yellow paint and battered chairs were evidence Richmond was still trying to come back from four years of war and siege. There was no sign of Clark and the others, but that was not a surprise. They had probably been put into a holding cell.

"What can I do for you?" the desk officer asked in a bored voice.

"I'm here in regard to the three gentlemen you arrested on the streetcar," Jeremy replied pleasantly.

The officer's eyes narrowed. "What do you care about that?"

Jeremy had planned his strategy on the way. "My sister was on that streetcar when the gentlemen chose not to leave." He figured a small untruth would be forgiven if he could stop more violence.

"Then you know they were hardly *gentlemen*," the officer snapped. "They get whatever is coming to them."

Jeremy kept his face blank, though his mind churned with the possibilities of what that statement could mean. "My sister was badly frightened," he confided. "She is certain there is going to be more violence. She implored me to come down here to try to stop it."

The officer looked at him impatiently. "And how do you figure you can do that?"

"I happen to know the group that followed you here after the arrest is planning on returning," Jeremy revealed, his voice lowering as if he didn't want anyone else to know.

The officer's eyes shot toward the front door nervously. "When?"

Jeremy shrugged. "They wouldn't tell me that. I just know they went back to get reinforcements." He kept talking, not wanting the officer to get any ideas about calling in reinforcements of his own. "We can stop all this," he said persuasively.

The officer looked at him more closely. "Who are you?"

"My name is Jeremy Anthony. Many of the men planning on coming back here work for me at Cromwell Factory."

The officer's eyes narrowed even more. "You own that factory?"

"My brother does," Jeremy said pleasantly. "I am the manager. I would like very much to stop any further violence."

"Because your *sister* is afraid of getting hurt?"

It was obvious the officer didn't believe his story about a frightened sister, but Jeremy had achieved his objective of being listened to. "That's right."

The officer switched his gaze to Marietta. "Are you the sister?"

"No, I am the wife," Marietta responded, giving the officer a bright smile.

Jeremy almost laughed when he watched the effect his beautiful wife's smile had on the officer. "May I make a suggestion?"

"I suppose so," the officer said grudgingly, his eyes still a little bemused by Marietta's smile.

"Let the men go," Jeremy said. "They have committed no real crime. No one was hurt."

"I can't let them go," the officer complained. "We *arrested* them."

"On no real grounds," Jeremy pressed. He leaned forward and lowered his voice to make it seem he was sharing a secret with the officer. "We may not like what is going on in our city, but things are changing. If I were you, I would not want to be responsible for holding men who have committed no real crime. It will not look good for Richmond if we have another Memphis or New Orleans on our hands." He dropped his voice even further, knowing he was getting through when the officer leaned forward so as not to miss any of his words. "It will not be good if Richmond has a riot. A lot of people will get hurt, and"—he paused for effect—"now is not a good time to have the attention of the federal government on our city." He was trusting the new army units that had taken control of Virginia in the last month would be a sufficient threat.

The officer stared at him for several long moments, and then he stood abruptly and disappeared.

Jeremy exchanged a long look with Marietta. He had done the best he could do. The man may have gone to get more officers to arrest the two of them, or he may have gone to consult about what to do. All they could do was wait to find out the results of their efforts. "That was quite a smile," he whispered.

"And I'm impressed with how protective you are of your sister," Marietta whispered back, her eyes dancing with fun.

Jeremy relaxed as he gazed into her beautiful eyes. He was once again blindingly aware that he was the luckiest man in the world.

"Can you stop that crowd?"

Jeremy spun around when the officer's voice came at him from a side entrance to the lobby. "I can," he said gravely.

"You're sure of that?" The officer pressed.

"I am," Jeremy assured him, completely confident since he knew no such group existed. "I promise you I can stop any violence."

The officer stared at him for several moments before, evidently satisfied with what he saw, he nodded. "You better be right," he growled. He beckoned behind him.

Three officers appeared, each of them holding one of the prisoners by an arm.

"Get them out of my station," the officer growled.

Jeremy fought the urge to laugh with victory. "Thank you, officer," he said somberly. "You have done a good thing for the city tonight."

"Just get them out of here," the officer snapped, eyeing the door nervously.

Jeremy bit back another burst of laughter and walked over to the door with Marietta, pushing it open before the officer realized he was playing nothing but a game. He wasn't going to give him time to change his mind. Clark, Ernst and Jubal were close behind him.

Everyone remained silent until they were several blocks from the station. The dark gave them a feeling of protection, but also made them aware danger could be lurking in any shadow.

Clark finally broke the silence. "How in the world did you do that?" he asked. "I'm pretty sure we was about to get beaten, and then all of a sudden this officer showed up. He said somethin' to the officers holdin' us, and they got real nervous lookin' and decided to let us go."

"My husband can be quite persuasive," Marietta responded with a chuckle, but she sobered quickly. "I'm glad y'all are all right."

"Me, too," Clark replied. "It seemed like a good idea at the time not to let the crowd keep us from gettin' arrested, but once we got down there, we realized things weren't gonna go well."

"I was afraid of that," Jeremy said grimly. "You can thank Eddie."

"Eddie?" Clark asked. "What does my brother have to do with this?"

"He asked me to go get you out. I had no idea how I was going to do it, but once I got down there, the words just seemed to come."

As they reached the outskirts of the black quarters, ten men stepped out to meet them. It was impossible to identify anyone in the inky darkness. "Who goes there?" one of the men called harshly.

"It's Clark, Ernst and Jubal," Clark called out.

"What?" Eddie stepped close enough to be identified. "Clark, is that really you?"

"It's me, brother. I hear we have you to thank for gettin' us out."

Eddie stepped forward to give his brother a hug and then slapped the other two men on their shoulders. The other militia men crowded close. "How did you get out?"

"Jeremy hasn't told us too much," Clark admitted. "I don't reckon I rightly know."

Jeremy smiled and shrugged. "Let's just say the police weren't excited about hundreds of black militia attacking the police station to free their friends."

"What?" Eddie breathed. "You told them that?"

"It seems they understood the federal government might frown on a repeat of the riots in Memphis or New Orleans," Jeremy said. He kept his voice light, but the reality of what he had done was settling in. He had freed the prisoners, but he also knew he had put Marietta and himself in more danger by revealing his close affiliation with the blacks in the quarters. They did not have to know he was mulatto; it was enough that he was aligning himself with the freed slaves who they believed were destroying the South. He couldn't help thinking about Robert. Would he and Marietta be next?

"We're going to walk you and Marietta home," Eddie said somberly.

Jeremy wanted to protest, but he was too relieved not to have Marietta's protection solely in his hands. He realized the city was buzzing with tension after today's events. He knew better than to tempt fate. "Thank you," he said quietly.

Eddie turned and spoke under his breath to one of the men in his group, and then he turned back to Jeremy. "Give me a few minutes. We're going to call more of the men out, and then we are going to walk you home. If there are enough of us, anyone will think twice before trying to go after us."

****

The entire group had not exchanged one word since they left the black quarters, because they did not want to call attention to their presence. Jeremy breathed a sigh of relief when they reached the house, but relief was quickly replaced by concern for his friends. He glanced up and down the tree-lined street, but he didn't see anything that indicated a threat. The elegant three-story brick homes were shrouded in darkness; the soft glow of streetlamps provided the only light.

"Don't worry about us," Eddie said quietly. "We know this city like the backs of our hands. We'll get home just fine."

Jeremy embraced him warmly, nodded his thanks to the rest of the men, took Marietta's hand, and climbed the stairs.

Thomas was waiting just inside the door. "What happened?" His eyes were dark with concern. "I wanted to come find you, but May wouldn't let me leave the house." He rolled his eyes with impatience.

"It would have been nothing but foolishness for you to go out there by yourself," May said, her black eyes crackling with worry.

"You were right," Jeremy replied. "It's not safe out there tonight." He explained while he gratefully accepted the hot cup of tea May handed him.

"I'm glad you did what you did," Thomas said, "but you know it makes you and Marietta more of a target, don't you?"

Jeremy understood the raw pain on Thomas' face. The death of Robert and his infant granddaughter was still a fresh wound. "I had no choice."

"Oh, you had a choice," Thomas replied, "but you made the right one," he added firmly. "I know you considered the risk and then decided you couldn't live with yourself if you didn't decide to help."

Jeremy nodded, grateful for Thomas' understanding.

Marietta leaned over and took her brother-in-law's hand. "Every single one of us in danger," she said steadily, "but we've known that for a long time. If we let fear stop us from doing the right thing, then the vigilantes and the haters have already won, without them having to do a single thing. We stopped something terrible from happening tonight. Your brother was absolutely brilliant," she added brightly.

Thomas took a deep breath and returned her smile. It was not as bright, but it was equally determined. "That doesn't surprise me a bit. Tell me what happened."

Laughter, even though it was a bit strained, rang through the house as Marietta regaled her listeners with Jeremy's performance at the police station. "You should have heard him," she declared as she finished, "he even had me almost convinced there was the potential of a riot in Richmond tonight."

Micah walked into the room in time to hear her last statement. "He wasn't far off," he said soberly.

Jeremy looked up, his searching gaze taking in Micah's strained eyes. "Where have you been?"

"Down in the quarters," Micah replied. "I was helping spread the word that Clark and the others had been freed." He took a deep breath. "Some of the men had gathered together a right large group to go after them."

Jeremy sucked in his breath. "They were actually going to do it?"

Micah nodded grimly. "The last men who got put in jail were beaten pretty bad. Oh, the police didn't do it, but they put them in a cell with other men that roughed them up. We weren't going to let that happen again."

"We?" Thomas asked.

Micah met his eyes steadily. "Yep. We."

Thomas sat back in his chair heavily but said no more.

Jeremy reflected on this new information. "It would have been a bloodbath," he murmured. The performance, which had promoted so much laughter minutes earlier, may have actually accomplished what he had predicted—saving Richmond from a riot. He sat down in the closest chair as the reality struck home.

Marietta took his hand. "Well done, Mr. Anthony," she murmured. "Even without knowing what you were doing, you saved a lot of lives tonight."

Jeremy returned her loving gaze. "I do believe that is what my father would have called a 'God moment.' "

"I do believe you're right," Marietta replied.

"You did a real good thing, Mr. Jeremy," Micah said. "A real good thing."

Chapter Twenty-Five

Felicia came rushing in from the library, her face alight with excitement. "They did it!" she yelled, waving a sheaf of papers in her hand.

Rose, home from the convention for only one week, looked up with a smile. "Who did what?" she asked as she spooned food into Hope's mouth, convinced her youngest daughter had grown leaps and bounds in the two weeks she had been gone.

"The protesters in Richmond," Felicia explained. "After what happened with the three men who were arrested, the streetcar company gave in! They have announced that from now on there will be six streetcars. Two will be reserved for white women and children, but the rest will be for black people." She did a little jig in the parlor. "They won access to Richmond streetcars, just like the people down in Charleston did!"

John looked up at her with a puzzled expression. "So what?" he asked. "You don't ride the streetcars. You live here with us where there aren't any."

Rose smiled, glad her young son's world could continue to be simple for a while. John talked about Robert, but he had no real grasp of what had happened that night. He had asked her once where Carrie's baby had gone, but he had accepted her weak explanation that God needed Bridget in heaven. Thank goodness he had not picked up on the grief and anger she had worked so hard to hide when she answered.

"It's important," Felicia explained patiently, "because it is a step for all black people. We may have our freedom now, but there are a lot of people who are fighting to keep us from having our rights. The blacks in Richmond showed that we can fight to get them." She waved the papers in her hand again. "It is a victory for all black people!"

Rose watched her, love pulsing in her heart for the passion Felicia showed every day. She tried to push back the hollow feeling of fear that followed hard on the heels of the pride she felt. She knew Felicia's passion and determination would bring trouble to her in the future, but that was not something she could control. Just like her mama had done when she had insisted on her secret school in the woods, all Rose could do was encourage Felicia, love her, and believe in her.

"What are you thinking, Mama?"

Rose took a breath. "I'm thinking I'm so proud of you I could almost pop." She was also remembering the feeling that Sojourner Truth had passed her baton onto her. Only time would tell what that would produce in her life – what dangers it would put her in.

Felicia's knowing gaze said she knew Rose was thinking far more than that, but she let it go, her eyes resting on John's innocent face.

****

Carrie was waiting outside the barn under the shade of an oak tree for Miles to bring Granite to her. It had been sixty-six days since the fateful night that had destroyed her life. She still had not found the courage to walk into the barn, but it no longer mattered to her. The days had all begun to blur together. She slept, she rode Granite because it made her feel close to Robert, and she sat by the river long into the night. She could tell by the concerned looks on everyone's faces that they were worried about her, but that didn't matter either. She really just wanted to be left alone. She could tell by how loose her clothes were that she was losing weight, but that was hardly a concern. She had started wearing Robert's breeches to ride in. They had started out being big on her, but she just kept pulling the rope tighter around her waist.

Miles emerged from the barn holding Granite, but the look on his face was stern. "Annie said you not eatin' enough to keep a bird alive, Miss Carrie."

Carrie shrugged and reached for the reins.

Miles pulled them back. "I ain't lettin' you go until you have somethin' to eat," he insisted. He handed her a small cloth bag. "I had Annie fix you some ham biscuits to take with you."

Carrie frowned. She wanted to tell him she wasn't interested in taking them, but she knew it would only delay her departure. It didn't mean she had to eat them. "Fine," she replied as she reached for the bag.

Miles still held it away from her. "You got's to promise me you will eat them," he said. "I know you be grieving, Carrie Girl, but you ain't never lied to me. I hope you ain't thinkin' about startin' now."

Carrie gritted her teeth, holding back the angry words she wanted to spew onto the elderly black man who had never been anything but a friend. She had become accustomed to the grief, but the anger still surprised her. If she was honest, she could admit she welcomed it because it offered a break in the endless gray that seemed to have become her world.   Still, Miles did not deserve what she wanted to say.   She took a deep breath and reached for the bag. "I'll eat it."   Somehow she would manage to choke down whatever Annie had put in the bag.

Miles' eyes were still suspicious, but once she had the bag, he handed her Granite's reins.   Carrie reached for them, stuffed the biscuits in her saddlebag, and prepared to mount. A sound in the distance made her hesitate. She glanced up the driveway. She didn't really pay much attention to what was happening on the plantation, but she didn't remember shutting out talk about a visitor arriving today. She knew she should mount and ride off, but something she couldn't identify held her in place.

The sound of the approaching carriage grew louder. Carrie's eyes widened with surprise when she identified the lone person occupying it. Her desire to leave intensified to something approaching desperation, but she seemed frozen in place as she watched Matthew catch sight of her and wave.

Carrie waited for him to approach, but she didn't return the wave. What was Matthew doing here? They had not talked since before Robert's death. She knew he and Janie had been on the plantation for a week after Robert and Bridget's deaths—she even had a vague recollection of his worried, sorrowful eyes during the funeral—but she had managed to avoid speaking to him.   She hadn't wanted to talk to *anyone*, but the devastation on Matthew's face was absolutely more than she had been able to deal with. That had not changed, but she could hardly ride away from him, even though the thought certainly occurred to her.

"Hello, Carrie," Matthew said as he pulled the carriage to a stop.

"Hello, Matthew," she replied. The look in his eyes made her uncomfortably aware that she must not look very good. The combination of shock and concern on his face made her glance down at the baggy breeches hanging from her body, and she reached up to push her tangled hair away from her face, remembering she hadn't bothered to pull it back this morning. The brief awareness made the anger surge back to the surface. What right did he have to make her aware of her appearance? Didn't he understand it didn't matter? She tightened her lips as she turned to put her foot in the stirrup. She had greeted him, so now she could leave.

"Can I come with you?" Matthew asked.

Carrie whirled around to stare at him. He had stepped out of the carriage and handed the team off to Clint, who had emerged from the barn to take them. "Riding?" Her thoughts spun. No one had gone riding with her in the months since Robert's death. Everyone seemed to accept that she wanted to be alone. That had not changed. "No, thank you," she said abruptly.

Matthew stepped closer, his blue eyes boring into hers. "It would mean a lot to me."

Carrie stared up at him and then looked away, not wanting to see the warmth in his eyes. Matthew reminded her too much of Robert. His very presence evoked memories she both welcomed and hated.

"Please, Carrie."

Carrie hated the hot burning in her eyes when Matthew's voice broke into her thoughts, but she was too tired to refuse his request. He could come, but it didn't mean she would have to talk to him. "Fine," she said vaguely.

"I'll get you a horse, Mr. Matthew," Miles said eagerly. "Won't take but a minute to throw a saddle on."

****

Matthew knew he had been unsuccessful at hiding his horror when he saw Carrie. Thomas and Abby had warned him that she had grown apathetic, but he had not been prepared for the thin caricature of the beautiful woman he knew. He had a sudden understanding of how he must have appeared to her when she came to visit him in Libby Prison during the war. She had tried then to suppress her look of horror, but she had been just as unsuccessful. The difference was that he looked like a scarecrow because he was not given enough food to sustain him; she was simply refusing to eat. A part of him realized it probably wasn't as much refusal as it was being incapable of swallowing the food given to her.

Abby had explained that Carrie's grief over losing both her husband and daughter at the same time was being compounded by the combined pressures and sorrows of the war years. The spirited woman he knew had obviously reached her breaking point. He had been warned, but the evidence of it took his breath away.

"Here you go, Mr. Matthew."

Matthew smiled at Miles and swung into the saddle of a new sorrel mare that Clint had purchased weeks earlier. "Thank you," he murmured. His mind was racing as he tried to figure out how to break through the grief that had trapped his friend. It was time to reveal what he had with him.

He rode side by side with Carrie down the path between the tobacco fields, vaguely aware that once again Cromwell Plantation was going to have a magnificent crop. The fields were full of sweating men who looked up with a cheerful wave before turning back to their work. He waved back, but Carrie seemed not to even be aware of their presence. Her eyes were set straight ahead as Granite trotted smoothly down the road.

Matthew was fine with the silence. The morning air was already hot, but a line of clouds on the distant horizon promised an afternoon thunderstorm that would cool things off for the evening. Watching Carrie from the corner of his eye, he recognized when she finally relaxed, obviously relieved he wasn't forcing conversation.

Once she relaxed, he found he could enjoy the ride. It had been a long time since he had been on horseback through beautiful scenery. The pressures of the country seemed to keep him trapped in the confines of one city after the other. He still managed to spend most of his time in Philadelphia, but the last weeks in the summer heat had begun to suffocate him. He was sorry Janie wasn't with him, but she was deep into an apprenticeship with a homeopathic doctor and didn't feel she could leave. Actually, he suspected she was relieved to have stayed behind. Carrie had not answered even one of her long letters, and she was discouraged that she would ever be able to help. He knew his wife would do anything to ease her friend's grief, but she had run out of ideas. She would be heartbroken when he reported Carrie's condition to her, but he knew he would have to tell her the truth.

Carrie abruptly pulled to a halt and turned to him. "What are you doing here, Matthew?"

Matthew took a deep breath, hardly able to believe she was handing him an opening. He could read the simmering anger in her eyes as she challenged him forcing his presence into her morning ride. He reached into his pocket and pulled out a letter. He had read it so many times he could recite it by heart, but still he opened the lined pages. "Robert asked me to come."

Carrie stiffened. "What are you talking about?"

Matthew could hardly stand the pain in her eyes. He should have come earlier, but he hadn't wanted to intrude on her grief. "Robert sent a letter to me a few weeks before his death," he said quietly, his heart heavy with regret. He held it up and began to read...

Dear Matthew,

I realize you will probably find this letter maudlin and melodramatic, but I feel the need to send it nonetheless. I never would have guessed my work on the plantation could put me and my family in danger, but your latest news on the vigilantes reveals I have done just that. I would like to believe nothing could happen, but the last years in our country have proven that anything is possible. My change of heart in regard to blacks has made me, and everyone else on the plantation, a target.

My reason for this letter is simple. If something happens to me, I ask that you take care of Carrie. I know she will have her family, but you have been my best friend since college. I know you love her. Oh, don't worry, I know that you love Janie desperately, but I also know how much Carrie means to you. I need to know you will be there for her. If something happens to me, I know she will take it hard.

I want her to live her life, Matthew, even if I am gone. Please help her do that.

Your friend,
Robert

Matthew carefully folded the letter and slipped it into his pocket, almost afraid to look at Carrie. When he finally did, the shattered look on her face made his heart skip a beat. The wild look in her eyes made him long to formulate words that would ease her heart, but he had no idea how to do that. He hated how helpless he felt and quickly realized that was the reason he had waited so long. He could not fathom how he might help her *live her life*. She had quite obviously decided to not do that. He could imagine his grief if something was to happen to Janie, but he couldn't possibly know what it truly was like.

"How do I live my life?"

The soft words from Carrie's lips were more a puzzled statement than a question, but Matthew grasped for it like a drowning man would reach for a buoy. "Robert loved you so much, Carrie. Seeing you like this would break his heart."

Carrie looked down at her thin body with a frown, and then looked up with a pleading expression in her eyes. "Would it? Why?" Her voice sharpened. "He left me here."

Matthew could tell by the shocked expression on her face that she was surprised by her own words, but she didn't take them back. "He didn't want to," he said gently, certain of that with all his heart.

"He told me to come back, you know," Carrie said as hot tears filled her eyes. "After Bridget died. I saw him." Her voice faltered. "Before I regained consciousness...he told me to come back."

Matthew's heart pounded as he looked into eyes filled with hopeless agony. "He wanted you to live, Carrie."

"Why?" This time Carrie's voice was simply puzzled. "Why would I want to live without Robert and Bridget?"

Matthew groped for an answer because he was quite sure he would feel just as Carrie was feeling if something were to happen to Janie. He opted for honesty. "I don't know," he admitted. "I just know that is what he wanted."

Carrie's eyes met his squarely for the first time. "Thank you for not trying to make up something that would make me feel better."

Matthew gazed at her. "We've always been honest with each other. I'm not going to change that now."

Carrie's eyes filled with something like sympathy. "So Robert asked you to do something that is basically impossible."

Matthew didn't care to acknowledge how close he felt that was to the truth. He wished he knew more about grief, a little stunned to realize how much this was being played out all over the country, as war widows dealt with the deaths of their husbands. Since Carrie seemed to appreciate his honesty, he decided to opt for more of it. "Do you hate that I asked to join you? Does it make it harder?"

Carrie considered his question. "I don't know that it makes me feel much of anything." She hesitated. "Nothing really does." She took a deep breath as she turned to stare out over the fields. "But it is also rather nice to have someone with me that is not pressing me to know how I feel."

"I do want to know, though," Matthew said honestly. He watched as a glimmer of something resembling amusement sparked her eyes, even though her face remained expressionless.

"Yes, I suppose I would feel the way you do," she admitted, cocking her head. "Are you here only because of Robert?"

"No," Matthew replied. "I would have come regardless. I knew you didn't want to see anyone after the funerals, but Janie and I think about you and talk about you every single day. We want to help."

"How?" Her expression was once again one of honest puzzlement. "How could you possibly help?"

Once again, Matthew didn't have an answer, but at least she seemed to be engaged. "Robert and I used to talk about you all the time," he said quietly.

Carrie studied him. "What did you talk about?"

"Robert was so proud of you," Matthew replied. "He loved everything about you, but he so loved your passion to make a difference in the world." He suspected he had said the wrong thing when her eyes shuttered closed again.

"I see," she said vaguely.

Matthew decided to press the issue. She might shut him out entirely, but at least he was trying. Since he had no understanding of how to deal with grief like this, he was simply going to follow his instincts. "What are you planning to do, Carrie?"

She stared at him. "Do?"

"Yes. Do." Matthew took a deep breath. It was clear the thought was foreign to her. "Dr. Strikener told Janie you have not responded to any of his letters. Abby told me Dr. Hobson has said the same thing." When Carrie's lips tightened with anger, he expected her to turn away from him, but he was surprised when her angry eyes met his levelly.

"There is no need." Her words were clipped.

"No need?" Matthew asked. "I don't understand." He could almost see a decision forming in Carrie's eyes. Her next words almost stole his breath.

"I am not going to be a doctor," Carrie stated quietly. Her eyes, no longer angry, had taken on a blank expression.

Matthew stared at her. It was all she had wanted from the day they had met the year before the war. "Why not?"

Carrie looked at him almost as if she pitied his stupidity. "What kind of doctor could I possibly be, Matthew? I let both my husband and daughter die."

Matthew felt as if she had punched him in the stomach. He opened his mouth to protest, but something inside him screamed to remain silent. She was not ready to accept anything different than what she had decided was the truth. "I see," he murmured, managing somehow to keep his voice level and noncommittal. "So do you plan to do anything other than sleep and ride Granite?" He wasn't sure he was taking the right approach, but everyone seemed to be walking around in complete terror of how she might respond. Maybe she needed something different.

Carrie's eyes widened slightly before they narrowed into angry slits.

Matthew watched her. There had been times when he was in Rat Dungeon that he had wanted to give up and let the cold and starvation finish him. One of the other men always had something to say to keep a spark of hope alive in him, and he had done the same for them. He realized Carrie was on the edge of giving up. He prayed he could find a way to reach her, hoping it was not too late.

"How dare you?" Carrie hissed.

Matthew continued to gaze at her. Anger was better than no emotion at all, though he suspected she was very uncomfortable with the rage.

"What do you know about how I am feeling?" Carrie's voice was slightly desperate.

Matthew continued to hold her eyes. "I don't know what it is like to lose a spouse," he admitted, "but I do know what it's like to feel no hope. I know what it's like to wish I could die to escape the pain. I know what it's like to want to give up." He realized with glaring clarity that he did understand how she felt. The knowledge gave him confidence.

Carrie swayed slightly in her saddle as her hands trembled on the reins. Granite snorted and swung his head back to stare at her.

"Do you really believe Robert would want you to feel this way?" Matthew pressed. "Do you think he would want you to throw your life away?" He saw Carrie open her mouth in protest, but she didn't respond. He pulled the letter from his pocket again. *"I want her to live her life, Matthew, even if I am gone. Please help her do that."*

Carrie gave a low whimper. "I don't know how," she whispered.

Matthew's heart almost broke when she looked at him, her green eyes full of hot tears, her face a mask of raw pain. "You have people who love you so much, Carrie. They want to help you."

"I don't know how to let them," Carrie whispered.

"Spending every night alone by the river probably won't help," Matthew said gently.

Carrie gasped. "How did you know?"

"Moses wrote Thomas a letter telling him Rose went into your room one night to ask you something and saw the tunnel door open. She's been checking it every night for the last month, and it is always open. She can hear from her room when it closes every morning right before dawn."

Carrie held her head defiantly. "What I do is no one else's business."

Matthew understood the need to hide her pain behind anger. "You're right," he agreed, "but when people love you with all their hearts, do you really think they're not going to care?" He paused. "What would you do if the positions were reversed?"

Carrie stared at him, shaking her head slightly. "I have no idea."

Matthew prayed for wisdom. He knew better than to say anything about her going back to school to become a doctor. It was far too soon for her to move beyond her grief and guilt. He didn't question his certainty—he just accepted it. "I went up the Mississippi on a steamboat last month when I was in Memphis covering a story and interviewing someone for my book."

Carrie watched him carefully, obviously wondering what he was talking about now.

"I thought I could never get on a steamboat again because it would always remind me of Joseph dying in my arms." Matthew struggled to keep his voice steady because the memory still evoked so many powerful visions of the *Sultana* explosion. "I didn't think I could stand passing the spot where the explosion had occurred," he admitted, "but I discovered something that day."

Carrie didn't respond, but her expression invited him to continue.

Matthew struggled for words to explain. "When I was on the boat I decided it was like salt. If one was forbidden all salt, you wouldn't notice its absence much more in any one food than in another. Every meal you ate would just be different—every day, and every meal. Living through that explosion changed everything in my life. It is like the sky, spread over everything I do." He took a breath, hoping he was making sense. "I think Robert's death must be like that for you. It has changed every single thing about your life. It doesn't really matter where you are or what you are doing. I also believe there is not one thing that will make it worse or better. I thought riding the steamboat past the point of the explosion, and also past the point where Joseph most likely died, would send me reeling. I didn't feel anything more than I have felt almost every day since it happened." He stumbled to a stop, not sure his words were communicating his thoughts.

Carrie was watching him carefully. A long silence followed before she spoke. "You think I should go into the barn."

Matthew had honestly not had that in mind when he started talking, but obviously that was where his story had taken her. He knew she had refused to step foot into the stables. He also knew she was terrified to walk over the spot where Robert's body had lain after he was shot. "I believe the act of walking into the barn will be no worse than the *thought* of doing it," he replied. "I also believe you go riding every day because it makes you feel closer to Robert." He could tell by the flicker in her eyes that he was right. "I can't imagine a way to feel closer to him than being with the horses he so loved." If she refused to be a doctor, perhaps she could at least open her heart to the horses. There had to be something to give her an outlet for her grief.

Carrie seemed to consider his statement. Granite shifted restlessly before settling down. A flock of blue jays exploded from a nearby maple tree, their raucous calls filling the air. A sudden burst of wind was accompanied by the rolling rumble of thunder. She looked up absently and turned her horse. "We should go back."

Matthew followed her as they cantered toward the house. He had done all he could do, said all he knew to say. He had no idea if it would have any impact at all, but he had tried to do what Robert had asked him to do, and he would continue to try. Robert had been his best friend. Matthew could swallow his own grief to try to help the wife Robert had loved more than his own life.

Chapter Twenty-Six

Matthew settled on the porch, watching as the storm blew through. He loved everything about thunderstorms. He loved the rolling thunder, the jagged lightning bolts, and the ear-splitting booms that followed. He loved the patter of the rain on the roof, and the way the trees swayed in the wind. He mostly loved the way the temperature dropped on the heels of a storm at the end of a blistering, humid day. He rocked quietly, relishing the cold lemonade Annie had brought him.

"We needed this."

Matthew looked up as Moses moved outside and claimed the rocking chair beside him. "The tobacco crop looks good."

Moses nodded, a satisfied look on his face. "It's going to be a good year," he agreed.

"No more signs of trouble?" Matthew asked.

"No. We have patrols out every night, though. I don't believe we'll ever let our guard down again," he said grimly. He glanced up at the window above him that had been closed in advance of the rain. "Were you able to get through to Carrie today?"

Matthew shrugged, wondering if she was in her room or down by the river. "I don't know," he admitted, hating the helpless feeling that engulfed him. He had done the best he could, but he wasn't certain it had achieved anything at all.

"My mama says she just has to have time," Moses said.

"How much time?" Matthew demanded. "If she loses much more weight she is going to blow away." He reached down deep to find hope. "I believe she heard me," he said. "I don't know if it will do any good, but someday our love will break through."

"That's what my mama says," Moses agreed. "She said to just keep loving her. One day her heart will open enough to accept it, and she will begin to heal."

Matthew stared out at the barn, noticing a small figure standing in the door. "How is Amber?"

Moses frowned. "Heartbroken." He followed Matthew's gaze. "Carrie won't go near the barn. No one can keep Amber out of it. She sleeps there at night unless Gabe or Polly comes to get her."

"She won't leave All My Heart?" Matthew guessed.

Moses shook his head. "I wish it was that, but it's not. Amber still feels Robert wouldn't have died if she hadn't been in the barn. Somehow she has turned that into feeling responsible for the safety of everything in that building. Even though Miles is in the room above it, she insists she has to keep an eye on things."

Matthew watched the young girl gaze up at the sky, her little body stiff and defiant. "Grief does strange things," he observed. "Is she still working with the foals?"

Moses nodded. "She pours her whole heart into it. She refuses to go to school. Polly and Gabe tried to force her, but they finally gave up, realizing she needs time to work through her heartbreak. She and Robert were as close as any father and daughter could be. The only time she seems to have any peace is when she is with the horses."

"I know," Matthew agreed. "Robert used to write me about Amber all the time. He was so proud of her." He decided to change the subject. Continuing to talk about the grief he could do nothing about was wearing him down. The topic he was bringing up was not any better, but he thought Moses should know about it. "A new organization has formed."

Moses eyed him. "I can tell by the tone in your voice that it's not one I'm going to be excited about."

Matthew nodded. "I'm afraid you're right. It's a group down in Louisiana called the Knights of the White Camellia."

"What a pleasant name," Moses said sarcastically. "My guess is they have the same agenda as most of the groups springing up around the South—to stamp out the blacks and punish the whites who try to help them," he added heavily.

"I'm sorry," Matthew said.

Moses shrugged. "In case you haven't figured it out, you are in as much danger as we are. Maybe even more," he added. "Robert's death should have shown you that."

"The men weren't trying to kill Robert," Matthew said. "He got in the way of them trying to shoot Amber."

Moses looked at him sternly. "You heard what Southerlin said. Those men came over to shoot Robert."

Matthew shook his head. "I think Stowe decided to take credit for it when his attempt to shoot a harmless little girl killed Robert instead." He seethed with anger as he thought of his best friend being shot down in cold blood. He gazed out into the darkness, almost wishing the vigilantes would try again so he could play a part in avenging Robert's death, but he sagged back against the chair, realizing more killing was not the answer.

Moses eyed him for a long moment. The expression on his face said he knew what Matthew was thinking. "Tell me about the Knights of the White Camellia."

Matthew sighed, wishing he hadn't started the conversation. He should have just enjoyed the cool breeze blowing soft rain onto the porch. "They are the Louisiana version of the Ku Klux Klan," he said. He realized he didn't really need to say anything else. Men were rising up all over the South to fight the Radical Reconstruction plan that had been in full effect since the beginning of May.

Moses remained silent for a long while. "If trouble comes, we will deal with it," he finally said. "I don't reckon there is anything else we can do." He shifted his massive frame in the rocking chair, causing it to creak in protest. "I am going to grow tobacco, I am going to raise my children, and I'm going to make certain Rose can teach her students. There is nothing more I can do right now." His deep voice somehow managed to be both stoic and bitter.

Matthew nodded. He knew Moses was right. All the man could do was what was in front of him to do. He and Rose had chosen not to start college so they could be here for Carrie, but he also suspected they felt their children would be safer on the plantation. Their decision to leave Cromwell and begin college would probably do nothing but make them more of a target. He was certain they would make that decision when they felt the freedom to move on, but he hoped they could enjoy this time as much as possible.

Matthew eyed Amber again, wondering if she was aware they were on the porch watching her. "Have you heard from Mark and Susan?" They had stayed for a week after Robert's death, long enough to be there for the funeral, but then they had to return to their own operation the same day he and Janie had returned to Philadelphia.

"Yes. They got all the yearlings back safely. It took four train cars to transport them all, but evidently they are creating quite a stir up in the Shenandoah Valley. I got a letter from them several days ago asking about Carrie and how things are going with the stables and the horses."

Matthew gazed at him. "How *is* it going? Everything seems to be running smoothly."

"It is," Moses agreed. "Robert trained Clint well, Amber is working harder than ever, and having Miles back has been a godsend."

Matthew glanced at him when his voice took on a funny tone. "What?"

Moses hesitated before he answered. "I'm just grateful Miles is here. It's like God knew what was going to happen. Miles knows Cromwell Plantation like the back of his hand, he has the maturity that Clint is still learning, and he loves Carrie so much. It helps that he has known her since the day she was born." He shook his head. "He even made her eat some of Annie's biscuits. That was a small miracle."

Matthew chuckled. "She made me eat one of them," he confessed.

Moses shrugged. "One is more than she has eaten for a while."

Matthew frowned. "Is she punishing herself?"

"I wish we knew. We've all dealt with grief, but I've never seen anyone that seems to have had their very soul ripped out."

Matthew nodded. "Abby says it is a culmination of everything that has happened in the last six years. Carrie finally reached the end of her endurance."

"She seems so broken," Moses murmured. "She has saved so many of us, and now we can't save her." He clenched his fists. "I hate feeling so helpless."

Matthew understood completely. "Carrie is strong," he said. "She will find her way back to us." He could feel Moses staring at him in the darkness. The skepticism in his unseen eyes vibrated through the damp air. "I believe that," he insisted.

"Why?" Moses asked bluntly.

Matthew knew Moses was reaching for hope. "I remember one night down in Rat Dungeon," he said. "I had held on to hope for so long. I had insisted on living down there so I could dig the tunnel faster. I thought I was strong enough to handle it." He paused as the memories that still haunted him poured through his mind and almost clogged his throat. "I wasn't," he said simply. "I laid down one night, freezing cold and hungry, and I decided I was going to die. I knew how close I was, and I knew that if I quit fighting, I would just die." His voice caught. He had never told anyone this before.

"Why didn't you?" Moses asked after a long silence.

"I couldn't." Even now Matthew wanted to be able to give a better answer than the one he had. "I wish I could say I had seen a bright light, or that God's voice spoke to me, but that wasn't the case. As I was lying there, praying I would die, there was a part of me that simply wouldn't give up. Was it God? Was it something within me that believed something better was going to happen? Was I simply too stubborn to just give up and die?" He shook his head. "I don't know. All I know is that I had to get up and keep trying, because I wasn't able to give up."

Moses pondered his words for a long while. "So you think Carrie doesn't have it in her to give up?"

"That's what I believe," Matthew agreed. "Carrie is special. She may not care much about living right now, but I believe the time will come when something sparks a desire to live."

Another long silence settled on the porch. The rain had stopped, and the rumble of thunder was far off in the distance. The noise had been replaced by the harmony of crickets and frogs, interspersed with whinnying horses. The cloying heat had been replaced by a cool air that wrapped around them. Neither man moved, both content to enjoy the night.

A sudden movement caught Matthew's attention. Carrie was walking down the road toward the stables, her posture both determined and hesitant. He felt the instant Moses noticed her because his whole body tensed.

"She must have walked all the way from the river," Moses whispered.

Matthew leaned forward, his eyes never leaving her. He watched as she walked within a hundred feet of the barn, the closest she had been since Robert's murder, and then stopped. He could feel the battle going on in her mind as she gazed at it. *You can do it!* His mind screamed the message, but he knew it was her own battle to fight. It would have to be nothing but her courage that would carry her past her fear.

Carrie walked several feet closer before she stopped again. An owl swooped overhead, its dark form outlined against the thinning rain clouds. She glanced up and continued to walk slowly, as if her body were encased in deep mud. She seemed to be pressing forward through a thickness so intense it seemed almost impossible to penetrate it.

Matthew gripped the arms of the rocking chair, every particle of him aching for her because he knew what she was having to conquer. *You can do it!*

When Carrie was only a few feet from the spot where Robert had lain, dying in a pool of his own blood, she stopped again and looked toward the sky.

Matthew could well imagine what she was feeling. Even though he couldn't see it, he was sure every muscle in her body was trembling with terror and determination. Something had shifted in her. Something had happened by the river that had brought her to this point. He wasn't sure she could actually walk into the barn, but what she had done was astounding.

Another movement caught his attention. His eyes shot toward the entrance of the barn, widening in amazement when Amber moved out into the darkness.

****

"I'm here, Carrie," Amber said somberly.

Carrie jerked. She hadn't known anyone was in the barn. For a moment she felt a flash of shame at the fear that must be obviously imprinted on her face. She wanted to whirl around and retreat before Amber could feel her pain, but a small voice inside told her Amber understood it better than anyone else possibly could. She remained rooted in place, her eyes fixed on the spot where her husband had been killed.

Amber materialized at her side. "I mostly come in the back way," she confided, "but when I take the horses out I have to bring them this way. It's real hard."

Carrie glanced over at her. "I imagine it is," she said softly, some small part of her recognizing the agony glimmering in Amber's voice. She had been so locked in her own pain that she hadn't been able to feel anyone else's. It was rather shocking to discover that recognizing the little girl's pain did not make hers any worse.

Amber's little hand slipped in hers. "I'll walk in with you," she said quietly. "The first time is the hardest."

Carrie jerked again. She had not planned on going into the barn. She had just wanted to see if she could actually walk up to the spot where Robert had thrown himself on Amber to protect her. She was relieved to discover there was no evidence of blood in the dirt. She knew, of course, that they would have gotten rid of any trace, but the image of it had never left her mind. She stared hard at the spot, trying to envision what must have been going through Robert's mind when he had felt the bullet enter his back. She swayed for a moment, but tightened her lips as she stared down at her hand encased in Amber's small black one.

The raucous sound of the crickets and bullfrogs seemed to fade as her mind roared with a refusal to do what was being offered. Suddenly a clear whinny split the air, followed by another one almost immediately. *Granite.* Carrie's heart surged forward, but her legs still felt incapable of movement.

Another whinny followed, this one more demanding. She knew her horse smelled her, but she felt something more responding in her heart. Granite was offering her courage. He was calling forth the memories of Robert riding him in the Tournament the day after she had met the man who would become her husband. He was reminding her of the months he had been missing with Robert after both of them had almost died in battle. Her horse's life was just as entwined with Robert as hers.

As another ringing whinny split the night air Amber tugged firmly on her hand. Carrie took a deep breath, willed her legs to move, and walked into the barn. Her first thought was one of pure astonishment. Walking over the spot...standing in the barn...it was not any more difficult than the thought of it had been. She remembered something Matthew had said earlier in the day, that the grief and pain were like the sky. It simply covered everything in her life. *It simply was.*

Amber stood quietly as Carrie took deep breaths of the barn scents that had been part of her life for as long as she could remember. She managed a smile when Granite thrust his head over his stall door and bobbed it joyfully. She walked forward, wrapped her arms around his warm neck and hugged him. Though she had been riding him every day for more than a month, this was the first time she had allowed herself to embrace him; the first time she had allowed him to comfort her. His solid warmth seemed to melt through the core of the coldness that had frozen her soul.

Somehow, the step into the barn had released something powerful within her. Just one tiny step, but it had ignited a spark of hope that someday her world might not be controlled by a dark grief that obliterated all the color. She didn't really feel any better, but she had hope that someday she would.

"All My Heart would like to say hello."

Amber's voice broke into her thoughts. Carrie looked over and saw the dark bay filly's head, the perfect heart-shaped marking glowing in the lantern light. All My Heart's eyes were locked on her with a bright intensity. Carrie stared at her, wondering what was going on behind the wise eyes. Almost against her will, Carrie reached over to stroke All My Heart's soft muzzle.

How had she lasted so long away from the horses? Granite evoked such powerful memories of Robert. All My Heart reminded her of the amazing heart of the man who had taken such joy in giving Amber the horse of her dreams. As she gazed around the barn, she realized every horse in it was a reflection of her husband. A reflection of his dreams. A reflection of the life he worked so hard to create when he believed his own hope was gone. As she took a deep breath of discovery, Amber seemed to read her mind.

"I feel Robert in here all the time." Amber's voice cracked, but the light in her eyes was steady.

Carrie realized she had been running from every memory of her husband, while Amber had run *toward* them, innately knowing she would need them to survive the pain. Not for the first time, she wondered where the little girl had gotten her wisdom, but she decided to just be grateful. She walked over to stare outside the barn and beckoned Amber to join her. "Tell me about the new foals," she invited. She knew several had been born since Robert's death. The moon breaking through the rapidly dissipating clouds cast enough light to distinguish the shapes milling around in the pasture. Half the herd was in this front field; the rest were in the back.

Amber smiled brightly and slipped her hand in Carrie's. "There are some mighty fine fillies and colts out there," she began. "Robert would be so proud of them."

Carrie accepted the catch in her heart when she heard his name come from Amber's lips, but she was relieved she could choose to focus on what Amber was saying. She pointed out a chestnut with four white stockings. "That one must be Lightning Lady's." The foals were clumped together, with the mares clustered beneath one of the oak trees.

Amber nodded. "That's right. She was born four weeks ago. She looks just like her mama, and she is just as sweet," she said proudly, her eyes reflecting the moonlight as she gazed up at Carrie.

Carrie lost track of time as Amber told her about one foal after the other. The sound of her voice, combined with the sweet smells of hay, grain and saddle oil, was a balm to her soul. Matthew had asked her what she was going to do. She had her answer now. She would carry on the legacy Robert had left her. She would raise horses on Cromwell Plantation, building the breeding program into the one she knew Robert had dreamed of.

She pushed down the swell of longing that rose inside her as the memory of being a doctor surged into her mind. That possibility was over. She would never be a doctor.

She had a new path now.

Chapter Twenty-Seven

Carrie could hear voices when she walked past the kitchen. She wanted to keep walking, but her stomach said she needed to eat some breakfast. Still, she stared at the closed door for several moments. She had managed to find energy to work with the horses each day for the last month, and there were moments when she actually felt little glimmers of joy when one of the foals learned something new, but anything outside the barn was simply more than she had the strength for. Whatever was being discussed in the kitchen, she simply had no desire to engage in it. A loud rumble in her stomach made her mind up. She was still too thin, but some of the weight she had lost was starting to return. If she stopped to think about it, it seemed somehow wrong that her body could respond in any positive way when her soul still felt so destroyed, but she figured it was just the way it was. She sighed as she pushed open the door and entered the sweltering kitchen.

The back door was open, letting in the sound of singing birds, as well as the aromas of biscuits baking in the cooking shed out back. It was too hot to cook in the house now that the end of July had pounced on the plantation like a horde of bloodthirsty mosquitoes. Each night seemed to bring a thunderstorm. It cooled things off briefly, but the mornings delivered another blistering day thick with humidity that seemed to suck the life from everything. Both Polly and Annie had sweat gleaming on their faces, but it didn't seem to really bother them that much. She wondered briefly if it had something to do with their African heritage. She was quite certain she couldn't take many more days of this heat, but she didn't suspect a break was coming anytime soon.

Carrie watched as Polly and Annie broke off their conversation abruptly. It didn't take a genius to realize they had been talking about her, but she didn't care. She nodded at them absently as she reached for a plate full of bacon and biscuits covered with gravy. She knew Polly was watching her closely, and she could almost feel the moment the older woman decided to say whatever she was thinking.

"There are a few people at the clinic that I don't know how to help," Polly said.

Carrie stiffened, but she felt rather detached from the words coming from Polly's mouth. There was a part of her that knew she should probably have some kind of response, but in all honesty she didn't care. She glanced at Polly, but didn't have anything to say. She just wanted to get some breakfast and go to the barn to be with the horses and Robert. She felt that way every day. When she was in the barn, or working with the horses, she felt close to her husband. She resented anything that seemed to keep her from that.

"Did you hear me?" Polly asked with a sharp edge to her voice.

Carrie nodded. She supposed she should say something, even though all she really wanted to do was walk out. "I don't work at the clinic," she said before she turned to leave.

"These men are hurting," Polly said more firmly. "I don't know how to help them."

Carrie tightened with anger. "I can't help them either," she snapped, rage surging to the surface so quickly it almost frightened her.

"You *won't* help them," Polly replied.

The rage disappeared almost as quickly as it had emerged. The whole conversation was not something she had the stamina for. "I'm sorry," she muttered, something telling her she probably *should* be sorry, even if she didn't mean it. It actually felt puzzling that Polly seemed to think she could help. Whoever the person was that Polly was thinking about, they no longer existed. Carrie started to push through the swinging door, but Annie's words halted her in her tracks.

"When you gonna stop feelin' sorry for yourself, Miss Carrie?" Annie's voice was not harsh, but it was blunt.

Carrie gasped as if Annie had punched her, and whirled around, fury loosening her tongue. "What would you know about what I'm feeling?" she snapped. Annie narrowed her eyes, but she remained silent. As Carrie glared at her, the understanding that Annie could understand better than anyone filtered through her bitter defiance, but the realization did nothing to make her feel better. Why couldn't everyone just leave her alone? Slowly, the compassion filling Annie's face broke through her defenses. As her walls lowered, the pain she had been holding at bay crashed through like towering waves and seemed to swallow her. Carrie doubled over as a ripping pain shot through her.

Then she turned and ran.

****

Carrie didn't know how much time had passed before she heard light footsteps. She wanted to jump up and run again, but she was too exhausted. She had run all the way here, and her tears had left her drained and empty. She wanted to tell whoever it was to go away and leave her alone, but her mouth wouldn't form the words. She remained silent and waited to hear the words of whoever had come to pass judgement on her for being cruel to Annie. There was some part of her that recognized she had not been kind, but she couldn't find enough energy to care. She was becoming quite adept at shutting out the world. She could certainly do it one more time. She was puzzled when she heard the crinkle of paper and then the sound of departing footsteps. When the expected voice didn't come, she finally looked down beside her and saw an envelope.

Curious, Carrie picked it up and stared at it, recognizing the handwriting immediately, but not seeing a postmark. How had Biddy sent a letter to her? She imagined Rose had followed her through the tunnel down to the river, but a quick glance told her she was nowhere in sight. There was a part of her that resisted opening the letter, and the very sight of Biddy's spidery scrawl evoked memories of the daughter named for her, but she loved the old woman far too much not to read what she had written. She opened the envelope carefully, pulled out the thick sheaf of papers, took a deep breath, and began to read.

My Dearest Carrie,

I have asked Abby and Rose not to give you this letter until the end of July because I don't believe you will be ready to hear anything I have to say until then.

You may still not be ready, but I fear waiting any longer would not help you.

Carrie frowned. Days had come to mean nothing to her so she had to struggle to determine the date. She vaguely remembered seeing a newspaper lying on the dining room table on her way to the kitchen this morning. Her eyes had landed on the day, July twenty-fourth. Her father always sent the newspapers to Felicia within a few days, so the best she could calculate, it must be the end of July. Her heart quickened as she realized it might even be July twenty-seventh, the third month anniversary of the deaths. She wasn't sure when she had begun to refer to them in her mind as *the deaths*. It somehow seemed easier than thinking of both Robert and Bridget dying separately.

Rose would be as aware as she was what day it was. That thought filled her with an instant remorse. She had been avoiding her best friend as much as everyone else. She couldn't face the sympathy in her eyes. The only peace she felt was when she was with the horses because they had no understanding that her whole world had been ripped into shreds.

Carrie shook her head and turned back to the letter. At this rate, it would take her all day to read whatever Biddy had to say. Just holding the pages in her hand, though, made her feel closer to the wise-eyed woman that had grown so dear to her.

You know my story, so there is no need to remind you while you are buried in your own grief.

Carrie stared out over the water, thinking of all Biddy had lost—her husband, all her sons, and all but one of her grandsons, most of them swallowed by the war. She had felt sympathy and horror before, but now the reality of her own loss had given her an understanding of how unbearable it all must have been. She could not imagine how Biddy had survived it.

I'm sure at this point that you are wondering how I survived it all, because you are questioning why you should survive your own loss.

Carrie gasped as the woman anticipated her thoughts from afar, and then she read on, suddenly desperate to hear what Biddy had to say. The words were clearly coming from someone who had walked where she was walking.

No one's grief is alike, Carrie. All of us have a different life, and we are all different people. We all lose our loved ones in different ways. There are many who are certain they understand your grief, but those are the ones who probably understand it the least. I certainly understand grief, but I'm not so arrogant to say I understand your grief. You do not need to explain your grief to anyone. It is mostly important for you to know your pain is unique to everyone else's. You can merely do the best you can to survive it.

Carrie sighed as she lowered the pages. She should have known Biddy would give her the space to do things her own way. She was also uncomfortably aware that neither Abby nor Rose had tried to tell her they understood her grief, or thought it should be a certain way. She had blocked them out, when there may have been no reason to block them out.

There will be people in your life who may feel you have grieved long enough, or that it is time for you to move on with your life. They will think about the strong Carrie they know and expect you to behave in a certain way. Sometimes, my dear, our very strength means our grieving is even deeper because our hearts are so passionate about everything. It can be both a blessing and a curse. Most days, four years after the loss of my final grandson, I can walk through life fairly normally, but then something will happen that awakens all the pain and makes it all seem fresh and new. All I can do is grit my teeth, wait for the worst of the agony to pass, and pray for my breath to come a little easier. Carrie, no one can dictate how you deal with the loss of Robert and Bridget. We all must find a way to embrace life again, though I'm quite certain that seems impossible to you right now. For so long I simply didn't care to try to make meaning or sense of all the death. There is no real sense in it, after all, but humans strive to find a way to move on since we are the ones still alive. You never truly get over it because the deaths leave a hole in your life that nothing else can fill.

Tears filled Carrie's eyes as Biddy spoke the words screaming in her soul. The conversation with Annie and Polly had seared her heart this morning, but there was also a part of her that realized Annie, because she was a slave, had barely had time to feel the grief of her losses because her life was not her own. She understood loss, but she had never had a choice to do anything but pick up the pieces and move on. Perhaps that was better, Carrie mused, but that was not her life, and not her experience. Biddy promised her that was all right.

There are people who will tell you that you have to let go of your loved ones. What rubbish!

Carrie couldn't help the smile that trembled on her lips as she envisioned Biddy's bright blue eyes snapping with indignation. She could hear her Irish accent clearly through the written words.

I've never told anyone that I have Faith fix birthday cakes every year for my husband, my sons, and my grandsons. The children in Moyamensing have no idea why Faith bakes so many cakes, but they know what the smells from the kitchen mean, and they are always lined up to eat them. Many would tell me I'm being maudlin, but it is simply my way of honoring their existence in my life. I treasure the memories of each one, even while I strive to live life each day and move into the future, however much more of it I have left. The day is coming soon when I will be with all those I have lost. You do not have that same knowledge, so do whatever feels right to you to honor the lives of Robert and Bridget.

Carrie lowered the pages again, thinking of her decision to carry on Robert's legacy with the horses. It was the only way she knew to live with her pain today, and it was the only way she knew to honor his existence in her life. She pushed aside the uncomfortable thought of how much he had supported her being a doctor. She wondered what he would think of her decision, but he hadn't known that the day would come when it was impossible for her to save her husband and her daughter. She swallowed hard to push down the bile of burning guilt that rose up in her throat to choke her. She turned back to the letter to escape her own thoughts.

Now I'm going to tell you something I am quite sure you don't want to hear, and you may not be ready to hear it, but still I am going to say it. We are enough alike that I know your first thought is to shut everyone out and endure the pain on your own. Carrie, my dear, you will never move through your grief unless you experience it. Hiding it or denying it will only prolong it. Talk about it, Carrie. Talk about it with Abby. Talk about it with Rose. Talk about it with anyone who will listen—even Granite, who may be the best listener of all!

Carrie could not believe it when she chuckled. She *chuckled*. It was the first thing resembling laughter that had escaped her mouth since she had seen Mark Jones' grim face on the train platform. She sobered quickly as the memory that had started this long nightmare rose up in her mind. Biddy was right that she didn't want to hear what she was saying, but there was also some small part of her that felt there might be truth in it.

Talk, Carrie. Talk about Robert. Talk about Bridget. Talk about the pain ripping through you. Talk about how you feel like you are a failure for not saving them. Talk about how you believe it is your fault.

Carrie gasped and put down the letter with trembling hands. How had Biddy known? Had Abby told her? She tossed the question aside as soon as it rose in her mind; Abby would never have done that. Biddy must know because she had felt responsible herself. But how could she? None of the deaths had been her fault. She had lost her sons and grandsons to a terrible war that had ripped the country apart.

I already know what you are thinking, Carrie. How do I know you believe it is your fault? I know you, dearest one. I've watched you go long, sleepless days and nights to save everyone you can possibly save. I've watched you fight the grain of society to help others because you believe it is the right thing to do. I watched you save so many here in Moyamensing from cholera. How it must ache that you could not save your husband and daughter. I'm not going to try to convince you it is not your fault, though it is most assuredly not. I'm just going to tell you to talk about it. Every time you do, you will breathe a little easier. It's okay that you don't believe me, but I urge you to at least try. You have so many people who love you so deeply. Let them love you, Carrie. Please let them love you.

Tears blurred Carrie's eyes and made it impossible to continue reading. She bowed her head as quiet sobs shook her thin shoulders. She finally was able to take a deep breath and pick the letter up again, eager to see what else Biddy had to say.

I fear I may have already tried to say too much, but I don't know how long it will be before I see you again. I wish we could sit in my parlor and talk for hours, but I understand why you don't want to leave the plantation. Grieving is a process, dear one. There will be days when it doesn't hurt quite so badly, and then it will come roaring back with an intensity you are sure will destroy you. There are days when the sadness consumes you, and then anger will make you want to lash out at every person around you. You will feel crazy at times. There will also be days when you will almost feel normal – but then you will feel guilty, because how could you ever hope to feel normal again. The spiral of feelings will seem to spin you around until you feel there is no life within you.

Now, do I believe it will get better? Yes. Though I will never quit missing the loved ones I have lost, my life is also full and good. The things I am doing will never replace what I have lost, but I have wonderful people that make the loss not quite so terrible. You are one of them. I have no idea how long it will take for you, Carrie, but there is one thing I encourage you to do. Every time you think of Robert dying in your arms, also try to pull forth a memory of you dancing together. Remember your first kiss. Remember laughing together. Accept the pain of the horrible memory, but also welcome the other memories that make you miss him so very much. *Remember him the way he is hoping you will remember him.*

I love you, Carrie. You are constantly in my thoughts and prayers.

Biddy

Carrie lowered the pages, and for the first time since Robert's death, she let her mind fill with memories of the good times. Until this moment, each memory that had tried to seep in had only increased her misery, not relieved it. She wasn't sure she was actually feeling relief now, but she could at least say the images filling her mind did not feel they were ripping her soul from her. A small glimmer of comfort filled her as she allowed her mind to replay many of the wonderful times with Robert.

Her breath caught with a gasp as she tried to do the same with Bridget. There were no memories of the daughter she had lost, only a black hole of emptiness that could never be filled. But then she realized something. She had the memories of the moments Bridget had been conceived. She had the memories of her growing in her womb, of her kicking and squirming as she moved toward life. Her throat locked as the memories threatened to choke her. She could only imagine how beautiful her daughter must have been. She had never seen her, though. Carrie understood why they had not been willing to pry open the tiny casket after five hot days, but she had nothing to remember. That knowledge, more than anything, rose up to overwhelm her. She cried out and leaned over as a new spasm of sobs racked her body.

"Carrie."

Carrie stiffened when the soft voice sounded beside her, and as an arm curled around her waist to support her. *Talk about it.* Biddy's words came to her as a command. She whirled to stare at Rose, not even questioning why she was there. "What did Bridget look like?" she cried. "What did my daughter look like?"

"She was beautiful," Rose murmured. "She had a perfect little face with tiny rosebud lips. Every toe and finger was there. She was so tiny, but she was so perfect." She paused. "And she had black hair." Somehow she managed to smile. "She had more black hair than I thought it was possible for a baby so young to have."

Carrie stared at Rose, trying to envision it. She had never asked before because she couldn't deal with one more image of the daughter she had killed. "What color were her eyes?" she whispered.

Rose's own eyes filled with sadness. "I don't know, Carrie."

Carrie finished what she didn't say. "She never opened them," she said numbly.

"No, she never opened them," Rose agreed, somehow knowing Carrie needed to hear it. "She was dead when she was born." Her voice was full of raw pain. "Abby held her for a long time. She held her, and talked to her, and stroked her tiny head so she would know how loved she was."

The tears came faster as Carrie imagined her daughter dying inside the womb that had sheltered and held her for seven months, yet she was also comforted by the knowledge that Bridget had not been alone, that her grandmother had held her close and wrapped her in love when she had been taken from her mother.

Rose kept her arm around Carrie's waist as she cried, but she said no more. Carrie simply enjoyed the connection until her tears ran dry, and then she moved back so she could see Rose. "Why are you still here?"

Rose cocked her head, but seemed to understand the true depth of the question she was being asked. "I'm here because you are here."

For the first time, Carrie looked at her with a thought to what Rose was doing. "You and Moses are going to college," she murmured, her eyes widening with sudden realization. "You should have already left."

Rose smiled tenderly. "Would you have left me?"

Carrie considered the question. "No," she admitted, "but it's time for you to go."

"Is it?"

Carrie stared at her friend's calm face, not able to miss the love radiating from her eyes. "I've been terrible," she cried.

"You've been grieving," Rose answered. "And you will be for a long time. I don't know what Biddy said to you in that letter, but I'm glad it seemed to help." She answered the questions in Carrie's eyes. "She gave it to us when we stopped to see her after the ERA Convention in New York City. She asked us to not give it to you until now."

"Until this exact date?" Carrie asked.

"No," Rose answered. "She told me you weren't ready for it yet, but that I would know when you were."

"How did you know?"

Rose shrugged. "I didn't. I was afraid I would give it to you too late, or too early. When I saw you run out of the kitchen this morning and head for your room, I knew where you were going. I hoped I wasn't making a mistake when I followed you and gave you the letter."

"It was the right time," Carrie murmured. Rose continued to sit beside her quietly. Carrie vaguely became aware of the sun blazing down on them. She could feel the sweat pooling in her armpits and beading on her forehead. It was the first time she had even been aware of her surroundings. "I'm not leaving the plantation," she said suddenly.

Rose turned to look at her, but she didn't say anything.

"I can't," Carrie said almost desperately. "I'm not going to be a doctor," she said, certain Rose would argue with her decision. She was surprised when Rose remained quiet, looking at her with a soft understanding. She grew uncomfortable when the silence stretched out. "Aren't you going to say anything?"

"What would you like me to say?"

Carrie shook her head with frustration. "I'm going to stay here on the plantation and make Robert's dream come true. The only peace I have is when I'm with the horses." She wanted her best friend to understand. She had to *make* her understand, because Rose had to leave.

"All right," Rose replied, her dark eyes glowing with compassion.

Carrie shook her head again. "I'm not leaving, Rose, but it's time for you and Moses to leave."

Rose met her eyes steadily. "I'm not leaving either," she announced. "I'm going to be here with you."

Carrie felt a surge of panic. Her life might be destroyed, but she couldn't let Rose's life follow suit. Rose had refused to escape the plantation earlier because she wouldn't leave her mother. Now she was making the same decision for Carrie. The last three months of dark pain had made her oblivious to what

Rose and Moses were going through. They had fought so hard, and given up so much, for their freedom. She couldn't entrap them on the plantation again. "You can't stay," she burst out. "You are meant to be a teacher. Moses is meant to be a lawyer."

"And you are meant to be a doctor," Rose said flatly. "As long as grief is keeping you from your path, I am going to walk the one you have chosen with you." She held up her hand when Carrie opened her mouth to protest. "It's already been decided, Carrie. I know you believe you are not meant to be a doctor. You certainly get to believe that, but I get to believe what I want too," she added. "This is not really open for discussion. Moses and I are staying here on the plantation with you."

Carrie closed her lips against the protest she was trying to find words to voice. She saw Sarah shining through her daughter's eyes. She recognized the same quiet strength; the same determination to do what she believed was the right thing to do. Sarah lived on through her daughter.

Carrie did the only thing she could do. She reached out and grabbed Rose in a tight hug, hoping it would communicate some of what was bubbling in her heart. When Carrie finally released her, she remembered she had seen Moses leaving that morning on horseback with Simon. They had not been headed toward the tobacco fields, and he had not been dressed for a day in the fields. "Where did Moses go this morning?"

"The Republican Convention in Richmond," Rose replied.

Carrie couldn't miss the tension in her best friend's voice. She sent up a thought of gratitude that at last she was able to recognize something more than her own pain. "You're afraid?"

Rose hesitated for a long moment as she turned her eyes away to gaze out at the river, but she finally turned back to look at her. "I'm trying to fight the fear, but we are all wise to be cautious right now."

Chapter Twenty-Eight

July 31, 1867

Moses was silent as they approached the Richmond city limits. The number of other black travelers said he and Simon were not the only ones coming in from the country for the GOP Convention. There was a part of him that was anticipating the event, but there was a bigger part that doubted his decision to leave the plantation. He was confident in the men he had left behind to guard his family, and he believed he should be involved in the politics changing not only his life, but all the people he cared about, but he could not rid his mind of the vigilante attack that had taken Robert from them.

He and Rose had talked about coming with the entire family. Abby had offered to watch the younger children so they could all attend, but in the end Rose had decided she couldn't leave Carrie. He knew the sacrifices she had made for her friend. He admired the decision, while also feeling uncomfortable about his own choice to leave the plantation. He stopped Champ and looked back over his shoulder, knowing it was not too late to change his mind. If he turned around and rode back, he would be home before nightfall.

Simon read his mind. "What about Felicia?"

Moses looked at his brother-in-law, realizing the simple question put everything back into perspective. Felicia had been heartbroken when they had decided not to attend the convention as a family. He managed a smile when he thought of the expression on Felicia's face when he had offered to let her ride with them into town on horseback. She knew how to ride, but hours in the saddle were not something she aspired to. When Thomas had been informed of the decision, he had sent one of his drivers out to pick her up two days ago. He was certain she was having the time of her life in Richmond with Thomas and Abby, but he also knew how disappointed she would be if they didn't attend the convention together. "You're right." Casting a final glance toward the plantation, he moved Champ forward, turning onto Broad Street.

Moses was astonished by the number of Federal troops in the city. "I haven't seen so many soldiers since shortly after the war."

Simon nodded grimly. "Things have changed since the Reconstruction Acts passed."

"You've spent more time in the city than I have recently," Moses observed. He knew Perry often sent Simon in for supplies. "Are things really this tense?"

"They have been," Simon replied. "I know you heard about the streetcar strike that got Clark thrown in jail."

Moses nodded, glancing at the streetcar they were passing. He was pleased to see black faces peering down at the clogged road. "It worked."

"Yes, it worked," Simon agreed, "but it hasn't all been going smoothly." He smiled at Moses' blank expression. "You've been too buried in tobacco stalks to pay any attention."

"And how do you have so much more time than I do?" Moses retorted. "You're growing tobacco at Blackwell Plantation the last I checked." It was sobering to realize just how little he knew about what was going on at Blackwell. Once he and Simon had hit the road, he had been content to ride in silence so that all the thoughts he had shoved aside for the last months could catch up with him. His thoughts had been full of Robert, Carrie, Bridget, and the heartache all of them felt every day. Simon hadn't seemed to mind, but Moses suddenly realized how oblivious he had become to most of the rest of the world. He didn't actually regret it, but he also suspected he should be paying more attention.

Simon grinned. "Not near the amount you are growing," he answered. "It's going to take some time to clear the amount of acreage you have over at Cromwell. I figure at the rate we're going it will take at least three years. Perry is a smart businessman. He realizes that if he grows too fast he'll outspend his limited capital and get in trouble."

"You're happy with it?" Moses asked keenly. He was also belatedly aware that Simon's speech was improving by leaps and bounds. Taking over as manager at Blackwell had given him the motivation to make sure his communication skills did not limit his potential for growth and income. His thoughts turned to the need for more teachers like Rose, but they were interrupted by Simon's answer.

"Absolutely. I love being in charge, and since my percentage of the profit is higher now, I will make as much as I made at Cromwell last year, and then it will just keep growing. Perry and I work well together. He lets me do things the way I know they should be done, but he also has some good ideas, and he is learning fast. He wants to understand every part of the operation."

"June is happy, too?"

The question made Simon grin. "She and Louisa have become thick as thieves. I swear, it would never cross my mind that Louisa used to think blacks were completely inferior to her. The boys have become best friends. I don't believe I've ever seen your sister happier."

"John misses Simon, but I'm glad June is happy," Moses said. Then his thoughts went in a different direction. "Any sign of trouble out there?"

"No," Simon said, "but that doesn't mean we're not expecting it. We have guards out every night, and I'm pretty sure all the men sleep with one eye open."

Moses nodded with complete understanding, and then noticed another clump of Federal soldiers eyeing the crowd. Their expressions said they were ready for trouble. He nodded his head in their direction. "What's been going on around here?"

Simon frowned. "The success of the streetcar strike seemed to give other groups ideas about what they could do. The Stevedore Society from down on the docks decided to strike about a week later for higher wages. They thought they had a pretty good chance of winning, but it failed."

"Why?" Moses asked.

Simon shrugged. "They found strikebreakers to do the work. All the men lost their jobs."

Moses grimaced. "What else?" He knew the looks on the soldiers' faces were not just because of a failed strike.

"Folks are getting more restless," Simon explained. "It ain't easy being black in Richmond."

"It's not easy being black *anywhere*," Moses reminded him tightly.

"Back in May there was a demonstration by firemen from Richmond and Delaware. There was a black fella who didn't feel like moving when he was asked. When one of the fire captains pushed him out of the way, he turned around and hit him."

"He was arrested," Moses guessed, able to see the scene in his mind.

"Yep. The crowd didn't like it too much, so they rioted. When the police arrested him, a bunch of them set him free. There was evidently a barber leading the way. The fella raised a barber pole over his head and yelled that it was time for the freedmen to save the nation."

Moses felt a surge of admiration, but he already knew the story was not going to end well.

"They managed to get him away from the policemen, and then after reinforcements came, they managed to free him again." Simon's voice grew grim. "There wasn't any gunfire, but there was an awful lot of rock throwing. Anyway, things ended when General Schofield and a group of his soldiers arrived on the scene. They put things back in order right quick."

Moses imagined they had. "Anything else?"

"A few days later, the policemen arrested one of us for drunken and disorderly conduct." Simon frowned. "There was another riot."

Moses eyed the soldiers again, better understanding the stern looks on their faces. "General Schofield laid down the law," he guessed. He could well understand the black frustration in a city that hated the fact that all the former slaves were now free, but he also knew they were hurting their own cause with the riots.

"Yep. He said the time had come to teach the Negroes that they could not be a law unto themselves. He issued a special order that disarmed the Lincoln Mounted Guard and threatened to disband all black militia units."

Moses frowned. "That's bad." He knew Richmond had become a boiling cauldron of frustration, but he didn't see a way for it to get better anytime soon. They had already seen what happened without the black militia.

"Real bad," Simon agreed. "So far it seems to have helped, though. There have been no more riots, and the militia can still protect the black quarters. No one is pretending the blacks in Richmond aren't in danger, but they are trying to establish control."

Moses continued to eye the soldiers. "They're expecting trouble with the convention."

"I suspect they are," Simon agreed.

****

"Daddy!" Felicia launched herself off the porch as soon as Moses and Simon rode into view.

Moses laughed and dismounted in time to catch Felicia in his arms. "Hello, beautiful daughter. I missed you."

"And I missed you," Felicia said. "But I've been having such a wonderful time. I've been to see the factory, and Thomas took me to the Capitol building." Her eyes grew large as saucers. "I've never seen anything so beautiful," she breathed. "Marietta took me to school with her so I could tell her students about what our school is like, and then Jeremy took me up to the bluffs above the river so I could see what is left of Chimborazo Hospital where Carrie worked."

Moses held her back so he could look at her. "Are you sure you've only been here two days?"

"Abby said she didn't want me to miss even one thing while I was here," Felicia confided before she grinned up at Simon. "Hello, Uncle Simon!"

Simon gave her a hug and turned toward the house. Moses watched him go and then knelt down to talk to his daughter. "What else have you been doing?"

"I had to get up very early this morning to read the newspapers in the library." Felicia's eyes glowed with unbridled excitement. "It was so wonderful to read the news the very same day the newspaper comes out!"

Moses laughed. "I do believe you may become a city girl."

Felicia considered his words, but shook her head decisively. "I don't think so."

There was something in her voice that made him lock his eyes on her. "Why not?" he asked softly, thinking about the fact that he and Rose were going to have to be in the city for college, which meant Felicia would have to join them. "Do you not like the city?"

Felicia smiled serenely. "I like the city just fine, but I would miss the country too much."

Moses stared at her. "What would you miss?" he asked in a bemused voice. "You are rarely outside. You spend most of your time in the library reading."

"But I'm looking *out* at the country," Felicia said earnestly. "I would miss all the beauty if I had nothing but houses and buildings to look at." She hesitated. "Even though Richmond is much nicer, it reminds me too much of Memphis."

Moses understood instantly. Being back in the city was a stark reminder of her parents' murder. Seeing the large numbers of policemen and soldiers would do nothing but cause her anxiety. He caught her to him in a close hug. "I'll keep you safe, honey." Felicia looked up at him with somber eyes that said she had seen too much. Moses knew just how much.

"I know, Daddy," she said softly. She pulled herself erect. "I'm real glad you're here."

Moses took her hand and walked with her up to the porch where Thomas, Abby and Jeremy were waiting. He was surprised when he heard the front door open and saw another man step out. "Matthew!"

Matthew grinned and raised a hand. "You didn't think I would let the Republican Convention happen in Richmond without being here, did you? I can't be at every one of them, so I decided this was the one I would cover."

Moses bit back his words before he asked if trouble was expected. He didn't want to put any more fear into his daughter's mind.

****

Felicia had eaten and reluctantly gone to bed before Moses asked the question on his mind. "Are they expecting trouble tomorrow?"

Jeremy sighed. "They are always expecting trouble."

"Do *you* expect trouble?" Moses pressed.

Jeremy thought about it, but it was Marietta who answered.

"Richmond blacks have become very serious about politics, Moses. They are well aware they are being given a chance to change their lives, and they believe being part of the political process is the only way to make that happen."

Moses decided to be more direct. "Is it possible to undo the damage President Johnson has done?"

"That's a very good question," Matthew said. "I don't think anyone knows the answer yet. No one can know what position our country would be in right now if Lincoln had lived, but it's certain it would not be where we are. Too many people want to think the choice of a vice-presidential candidate is not very important, but they neglect to consider the consequences of what America will be like if the vice president is suddenly the president."

"A lot of people don't think about any consequences at all," Abby stated. "Next year we will be electing another president. I don't believe President Johnson has even a remote chance of being reelected, but his actions have unleashed a torrent of hatred that will be very difficult to get rid of."

Matthew nodded. "President Johnson is an arrogant man who believes blacks are totally inferior to the white race." He paused. "Actually, he believes any other race is inferior to whites, and his definition of whites is also very limited. In the months before Congress was able to regain control, he unleashed a darkness in the South that is going to be very difficult to eradicate. It's not just about changing policy because he has poured fuel on the hatred in the hearts of many Confederate veterans."

"The Ku Klux Klan," Moses said grimly.

"Yes, but they are just a part of it," Matthew responded. "There are many other groups that have sprung up to try to maintain the order of the Old South. The Federal troops are here now, but they have what I believe is an impossible task. There are not enough of them to control what is happening, and what is *going* to happen. They can probably maintain order in the larger cities, but most of the South is rural and sparsely populated. It will be difficult to stop the violence everywhere."

Moses thought about Robert. He knew things like his murder were going to be repeated all over the country. The thought made him feel sick.

Marietta shook her head, her hair glowing in the lantern light. "People don't think about the consequences of their choices. Someone can stand up in front of them, and as long as they can talk with power and persuasiveness, the listeners find it easy to believe them. That's what happened with President Johnson. They don't listen long enough, and they don't question enough to realize he is lying to them to get their support."

"Especially if they *want* to believe them," Thomas added angrily. "President Johnson came down here and told the South there would be no real consequences for four long years of war. He wanted the Southern vote, so he made promises he couldn't begin to keep, and broke the trust of millions of people who sacrificed so much in the war. That may sound strange coming from a Southerner, but now that the war is over I want the South to rebuild. What President Johnson has unleashed will probably set things back for generations."

Moses drew a breath. "You really believe that?"

Thomas sighed. "Unfortunately, I do. The war happened in the first place because too many people could only focus on their own agendas. They refused to make decisions that would benefit the entire country. Those decisions went back decades—it wasn't just those made in the last few years before the war started. People want to think their decisions only impact the things right around them, but they have the same ripple effect as throwing a stone into the water." He sighed again and his eyes turned sorrowful. "Just the war alone will create consequences for generations to come, but add in what President Johnson's attitudes and beliefs have created..." Thomas spread his hands and looked at

Moses apologetically. "I'm afraid the battle your people are going to face is going to be much harder and longer than it should have been."

"Do you think people really knew?" Simon asked.

Thomas raised an eyebrow.

"Who President Johnson really was," Simon clarified. "Did he have everyone so fooled that they truly did not see the man he is?"

Thomas' face grew very thoughtful. "I think there is not an easy answer to that question," he finally said. "The Republican party believed Johnson would help unify the vote for Lincoln because Johnson was a Unionist. They were right about that, but I don't think they looked deep enough to see the danger." He paused thoughtfully. "I believe politicians always reveal who they truly are. Oh, in some ways they will say whatever they believe they need to in order to get elected, but I think the real person always comes through. If," he qualified, "people are willing to look hard enough to discover the truth. There were so many things Johnson said as a senator from Tennessee that showed his beliefs. It was easier not to pay attention, but in the end, the problems we are facing now are because people were too lazy to recognize reality."

Moses knew he was right. "It is imperative that blacks have the vote," he said suddenly. "I know it is only right that women have the vote, too, but if blacks miss this opportunity it is going to make things even more horrible for my people because we will have absolutely no voice to stop the atrocities that are happening now." His mind filled with the conversation he'd had with Rose when she returned from New York. He gazed at Abby, and then turned his eyes to Marietta. "I'm sorry I feel that way."

Abby smiled sadly. "I'm sorry, too, but I certainly understand why you feel the way you do."

When he turned to Marietta, she was looking at him with a scowl.

"I have no desire to be a sacrificial lamb," she said.

Moses knew she was trying to temper her anger, but her eyes were snapping fire. "I understand."

"Do you?" she snapped. "Rose and I had a conversation when she was on the way back from the convention. She told me about the moment she looked around the room and realized every woman in that room was as enslaved as she had ever been, because the government refused to allow them control of their own lives. I am tired of having no control. Rose realizes things are going to get even worse for black women if they are refused the vote while their husbands gain that power. You can't possibly know what that is like."

Moses took a deep breath. "That is true," he admitted. "There is no way I can know what it is like to be a woman, but I do know what it is like to love my wife with every fiber of my being. I know what it is like to want my two daughters to have the best world they can possibly have." He stopped to form his next words, knowing they were important. "The best solution is for everyone in this country to have the right to vote, without regard to race or gender, but I understand that is not possible right now. If that is true, then I at least want to have a voice in trying to make that right—in making the world better for the women in my life that matter so much to me."

Marietta stared at him for a long moment before she released the breath she had been holding. "And I only wish every black man who will get the vote would be like you, Moses, but I already know that is not the case." Her face hardened. "I realize women are not going to get the vote now because we have absolutely no voice in the arguments for and against. We can have our conventions, and we are certainly making waves, but the men in Congress are determined to block it." She turned to lock eyes with Abby. "Do you disagree with me?"

Abby returned her gaze steadily. "I would give just about anything to be able to, but no, I believe you are right. That does not mean, however, that I intend to give up fighting."

Thomas reached over to take his wife's hand. "I would give just about anything to assure the female vote. I believe this country needs the voice and the perspective of women. Without it, we are rather one dimensional." He cocked his head. "You told me about the woman who accosted you and Rose on the train. Are there quite a lot of women like that?"

"A growing number," Abby admitted. "I find it inconceivable that there are women who truly wish to abdicate their life to men, but I know they find it equally inconceivable that I wish to make all my own decisions, and that I want to have a say in what America becomes."

"They're idiots," Marietta said with an indignant snort.

Jeremy chuckled. "I suppose it's a good thing that I agree with my wife. I have doubts of a happy marriage if I did not believe as she does."

"You would have no marriage at all if you didn't agree with me," Marietta said hotly. Somehow she forced a smile. "The women in my family have been fighting male arrogance for a while. My grandmother and my mother have been deeply involved in the women's rights movement since it first began. They are devastated by this latest turn of events. My grandmother wrote me recently and told me she had always believed she would live long enough to vote in a presidential election. She no longer believes that."

Moses thought about her words. "Do you believe if black men weren't getting the vote that women would be?"

Marietta considered his question, and then shook her head. "I wish it were that simple. I also wish I believed black men are getting the vote because people believe it is the right thing, but I believe it is mostly a political move on the part of the Republican Party to gain the vote of a million black men. If they do, they can almost certainly block the Democratic vote in many elections."

"It's not quite that simple, either," Abby protested. "I do believe there is political motive, but I also believe the abolitionists who have fought to end slavery are willing to use that motive in order to finish this battle in the only right way—by giving blacks the right to vote. There are many, many people who want to do the right thing."

"Then I wish they would see fit to do the right thing for women, too," Marietta retorted. She quickly held her hands up in apology. "I'm sorry. I know the people around this table are not the enemy."

"Passion seems to always get America into trouble," Thomas said ruefully.

Laughter riffled through the room before Jeremy turned to Moses and Simon. "Will black men vote?" he asked bluntly.

"They'll vote," Simon responded. "They'll vote in the same way white men vote."

Jeremy raised a brow.

"I believe he means there are black men who won't vote just as there are white men who don't vote," Thomas said. "He's right. There is not a man in this country, of either color, who does not have strong opinions about how things should happen, but there are a lot of them who merely want to voice their opinion or complain. They don't want to take the time to vote, or they simply don't believe their vote will matter."

"Every vote matters," Jeremy stated.

"It's more than a vote," Marietta added. "It's a person's way of saying they care about what happens in America. It's a way of saying you have an opinion that you believe matters." She paused as she stared into the flame of a candle flickering on the table. "I also want to believe it is a statement that a person cared to be become educated enough to even deserve to have a vote."

"Well said," Abby agreed. "I would like to add that a vote is a statement that every single person who ever holds an office is important. That every single person has the power to change the course of this country for generations to come. Voting is a privilege, but first it is an awesome responsibility."

Her words hovered in the air. There seemed to be nothing more to say as each of them contemplated what the future was going to hold.

****

The lines had begun to form at the First African Church at seven o'clock the next morning. Moses had been sure to be there with Felicia first thing. They munched on a basket of biscuits and jam that May had fixed for them while they waited four long hours for the doors to open. He and his daughter talked while they waited.

"This is a real important time, Daddy," Felicia said, her serious eyes scanning the growing crowd.

Moses knew she was scanning for trouble. His brave daughter was determined not to miss this historic event, but he knew she was also frightened of what might happen. In the only world she had known before she'd come to the plantation, crowds had meant a riot where defenseless blacks were being slaughtered. She only seemed comfortable when her hand was tucked securely into his. Talking would keep her mind off the growing crowd. "Tell me why," he invited.

Felicia looked up at him indulgently. He was sure she knew what he was doing, but she obliged him with an answer. "Now that Congress has taken over Reconstruction, every Confederate state has to rewrite its constitution before it can be readmitted to the Union and have their political rights restored."

Moses bit back a smile when he saw several nearby people turn their heads to see who was giving such a clear answer. He understood their surprised looks when they realized the speaker was a young girl.

"The new constitutions have to reflect our freedom," Felicia continued, "and they also have to ratify the Thirteenth, Fourteenth, and Fifteenth Amendments. This one is especially important to our people because it is going to decide the Republican platform going into the constitutional convention later this year." She took a deep breath and looked around, her eyes slightly alarmed by how the crowd was continuing to grow. "Where are all these people coming from, Daddy? Don't these men have to work?"

"We do." The answer came from a wiry man standing close to her at the beginning of the line. "Most of the men you see right now came from the tobacco plants. Our tobacco worker societies informed all the factories that we was coming to the convention today. They had no choice but to close up." His voice was full of deep satisfaction.

Felicia grinned. "I bet they didn't like that."

"Probably not," the man confided with a smile, "but things ain't gonna be the same now that we're free. We got rights."

Felicia looked around again, but now her gaze was calculating. "There are people in Washington that won't like this," she told the man.

His eyes narrowed. "Why not?"

Moses hid a smile as other listeners leaned in to hear what his daughter had to say. He stuffed down an uncomfortable feeling that he was watching the emergence of a powerful woman who would constantly put herself at the forefront of danger. He had always known Felicia was special. All he could do was protect her to the best of his ability, and encourage her to be all she could be.

"I read about this," Felicia said confidently. "There are two parts of the Republican Party. There are moderate ones who believe delegates should dictate the policy of our party. Then there are the ultra-Radicals who believe decisions should be made by mass meetings where everyone has a say."

"That's the only right way to do it," a woman snorted. "If we want things in the South to ever be right for the black folks, we got to make sure them white men who enslaved us can't vote, and we got to make them give up their lands so we got a chance to build a life of our own."

Felicia turned to her with a warm smile. "I agree there should be mass meetings," she answered.

Moses was aware Felicia had made no stance on whether she agreed with the ultra-radical position. She was simply affirming the right of everyone's voice to be heard. He hid another grin. His daughter was already becoming quite a little politician. It would be the world's loss if she didn't have the right to vote and govern when she grew up just because she was a woman.

Oblivious to his thoughts, Felicia continued her discussion with the woman. "National Republican leaders know the power of the radicals rests on the black popular movement here in the city. That bothers them because they know they will actually have little say in making party policy." She grinned. "I don't know a man alive who would be happy with that. Politicians will be less happy."

Moses couldn't stop his chuckle this time.

The wiry man eyed him. "This your daughter?"

"She is," Moses confirmed.

"She always been this smart?"

"For as long as I've known her," Moses agreed. Felicia's story was her own to tell.

When they were finally able to enter the church, Moses knew many of the thousands clogging the streets would not have room to crowd in. He suspected there would be some kind of meeting held outside for the ones who were not allowed to enter.

****

When he walked back out, he knew the country was in for a bitter battle. Though he knew many Richmond blacks truly felt this way, he suspected the passion vibrating through the building for the last several hours had been brought on by heated rhetoric from speakers determined to promote their agenda. The crowd, frustrated by all they had experienced since emancipation, was easy to sway to their side.

Moses was silent as he and Felicia pushed their way through the buzzing crowd. He overhead many conversations as people who had been inside explained the proceedings to those who had not been able to enter. It didn't take him long to realize the outside proceedings had echoed the interior ones.

Thomas and Abby were waiting for them when they arrived home. A tray of tea and cookies perched on the table next to the porch swing.

Moses sat down, took a glass of tea, and drank deeply.

"That bad?" Thomas asked.

Moses shrugged. "Perhaps it was that good." He really wasn't sure.

"Felicia?" Abby asked.

Felicia gave a succinct report. "The Ultra-Radicals had their day. When it was all said and done, there was almost complete support for the radical program that includes disenfranchisement for anyone who supported the Confederate cause, and also the belief that Confederate lands should be confiscated and given to the blacks."

"Why does that make you frown?" Abby asked gently.

Felicia met her eyes squarely. "Because the people at that meeting don't understand what they did. Instead of finding a way to make things work for everyone, they just want to punish anyone who played a part in making them slaves."

"And you don't think that is good?" Abby probed.

"I don't think they understand the backlash," Felicia answered. She shook her head. "I wish they did more reading because they would realize their stubborn position is going to make white people angrier, which means they are going to make life more miserable for everyone." Her voice wavered. "It made me very sad because I felt like the leaders really were using the people there to support their own agenda. Everybody seems to be after just one thing..."

"Power," Moses finished for her. She had easily explained the turmoil he had been feeling since the first few moments of the convention. He totally understood why people were so angry, but he didn't believe they comprehended the best path to helping them attain the freedom they wanted. He finally found the words he was looking for. "They are pushing white Americans up against a wall. No one likes to be up against a wall, and they already have everything in place to fight back." His mind filled with stories of vigilante atrocities. "They are going to fight back just as hard as we are fighting."

"And in the end everyone loses."

Moses looked up as Matthew walked up the steps. They locked eyes as a silent message passed between them.

Things were going to get much worse before they got better—if they ever could.

Chapter Twenty-Nine

Carrie had discovered it was impossible to be consumed with grief when she was surrounded by a dozen foals prancing through the pasture with their heads and tails lifted high. She longed for Robert to see the results of his careful breeding, but the thought no longer brought nothing but searing agony. It was easy to envision the pride and pleasure shining on his face if he had been standing beside her. The nights were still endless, but the days had become almost bearable.

Amber clambered over the fence and joined her.

"There is a gate," Carrie reminded her gently.

"It takes too much time," Amber explained. She giggled as All My Heart trotted up and pushed her with her beautiful head. Amber pretended to ignore her. All My Heart snorted and nudged her once more, a little harder this time. Amber giggled again and wrapped her arms around her filly's neck.

Carrie watched with something approaching awe. She wondered if the little girl was simply more resilient than her, or if she had dealt with her grief better in the beginning, so she was able to laugh sooner. She remembered Biddy's letter telling her that everyone grieved in their own way, and decided it didn't matter.

"All the foals are leading now," Amber announced.

"They are," Carrie agreed, feeling the same pride she saw shining on Amber's face. "Robert would be so proud of you."

"You helped," Amber reminded her with a glow of pleasure. "Robert would be real proud of you, too."

Carrie's heart caught for a moment as she envisioned the look of pride on Robert's face that had so often been there for her. She saw the look of sudden anxiety gleaming in Amber's eyes.

"Was that the wrong thing to say, Carrie?"

"No, honey," Carrie murmured as she stroked All my Heart's shining neck. "Robert would be proud of both of us." Just the fact she could say his name was a victory.

"There are men coming to see the new babies, aren't there?" Amber asked, obviously relieved she hadn't said the wrong thing. "To buy them like Mark and Susan did?"

"There are," Carrie agreed. "They will be here in a month, after we have weaned the foals from their mamas." She understood the frown on Amber's face. "I know the weaning is a very hard time," she said softly.

"I hate it," Amber said fervently. "It almost rips my heart out to hear the mares and babies crying for each other."

Amber buried her face in All My Heart's neck, but not before Carrie saw the glimmer of tears in her eyes. She instantly understood Amber's sadness was not just about the babies. "Robert always hated this time, too," she confided.

Amber peeked up. "He did?" she whispered.

"He did," Carrie confirmed, remembering the pain on his face. "He know it had to be done, but it never got easy for him. He just figured he had to get through it so all the foals could go on to become great horses."

Amber lifted her head and put her hand on All My Heart's muzzle. "All My Heart is going to be a great horse," she said confidently, the misery disappearing from her face when she realized her hero had also hated the weaning process.

"Yes, she is," Carrie said. "Just like you are going to be a great woman."

Amber cocked her head, fixed her with a steady gaze, and then nodded shyly. "Robert used to tell me the same thing all the time."

Carrie took a deep breath to hold back the sob that wanted to explode from her chest. It broke her heart that Amber would not have Robert to believe in her as she grew up. It broke her heart to know Robert had never had a chance to know his daughter. He would have been such a wonderful father. Her thoughts were interrupted by Amber's hand on her arm.

"Robert used to tell me that someday I would be a great woman like you," she said, her dark eyes gleaming with a bright intensity. "He told me you were the greatest woman he had ever known."

Carrie stared down at the little girl, hardly able to breathe. As glad as she was to hear those words, the knowledge of all she had lost was almost more than she could fathom. Now that the numbing grief had lifted, the sharp pangs of loss that could strike her at any moment were no easier to bear. She was saved from having to respond by the sound of Clint's voice.

"We have another letter, Carrie!"

Carrie looked up, sheer relief allowing her to smile almost naturally. "A letter?"

"From another potential buyer," Clint informed her. "Captain Jones and Susan said they were going to spread the word. They sure have!"

It warmed Carrie's heart to see the young man's enthusiasm. He had taken Robert's death hard too, going off for many long rides on his own in the weeks following the murder, but having the horses to concentrate on had helped. She noticed a flash of worry in his eyes. "Is something wrong, Clint?"

Clint hesitated. "I'm real good at raising the horses and training them, but I don't know much about selling them. I'm afraid I won't be very good at negotiating their price," he admitted. "I don't want to let you and Robert down."

Carrie smiled. "You don't have to worry. I'll be handling that end of it."

Clint sagged in relief. "You'll still be here?"

Carrie had not yet told Clint and Amber about her decision. Now was as good a time as any. "I'm not leaving the plantation."

Clint stared at her. "You're not?"

Amber stared up at her too, but her eyes were cautious. "You're not?"

"I'm not," Carrie assured them, wondering about what she was seeing in Amber's eyes. "I've decided to stay here and run the horse operation for Robert. All of us working together can make his dreams come true." The delight in Clint's eyes was unmistakable, but Amber's eyes looked troubled.

Carrie knelt down to the little girl's level. "Aren't you glad, Amber?"

Amber nodded her head quickly. "I'm real glad you're not leaving, Carrie, but..."

"But what?" Carrie prompted, wishing she hadn't started the conversation because she was almost certain where it was going to lead.

"You're supposed to be a doctor," Amber said bluntly. "Robert told me so. How come you're not going to be a doctor?"

Carrie flinched but didn't look away. "I'm not going to be a doctor after all," she said softly. She held her finger to Amber's lips to keep her from asking the question that evoked memories still capable of destroying her heart. "Can you accept that and be happy I'm going to stay, honey?"

Amber stared at her for a long moment, uncertainty radiating from her eyes, but she finally nodded. "I *am* real happy you're staying, Carrie." She paused for a long moment before she added, "But if you change your mind about becoming a doctor that will be all right, too!"

Clint saved her from having to respond again. "So you'll meet with the horse buyers when they come?" He was more than happy to focus on the fact that he wouldn't have to do something he didn't feel capable of doing.

"I will," Carrie promised. She planned on talking to Abby about how she had handled taking over her first husband's business when he had died. "But," she added, "I want you to be there with me so you can learn, too. I want everyone in the South to know what an amazing horseman and stable manager you are. The time will come when you will be able to negotiate the sales yourself."

Clint smiled broadly and his shoulders went back proudly. "Yes, ma'am!"

Carrie watched as Amber ran off with All My Heart, and Clint strolled away whistling.

"I'm real proud of you, Miss Carrie."

Carrie looked up as Miles walked down the stairs from the room above. She suddenly felt very fatigued. She recognized she was doing better, but the energy it took to operate normally was almost more than she could produce sometimes. She knew she didn't have to pretend with Miles. "I'm tired," she confessed.

"Of course you are," Miles agreed tenderly. "You serious about staying here on the plantation?"

Carrie nodded. She felt caught somewhere between a place of peace and uncertainty, but it was the only decision she felt she could make. She was sure Miles could read the expression on her face, but he didn't question what she had said.

"I'm real glad," he murmured before he turned away to start work.

Carrie gave a sigh of relief and then frowned when she realized there was also a twinge of disappointment. There was a part of her that had expected Miles to disagree with her, to tell her she had to go back to medical school. She knew she should be glad he hadn't, but there was still the twinge she couldn't ignore. She shook her head heavily, unable to understand her own jumbled feelings and thoughts. Granite's whinny pulled her out of her own reflection. He had gotten used to their daily rides, and she wasn't going to disappoint him. When she turned to him, though, he wasn't looking at her. His eyes were focused on the drive leading away from the house.

Carrie walked to the door, certain they weren't expecting anyone, but now that she was paying attention there was no mistaking the sound of a carriage approaching the house. She patted Granite and walked out to discover who their company was.

"Carrie!"

Carrie's eyes widened in shocked surprise as the call floated to her through the thick afternoon air. "Abby?" She ran to the porch, arriving just as the carriage pulled to a stop. "Hello, Spencer," she said warmly to the driver. "It's so good to see you again."

"You too, Miss Carrie," Spencer replied before he glanced at the house. "You reckon Annie got any cookies in there?"

Carrie smiled and waved him into the house before she turned to Abby. "What are you doing here?"

"Disappointed to see me?"

Carrie smiled again. "Never. I just had no idea you were coming." She was aware Abby was staring at her with a look of delighted surprise. She understood why. The last time she had seen her stepmother, she was a complete mess. Most of her weight had come back on, and she at least cared enough to take care of her appearance.

"I like surprises," Abby said lightly as she climbed down from the carriage and enveloped Carrie in a warm embrace.

Carrie sighed as she fought back the tears that threatened to erupt whenever she let her guard down. She relished the feeling of Abby's arms, realizing she hadn't let her stepmother hold her enough since Robert and Bridget's death.

"I love you so much, Carrie," Abby whispered, her voice clogged with tears.

Carrie just held on, not trusting her voice. *Talk Carrie. Talk about it.* The advice from Biddy's letter echoed in her heart. "We have a lot to talk about," she finally managed.

Abby laughed shakily and released her. "Yes, we do," she agreed.

****

It wasn't until Carrie had led Abby through the tunnel down to the river that she could finally relax. She understood that everyone else wanted to visit with Abby, and dinner had been a necessity, but as soon as she had felt it was polite, she had beckoned Abby to join her for a walk.

Abby gazed around, taking a deep breath as the sun dipped below the horizon, painting the sky with brilliant hues of orange and purple splashed on a canvas of cobalt blue. A masked raccoon looked up, calmly went back to washing himself, and then slowly lumbered back into the brush. "I see why this has become so special to you," she said quietly.

"I don't stay out here all night anymore," Carrie revealed, "but I still come every day."

"I understand why." Abby turned and caught Carrie's face in her hands. She peered deeply into her eyes.

Carrie squirmed slightly, but let Abby examine her closely because she knew how badly she had scared everyone.

"You've come a long way," Abby said before she dropped her hands and sat back.

"I have," Carrie replied. "I still have a long way to go."

"Yes," Abby agreed. "Tell me."

Carrie smiled, knowing Abby would let her tell everything in her own way, and wouldn't ask for more than she was willing to reveal. "Thank you," she whispered.

Abby cocked her head and raised a brow.

"For giving me time. For not thinking badly of me when I simply couldn't deal with anything." She paused, knowing Abby wouldn't interrupt her as she processed her thoughts. She already knew Abby understood what she had gone through. It was true that everyone dealt with grief in their own way, but Abby had known deep grief too. For just a moment she felt a flash of awareness that she would be able to understand someone else's grief in the future, but her own was still too raw for her to be truly grateful. She still doubted she would ever feel anything but brutal agony when she thought of Robert and Bridget, but the fact that she could even *consider* reaching a place of gratitude was a huge step for her.

"I'm not going to be a doctor," she said bluntly. She wanted to get the hardest revelation out of the way first.

"I know," Abby answered.

"Did Matthew tell you?" Carrie wasn't sure if it bothered her or not, but she understood why if he had.

Abby nodded. "He was still at the house when Dr. Hobson came by one day to ask about you."

Carrie stiffened. "He told Dr. Hobson?" She wasn't sure why that bothered her, but it undeniably did.

The look on Abby's face said she was wondering the same thing, but all she did was shake her head. "No, but when Dr. Hobson left, Matthew told me and your father."

Carrie searched her face. "Are you angry?"

Abby's eyes widened in surprise. "Angry? Of course not. Why in the world would I be angry?"

"You've invested so much in me becoming a doctor," Carrie protested.

Abby waved her hand in the air. "Nonsense. No one could have possibly anticipated what would happen in your life. Anyone who could respond with anger doesn't understand your life is your own to live." She paused. "They don't understand you are the only one who can live with the consequences of your decision."

Carrie knew there was no ulterior motive to Abby's quiet statement. She waited for her to question the decision she had made, but Abby remained silent. Carrie was sure her stepmother knew the reason for her decision, and was also sure she disagreed with it, but Abby was giving her the freedom to do what she believed she needed to do.

The splash of a fish made her turn to catch the last glowing rays of the sun before it slipped away to continue its revolution of the Earth so it could bring a new beginning in the morning. For a moment she wondered about the people watching it beginning to rise in their part of the world. Were they as desperate as she was to relish the beginning of a new day, instead of dreading the feelings it would bring? Did they appreciate the beauty of the sunset or did they wish it would never come, like she did? "The nights are the hardest," she murmured.

Abby reached over and took her hand. "They will be for a long time," she said somberly. "It was years before I could go to bed without crying myself to sleep after Charles died. As time went on I could function fairly normally during the days, but the nights seemed to mock me."

Carrie relaxed, glad that Abby understood. Another long silence passed before she spoke again, not ashamed when her voice cracked. "Thank you for holding Bridget."

Abby squeezed her hand tightly. "Bridget was beautiful," she said softly, before her voice strengthened. "She wasn't alone, Carrie. I don't know if she had any way of knowing, but my granddaughter was held and loved when she came out of your womb."

Granddaughter. The simple word made Carrie realize how much Abby and her father must have grieved. *Robert. Bridget.* They had lost so much too, but her own grief had been so dark she hadn't been able to even acknowledge anyone else's. The unwelcome recognition brought huge tears to her eyes. "I'm sorry," she whispered. "I've been so selfish."

"Hush," Abby said. "You have been buried by a pain that is greater than you. There is no shame in that, Carrie." She leaned over and kissed her cheek. "I'm thinking you must have read Biddy's letter."

"She is a very wise woman," Carrie answered, a smile forming among her tears.

"That she is," Abby agreed. "I don't know what she said, but I knew it would be what you needed to hear."

"It was," Carrie replied, relishing the soft breeze that sprang up off the water as the sun was swallowed by darkness. She gazed up at the canopy of stars winking their way into existence as the night sky revealed them. She stiffened suddenly.

"Carrie...?"

"I just realized something," Carrie breathed as she continued to stare upward. "Stars are always in the sky, but we can't see them until it gets dark." Abby smiled, but remained silent as Carrie's thoughts formulated. "I suppose it's only natural to always want your life to be brilliant sunshine, but the stars are so beautiful," she murmured. "The darkness is usually not a fun place, but it is the only way to reveal the beauty of the stars." She smiled as the glowing orbs seemed to twinkle more brightly in response to her appreciation.

Abby leaned back against the log to fully absorb the shimmering canvas. "Nothing is ever wasted. I don't believe God ever *brings* pain into our life, but I do believe good can come from every single thing. I will never be glad Charles died, but I'm grateful for who I became through it. I will never be glad Robert and Bridget died, but I've at least learned that good *can* come from it *in time*." She put a strong emphasis on the final words. "We are all waiting for the good things to be revealed. I believe they will be."

Carrie couldn't say she agreed, but she had at least come far enough not to lash out in anger or dissolve in tears. It was enough for her to realize the beauty of stars could only be revealed in the darkness. That was quite enough revelation for one night.

"I need your help," Abby said.

Carrie whipped her head around. In all the time she had known Abby, the older woman had never asked for her help. It had become too dark to see her eyes, but Carrie could feel a strange tension radiating from Abby now that the question had been asked. "What do you need?"

Abby took a deep breath. "I need you to go to Kansas with me."

Carrie's eyes widened and she couldn't seem to find enough air to respond. She finally managed to squeak, "You need me to do what?"

"Come to Kansas with me." Now that she had broached the subject, Abby's voice seemed more certain.

Carrie stared at her, wondering if she was speaking a foreign language. "Kansas? As in the state?"

"That would be the one," Abby replied, and then she continued in a hesitant voice that said she knew she was asking a lot. "I have been asked by the ERA to go to Kansas to work for the passage of the woman's suffrage vote there."

Carrie's head was spinning. She had no idea what was going on outside the world of the plantation, and she was completely unable to comprehend the possibility of leaving.

Abby seemed to understand her confusion. "Kansas is holding a referendum on November fifth. It is the first ever referendum on women's suffrage in United States history," Abby explained. "They are trying to amend the section in the Fourteenth Amendment that adds the word *'male'* as being one of the qualities of a voter."

Carrie had talked to Rose enough in the last weeks to understand what Abby was saying, but it still seemed like a language she didn't understand because there was absolutely no part of her that cared.

"It's important, Carrie," Abby said, her voice becoming urgent as if she were trying to break through her apathy. "Kansas is also trying to get the word *'white'* taken from the amendment so that blacks also have the right to vote. So many people have fought for both of these things for a very long time. We finally have a chance for it to happen."

Carrie gazed at her, glad the darkness covered just how much she didn't care—*couldn't* care—because she simply didn't have the energy to.

"I need you to come with me," Abby repeated.

"Why?" Carrie asked bluntly.

Abby laughed softly, the sound rising up to be swallowed by the stars gleaming down on them. "Because I agreed to do it before I really thought about it." Her voice became hesitant. "I know you think I'm asking you to do this only to get you off the plantation, but the truth of the matter is that I have no idea what I'm doing. I'm nervous about going alone."

Carrie was glad it was dark, because now Abby couldn't see the skepticism on her face. "And there is no one else who can go?" She was sure there were many people more qualified than she was to go to Kansas to fight for women's right to vote, especially since she didn't even have the qualification of *caring*.

She was more certain than ever that this was a plot Abby and her father had devised.

"There is no one else I *want* to go with me, darling daughter," Abby said. She hesitated. "I probably shouldn't be asking..."

Carrie tensed, struck by the vulnerability vibrating in Abby's voice. She had never heard Abby sound that way. Suddenly she believed her. It may all be part of a plot to get her to leave the plantation, but she also realized Abby was being asked to do something she felt completely uncomfortable with. It was hard to imagine that her stepmother, the successful businesswoman who had stepped in to take over her husband's factory, was afraid of anything, but Carrie couldn't deny the authenticity of the tremor in her voice.

"I'll make a deal with you," Carrie finally said.

"A deal?" Abby asked in a bemused voice.

"Yes," Carrie answered. "A deal. I will go to Kansas with you if you will teach me all you know about running a business. Now that I'm taking over the horse operation, I realize there is much I don't know how to do. I'm great with horses, but I've never been interested in business. I assume it will be a grave error if I don't learn as much as I can before the first batch of buyers show up."

"When are they coming?" Abby asked.

"One month from today. When do you want me to go to Kansas?"

"We leave on September tenth," Abby replied, her voice hopeful.

Carrie was almost sure Abby had already bought round-trip tickets for two people, but she decided not to challenge her. After all Abby had done for her, it was impossible to deny the request of the woman she loved so much. "So you have time to teach me what I need to know?"

"Starting tomorrow," Abby responded. "I will stay for a week and pour everything I can into your head, and then I will be available by letter until we leave for Kansas. I have only one condition," she added.

"And that is?"

"I want to teach Clint, as well. He will need to know more about running operations. It is never a good idea to have only one person that can handle the business end of things."

Carrie wondered if Abby had ulterior motives, but she certainly couldn't debate the truth of the statement now that Robert was gone and no one knew how to do what he had done. "All right." She took a deep breath as she reached out to take Abby's hand. "We have a deal then," she murmured, wondering if she looked up if she would see the stars laughing.

She was going to Kansas.

Chapter Thirty

Carrie was uncomfortable, but ready, when the first buyers arrived a month later.

Annie smiled at her when she walked into the kitchen. "You look pretty as a picture, Miss Carrie!"

Carrie scowled. "I look like I should be going to a dance, not out to the stables I own," she complained as she looked down at the light blue dress she had selected from her closet the day before.

"I reckon you've gotten real used to wearing Mr. Robert's breeches," Annie agreed.

Carrie shot a look at her, but she could hear no reproach in her voice. "Dresses are useless in a barn," she sniffed. "I can't believe I used to ride around the plantation in the dresses my mother insisted on. Brecches are practical."

"That's so," Annie said with a nod while she finished filling a bowl of fresh fruit to go with the plate of eggs waiting on the counter. "They're not so practical, though, if you lose a sale or can't negotiate effectively."

Carrie couldn't stop her snort of laughter. "Has Abby been training you, too?"

"I got two ears," Annie retorted. "All a body has to do is listen around here if you want to know something."

Carrie knew she was right. She could still hear Abby's voice in her head. *If you want a man to take you seriously in the business world, you have to be a professional. You might be more comfortable in breeches, and they might indeed be more practical in a barn, but when you are negotiating a sale you want every advantage you can get. You are a beautiful woman, Carrie. Don't throw away that advantage.*

"You still bothered about this aren't you?" Annie asked.

"Yes," Carrie said honestly. "It feels wrong to use being a woman."

Annie snorted. "Girl, women got to use what we got."

Carrie stared with disbelief. She would never have expected this to come from Annie's lips.

"What you looking at me like that for? I may not be much to look at anymore, but I know enough to know that if I looked like you, I would use it for all it's worth. Those men are probably planning on coming down here to do some hard-nosed negotiatin'. You gonna throw 'em for a real loop when they find out they are negotiatin' with you. "She stopped and eyed Carrie. "The first thing they gonna think is that you will be a pushover 'cause you be a woman, so they are gonna have their guard down. Then you gonna knock them over with how much you know about horses, and they gonna be even more surprised." She cocked an eyebrow. "By the time you get around to naming a price for them beautiful babies out there, they just gonna nod dumbly and give you what you want."

Carrie burst into laughter. Annie seldom talked for so long, but it was clear she had listened to Abby carefully, and had absorbed everything she said. "Would you like to go do the negotiating for me?" Carrie finally sobered enough to ask. She still felt uncomfortable with laughter—almost as if it dishonored Robert and Bridget's deaths—but she suspected Robert would be doubled over with laughter right now, too. That knowledge made her own mirth easier.

Annie shook her head firmly. "I ain't got what you got," she said. "Girl, you know more about horses than any of them men coming here to see our stock. The advantage you have is that you also know how to use being a *woman...*"

Carrie grinned again as Annie drew out the word *'woman'* as if to make it sound like something very mysterious, and also rolled her eyes dramatically.

"One of these days men are gonna realize just how powerful women are," Annie stated. "When they do, they gonna have to give us the vote...and more."

Carrie sobered as she realized that in only five days she would be leaving for Kansas to fight for the vote. It hadn't truly sunk in that she was leaving the plantation, but there was no way she would go back on her word to accompany Abby. She reached for the bowl of fruit and began to eat the eggs. The buyers would be here in a few minutes. She hadn't dared go near the barn in her dress, but she knew Amber, Clint and Miles would have the foals ready for their showing.

****

Carrie had watched the group of three men arrive in their luxurious carriages, and she had watched for a few minutes while they hung over the fence to view the foals. She waited a little while longer, giving Amber and Clint time to catch several of them, slip their halters on, and lead them around the pasture. Every one of them performed perfectly, their heads held high as if they knew they were on display. Just when she was sure the men were probably drooling, she sauntered outside, her face shaded by a hat the same shade as her dress.

"Good afternoon, gentlemen." She hid a grin as the three men turned to look at her. Their eyes widened, and they straightened, trying not to ogle her. Maybe Abby was right - negotiating might turn out to be fun after all. The memory flashed into her mind of the time just before the war when she had charmed the overseer from Blackwell Plantation long enough for one of the plantation's escaped slaves to slip deeper into the Underground Railroad. She had been surprised by how much fun it had been then. This was reminding her of the sense of power she had felt.

"I see you have had time to take a look at our newest crop of foals," Carrie said. "They are rather nice, aren't they?" she asked casually.

"They are," one of the men responded. "They are some of the finest horses I have ever seen."

Carrie nodded pleasantly as she realized Abby had been right. These men had not received the news of Robert's death, so they assumed they would be negotiating with him. "They *are* rather special," she agreed. Amber and Miles had disappeared into the barn, but Clint had moved closer so he could hear the conversation.

"They certainly are," another of the men said as he wiped sweat from his balding head. His face was flushed red, but Carrie wasn't entirely sure it was because of the heat.

"Mark Jones told us about the operation down here," the final man offered.

Carrie observed him carefully. Of the three of them, he seemed to be the one least affected by her charm. His gaze was pleasant, but he was strictly business.

"How old are the foals?" the third man asked keenly.

Carrie decided it was time to take control. She turned to the first man. "First, who do I have the pleasure of speaking with, gentlemen?"

"My name is Lester McMinnville," the oldest said. He was thin, looked to be in his early fifties, and had the air of elegant wealth.

"It's nice to meet you, Mr. McMinnville," Carrie said pleasantly, and then looked to the balding man.

"I am Tobias Smithfield."

Carrie extended her hand graciously. "A pleasure, Mr. Smithfield." His face reddened even more when he took her hand. Carrie wondered briefly if he spent so much time in stables that he had forgotten what a woman looked like, but she pushed it aside because she knew she was dangerously close to laughing already.

She turned to the third man, allowing her eyes to become more direct. "And you are?"

The man looked at her carefully. "Anthony Wallington." He accepted her hand but gazed over her shoulder. "And you are?"

"I am Carrie Borden."

Anthony met her eyes briefly before he looked at the house again. "Will your husband be out soon?"

Carrie steeled herself to answer the question without a catch in her voice. "My husband is dead," she said steadily. "I own Cromwell Stables." She watched all the men's faces change as they absorbed her words and realized how enthusiastic they had been in their admiration of the foals. Their looks said they knew they had already lost negotiating power.

"I see," Mr. Wallington murmured, amused appreciation glowing in his eyes.

Carrie smiled at him brightly. "Would you like to see the rest of the foals perform?"

He shook his head. "I'm sure they are exactly what Jones told me they are." He glanced over at Clint, his eyes taking in Amber who had appeared at the door of the barn. "They are the ones that trained the yearlings he brought home this spring?"

"They are," Carrie assured him. She made no mention of the fact that she had also been involved in their training. She was simply the business owner on this day. "Are each of you gentlemen interested in buying some of the foals?"

Lester McMinnville stepped forward quickly, realizing he could be at a disadvantage. "Mr. Smithfield and myself are partners," he said haughtily as he tried to establish some kind of control of the situation.

"How nice," Carrie murmured.

"Yes," he continued in a firm voice. He glanced back over his shoulder, trying to project a skeptical interest.

Carrie hid another smile. She wondered if he had forgotten his earlier statement that they were some of the finest horses he had ever seen, but then decided it was more likely he thought her feeble female mind might have forgotten his words.

"I would like to know more about their bloodlines," he said imperiously.

Carrie was quite certain he thought she would be clueless. "Certainly," she replied, dropping all pleasantries as she allowed herself to go into full negotiating mode. "The sire is Eclipse, a son of Lexington. I'm sure you gentlemen are aware that Lexington was bred in Lexington, Kentucky. He is a racehorse who won six of his seven race starts. He is a son of Boston, another Thoroughbred legend." She paused as she watched their faces try to absorb her rapid transformation into an equine expert. "Lexington is known as the best race horse of his day, gentlemen. Unfortunately, he had to be retired in 1855 because of bad eyesight, but it's not genetic because he hasn't passed it on to his progeny. He's claimed the title of leading sire in North America many times since his retirement."

"And the mares?" Wallington asked, his amused eyes saying he appreciated what was happening.

Carrie was suddenly certain she liked this man. "The mares come from a variety of lineages, all carefully picked to maximize the progeny they produce with Eclipse. We, of course, have papers for every one. I can assure you Cromwell Stables chose nothing but the best, and I also believe we have the best trainers in the industry for young horses."

She swept all three men with her gaze. "Whatever you decide to do with these foals, you will not find better horses in the country," she said. This part was easy to do because she believed it with all her heart. She saw McMinnville take a breath to talk, but she decided to maintain control. "We have fifty foals available for this season. I have four more buyers competing for the right to purchase them. I have checked to make certain all you gentlemen run viable operations because I want our horses to be well cared for. You seem to all meet that criteria, as do the other gentlemen who have inquired, so it is really just a matter of finances." She smiled pleasantly, hardly able to believe how much she was enjoying this. It almost made having to put a dress on worth it. "Look at the foals for as long as you wish. Clint and I will be on the porch. When you are ready to make an offer, you may join me." Not giving any of them a chance to respond, she turned slowly and sauntered up onto the porch where Annie had placed a large pitcher of tea and a plate of cookies.

Clint joined her, his eyes filled with glee. "You were sure something out there, Carrie. Those men don't stand a chance with you."

Carrie smiled graciously, wanting to be sure she kept up the act in case any of the men were watching her, but her words were just as gleeful. "I do believe you're right, Clint." She batted her eyes as Clint snorted back a laugh.

****

Mr. Smithfield and Mr. McMinnville were the first to approach the porch.

"Would you like some tea, gentlemen?" Carrie asked graciously.

They both nodded, and then McMinnville started the conversation. "We are prepared to make an offer for twenty of the foals," he began. He pulled out a sheet of paper from his pocket and handed it to her. "I believe you'll find the terms agreeable," he said smoothly.

Carrie glanced at the paper, careful to keep her face expressionless as she read it, but inside she was shouting with joy because the price was even more than Robert had gotten for the foals the year before. She examined the paper carefully, folded it, and put it in her pocket. "Thank you, gentlemen." She saw Anthony watching her on the porch and knew he was waiting his turn. "I will meet with Mr. Wallington, and then let you know. There are chairs set up under the oak tree so you will be comfortable while you wait."

McMinnville scowled but quickly smiled to cover it up. The overall effect was one of a twisted grimace. "We would appreciate it if you would give us an answer now," he stated. "We believe this is a fair offer."

Carrie nodded. "I'm sure you do, but I'm also sure that as a businessman you would want to know all the offers before you accepted one." She held his gaze until he nodded reluctantly. "I'm sure you won't have to wait long, gentlemen." She inclined her head toward the chairs positioned far enough away so that any conversation could not be overheard, and then beckoned Mr. Wallington forward. The other two men had no other choice but to leave the porch, their faces filled with frustration.

Carrie smiled up at Anthony Wallington. "You are pleased with the foals?"

Wallington grinned. "You know I am, Mrs. Borden."

"I know you look intelligent," Carrie agreed, "so I imagine you are." Even though he seemed very likeable, she was not about to let her guard down. She was a businesswoman negotiating the best deal possible for her business. Abby had drilled into her that she could not forget that for even one moment. Some men would try bullying to get their way, but just as many would try to charm her. Either would diminish her effectiveness. She sat back and waited.

The appreciation in Wallington's eyes intensified as he leaned forward. "What did the other gentlemen offer you?"

Carrie laughed lightly. "Surely you can do better than that," she chided him, deciding to be just as blunt as he was. "I suggest you make the best offer you can and we'll go from there."

Wallington settled back in his chair, holding her eyes with his direct gaze. "I recognize quality horseflesh when I see it. I represent several gentlemen who will pay well for the best."

Carrie nodded but remained silent. Her research had already revealed what he had just told her.

Wallington smiled again. "But you already knew that."

Carrie inclined her head in agreement and continued to watch him.

"I will increase whatever McMinnville and Smithfield offered by twenty percent." Wallington made his offer, and then sat back in his chair as he reached for a glass of tea.

Carrie fought to maintain her composure, but the knowing glint in Wallington's eyes said she had probably failed. "How many are you interested in?" she asked briskly.

"All of them," Wallington answered. "I'm willing to offer a more than fair price because I don't want to have to haggle over a few dollars with any other buyers. I would rather finalize this deal and be on my way." He paused. "Am I right in assuming it will be the same as with Mark Jones—that Amber and Clint will train them, and then I can pick them up next spring when they are yearlings?"

"Yes," Carrie managed in what she hoped was a natural voice. That in itself was a small miracle, because in all truth, she was having difficulty breathing.

"Then I may buy them all?" Wallington pressed.

Carrie smiled naturally and allowed her delight to shine through. "Yes, you may, Mr. Wallington." She reached out a hand and shook his firmly, feeling a brief sympathy for the disappointment she saw on the other two men's faces, but too elated in her success to be concerned for long. Abby had assured her it was just business, so she should treat it that way.

Mr. Wallington shook her hand, stepped back, and smiled again. "Your husband would be very proud of you, Mrs. Borden," he said quietly. "I'm sorry for your loss."

"Thank you," Carrie managed to say around the sudden lump in her throat. She did know Robert would be proud of her, but she would give anything in the world for it to be him making this deal. The dream he had nurtured since he was a child was coming true. It broke her heart that he couldn't see what he had accomplished.

"May I ask another question?"

"Of course." Carrie was completely relaxed now that the business transaction had been taken care of.

"I saw a stunning mare in your barn. I'm afraid I didn't recognize the breed. I see the Thoroughbred in her, but there is something more. She is quite regal."

Carrie smiled. "You met Chelsea. She is a Cleveland Bay. I didn't recognize her breed the first time I saw her either. They are Great Britain's oldest breed of horse, but they haven't been in the United States for very long. The breed started up in an area northeast of England that used to be called Cleveland."

"She appears to be quite athletic," Mr. Wallington said with a voice full of admiration. "What is she used for?"

"Chelsea is a carriage horse," Carrie answered. "The Cleveland Bays, because they seem to almost always carry the same colors, are being used quite extensively for matching pairs."

"You're expanding into Cleveland Bays?"

"I have no idea," Carrie answered honestly. "Miles, one of our stable hands, brought Chelsea down from Canada."

"Canada?"

Carrie had become very comfortable talking to the man who obviously had a deep love for horses. "Miles used to be a slave here. He worked in Canada after he escaped the plantation before the war. He returned several months ago looking for a job. We were thrilled to give him one because he is wonderful with horses."

"And he brought Chelsea with him?"

"I do believe you're having a hard time believing my story, Mr. Wallington," Carrie murmured.

"Not at all, Mrs. Borden. I heard life on Cromwell Plantation was rather"—he paused as he searched for the right word—"unique."

Carrie laughed, watching out of the corner of her eye as the other two men left. She had seen Clint tell them the foals had all been sold. She could see the disappointment in the lines of their body, but their faces were resigned. She turned her attention back to Mr. Wallington ."I believe unique is an appropriate word," she said lightly. She wanted to ask what else he had heard, but didn't want to start a discussion that would harm the business arrangement they had just struck.

Mr. Wallington looked at her for a long moment and seemed to make a decision about something. "I did my homework before I came, too."

Carrie cocked her head and waited.

"I didn't know about your husband's death, but I did research your family after I realized Abby had married your father."

"You know Abby?"

Mr. Wallington smiled. "I used to be a manufacturer's representative in the textile industry," he revealed. "I met Abigail Livingston shortly after she took over her husband's business."

Carrie's eyes narrowed. "May I trust you treated her better than many of the other men did?"

"You may," he assured her.

Carrie decided she believed him. He had honest eyes, and his smile was genuine. "And now you're into horses?"

"Horses are far more fun," he admitted with an easy smile. "I was raised on a horse farm in upstate New York. That's where I met Mark and Susan. We grew up together as children."

"How delightful," Carrie cried.

Annie walked out onto the porch with a plate full of fried chicken and biscuits slathered with butter. "If I heard everythin' right from behind the door, I believe business is finished, and it's time to eat."

Carrie laughed, quite sure Annie had indeed had her ear plastered to the door during negotiations. "This is Mr. Wallington, Annie. He has just bought every one of the foals."

Annie fixed him with a steely gaze. "For a good price?"

"For a very good price," Carrie agreed happily.

Mr. Wallington laughed. "Has Abby trained *all* the women on Cromwell Plantation? I recognize her very effective techniques."

Annie snorted, her eyes twinkling with fun. "Then you know we ain't gonna tell you our secrets. I reckon you just ought to eat this food and be thankful you got the best horses in Virginia!"

Chapter Thirty-One

Carrie gazed out the train window, wondering what had ever possessed people to move west of the Mississippi River. She and Abby had long ago left behind the mountains, lush fields, and thick forests of the eastern United States. Now there seemed to be nothing but empty green flatness, limestone ledges, and dilapidated log houses or homes made from sod. Tired-faced women, standing herd over children in simple clothing, stared up at the train as they passed. Their eyes seemed glazed with fatigue, but they also had looks of determination that revealed how they had survived for so long in the brutal environment.

"Does the wind ever stop blowing in Kansas?" Carrie asked, alarmed when a particularly hard gust made the train car sway even more than the tracks could account for.

"Evidently not," Abby said. "I was warned before I came, but I had no idea what it was really going to be like."

Carrie looked away from the unfolding scenery, or lack thereof, and fixed her eyes on her stepmother. "Have you ever lived a life of anything but luxury?" she asked.

Abby shrugged. "No more than you have, my dear," she said blandly. "But I have been assured it won't kill us to live without comforts for a few weeks." Her lips tightened. "We have our work cut out for us," she said. "We have much bigger things to worry about than whether we will have a comfortable bed at night, or just how hard the wind is blowing."

Carrie knew Abby was right, but still, she missed the plantation with every fiber of her being. In her most honest moments, however, she admitted there was some relief in not being reminded of Robert by every single thing she saw. He was never out of her mind, but the sharpest edges of grief had been somewhat dulled the farther the train had chugged away from Virginia. "Tell me where we stand," she invited, knowing she needed to think about something else.

Abby knew her daughter needed distraction because they had already talked about this at length. "Things are not going as we hoped," she admitted. "Susan Anthony, Elizabeth Stanton, Lucy Stone, and others have been here since July, campaigning tirelessly, but I fear they are fighting an uphill battle they have no hope of winning."

"Because the Republicans and abolitionists are blocking their efforts in an attempt to make sure the black vote passes?"

"That would be the crux of it," Abby replied, her lips tightening with anger. "I am watching it happen, but I still have a hard time believing they are working *against* us after all we gave up. We put away the cause of women's rights during the war and put all our efforts into freeing the slaves—and were happy to do so." She shook her head. "We were obviously fools to believe we would be rewarded by a grateful country, and that the Republicans would fight for us. We have become accustomed to the predictions of the conservatives who believe women getting the vote will mean the downfall of home, church, and state, but we were totally unprepared for the opposition of the very politicians who have said they support us."

Carrie, prodded out of her memories of home, thought about what Matthew had told them before they left. She knew he was trying to prepare them for disappointment, but Abby had made a commitment, and she wasn't the type to walk away from a promise. Even if it was too late, she would fight. "Evidently politics are much more complex than everyone understands," Carrie said quietly. "The Republicans have their gaze fixed on the potential of two million black male voters in the South." Her voice sharpened with sarcasm as she saw the pain of futility glaze Abby's eyes. "Of course they are not going to jeopardize that by stirring up a tempest over women's suffrage." She thought about how hard Abby had fought for abolition of the slaves. "It is ludicrous that even the abolitionists are deserting women," she said hotly.

Abby sighed. "They are convinced this is the 'Negro's hour' and that nothing must be allowed to interfere." She lifted her head with defiance. "I refuse to believe it is not possible to do both. Blacks should have the right to vote, but I will not give up fighting for women to have the same right." Her shoulders slumped a little when she made her next statement. "I'm afraid Elizabeth is right. If the Fourteenth Amendment passes and puts the word '*male*' into the Constitution, it will no longer be possible for individual states to give women the right to vote. It will take another amendment to even give women the status of *citizenship*." Her voice sharpened with disbelief. "It could be decades before we have another chance. Elizabeth believes it could set us back a full century."

Carrie absorbed that prediction. It was likely she would never have the right to vote. Even little Hope might never be granted that freedom. And Hope's children, the next generation that was counting on them? It was inconceivable that they might not be able to have a voice either. She stiffened and looked out the window again, oblivious to the tall grasses bent flat by a roaring wind. She only saw an opportunity to change reality for women all over the country. "We'll fight hard, Abby," she said staunchly. "We may lose, but it won't be for lack of trying."

Abby smiled and reached out to take her hand. "Which is exactly why I wanted you with me, Carrie," she murmured.

****

Carrie had felt bone-searing fatigue many times during the war years, but she honestly couldn't remember ever being this tired. All the exhausting days seemed to blend into each other. She and Abby had arrived in Junction City, a rough and tumble town tucked up almost against the Texas border, ten days ago. Earlier campaigners had covered the sizeable towns in the months before their arrival, so she and Abby's job had been to go out into the smaller settlements to distribute pamphlets and talk at impromptu meetings. She had ceased being astonished at the living conditions, but the itching welts that were the courtesy of bedbugs had made every night miserable.

"We should be able to stop in an hour or so, Mrs. Borden," Kyle said.

Carrie looked at the man who had been selected by the Kansas Women's Rights Committee to accompany them. He was as rough and rugged as he looked, but the scruffy exterior covered in dust hid a heart of gold that truly believed women should have the right to vote. Without Kyle they would have left in defeat after the first couple of days, and without his knowledge they would have been hopelessly lost in a terrain that had begun to all look the same. "We'll be fine," she said firmly.

Kyle said nothing, but he cast a glance toward Abby.

Carrie didn't have to look to know why he had such a concerned expression on his face. If it was possible, Abby looked worse than she did. Her mother had an iron will and a determined spirit, but the hot, dusty days, combined with a howling wind that seemed to never lose its intensity, had seemed to suck the life right out of her. She still managed to stand in front of the crowds every night, whether they were in a schoolhouse, a church, or simply talking to people perched on rugged benches hastily assembled under the stars, but a particularly hot day had seemed to bring her to the end of her endurance. Carrie hoped the thunderstorm that had both drenched and cooled them would have restored some of her energy, but Abby seemed to be wilting even more. "Abby needs some water," she said urgently.

Kyle nodded and pulled out an oilskin he had filled from a stream they had passed earlier. "I have a few apples, too," he offered.

Carrie acknowledged his kindness with a nod as she reached for the water, but the shriveled fruit he called apples hardly resembled what they ate at home. She pushed aside the thought that they were ripening on the trees even now because the thought of the plantation made Kansas harder to endure. She was certain Abby's stomach couldn't handle what he was offering. She held the water up to her mother's lips. "Drink this," she said gently.

"I'm fine," Abby said weakly, working hard to summon a smile. "We'll be somewhere we can stop soon. I just need some sleep."

Carrie returned the smile, but she knew Abby needed far more than sleep. Ten days of living off bacon swimming in grease, rock-hard biscuits, and coffee strong enough to curdle your hair had taken its toll on her. She glanced at Kyle. "Will you hand me some of the slippery elm we bought today?" The purchases they had made earlier that day in a settlement they passed had been sparse—dried herring, crackers, gum Arabic, and slippery elm—but they were better than nothing.

"I saw you buy that today," Kyle commented as he rooted around in a bag he had tied to the carriage. "What's it for?"

Carrie pulled out the pieces of bark and handed one to Abby. "Just chew on it," she said. "It will help." She smiled when Abby followed her orders, closing her eyes as she chewed.

"Slippery elm bark is remarkable," Carrie replied to Kyle. "It was first introduced to whites here in America by the Indians as a survival ration. You can eat it just like Abby is now because it is very nutritious, but it tastes better when it is ground into a coarse meal and boiled into a porridge. It actually has a creamy, sweet flavor. You can also use it as a powder to extend ordinary flour." She glanced at Abby. "What she is chewing now is like a sweet, long-lasting chewing gum."

Kyle looked at the slightly slimy bark that glowed in the moonlight, and grimaced. "What does the porridge taste like?"

"Oatmeal," Carrie said with a smile. "You can probably thank the existence of our country to slippery elm bark."

Kyle raised a brow. "Really?"

Carrie nodded, glad to have something else to think about besides the endless carriage ride. "During the Revolutionary War, George Washington's soldiers had to survive for twelve days during the brutal winter at Valley Forge with little more than slippery elm porridge. I'm sure they were still hungry, but it kept them alive, and it kept them fighting." She paused, looking out over the harsh landscape of southwestern Kansas. Carrie couldn't imagine living in Kansas during a winter snowstorm. The very thought made her shudder. "We'll probably never know how many families have survived their first winters here because of slippery elm bark."

Kyle looked impressed. He was also staring at her a little more closely. "How do you know all this?"

Carrie was uncomfortable with the turn in the conversation. The endless exhaustion of the unbearably long days had actually produced moments when Robert and Bridget weren't the first things on her mind, but Kyle's innocent question brought it all roaring back with an intensity that almost took her breath away. She struggled to make her voice sound natural. "I mostly learned it from a woman on my father's plantation." She couldn't bring herself to say anymore, so she decided to change the subject. "I'm surprised you don't already know this. Slippery elm bark is fairly common in the settlements because it has so many uses."

"I haven't been in Kansas very long," Kyle admitted.

Carrie looked at him with surprise. He fit right into the rugged environment like he had been here all his life. "How long have you been here?"

"About six months."

Carrie was intrigued now, and once again happy to have anything keep her mind off the endless day. "Where are you from?"

"Boston."

Carrie stared at him, certain she had not heard him correctly. "Did you say Boston?"

Kyle grinned. "I don't much look like it now, I know."

Carrie couldn't think of a way to respond, but Abby saved her.

"What brought you to Kansas, Kyle?" Abby asked quietly.

Kyle shrugged, his look saying he would rather not be having this conversation. "I got the Westward Fever," he finally said. "My family thought I was crazy, but they couldn't talk me out of it. I was convinced everything was bigger and better out here."

"It's certainly bigger," Carrie muttered. Even under moonlight the countryside stretched on for endless miles because there was nothing to break it up. The last tree she had seen had been hours earlier by a creek, and there was hardly even a bump in the ground to break the flatness.

"You've decided to stay?" Abby pressed.

"I don't think I've decided anything," Kyle admitted, "except that I am going to help women try to get the vote." He answered Abby's next question before she could ask it. "My mother and sisters have been fighting for suffrage for years. I owe it to them to help however I can."

Carrie smiled at him. "Thank you. I figured you were doing this just for the money. I'm glad to know you believe in our cause."

Kyle laughed. "I'm not sure anyone could pay me enough to keep up with the schedule you ladies are keeping." Suddenly he cursed and drew the horses up sharply.

"What is it?" Carrie asked with alarm. She heard it before she saw it, remembering the thunderstorm she had welcomed because it would cool things off. She had neglected to take into account that the rain would fill the streambeds as well. She peered into the darkness. The moonlight was glistening off the water, and she could tell by the noise that it was moving swiftly, but she couldn't tell how deep it was, nor how wide the creek had become.

Abby was the first to voice the thought all of them were having. "Can we get across it?"

Kyle sat silently for several long moments as he stared at the water. "Only one way to find out," he finally said. He jumped down from the carriage and then looked up at Carrie. "Can you drive this thing?"

"Yes, but you can't walk into that water," she said with alarm. "You have no idea how fast it is moving. It could wash you away."

"It might," Kyle said casually, "but I don't think we got that much rain. This creek is little more than a trickle on most days."

Carrie looked at him with suspicion. "You've only been here six months. How do you know Kansas so well?"

Kyle grinned, his teeth flashing white in the moonlight. "I don't, but they tell me most streams are usually just a trickle around here. This one is probably the same."

Carrie laughed, but his answer did nothing to ease her concern. "At least hold on to the horse's bridle. It will help keep you steady."

"And you can handle the team if you have to?" Kyle persisted.

Carrie frowned. "Yes, but why don't we just turn around and go back?" As soon as the question was out of her mouth, she knew it wasn't a viable option. The last house of any kind had been at least two hours back, and there were two other streams between them and civilization. Kyle's silence said he knew she had answered her own question.

"Carrie?"

There was something about Abby's voice that set off alarm bells in Carrie's head. She turned to her quickly. "What is it?"

"We need to go forward and find our lodging."

Carrie, frightened by the almost desperate tone, knew what she would find when she reached out her hand, but it took all her self-control to stifle her reaction when she felt Abby's burning forehead. Her stepmother wasn't just tired; she was sick. She looked down at Kyle. "Lead the way," she said. "And be careful."

Carrie clambered onto the driver's seat and picked up the reins. She knew both horses were willing and well-behaved; she also knew they were tired. She wasn't at all sure they could battle a raging creek.

Kyle looked up at her, his eyes grim but steady. "It will be fine," he assured her. "I'm going first because it's the only way to know what is waiting for us."

Carrie chose to believe it would be fine, because the alternative was simply more than she could bear to consider. "Let's go."

Kyle moved to the head of the team, grasped the bridle, and began to walk toward the rushing water. He moved steadily, slowing only a little when he reached the flooded stream. Within moments, water had reached up to the footboard of the carriage and begun to flow in.

Carrie knew their clothes were getting soaked, but their luggage was tied in to protect it from jostling, so there was no worry about it washing away. She glanced at Abby, her worry increasing as she saw Abby's eyes remained closed. There was just enough light to see the deep lines of pain on her face. Carrie urged the horses forward as she watched Kyle stride into water up to his waist. She tensed, but he didn't seem to be struggling.

She breathed a heavy sigh of relief when he stepped out onto dry land and pulled the horses up the slight rise on the other side. "Well done!" she called.

Kyle grinned, patted the horses on their necks, and climbed back into the driver's seat. Carrie slipped back to be with Abby, and shot Kyle a look that said they had to hurry. All Carrie could do was hold Abby's hand as they rattled on through the night made much darker by a bank of clouds that had swallowed the moon. She refused to consider Indian attacks or any of the other hazards they had been warned about. Nothing that was out there could cause her more concern than what she was feeling right now.

Carrie bit her lip to keep from crying. It was bad enough that Abby was sick, but what made it even worse was that she had no way of helping her. In spite of her determination not to be a doctor, she thought longingly of the medicine bag at home full of remedies that could help Abby. She had been a fool not to bring anything along at all. She was so resisting the idea of being a doctor that she had put Abby at risk. "How long before we get there?" she snapped, instantly sorry because she knew none of this was Kyle's fault.

"We're close," Kyle assured her, nodding with satisfaction. "I can see a light over there on the horizon. "We're only a couple miles away at the most."

Carrie took notice of the fact that the house could be seen from two miles away, something not even conceivable in Virginia, and then she turned back to Abby. The only thing she could do was wet a bandana with cool water to wipe Abby's face, but it seemed to be offering at least a little relief. She tried to push down the fears of what could happen if Abby was seriously ill, but she knew she couldn't slip into the dark space of remembering Robert and Bridget's deaths. She had to stay in the present if she was going to make a difference.

"Carrie," Abby said weakly, forcing her eyes open.

"I'm here, Abby," Carrie replied soothingly. "Just close your eyes and rest. We will be there soon."

Abby shook her head, the effort causing her to grimace. "My bag," she whispered. "My bag." It seemed that was all she was capable of saying before her eyes drifted shut again.

Carrie had no idea why the bag was so important, but she reached for it where it was lashed onto the back of the wagon just above the water line from their trek through the flooded creek. She untied it quickly, wondering why it weighed so much more than her own, and then laid it on the seat and opened it. "My medical bag!" she gasped. She looked at Abby and saw her eyes were open again.

"I thought you might need it," she gasped before she went limp.

Carrie leaned forward to test Abby's pulse, relieved when she found it weak but steady. The fever and the long day had simply become too much for her to bear. She continued to bathe Abby's face, and prayed for the house to appear soon while she formulated her plan. She wouldn't know for sure what was in the medical bag Abby had brought until she had light to examine it, but she trusted there was something that would help.

****

Carrie breathed a sigh of relief when the carriage finally pulled to a stop in front of a simple log house. A light glowed steadily in the window. She prayed whoever lived here would let her bring a sick woman inside. She didn't know what was wrong with Abby, but she knew she needed medical attention quickly.

What if you kill her, too?

Carrie tensed as the question reverberated through every part of her being. She pushed it down, along with thoughts of Robert and Bridget. Fear had crippled her for four months since their deaths, but she couldn't afford to be crippled right now. She breathed a sigh of relief when the door opened and outlined a man's shape.

"Is this the Marlton residence?" Kyle called.

"Are you the suffrage folks we were told were coming through?" the man called. "You're awful late."

"You're right," Kyle said apologetically. "The storm and swollen creeks delayed us."

"Come on inside," the man invited. "We made some room for you. It will be tight, but we're going to make it work."

Carrie stepped from the carriage and approached the house. She needed to tell him about Abby, but she also needed to discover why his voice sounded so distraught. She was slightly alarmed by his appearance when she was close enough to see him clearly. A tall, gangly man, his face was tight with stress, and his eyes gleamed with something bordering on panic. "Is everything all right here?" she asked quietly.

"No. Three of my kids are sick." He shook his head. "We put them in a back room. I know this probably isn't the best place for you to be staying, but there isn't another house for miles and it is getting real late."

Carrie took a deep breath. "What's wrong with your children?"

"I don't know," the man admitted. "They were doing fine this morning, but then they got a fever and just kept feeling worse."

Carrie nodded as she thought quickly. "The woman with us is sick, too," she revealed. "Abby Cromwell is my mother." She took a deep breath, breaking the vow she had made to herself. "My name is Carrie Borden. I am a doctor. I can help everyone if you will let me." She could feel Kyle's surprised eyes boring into her back, even as the man's face went slack with relief.

"A doctor?" he exclaimed as he stepped aside. "My name is Stanley Marlton. Please come in."

Carrie stepped into the house and looked around. "Kyle and I will be fine on the floor, but is there a bed for my mother?"

Stanley nodded quickly. "She can sleep in my bed. It's in a curtained off area next to where my kids are."

Carrie analyzed the situation in moments. The little house was home to Stanley, his three sick children, and four more who stared back at her from the kitchen table. The home was crowded, but looked clean and orderly. She locked eyes with the oldest child, who looked to be in her late teens. She didn't see a mother, but now was not the time to ask about it.

"You can help my brothers and sister?" the girl asked.

Carrie immediately liked her direct gaze. "I believe I can. What is your name?"

"My name is Bridget."

Carrie gasped and felt herself sway slightly before she could regain control.

"Ma'am?"

Carrie somehow managed a smile when Bridget's voice broke through the roaring in her head. "I'm sorry. I must be more tired and hungry than I thought."

A little boy who looked to be about ten jumped up from the table. "We got some cornbread and buttermilk left over from dinner," he said brightly. "Bridget is a real fine cook. Would you like some?"

Carrie wasn't sure how she was going to survive hearing the name Bridget over and over, but she knew she would have to. "I would love some," she said, "but first we need to get my mother in the house, and make sure everyone is taken care of." A movement at the door made her glance in that direction.

Stanley stood there, Abby held securely in his arms as if she weighed nothing. He strode in and deposited Abby's limp form on the bed. Carrie bit back her panic, and then turned to go get her medical bag from the carriage. Kyle walked in the door just then and handed it to her. "Thank you," she murmured. Her emotions jumped from dread to relief and back again, as she felt the familiar weight in her hands.

Bridget beckoned to all the children. "Go sit down somewhere else. Mrs. Borden is going to need this table to work on."

"Please call me Carrie," she said as she set the bag down and began to pull things out. Her eyes widened at the vast array of herbal and homeopathic medicines. Where had Abby gotten all this? As she laid it out on the table, she realized Dr. Hobson must have put it together. It was the only possible explanation. Abby had known better than to let them come to the western wilderness without medical supplies. She breathed a prayer of gratitude as she sorted through everything and chose several small bottles. She turned to Bridget. "Please show me where the children are."

Bridget pulled aside the curtain next to the bed where Abby lay. Three small children gazed up, their faces flushed, and their eyes filled with fevered misery.

"Hello," Carrie said softly. "Who do we have here?"

The smallest, a little girl with blond curls, gazed up at her. "I'm Camille. I'm four."

"It's a pleasure to meet you," Carrie murmured, relieved to discover that while the little girl was definitely sick, the fever did not yet appear high enough to be dangerous.

One of the little boys managed a weak smile. "I'm Abraham," he said shyly. "I'm six." He tried to smile again, but the best he could manage was a whimper. "I don't feel so good."

"I know you don't," Carrie said soothingly. "We're going to fix that. Can you tell me what hurts?"

"My head," the boy answered. "It hurts something fierce. So does my throat."

Carrie almost sagged with relief. She had been afraid of cholera, but the symptoms didn't support that. She was fairly certain she was dealing with the flu.

"And how about you, honey?" she asked the third child.

"I'm Belton. I'm eight." His eyes gazed into hers with fierce intensity. "You can help the younger ones first," he said bravely.

Carrie's heart swelled with emotion as she laid a hand on his forehead. He had a fever, too. "Does your throat hurt?"

"Real bad," he agreed. "Are we gonna die?"

Something about the stoic acceptance in his voice told Carrie he had experienced death before.

"No one is dying, Belton," Bridget snapped.

Carrie recognized the fear in her voice as well. She reached down and gripped Belton's hands. "Your sister is right. No one is going to die."

"You promise?" Camille whispered. "Baby James already died. And then Mama died. And then Mary died," she said sadly.

Carrie's heart almost broke, but she managed to smile tenderly as she pushed back hair from Camille's damp forehead. "I promise," she said. She looked up when she heard Stanley step to the opening in the curtain. "Have you been to town recently?"

Stanley nodded. "Two days ago. The kids like to go in, so I take them once a month." His forehead creased. "Did they get sick there?"

"I think so," Carrie informed him. "We were there the last two days. My mother started feeling badly this afternoon, and your children got sick as well." She breathed a sigh of relief. "I think everyone has a bout of the flu." Fear sprang into Stanley's eyes, and Carrie heard Bridget gasp.

It was Camille who cleared up why there were so afraid. "You said we wouldn't die," she cried. "My mama died from the flu. So did Baby James and Mary. I reckon we're gonna die, too."

"No one is dying," Carrie repeated firmly. "In fact, I think you'll feel better by morning," she said cheerfully. "You probably won't feel like running around for a couple more days, but you won't be as miserable as you are now."

The look on Stanley's face remained skeptical, but he seemed desperate to believe her. "You can really help them?"

"I can," Carrie said confidently, not bothering to question her certainty when the last four months had been a haze of belief that she could never help anyone again. There was no time to analyze feelings when she had Abby and three sick children counting on her for help. She turned to Bridget. "Do you have a garden?"

"Yes."

"Onions?"

"Yes," Bridget replied, though her gaze said she had no clue why Carrie was asking. "I have a basket here in the house that I dug up this morning."

"Good," Carrie said. "I want you to cut eight of them into thick slices." She raised a hand when she saw the question forming on Bridget's lips. "I'll explain later. For now, I just need you to do it."

Bridget snapped her lips shut and turned away to do what had been requested.

"What can I do?" Stanley asked.

"I need four glasses of clean water," Carrie replied. "Is your well a good one?"

"Probably the only good thing about this disaster we call a farm," Stanley said wearily. "I'll be right back with a fresh bucket."

Carrie pulled out the bottle of *Gelsemium* that Dr. Hobson had packed. Her earlier research had told her the homeopathic remedy best represented flu symptoms, so it was the best medicine for her patients. When Stanley put four glasses of water on the table, she put several drops in each one and stirred them.

She handed the first glass to Kyle, who had been watching quietly the whole time. "Please lift Abby up and give this to her very slowly. Even if she is still unconscious, she will have automatic swallowing instincts if it goes in slowly enough." She put the other three glasses on a wooden tray Bridget had pulled down from the wall. "I'll take care of the children."

"Here we go," she said brightly as she entered the curtained off area. "I want each of you to drink this. It will take a few minutes for it to start having an effect, but then you will want to go to sleep." She saw alarm spring into Camille's eyes. The little girl had probably watched her mother and siblings go to sleep and never wake up. "There is nothing to worry about," she said softly as she pulled the little girl into a warm embrace, knowing how badly she needed reassurance. "I promise you are going to be all right. When you wake up in the morning, you're going to feel better."

Camille's eyes filled with trust. "I believe you," she whispered. Then she looked over at her sister. "Why is Bridget cutting up onions?"

Carrie smiled. "Because we are going to put them on your feet," she said in a mysterious voice.

"Our feet?" Belton demanded. "Why?"

"It's magic," Carrie said, maintaining her mysterious tone. "The onion will suck all the flu right out of you."

Belton eyed her skeptically. "I'm eight," he reminded her. "You don't have to lie to me."

Carrie laughed, appreciating the intelligent shine in the little boy's eyes. "The onion is a natural remedy that truly does take fever and sickness from your body," she said in a more serious voice. "I use it on many of my patients. It works every time." She watched the suspicion slowly fade from Belton's eyes.

"Okay then," he finally said.

Stanley stepped forward with four pairs of socks. "I imagine you will need these."

"Thank you." Carrie reached for the plate of onion slices Bridget had prepared, placed them on the soles of all the children's feet, pulled the socks on, and told them to lie still.

She moved to Abby's bed and did the same thing, trying to bite back her concern that she had not regained consciousness. She knew the long day in the carriage, combined with a searing hot sun and a case of influenza, had sapped everything from her. She fought her fear as she told herself she should be grateful Abby was still asleep, because that was the most important thing for her healing, but still the whispers besieged her. *You let them die. You let them die.*

"Are you all right, Carrie?"

Kyle's voice broke through her thoughts, allowing Carrie to regain control. "Yes," she said with conviction. She had decided to treat these sick people. It was no time to let her fears cloud her judgement. "Did you get Abby to drink all the water?"

"I did." Kyle gazed down at her. "Is she really going to be all right?"

"Absolutely," Carrie responded. "She needs sleep more than anything."

"So do you," Kyle observed.

Carrie shook her head. "Each of them will need the remedy every three hours through the night. I'll stay awake to make sure they get it." As fatigue pressed in on her, she hoped she could do it.

"Nonsense," Stanley said briskly. "I don't want to mess up the remedy by doing it wrong, but I can wake you when you need to give it to them." He gestured toward the bed where Abby was asleep. "There is room enough for both of you. You get some rest. I'll wake you up in three hours."

Carrie nodded, struck by the agony in his eyes. She recognized that look all too well—the haunted look that said he was thinking about the nights he had lain in bed with his wife before she had died. She knew he needed reassurance more than anything else. She stepped forward and grasped his hands tightly. "No one is going to die," she repeated again. "Your children are going to be just fine." She knew she couldn't restore the family he had already lost, but if she could relieve his fears, it would also help the rest of the children who were watching silently.

Stanley stared into her eyes and finally seemed to reach a conclusion. "Thank you," he said gruffly. "Now you get some sleep. You look all done in. I'll wake you up."

Carrie lay down on the bed and was asleep in moments.

An Invitation

Before you read the last chapter of Carried Forward By Hope, I would like to invite you to join my mailing list so that you are never left wondering what is going to happen next. ☺

<u>Join my Email list so you can:</u>

- Receive notice of all new books & audio releases.
- Be a part of my Launch celebrations. I give away lots of gifts! ☺
- Read my weekly blog while you're waiting for a new book.
- Be part of The Bregdan Chronicles Family!
- Learn about all the other books I write.

Just go to <u>www.BregdanChronicles.net</u> and fill out the form.

I look forward to having you become part of The Bregdan Chronicles Family!

Blessings,
Ginny Dye

Chapter Thirty-Two

Carrie wasn't sure what jolted her awake, but her still weary mind refused to process the information it was receiving as she gazed around the strange room. Slowly, it all filtered back—the long carriage ride, fording the swollen creek, Abby and the children having influenza. As the last piece of information settled in, she sat up quickly and looked beside her. Abby was still asleep, but even in the dim lantern light, she looked like she was better. Carrie laid her hand on her forehead, relieved beyond words to find the fever almost gone. Abby would be too weak to travel for a few days, but she was going to be fine.

Carrie swung her legs off the bed and looked around the small cabin, taking in details she had not noticed the night before. The log cabin was as rustic as she remembered, but there were touches that said the Marlton family had not always lived in such dire circumstances. A fine oak dresser was tucked up against the wall, with delicate lace doilies beneath a gleaming silver comb and brush. She suspected the comb and brush had belonged to the mother who had died. Carrie felt a wave of sadness, but along with the sadness came a depth of understanding she had never experienced before.

A quick sweep of the room told her she was the only one awake, and a slight glow coming from one of the two windows in the house told her the sun was about to make its appearance. Suddenly desperate for fresh air, Carrie stepped silently to the door, eased it open, and walked outside. The sight that met her took her breath away.

The clouds that lingered from last night's thunderstorm danced across a verdant green landscape that stretched as far as she could see. The sun kissed the clouds as it rose toward the horizon, touching them with hues of purple, pink, and orange. She had seen many beautiful sunrises over the James River, but had never seen one that seemed to stretch on for endless miles. Carrie stood quietly, taking deep breaths of the cool morning air, knowing the sun was going to deliver another stifling day. For just a moment, she understood why people had moved to Kansas.

"It's beautiful, isn't it?"

Carrie turned her head, somehow not startled to find she wasn't alone. She smiled at Bridget. "I can almost understand why people live here," she said softly, not wanting to break the magic of the morning.

"It's about the *only* thing that makes it worth it," Bridget responded in a voice that was both bitter and stoically accepting.

"Have y'all been here long?" Carrie wanted to know more about the young woman standing before her with eyes full of sharp intelligence and aching sadness.

"Long enough," Bridget replied with a sigh. "We left Ohio less than a year ago." Her eyes took on a faraway expression. "My mama didn't want to leave home. We had a good farm, and we were surrounded by family."

"Why would you leave that?" Carrie pressed, knowing Bridget needed someone to talk to. Since she was the oldest child, Carrie was sure most of the care and burden had fallen on the young woman.

"I believe they call it Westward Fever," Bridget said. "My papa caught a bad case of it. He believed everything would be even better out here. Nothing Mama said made any difference, so we sold our farm, said good-bye to friends and family, and headed for Kansas."

Carrie waited, knowing Bridget had more she needed to say.

"Baby James was only six months old when we left," she continued, her words twisted with pain. "He didn't make it even a month before he died on the trail."

Carrie shuddered, wondering how Stanley had been able to take such a young child on a long, arduous journey, but just as quickly realized he had probably believed he was doing the best thing for his family, and had no comprehension of how hard the trip would be. "I'm so sorry," she murmured.

"I think it broke Mama's heart. She died a few weeks after we got here, and then my two-year-old sister, Claire, died right after." She shook her head. "The dying seems to have stopped for a while—at least once you got here last night. I was sure I was going to lose my other brothers and sisters, too."

Carrie reached out and took her hand. "I'm so sorry, Bridget."

"Thank you," Bridget whispered. She lifted her head with determination. "You're sure they are going to be all right?"

"Abby's fever is almost gone," Carrie replied. "I'll check on the children when we go back in, but I already know they are fine. We caught it quickly, and children are much more resilient than adults when they catch the flu."

Bridget cocked her head. "Are you really a doctor?"

Carrie hesitated, not sure how to answer that question. "I was," she said finally, looking away from the girl's searching eyes to gaze at the sunrise again.

"Was?" Bridget pressed. "What do you mean?"

Carrie sighed. She would rather not have this conversation, but she supposed there was no getting around it. "I was in my final year of medical school, and also in an internship with a homeopathic physician..." Her voice trailed away because she couldn't find the words to finish the explanation.

"Something real bad must have happened," Bridget said, her voice thick with understanding.

Carrie shot her a glance. "Yes." She remained silent as she watched the sun slip through the lowest layer of clouds and perch on the horizon like a blazing ball of fire. The dew clinging to the grasses around her sparkled and danced as a light breeze sprung up. "My husband was murdered five months ago," she explained in a halting voice. "I went into early labor and lost my daughter." Her voice cracked with the memory. "Her name was Bridget," she whispered.

Bridget reached over to take her hand and held it firmly. "I'm so sorry." Her voice was both compassionate and heartbroken.

Carrie recognized it for what it was—the voice of someone who had walked through their own dark pain. Somehow it comforted her. She stood quietly, glad for the connection of their linked hands.

"You blame yourself," Bridget said after several minutes.

"Yes," Carrie said. It didn't matter how the young girl knew; it was simply the truth.

"I blamed myself, too," Bridget said. "When Mama died."

Carrie looked at her. "It wasn't your fault," she protested. "You couldn't have possibly stopped it."

"Maybe," Bridget said, "but I don't think I tried hard enough to talk Papa out of coming here. I've always been his favorite, I guess because I'm the oldest. Anyway, Mama asked me to talk him out of it, but I think I caught something of the Westward Fever too," she said sorrowfully. "I didn't try to convince him to not come. Mama died. So did James and Claire."

Carrie understood the desolate look in the girl's eyes. "Bridget..." She couldn't say anymore as stark realization stole her breath.

"What is it?" Bridget asked, a slightly alarmed tone in her voice.

Carrie turned away and watched as the sun baked away the sparkling dew on the grass. Everyone had tried to tell her the *deaths* had not been her fault. She had not believed them, perhaps had not *wanted* to believe them, because blaming herself gave her a target for the rage and grief that consumed her. Blaming herself gave her a point of understanding, when the reality was that the deaths had been so senseless that understanding was not even an option. Perhaps Bridget would have lived if Carrie had not ridden home to be with Robert, but her medical training said she might well *not* have lived either. In reality, a four-hour horseback ride should not have killed a healthy child coming from a healthy mother. She would never know what might have happened, but hanging on to the guilt, trying to attach understanding when there was none to be had, was as senseless as the deaths that had spawned it.

"Carrie?" Bridget's voice, more insistent this time, broke through Carrie's thoughts.

Carrie turned to her, hearing the vulnerability in the girl's voice. "It was not your fault," she said firmly. Truth pulsed through her as she accepted what had just poured into her soul. "You want to blame yourself because it helps make sense of it, but the truth is that there *is* no sense to all the deaths. Your mama and siblings were taken by a disease that has killed millions across the country." She took a deep breath. "The worst part of it is that there is medical care to keep that from happening." Her mind raced as she realized, perhaps for the first time, just how much power she had to lessen the number of senseless deaths in the world. She couldn't stop Robert and Bridget's, but she *had* stopped influenza deaths in the cabin behind her.

She gripped both of Bridget's hands. "Blaming yourself will not change what happened, honey. And your mama would be heartbroken to know you believed it was your fault." She peered into her eyes, praying the girl was ready to hear what she was saying. "Death just *is*, Bridget. It happens to every single person. When it happens sooner than we believe it should—before someone has had the opportunity to live a long life—it is even harder to bear losing the people we love. We feel guilty because we are still alive, so perhaps we decide to take on the guilt of the death as well." As she talked, deeper understanding poured into her. "Your mama loved you, didn't she?"

Bridget nodded, tears shimmering in her eyes. "Mama had more love than anyone I ever knew," she whispered.

"Then hang on to that love," Carrie said, a powerful vision of Robert's loving eyes filling her mind. "That love will carry you through all the days to come. I don't know why your mama and your siblings died, but I do know that *you* are still alive. We both..." Carrie shivered as the truth of her words penetrated the remaining layer of guilt. "We both have the privilege of letting our lives be a reflection of the love we lost."

Bridget swallowed hard and turned to look out over the horizon, which had lost its magic once the sun had risen high enough in the sky to remind lookers that Kansas was an endless, often brutal plain, which would demand everything from a person in order to survive.

Carrie stood silently as tears coursed down Bridget's cheeks. She didn't say anything when the tears stopped and Bridget lifted her head with a touch of defiance, and an abundance of courage. She simply stood with her, offering her the strength to reach her own conclusions.

Bridget finally turned to her. "Thank you," she said quietly. Then her gaze sharpened. "Does this mean you are going to be a doctor again?"

Carrie managed a smile. "I think it does," she murmured.

"Good," Bridget replied. "Can you start by checking on my sister and brothers?"

Carrie laughed and linked arms with her. Together they strode into the cabin. The first thing she saw was Abby sitting up against the pillows, drinking slowly from a glass of water Stanley had given her.

"Good morning," Abby said quietly.

"Good morning!" Carrie responded, happy to see the light back in her mother's eyes. "You look better."

"I feel better," Abby replied. "I understand I have you to thank."

Carrie shrugged. "I believe you should thank yourself," she said wryly. "If it weren't for the medical supplies you had brought along, I wouldn't have been able to help anyone."

Abby smiled. "Oh, you would have probably pulled some plants out of the woods if you had to."

Carrie laughed. "I'm a good doctor, but I'm not sure I'm that good." She understood when Abby's eyes widened, but she wasn't ready to talk through her revelations yet. "I have some patients in the other room to take care of," she said. "Drink all of that water."

"I'll make some cornbread," Bridget said eagerly. "We've got some honey to put on it that I pulled out of a hive last week."

Abby looked relieved. "As long as I don't have to eat soggy bacon and hard biscuits, I will be so grateful."

"My mama made sure I could cook better than that," Bridget promised her. "I'll have it for you soon."

Carrie winked at Bridget, and then pulled back the curtain to the other alcove. Her heart leapt with gladness when she saw the three children sleeping peacefully. As she watched, Camille stirred and opened her sleepy eyes. The little girl stared around for a minute before she focused on Carrie.

Gradually, her eyes grew wider. "I didn't die, did I?" she asked in wonder.

"You didn't die," Carrie agreed, moving over to touch her forehead. "And your fever is all gone, too."

Camille grinned and swung her gaze toward her brothers. "Are they alive, too?"

"They are," Carrie assured her, happy when both little boys opened their eyes in response to her voice. "Good morning, Abraham. Good morning, Belton."

Belton rubbed his eyes and then shot a look toward Abraham and Camille. When he was satisfied both of them were all right, he looked back at Carrie with an appraising gaze. "I guess you were right," he said. "You're a real doctor."

"Yes, she is!"

Carrie smiled when Abby's voice floated through the house. They had so much to talk about, but the conclusion was already obvious.

Stanley walked in just then, his hands holding a heavy pail of fresh milk from the lone cow in the stable. "I don't know how to say thank you," he said awkwardly.

Carrie smiled. "I think we all have reason to be grateful. Without a bed for Abby to sleep in last night, I'm not sure what would have happened." It made her uncomfortable to realize how true that was, but she decided to focus on gratitude. After five months of dark grief and guilt, it felt liberating to make a different choice. She gestured toward the bucket. "Can we dunk our cornbread in that?" Her growling stomach was reminding her she was famished.

Stanley nodded. "My Bridget makes the best cornbread in the world," he said proudly, and then his voice faltered. "Her mama taught her."

Carrie stepped forward and held his eyes with her own. "Her mama would be so proud of all of you," she said. "She would be proud of you for making such a comfortable home for your family, and she would be proud of every one of her children."

Stanley's eyes bored into hers before he nodded abruptly. "I made a decision this morning," he announced as he reached out to pull Bridget to his side. "We're going back to Ohio."

Bridget gasped. "I didn't think we had enough money, Papa. How can we go back to Ohio?"

"I got just enough," Stanley replied. "And last night destroyed the rest of my pride about not admitting defeat out here."

Abby's voice broke in. "It's not failure to want the best for your family."

"You're right," Stanley agreed, his face beaming when Bridget kissed him on the cheek. "I'm taking all my children back where they have family and folks that love them."

"I'm glad," Carrie said softly, exchanging a long look with Bridget.

"I've got you to thank for that," Stanley said.

Carrie's eyes widened with surprise. "Me?"

Stanley nodded. "I was out in the barn when you and Bridget were talking this morning." He took a deep breath. "My Angela's death almost killed me, too. I've felt nothing but dead the last months since she passed. I know it was my fault that all of them died." He held up his hand when Carrie opened her mouth to protest. "I know what you're going to say—that it was influenza that killed them. Part of me knows that is true, but the other part of me knows they probably wouldn't have gotten sick, or they would have gotten care sooner, if I hadn't left on that wagon train." He pulled Bridget close to him. "I'm sorry, honey. You were never to blame. It was always me. There comes a time when you are truly responsible for something that you need to admit it, but then you've got to find a way to forgive yourself if you want to keep living."

"And you found that way, Papa?" Bridget breathed.

"Let's just say I'm on the way," Stanley answered. "I know I made a mistake when I brought all of you out here. I'm not going to keep making that mistake. I've talked to enough men out here who have too much stupid pride to admit they were wrong to come to Kansas. Oh, it's fine for some, but not for *my* family. I almost lost three more of you last night." He locked eyes with Carrie. "I'm taking all of you home."

Carrie sucked in her breath, overwhelmed with an avalanche of feelings. Sorrow that Robert was gone. Sorrow he would never be a father to his own Bridget. Gladness she had saved Abby and the children. Gladness for the light of love and pride in Bridget's eyes as she gazed at her father. And for the first time in many months, anticipation of what lay ahead for her. Oh, she knew she would carry the grief for a long time to come, but finally, it wasn't controlling every aspect of her life.

****

Carrie breathed a sigh of relief when the train pulled out of the station in Grand Junction. There was not one thing she would miss about Kansas, but she would always be grateful she had come on this journey.

"It's good to be headed home."

Carrie turned to Abby. "You're sure you feel up to this?"

Abby gave her a mock glare. "If you ask me that one more time, I may have to strangle you. How many times do I have to tell you I'm fine?"

"Evidently a few more times," Carrie said ruefully. It was possible Abby didn't understand how likely her death would have been if she hadn't had the medicine to treat her, but she had decided not to explain it in depth. All that really mattered was that she *did* have the medicine to treat her. Stanley's younger children had all been playing happily in the yard when they had left, stopping long enough to wave wildly and call good-bye to them. Bridget had hugged her as if she would never let her go, and Carrie had promised she would write.

Abby seemed to read her mind. "So Bridget wants to be a doctor, too?"

"She does," Carrie said softly. "She'll be a good one."

"Because she has seen so much death?" Abby guessed.

Carrie considered the question. "Because she has learned how precious life is," she answered. Abby sat back and stared at her. They really hadn't had much time to talk in the crowded cabin, or when Kyle was driving them back. This was their first time being truly alone since everything had happened—if you could count a bench in a crowded train car as truly alone.

"As you have learned it?" Abby asked tenderly.

"Yes," Carrie admitted. She knew it was time to tell Abby more of what had happened. "I've always been good at medicine, but I didn't truly understand the fear inside people's hearts when their loved ones were ill. I probably thought I did, but..."

Abby picked up when her voice trailed off. "But now you know exactly what it is like."

"Yes. It will make me a better doctor." She turned to gaze out the window for long moments before she swung back to look into Abby's compassionate gray eyes. "I will never believe Robert and Bridget's deaths were anything but a senseless loss, but just as you predicted, I have at least reached the place where I can acknowledge the good things that have happened in me because of them."

"That takes great maturity and wisdom," Abby said softly.

Carrie frowned. "I had a conversation with Rose shortly after I found out I was pregnant," she murmured, her mind back on the plantation in the clearing around Sarah's grave. "Sarah told me once that greatness comes from great suffering. I wondered then if Rose and I had suffered enough to be great." She took a deep breath. "Obviously, the answer was no."

"All of life is a cycle, Carrie," Abby said. "You were a great woman when you had that conversation with Rose. You are a great woman now, and you will be even greater in the future, but life will always be full of ups and downs, suffering and joy. I have found that it is so important to embrace the joy fully, pulling it into every part of your being, because you will need it there when the next hard times start. You'll need the joy to balance the grief, and to remind you that the sunrise always follows the darkness."

Carrie smiled, knowing she was right. "I don't have to be excited about that, do I?" she asked dryly.

"I would think you were strange if you were," Abby assured her.

The two women rode in silence for a long time, watching the Kansas plains roll by as their train headed east. Carrie's mind flew ahead to the plantation.

"What's next, daughter?"

Carrie sighed. "Life seems to be nothing but one transition after another."

Abby laughed. "And again you have discovered a great truth about living."

"Another truth I wish weren't true," Carrie complained, managing a slight smile. "I have some things to figure out. I know I am a doctor, and I know I'm meant to finish my education, but there are so many unknowns."

"Like who will handle the horse operation?" Abby asked with a strange smile on her face.

"Yes," Carrie agreed. "Clint has come so far, but I don't think he's ready to take on the business operation of things yet. That time may come, but it will take a lot of training before I would feel good about it, and I suspect before he would feel good about it." She cocked her head and peered at Abby more closely. "Why are you looking at me like that?"

Abby grinned. "I didn't just bring a medicine bag with me."

Carrie was confused. "I don't understand."

Abby grinned again, rummaged through her bag, and pulled out an envelope. "You should read this."

Carrie took it, not recognizing the handwriting. She slit the seal, unfolded the letter and read it, her eyes growing larger with each sentence. "I don't believe it!" She looked up. "Do you know what this says?"

"I think so," Abby admitted. "Susan sent your father and me a letter, too."

Carrie looked at the top of the letter more closely. "Susan sent this almost two months ago."

"Yes. She asked your father and I to give it to you only if we felt it was the right time."

Carrie stared at Abby, her mind racing through what she had read. "Mark is in love and is getting married," she murmured. "Susan is welcome there, of course, but she has always wanted a stable of her own, and is wondering if she could run Cromwell Stables, with an eye to buying it one day if that is ever a possibility."

"What do you think?" Abby asked.

Carrie's mind wouldn't quit spinning, but she knew this was the perfect solution, and that it would give her time to decide what she wanted to do about Cromwell Stables in the future. She could never imagine selling Robert's dream, but then, she had never imagined she would go back to medical school either. All she could do was continue to take life one step at a time. "I think I have to keep walking forward into the unknown," she replied. "Everything still seems a little foggy, but it is certainly getting clearer."

"Making decisions as they come to you is the best way," Abby agreed. "I could never have imagined the way my life would turn out after Charles' death."

Carrie shook her head. "After the last three weeks, the only thing I can really think about is getting home." She smiled. "The leaves will just be starting to turn, and the harvest should be almost finished."

"Your father and I are coming out for the Harvest Celebration," Abby said happily. "Being on the plantation will be wonderful after being stuck on the Kansas plains."

Carrie sobered as she thought of the last few weeks. "Our being there was pointless, wasn't it?"

"Not if you have decided to be a doctor again, Carrie. I'd say it was worth every minute of greasy bacon, bedbugs, and influenza," Abby replied happily.

"But the reason we went in the first place?" Carrie persisted. "It's not going to happen is it? I don't believe Kansas will vote for woman suffrage."

Abby sighed. "I believe you are right," she said sadly. "We all did the best we could, but in the end we couldn't fight the determination of the Republican Party to focus only on the vote for black males. The vote won't happen until November fifth, but I think we all know what the decision will be."

"What now?" Carrie asked.

"We keep fighting," Abby responded passionately. "America will never fully realize its potential until women have the vote. Our country will never be balanced by women's perceptions as long as we are silenced. I will never give up fighting."

"So much to be done," Carrie murmured, wondering just when she had started to feel like such an adult.

"Strong women never quit fighting for what is right," Abby said quietly. She reached over and grasped Carrie's hand. "We will walk into the unknown together, and we will fight together."

Carrie looked down at their linked hands. "*Together*," she promised.

To Be Continued...

Would you be so kind as to leave a Review on Amazon?

Go to www.Amazon.com
Put Always Forward, Ginny Dye into the Search Box
Leave a Review.

I love hearing from my readers!

Thank you!

<u>The Bregdan Principle</u>

Every life that has been lived until
today is a part of the woven
braid of life.

It takes every person's story to create
history.

Your life will help determine the course
of history.

You may think you don't have much of
an impact.

You do.

Every action you take will reflect in
someone else's life.

Someone else's decisions.

Someone else's future.

Both good and bad.

The Bregdan Chronicles

Storm Clouds Rolling In
1860 – 1861

On To Richmond
1861 – 1862

Spring Will Come
1862 – 1863

Dark Chaos
1863 – 1864

The Long Last Night
1864 – 1865

Carried Forward By Hope
April – December 1865

Glimmers of Change
December – August 1866

Shifted By The Winds
August – December 1866

Always Forward
January – October 1867

*Many more coming... Go to
DiscoverTheBregdanChronicles.com to see how
many are available now!*

Other Books by Ginny Dye

Pepper Crest High Series - Teen Fiction

Time For A Second Change
It's Really A Matter of Trust
A Lost & Found Friend
Time For A Change of Heart

When I Dream Series – Children's Bedtime Stories

When I Dream, I Dream of Horses
When I Dream, I Dream of Puppies
When I Dream, I Dream of Snow
When I Dream, I Dream of Kittens
When I Dream, I Dream of Elephants
When I Dream, I Dream of the Ocean

Fly To Your Dreams Series – Allegorical Fantasy

Dream Dragon
Born To Fly
Little Heart

101+ Ways to Promote Your Business Opportunity

All titles by Ginny Dye
www.AVoiceInTheWorld.com

Author Biography

Who am I? Just a normal person who happens to love to write. If I could do it all anonymously, I would. In fact, I did the first go round. I wrote under a pen name. On the off chance I would ever become famous - I didn't want to be! I don't like the limelight. I don't like living in a fishbowl. I especially don't like thinking I have to look good everywhere I go, just in case someone recognizes me! I finally decided none of that matters. If you don't like me in overalls and a baseball cap, too bad. If you don't like my haircut or think I should do something different than what I'm doing, too bad. I'll write books that you will hopefully like, and we'll both let that be enough! :) Fair?

But let's see what you might want to know. I spent many years as a Wanderer. My dream when I graduated from college was to experience the United States. I grew up in the South. There are many things I love about it but I wanted to live in other places. So I did. I moved 42 times, traveled extensively in 49 of the 50 states, and had more experiences than I will ever be able to recount. The only state I haven't been in is Alaska, simply because I refuse to visit such a vast, fabulous place until I have at least a month. Along the way I had glorious adventures. I've canoed through the Everglade Swamps, snorkeled in the Florida Keys and windsurfed in the Gulf of Mexico. I've white-water rafted down the New River and Bungee jumped in the Wisconsin Dells. I've visited every National Park (in the off-season when there is more freedom!) and many of the State Parks. I've hiked thousands of miles of mountain trails and biked through Arizona deserts. I've canoed and biked through Upstate New York and Vermont, and polished off as much lobster as possible on the Maine Coast.

I had a glorious time and never thought I would find a place that would hold me until I came to the Pacific Northwest. I'd been here less than 2 weeks, and I knew I would never leave. My heart is so at home here with the towering firs, sparkling waters, soaring mountains and rocky beaches. I love the eagles & whales. In 5 minutes I can be hiking on 150 miles of trails in the mountains around my home, or gliding across the lake in my rowing shell. I love it!

Have you figured out I'm kind of an outdoors gal? If it can be done outdoors, I love it! Hiking, biking, windsurfing, rock-climbing, roller-blading, snow-shoeing, skiing, rowing, canoeing, softball, tennis... the list could go on and on. I love to have fun and I love to stretch my body. This should give you a pretty good idea of what I do in my free time.

When I'm not writing or playing, I'm building I Am A Voice In The World - a fabulous organization I founded in 2001 - along with 60 amazing people who poured their lives into creating resources to empower people to make a difference with their lives.

What else? I love to read, cook, sit for hours in solitude on my mountain, and also hang out with friends. I love barbeques and block parties. Basically - I just love LIFE!

I'm so glad you're part of my world!

Ginny

Join my Email List so you can:

- Receive notice of all new books
- Be a part of my Launch Celebrations. I give away lots of Free gifts!
- Read my weekly BLOG while you're waiting for a new book.
- Be part of The Bregdan Chronicles Family!
- Learn about all the other books I write.

Just go to www.BregdanChronicles.net and fill out the form.

DISCARD

Made in the USA
Lexington, KY
07 April 2016